Readers love
the Long Con Adventures
by Amy Lane

The Mastermind

"This story is a prime example of a highly complicated long con complete with a family of the heart, a reunion of two souls destined to be together forever, and Revenge with a capital R."
—Rainbow Book Reviews

The Muscle

"...Amy Lane has a way with surrounding her self with many characters and melding them into a great family. I saw this book was no exception."
—Paranormal Romance Guild

The Driver

"I just can't get enough of this crew of heroic outlaws."
—Love Bytes

The Suit

"This story was incredible, everyone using their talents was essential! It was a mystery, an education on birds... and best of all a love story."
—Paranormal Romance Guild

The Tech

"As always, I enjoyed the parts most where the whole team worked together."
—Love Bytes

By Amy Lane

An Amy Lane Christmas
Behind the Curtain
Bewitched by Bella's Brother
Bolt-hole
Christmas Kitsch
Christmas with Danny Fit
Clear Water
Do-over
Food for Thought
Freckles
Gambling Men
Going Up
Hammer & Air
Homebird
If I Must
Immortal
It's Not Shakespeare
Late for Christmas
Left on St. Truth-be-Well
The Locker Room
Mourning Heaven
Phonebook
Puppy, Car, and Snow
Racing for the Sun • Hiding the
Moon
Raising the Stakes
Regret Me Not
Shiny!
Shirt
Sidecar
Slow Pitch
String Boys
A Solid Core of Alpha

Three Fates
Truth in the Dark
Turkey in the Snow
Under the Rushes
Weirdos
Wishing on a Blue Star

BENEATH THE STAIN
Beneath the Stain • Paint It Black

BONFIRES
Bonfires • Crocus

CANDY MAN
Candy Man • Bitter Taffy
Lollipop • Tart and Sweet

COVERT
Under Cover

DREAMSPUN BEYOND
HEDGE WITCHES LONELY
HEARTS CLUB
Shortbread and Shadows
Portals and Puppy Dogs
Pentacles and Pelting Plants
Heartbeats in a Haunted House

Published by DREAMSPINNER PRESS
www.dreamspinnerpress.com

By Amy Lane (cont)

DREAMSPUN DESIRES
THE MANNIES
The Virgin Manny
Manny Get Your Guy
Stand by Your Manny
A Fool and His Manny
SEARCH AND RESCUE
Warm Heart
Silent Heart
Safe Heart
Hidden Heart

FAMILIAR LOVE
Familiar Angel • Familiar Demon

FISH OUT OF WATER
Fish Out of Water
Red Fish, Dead Fish
A Few Good Fish • Hiding the Moon
Fish on a Bicycle • School of Fish
Fish in a Barrel

FLOPHOUSE
Shades of Henry • Constantly Cotton
Sean's Sunshine

GRANBY KNITTING
The Winter Courtship Rituals of
Fur-Bearing Critters
How to Raise an Honest Rabbit
Knitter in His Natural Habitat
Blackbird Knitting in a Bunny's Lair
The Granby Knitting Menagerie
Anthology

JOHNNIES
Chase in Shadow • Dex in Blue
Ethan in Gold • Black John
Bobby Green • Super Sock Man

KEEPING PROMISE ROCK
Keeping Promise Rock
Making Promises
Living Promises • Forever Promised

LONG CON ADVENTURES
The Mastermind • The Muscle
The Driver • The Suit
The Tech • The Face Man

LUCK MECHANICS
The Rising Tide
A Salt Bitter Sea

TALKER
Talker • Talker's Redemption
Talker's Graduation
The Talker Collection Anthology

WINTER BALL
Winter Ball • Summer Lessons
Fall Through Spring

Published by DREAMSPINNER PRESS
www.dreamspinnerpress.com

By Amy Lane (CONT)

Published by DSP Publications

ALL THAT HEAVEN WILL
ALLOW
All the Rules of Heaven

Published by Harmony Ink Press

GREEN'S HILL
The Green's Hill Novellas

BITTER MOON SAGA
Triane's Son Rising

LITTLE GODDESS
Vulnerable
Wounded, Vol. 1 • Wounded, Vol. 2
Bound, Vol. 1 • Bound, Vol. 2
Rampant, Vol. 1 • Rampant, Vol. 2
Quickening, Vol. 1 • Quickening, Vol. 2
Green's Hill Werewolves, Vol. 1
Green's Hill Werewolves, Vol. 2

Triane's Son Learning
Triane's Son Fighting
Triane's Son Reigning

Published by DREAMSPINNER PRESS
www.dreamspinnerpress.com

The Face Man

AMY LANE

DREAMSPINNER PRESS

Published by
DREAMSPINNER PRESS

5032 Capital Circle SW, Suite 2, PMB# 279, Tallahassee, FL 32305-7886 USA
www.dreamspinnerpress.com

This is a work of fiction. Names, characters, places, and incidents either are the product of author imagination or are used fictitiously, and any resemblance to actual persons, living or dead, business establishments, events, or locales is entirely coincidental.

The Face Man
© 2023 Amy Lane

Cover Art
© 2023 L.C. Chase
http://www.lcchase.com
Cover content is for illustrative purposes only and any person depicted on the cover is a model.

Mass Market Paperback ISBN: 978-1-64108-690-5
Trade Paperback ISBN: 978-1-64108-662-2
Digital ISBN: 978-1-64108-661-5
Trade Paperback published October 2023
v. 1.0

Printed in the United States of America
∞
This paper meets the requirements of
ANSI/NISO Z39.48-1992 (Permanence of Paper).

This was hard to write. Not the story—I've had Tor's story planned for a while now—that part was cake. It was literally hard to type because age has caught up to me, and suddenly arthritis is a thing. I do not take "things" well. I bitch, moan, whine, and sometimes give up and go to bed when I should be writing because I'm just done. To Mate and the kids—of course. OF COURSE. And to everyone who heard me bitch, moan, and whine and DIDN'T smack me across the face and say, "Lots of people deal with this, Amy. For hell's sake, suck it up."

Acknowledgments

MY FAMILY is a weird mix of European lineage, one or two per grandparent, with a dash of Indigenous Peoples too obscure to identify for certain on my maternal grandfather's side. The one culture to beat the others into submission and announce that, "Yes, this child can claim me!" has been Italian, and part of that is my Grandma Olga's doing. (Do not ask about the name, that woman told the best and most amazing lies, and I have no idea why two Italian immigrants should name the first child they had in America "Olga.") Anyway—Grandma gave birth to five kids, which was three down from the family of eight she'd grown up in, and taught me everything I know about Italian families (including forgetting the name of the kid you're mad at and just calling random names until the guilty party shouts "I didn't do it!")

The point of all of this is to say that Marco's family is loosely structured on my grandmother's matriarchal dream family, and while Grandma passed away many years ago, I should acknowledge that yes, in this one case, the Italians beat the Germans, Scots, Greeks, and French, and that is all Olga Gaudioso Chaney's doing.

Thanks, Grandma. We all still miss you. I'm sure there's a collection of hats in heaven that you're saving to show us when we reunite.

Author's Note

STILL ALL fantasy. I hope it's a fun one.

The Face Man

TORRANCE GRAYSON stared at the body blankly.

The alley where he'd found it was awful—fetid, full of restaurant trash, stinking of frozen piss and feces and death.

The true definition of human waste.

The body, on the other hand, was almost peaceful, for all that it was blue. A girl, maybe fifteen, dressed in jeans and a hooded sweatshirt. Northeast High School Roosters.

It was that last part that was the kicker. She was fifteen, and her name was Jancy Anne Halston.

Stupid name, he thought with a swallow. He'd thought that when her father had first asked him, desperately, to investigate his daughter's disappearance. *Too many liquid consonants. Hard to pronounce.* It was a newsperson's nightmare, fumbling a name. Saying "janky" instead of "Jancy." *Jancy Anne. I bet she caught shit for that all through school. Poor kid.*

There'd be no more school for this one. No more sleepovers. No more passed TikTok videos or secret texts. Jancy had caught the bus into the city one day, found her friend's fentanyl hookup for a "refill," and had taken two for herself, because her friend said they were "just so chill." But Jancy weighed twenty pounds less than her friend and had never taken opioids before and….

And Torrance Grayson had just finished running a series on the face of the opioid epidemic, and Hugh Halston had been a professor of Tor's, long before Tor had landed his first job. Hugh had gotten the basic story from Jancy's semihysterical friend the night before, and minutes later Torrance had gotten a call begging him to use some of the sources he'd cultivated while doing his award-winning YouTube news show to find the missing Jancy.

And hey, Torrance had found her, right?

His face crumpled. He had a pretty strong stomach, so he didn't retch, didn't throw up, but he didn't cry either. He was a hard-bitten news reporter. He didn't cry. This was not his first dead body. Why cry? This wasn't even his first dead body this *month*; he knew better than that. But this pretty girl in the corner of the alley, face and hands blue in the late-November cold, wearing a sweatshirt because she thought she'd only be off the bus for a few moments…. God. She had spots. *Spots*. She was a baby. She should get up, go back to the suburbs, and tell everybody what a bad idea *that* had been, but she couldn't, because she was here, in the alleyway, dead.

With trembling fingers he pulled out his phone and managed to keep his voice crisp as he talked to his contact in the police department. Nick Denning technically worked organized crime, but he would know who to call to get someone out here who could deal with a grieving father from the suburbs and a tragedy.

Ten interminable minutes later, what he got was Nick.

Nick was a relatively young detective—barely thirty—with a wife and a baby and a helpless crush on the same guy *Tor* had been crushing on over the last year. Not that the two of them had ever confessed their helpless attraction to Josh Salinger to each other—Tor was pretty sure Nick hadn't confessed it to *himself*—but Tor recognized the signs.

"So," Nick said, hopping on his toes as he supervised the girl being deposited—gently, thank fuck, because these coroner's assistants were old enough for some compassion—into the black void of the coroner's bag before they put it on the stretcher.

"So?" Tor replied, hopping on his toes too. He wished he could be stoic, go someplace in his head other than Jancy Halston's poor blue face and the hell Nick was going to have to endure informing her father.

"You heard from Josh or his family lately?"

Tor frowned, not sure how much Nick knew. "He's getting better." Felix Salinger, Josh's father in name and affection if not in bloodline, was a *good* friend. Tor ate a meal at the Salinger mansion once or twice a week. He claimed it was because the Salingers gave him such good stories for his independent YouTube news channel, but he was pretty sure Felix and his partner, Danny, knew the truth.

"For sure?" Nick asked, his voice trembling with apprehension.

Tor nodded, feeling the ache of unrequited love to his bones. "Yeah. Josh's mom found a family member who gave him a bone-marrow transplant." He grimaced, because nobody had needed to tell him this. He'd guessed. "Two, actually. He was… he was close, I think, although his dads don't want to admit it."

"Two family members or two transplants?" Nick asked, but the relief in his voice—so damned similar to Tor's, actually—told Tor that wasn't what he was worried about.

"Two transplants," Tor told him, swallowing. The zip of the coroner's bag interrupted his memory of that frightening, fraught September, the whole family knowing Josh wasn't doing well, nobody sure what to do about it.

He shuddered. God. Poor Jancy. Her poor father, having to live through this news. Josh's family had been close... so close.

"I'm...." Nick's voice wobbled, and Tor turned his head in time to see the young detective wipe his eyes on his shirtsleeve. "I'm glad to hear he's going to be okay," he said, trying hard to firm up his voice.

"Me too," Tor said. He shuddered. "You, uhm... you want a drink?"

Nick shuddered too but declined. "It's only four in the afternoon. I've got two more hours on shift, my friend. Want to meet up afterward?"

But Tor only wanted to get warm. "No, I've got some work to do," he said, and it was true. He had some editing on a segment he was planning to release the next day, but that's not what he was thinking about. What he was *really* thinking about, what he was *dreaming* about, was the bottle of celebratory whiskey his cameraman had given him in October when their segment on the murder birds and genetic engineering in Napa wineries had gotten over three-million hits and their sponsors had started throwing money at them to keep the now-valuable spots.

It had just sat there, really. A dash here, a nip there, and now in the end of November, more than three-quarters of a bottle was left for him to pour into his hot chocolate as he curled up under a blanket on his couch, watching cartoons and trying to forget about his day.

A week later....

"TORRANCE, GET up."

A blinding shaft of light pierced Tor's eyeballs, and he tried to scream. It came out as a whimper, and he raised his blanket over his head with aching arms.

"Fuck off," he mumbled.

"Torrance Robert Grayson, I said *wake up*."

With a violent jerk, the blanket was yanked off his body, and he was left shivering on his couch, wearing his briefs and the suspiciously stained sweater he'd been wearing a week ago in the alleyway. His black jeans— sort of a trademark—were crumpled in a heap at the foot of his squishy corduroy couch, and some sort of... of *smell* was coming from his corner of the room.

"You're not the boss of me," he said tearfully, although he knew this voice. This man *had* been the boss of him, once upon a time.

"Only because you make more money than I can pay you," Felix Salinger said. "Danny, he smells."

Tor worked hard to pry his gummy eyelids open. "Danny?" he mumbled to himself. "You brought *Danny* to my apartment to see me drunk?"

"It gets worse," Danny said. "Josh, Hunter, go prepare a bath."

Tor's eyelids actually shot open so fast he thought he might have torn all his lashes out. "You bastard," he croaked. "Felix Salinger, you're no longer my friend."

"I can deal with that," Felix said softly, his voice coming from surprisingly close. Tor blinked rapidly and managed to focus on that classically handsome face, the mane of silvering blond hair barely contained by a very skilled barber. "I can deal with any name you call me, Tor, but you've got to tell me what happened."

To his horror, Tor's eyes started to burn. "Just… you know. Came home, had a drink—"

Following a clatter in the kitchen, a deep, masculine voice with more than a hint of country boy called out, "I count six bottles here. Oh my God, son, is that some sort of a record?"

"A record for DoorDash receipts!" came a younger, more pointed voice. "Fuck *me*, Grayson. You've been doordashing Jim Beam?"

"Any food with that, Charles?" Danny called to the country boy— who usually went by Chuck. "Grace, help him throw that crap away. And both of you stop yelling. His head's going to explode."

Gratefully, Tor's eyes were drawn to the slender, graceful man in the stretchy black jeans and black sweatshirt. Danny Mitchell, now known publicly as Dr. Benjamin Morgan but never to the insiders of his extended "family," had been a system throwaway, a hustler, a con man, and a thief— and was the love of Felix Salinger's life.

And he had been, Tor recalled now, a raging alcoholic, until he'd left Felix nearly eleven years ago to get clean. They'd reunited last spring, and now they were very rarely apart, but something in Tor relaxed a little. Danny…. Danny might not judge him. Danny would know what to do.

"No food," said Chuck Calder sadly as he swaggered into the front room. A solid six foot four, Calder had bright auburn hair, sparkling green eyes, and a personality so big Torrance felt pushed out of his own living room. "Danny, would you like me to go get some?"

Danny nodded. "I saw a bodega downstairs. Have Grace run and bring back some fried-egg bagel sandwiches for Tor and anything else you all would like. But the sandwiches are *only* for Tor, do you understand me, precious?"

Grace had come in on Chuck's heels, and he blinked his tawny eyes slowly as Danny spoke to him. Someone who didn't know the ethereally beautiful young dancer would suspect him of being slow on the uptake, but the opposite was true—Dylan "Grace" Li possessed a genius-level IQ and a proportional level of ADHD. He understood Danny perfectly, but the slow blink was probably his attempt to make the words stick so he didn't screw up the assignment.

"I got you, Uncle Danny," Grace said, and then he had one of those surprise moments that often gave his friends whiplash. "I'm sorry you're sad, pretty news guy. Don't worry. We'll clean you up. Danny and Felix are good at it."

And with that he turned on his heel and ran out of the apartment. Danny had his hand out as if to stop him, and Felix made a gentle tutting sound.

"He's not twelve," Felix said softly. "He has his own money. Scads of it."

"I know," Danny muttered. "I get protective over that kid. Can't help it."

Torrance made a sound. It was meant to be a chuckle, but it came out like a chuckle through a meat grinder, and suddenly *he* was the center of their worry again.

"Okay," Danny said thoughtfully. "I'm going to have you undress and drop your clothes there, and Chuck can gather them into a plastic bag and have them burned."

Tor was about to protest, but then a burst of smell wafted up from his crotch and his pits and his generally unwashed body and—oh God, his *sweater*—and he had to fight off a sudden bolt of nausea.

"Sure," he rasped. Then he tried to stand and stumbled and was borne up by Felix on one side and Danny on the other, and neither one of them seemed to be gagging over his smell. "Sorry," he said in a small voice. "Don't know what's wrong with me."

Danny let out a long, slow breath. "What's wrong with you, son, is that you supped full with horrors," he said softly, and Tor squeezed his eyes shut.

"*Macbeth*," he managed, wondering how *that* brain cell had survived.

"Indeed," Danny said, breaking away to help Tor strip his turtleneck up off his torso. For the first time he reacted to Tor's BO, and Tor had a feeling it was on purpose. "Whoo, boy. That's strong. My eyes are going to be stinging for a while."

"Sorry," Tor whimpered, and then he found himself naked in his own living room while two men whose friendship he treasured offered him their arms so they could escort him to the bathtub. "I still have no idea what happened."

As they made their way—slowly—he heard about how his assistant had called them after Tor had gone dark for a week. He'd missed posting a segment on the opioid crisis six days ago, and his last known contact had been tracked down to Nick Denning, who had told them that he'd seemed particularly green around the gills after finding the body of a teenager who'd OD'd.

The rest hadn't been hard to put together.

His apartment had an old-fashioned claw-footed bathtub with a standing shower and a frothy curtain. The curtain had been pulled back, and the tub—painted a stunning indigo glaze—had been filled with foamy hot water that smelled like Old Spice bodywash used as bubble bath.

Suddenly Tor's eyes teared up again, and he wasn't sure if it was the lack of food or the lost week or the fact that all that drinking hadn't erased the image of the girl's face one bit—hadn't even faded it. But suddenly the simple humanity of the bathtub full of hot water seemed like too much grace for his battered heart to bear.

"Here we go," Felix said softly, helping him into the tub by main force. Tor realized that he was getting his nasty, smelly body all over what was probably a thousand-dollar suit Felix was wearing, and he fought the urge to sob. He searched discount sales and bribed tailors; he *knew* what Felix Salinger's wardrobe cost, and he hated that he was helping to destroy a perfectly good winter wool concoction.

"I'm sorry," he whispered, and to his utter mortification, he felt a kiss in his greasy hair.

"Don't be," Felix murmured. "Everybody needs a hand up. Now Danny and I are going to go take care of your business and your living room, and then we're going to move you into the mansion for a month or two. Are you ready for that?"

Torrance's breath stopped. He'd been on his own since he'd left home for school—he'd pretty much given his parents the "I'm gay, bitches, and I've got a free ride!" salute as he'd left. They hadn't written, and neither had he. He'd had dormitories since then, and shitty apartments too. After Felix had given him his start as an anchor for his cable news station, he'd leased this retro-stylish apartment in an old building overlooking the river off the Loop and had loved it.

But he'd drop anything—dates, award ceremonies, meetings with sources—to go stay in the room that Felix, Danny, and Felix's ex-wife, Julia, had designated as *his* in a corner of their spacious Glencoe mansion.

Whether they were meeting for a project or invited him to come out for dinner and stay rather than drive the hour back into the city, that room—masculinely appointed, with a selection of Marc Chagall paintings for color against clean white walls with teak hardwood—the room was comfortable and pretty and… safe. Torrance Grayson had never felt as safe in his life as he did in that room. He'd started to bring clothes there—a simple suit, jeans, sweats, pajamas—and also a toothbrush so that he could lay some sort of claim to that room in the mansion. It was by far the smallest guest room, but he thought maybe that was on purpose too. Not because the family found him unimportant, but because they knew his apartment was small, and they were trying to let him know they had room.

"Like a home," he rasped, settling into the hot water with appreciative moans. "God… this is blissful. Can I just die here?"

"No," rasped a voice. Once a strong, dynamic voice, but now it was weaker and gruff—chemo and radiation therapy could do that to a young man. "You can't die in the bathtub, you can't die on the couch, and you can't die in your bed at our house. All these people are here to clean you up and you sort of need to live, right?"

Tor squeezed his eyes shut. Oh Lord. No. Not… it couldn't be. Had he really heard Felix give an order to his son?

"Josh?" he said, begging it not to be true. "Why are you here?"

There was a frustrated grunt, and then warm water poured onto his hair while gentle fingers scooped it back from his eyes. "I'm here to help my family's friend," Josh said gently. "And apparently wash your hair. Keep your eyes shut so I don't get soap in them."

Tor couldn't help the noise he made then—partially a moan of pleasure as Josh massaged the soap into his nasty, greasy hair and partially a moan of embarrassment because… oh God. Of all people.

"Nick and I are helplessly in love with you," he mumbled after Josh had finished and then wiped Tor's face off with a dry towel for good measure. With every minute soaking in the hot water, Tor felt a little more awake—and a little more mortified. It felt like the time to confess to unrequited love, to make his humiliation complete.

Josh's gruff chuckle was not the response he'd expected to that information.

"You are not," Josh replied stoutly. "You've got a crush. It's fine. It used to make me uncomfortable, but then you turned out to be an outstanding guy and not just my father's show-offy friend, and I realized what an honor it was. But it'll fade. It's fine."

Tor glared at him. "I have been *pining* for you for over a year now! Remember your family Christmas party last year? We sat in a corner and talked all night and…." He sucked in a breath that sounded suspiciously like a sob. To his surprise, Josh sank down and kissed his temple, and Tor was treated to the sight, the *smell*, of him up close and personal. Bright brown eyes beginning to regain their sparkle, neatly cut black hair just starting to shine again. He had a piquant, pixieish face and a full mouth that seemed almost perpetually amused and this look—this stunning look of *kindness*— on his features that seemed to cut Tor to the bone.

The kiss on the temple was as physically close as they'd ever been.

"It was a good night," Josh said softly. "Books and poetry, music and politics. Grace doesn't focus long enough to talk about things linearly. I thought, 'Wow, I've discovered an amazing friend.'"

Tor closed his eyes, suddenly getting Josh's standoffishness over the last year and hating himself. "And then I hit on you," he muttered.

"I was flattered," Josh told him, smoothing Tor's wet hair back from his brow. "But…." He shrugged. "I told you that night, I was crushing on someone else. I wish I could play that way, date one person to forget another, but I can't. I couldn't do it to you. I *liked* you."

"Liked?" Tor begged pitifully.

"*Like*," Josh told him, because that kindness went down to the bone. "As in care about as a friend. I care about you very much. I consider you a friend. That's why I'm here. Because when Nick told us what you'd seen, where you'd been, I knew you were in trouble. Everybody here—even Grace—cares about you, and that's hard, you know. Grace doesn't always see other people."

Tor snorted. "He's going to get me bagel sandwiches. Let's see how that works." For the first time since the light had stabbed his eyes like the piercing sword of justice, he started to realize how his nausea might be disguising hunger.

"Well, we can cross our fingers," Josh said philosophically. He backed away and handed Tor a washcloth. "My point here is you can't crawl into a hole and die because your heart was broken by Jancy Halston."

Tor sucked in a pained breath. "You… you know about her?"

Again that comforting hand on his brow. Tor's mother hadn't been big on comfort. Her next party, her next dress, the diamonds his father bought her—yes. Comforting her son? Not so much. But the Salinger clan seemed to thrive on it, and Tor's upset stomach and shaking hands were soothed somehow, warmed and strengthened by the knowledge that Josh Salinger, platonic friend, was still not going to let him die. Not in a puddle of his own body odor—oh God, it had been vomit, hadn't it!—and not in the lovely warm bath either, apparently.

"Nick told us," Josh said softly. "I'm sorry. That must have been awful."

"I didn't know her," Tor said, trying not to take sympathy where it wasn't deserved. "Her family, though… they're going to be devastated. I…." He wouldn't know what it was like to have a family like that, he thought wretchedly.

"They were," Josh said softly.

Tor cast a quick glance at him and saw him sitting on a stool near the tub, resting his weight on his elbows and regarding Tor with a sort of steady strength.

"Nick also told us that they were grateful. He did the notification and said you were the one who had found her. They've written you emails, you know. About how much less awful it is that somebody who cared went searching for their little girl."

"I didn't…." Tor swallowed. "I haven't checked my computer." He remembered watching cartoons—lots and lots of them—and his phone buzzing until he'd thrown it across the room. Besides that and tipping the DoorDash guy, a whole lot of drinking and some throwing up and a massive quantity of wanting to forget.

"Color me surprised," Josh said dryly. Then his expression sobered. "Look, you're going to get the full-court press from Danny and Dad. They're going to want to know how bad this is. They grew up in the eighties, you know. One bender does not an alcoholic make. Was this just a really bad reaction to a really bad moment, or is this going to be your go-to every time things get grim?"

Tor gasped sharply, suddenly understanding the import of that moment. If this was a bad reaction to a bad moment, he could overcome it. He could recognize the signs. He could call his friends. His mouth parted softly as he looked at Josh, young and frail and brilliant, and realized, in a flash, that he hadn't needed to.

His friends had come anyway.

"If I let this get the best of me," he said, reasoning, "I'll have to walk away from what I do."

It was a wrenching admission. He'd been the driving force behind his high school newspaper and then been the editor-in-chief for three years. Had broken a story about co-ed assaults in his college paper, one that had been picked up by national news networks and had caught the attention of Felix Salinger. When Felix had been under attack at work, Tor had quit, not able to work for the manipulative bitch distorting the truth to ruin Felix, wanting to make a statement because he knew his own worth. Working for himself, going independent, had been scary and hard, but he'd gotten successful at it and, with the help of Felix's family, had become known for not only hard-hitting stories, but also for unusual ones, stories that would never have caught the attention of local law enforcement *or* journalism if not for Tor's connection to the group of people quietly investigating crimes that nobody else had seen.

He loved what he did. Was *proud* of what he did. Had developed a polish and a reporting style that was concise, clear, and relied on facts rather than editorializing.

Who am I without my job? he thought wretchedly, and then he had his answer.

"A onetime thing," he said, almost to himself. "I'll… I'll get a handle on this—"

"You'll ask for help," Josh said, sounding so adult Tor almost checked to make sure Josh was still twenty. One of the most depressing things about Tor's crush had been the age difference—Tor was getting close to the big 3-0, and Josh wasn't old enough to buy beer.

Tor grimaced. "I… I have no idea how this happened," he said, aware of sounding very young.

"Oh, that's easy," said Danny Mitchell, coming back into the steamy bathroom with a burst of cold air. Tor shivered involuntarily, and Danny shut the door with a quick slam. "Sorry, my boy—we had to open your windows as we were cleaning. I hope you weren't too attached to that couch, by the way. Felix ordered a new one to replace it, and the area rug beneath as well."

Tor frowned. "What did I do to the area rug?" he asked, wondering how bad things had gotten.

"Nothing, as far as I know," Danny said, shrugging. "I just don't think Felix liked it very much. Anyway, we'll be requesting a ritual burning when the movers come to take the couch away. Do you need to witness it?"

Tor thought about the past week, what he remembered of it, and shuddered. He'd made it to the bathroom, but he hadn't been neat about it, and as he looked around, he realized that Josh and Hunter—Grace's decked, scary mercenary boyfriend—had probably sanitized the bathroom while Danny and Felix had been giving him a literal dressing-down.

"Probably not," he said weakly, and he heard it—the fragility in his voice. He turned his face to Josh's other "dad," the avuncular figure who had brought the family together. "Uncle Danny, I don't even know how this happened. I don't even *like* Jim Beam." His voice wobbled and fractured, and his eyes burned until finally the tears broke through and washed them clear.

"Sh…." Danny was kneeling on the mat next to the tub, doing that same thing with the wet hair at his brow that Josh had done. "Hush, sweet boy. You had a really bad moment here, I think. And next time you feel like crawling into a hole and drinking *bottles* of alcohol, I think you need to do one thing first. You know what that is?"

Tor sniffled, barely holding it together to answer. "Call you?" he asked.

"Any of us," Danny said softly, reaching to pull Tor's head against his chest. "Call any of us, son. You're ours now, do you understand? Nobody in this crew is going to let you fall."

Tor sniffled again and nodded and thought, *He's going to let me go in a minute, and I'll be fine.* But Danny stayed right there, and at the moment Tor thought he was going to move, his hands came out of the water and he fisted them into Danny's black hoodie and sobbed, embarrassed, ashamed for practically dragging this nice man into his mucky water with him but unable to let go.

HE DIDN'T remember much of that day. The bagels arrived, and Danny and Felix helped him into clean clothes and fed him while Josh and Grace packed him a bag. Then Chuck bundled him into an SUV—prewarmed because apparently Chuck was a gentleman and a miracle worker—and he'd been spirited away to the mansion in Glencoe and his blessed, precious little room with the attached bath and the pictures of Chagall's cats.

He'd slept a lot that first night, but that morning he'd been awakened by a tap on his door and the smell of hot coffee, croissants, and something decadent and fattening that he couldn't identify.

"Immnotup," he slurred, swinging his feet over the side of the bed, surprised when his leather moccasins were right in the exact place they needed to be.

"Well, don't get up" was the feminine, almost musical reply. "Josh, darling?"

"Got it, Mom."

Tor had just enough time to cover his pajamas with the thick blue flannel duvet before the door opened and Julia Dormer-Salinger, Felix's ex-wife and Josh's mother, walked into the room, blond, blue-eyed, in a casual outfit of khaki slacks and a pale pink sweater, and soigné as fuck.

"How are you doing, sweetheart?" she asked, setting the tray over his legs and plumping the pillows behind him.

"I'm trying to remember when a drunken bender got this much coddling," he said, smiling at her in embarrassment.

"It wasn't the drunken bender," Josh said baldly, pulling a chair away from the corner of the room and gesturing for his mother to sit down in it. "It was the nervous breakdown that preceded it."

"Are we even using that term?" Tor asked. "I don't think that's the current terminology. I—"

"You couldn't deal anymore," Josh replied. "Sorry. I wish I had a degree in psychology, but I was majoring in…." He grunted.

"Everything else, darling," his mother said sympathetically. "Engineering was in there, politics, business, drama, art history. I can see why you're so excited about going back. You'd been planning to make the place your second home for at least ten years."

Josh grinned, looking tired but animated, and Tor could suddenly see how hard it had been for the young man to put an active, vital life on hold while his body recovered. "Grace and I are going to burn the place down next year. It'll be great."

Tor was suddenly curious. "But what's your degree going to be in?"

Josh rolled his eyes. "Who cares? I can make a living legally about six different ways right now without the degree. I just want to take the classes!"

Tor snorted softly. He was pretty sure Josh could make *more* money *il*legally, but he didn't say so.

"So," Julia said smoothly, steering the conversation back and lowering her voice. "Torrance, most people know you're here, but *being* here does not necessarily mean you have to participate in all of the madness that *is* here. The mansion is a big place. Feel free to work out with everybody in the morning or use the gym when everybody's left, to be alone. There is always food in the fridge, and we've hired extra staff in recent months. We even have a full-time chef! If you're hungry, go into the kitchen, be sweet to Phyllis or one of her minions, and you shall have whatever your heart desires. Do you understand?"

He took a grateful sip of his coffee. "Julia, I don't know what to say. But I left my business sort of in the middle. I can't just move in here."

Her hand on his arm was a touch of graciousness he hadn't known he'd needed. "Sweetheart, you've dined with us and played with us before. You know we can be a lot, and sometimes a lot is exactly what people need." She made meaningful eye contact with Josh, who nodded in agreement, and Tor wondered who they were thinking about. "But sometimes what people need is a quiet retreat, while at the same time knowing they're not alone. You are not alone. You never *need* to be alone here. But if you need or prefer solitude, we get that. You…." She took a liberty and caressed his cheek. "You look exhausted. Please rest here. I get that you will need to visit your flat and stay there part of the time—but not for a few days. In less than a month we will celebrate Christmas and whisk you away on vacation afterward, and there's always a story if you're up to it. Or not. But I promise you, my darling, this is the one place you can know you're not alone. Are we clear?"

He wiped his suddenly watery eyes on the shoulder of his T-shirt. "Now I *really* don't know what to say," he rasped.

She stood and kissed his cheek. "Just tell us when you're ready to join us for dinner. Phyllis will be happy to set the extra plate."

With that she left him to his croissant, which was delicious.

Two Weeks Later

PHILLIP, HIS assistant who doubled as his extra cameraman sometimes and who worked hard to keep the YouTube channel current, monetized, and troll free, peered at Tor through his computer screen and let out a low whistle.

"Nice digs, man. You sure you're okay?"

Tor sat cross-legged on the bed of his little room and smiled tiredly into the camera. "Yeah. I mean, I'm getting there." The fact was, much like Julia's prediction, he'd spent the first week *sleeping*—or pretending to sleep—in his room in the Salinger mansion while they claimed to be fumigating his apartment. Since he was pretty sure the new couch and rug had already arrived, along with an army of cleaners employed to clean up his very rank, very nasty mess, he sort of doubted that. He was also sure he was there so they could keep an eye on him. Make sure he ate. Make sure he didn't drink. Make sure he woke up enough to move.

He had, in fits and starts at first, but after the first week, solidly enough to go back to his apartment for most of last week. Those first few days, though…. He shuddered. When he *had* slept, for real, awakened with nightmares, terrified and alone. But each time, *somebody* had shown up in his room. Once it had been Felix and Danny, both of them dressed in flannel pajamas, looking young and vulnerable as they rushed in like new parents comforting a child. Once it had been Chuck Calder, who somehow managed to appear *more* dangerous than usual in flannel bottoms and a T-shirt, probably because his sizable muscles were usually covered by jeans and a leather jacket.

Once he'd awakened, heart pounding, whimpers sounding from his throat, to find a wraith in black yoga pants and a black microfiber shirt perched on the foot of his bed.

"Are you fine, Mr. TV man?" Grace asked irritably. "Josh was all worried about you, and I told him I'd check to see if you were sleeping. You have to be okay because he's got chemo in the morning and he's only got a few more rounds left, you understand?"

"I understand," Tor said, trying to keep his eyes from rolling wildly out of sheer fright. "I'll try not to let my screaming scare you."

Grace was not known for his patience. He huffed out a little breath and then scooted to the side of the double bed. "Move over. Hunter's out in the city doing investigative things for our forger right now, so I can keep you company. It's cold. Don't argue."

Torrance didn't argue, but he did scoot over as far as he could. Hunter, Grace's boyfriend, was *really* scary. Big muscles and no survivors kind of scary. He always identified himself as the family's muscle, and between him and Chuck—who was in charge of munitions and transport—Tor figured they could probably beat back any army.

Tor did *not* want to get caught in bed with Hunter's boyfriend.

"Oh, relax," Grace muttered, turning on his side away from Tor. "I stopped being a manwhore when Hunter and I got together. I'm not grabbing anybody's wiener but his. Besides, I didn't pity-fuck the guys in love with Josh *before* I got with Hunter, so I don't know why I would *now*."

Grace and Josh had been friends since grade school, but Grace had frequently professed to not have an attention span big enough for morals. Color Tor surprised to find that wasn't entirely true.

"That's probably wise," Tor said, scooting closer to the middle of the bed. "Why are you doing this again?"

The sigh next to him was long-suffering. "Because you did something stupid because you got really sad. Believe it or not, Mr. Fancy TV Person, *I've* done something stupid because *I* got really sad. Josh's family bailed me out too, and they brought me here so I'd never have to be alone and sad or with the wrong person and sad again. So go to sleep now. It's okay. No scary monsters tonight. They have to come through me to get to you, and if they tried that, my terrifying mercenary boyfriend would paint the walls with their blood."

Tor sputtered laughter, but Grace just grunted in disgust and curled up into a tighter ball. Tor's laughter subsided, but he was left knowing that he wasn't alone, and that the person in bed with him wanted nothing from him but his own peace.

The thought was amazingly soothing, and he curled up next to Grace and fell asleep almost immediately. No dreams disturbed him, and he woke up feeling like he'd slept well for the first time in *months*.

It wasn't until that moment—that moment of waking up alone and remembering how he'd gotten to sleep at all—that he realized how *tired* he'd become since March, when he'd quit his job to protest the unlawful takeover of Felix's business and started his own independent channel. He'd been pushing himself *hard* since then, sometimes in service of the Salinger family, who had fed him some *really* juicy stories, but often on his own pursuits as he endeavored to do important things that made the world a better place.

That moment after Grace had crawled into bed next to him, he remembered that his heroes in the news industry took vacations—often month-long ones—in order to recharge and do their job better.

It was time for him to do the same.

Phillip—who had just helped him edit, upload, and schedule two segments on Tor's channel, seemed to know what was coming.

"Well, we caught up with all the work left hanging when you were sick," he said, like he got it. "But you're not rested yet. I don't want to watch you wither and die. Tell me you're taking a holiday?"

Tor shrugged sheepishly. "Yeah. I've got one more segment that I can have to you next week for polishing, but then I'm going to be offline for Christmas and about two weeks after."

"Woo-hoo!" Phillip pumped his fist. "Margaritas and boys in tight shorts?" Phillip was 100 percent heterosexual, but he was also a really good friend who liked to support Tor in any endeavor.

"Kind of you to wish that on me," Tor said dryly, "but mostly it's just friends, most of whom are paired off." He shrugged, and he was sincere—after the last couple of weeks, it really didn't matter. "I think we're going on some sort of surprise destination vacation. I haven't gotten details, but I've been told what to pack and asked to take a certain amount of time off." He winked. "Lots of board shorts and Hawaiian shirts. I think I'm in good hands."

Phillip's nod was sober. "Good. I'm glad. I've got enough work to keep me busy until Christmas and beyond, but you know I'm your boy first, right?"

"Absolutely," Torrance said, and held his fist to his chest. "Always." Phillip had followed him off his union job at Felix's station, partly in support of Felix, but mostly because he wanted to follow Tor. They'd been working together for three years, and the last nine or so months they'd been on their own. Phillip and his girlfriend had a toddler to provide for and another one on the way, so it hadn't been an empty gesture, following Tor into the great beyond. "I count on it." He smiled a little. "Also, I'm sending stuff to your apartment. I may not get a chance to see you or the munchkin before Christmas, but Santa's not skipping your place by any means, right?"

Phillip's face—a rough-hewn salute to all stubbled bros everywhere, complete with backward-facing ball cap—grew fond. "I may have gotten you a T-shirt or something. For you, I'll drive out to Glencoe, even. 'Kay, bro?"

"I'd love to see you. And"—he lowered his voice conspiratorially— "dude, they've got a kitchen staff here twenty-four seven around the holidays. You show up and I guarantee you some hot chocolate and pastry to die for, you feel me?"

"Ooh… you do a brother proud," Phillip said appreciatively. "I've got to sign off here, but I think we're good to go. I'll let you know if we've got any glitches, but"—his voice dropped—"I think some vacay and some time with your friends is a good idea, Tor. You were looking sort of drug out since before this bout with the flu. I mean, that trip to Napa for the murder birds, that was some good shit, but you've been running balls-out ever since. Chill. Get better. You can't be a truth warrior if you don't take care of yourself, yeah?"

Tor swallowed, that moment from the bathtub flashing behind his eyes. Danny had said he had people to call. Suddenly he realized that maybe he had more people than he thought.

"I feel you," he said soberly. "Keep in touch. You have the only baby I know, so I need to practice being Uncle Tor."

On that note Phillip laughed, and Tor closed his laptop. At that moment there was a brief tap on his door.

"I'm decent," he said, stashing the laptop on the end table. The door opened, revealing a young woman with pale, freckled skin and dazzling red hair, corkscrew curls intertwined with dyed strands of purple, burgundy, and blue. At her shoulder was her brother, a couple of years younger, Black with green eyes and a stoic, determined expression.

"You are not decent," said Molly Christopher impishly. "Decent people don't rate a room here. You may have a legit job, but you're a con artist like the rest of us."

Torrance grinned at her because in his heart he took that as a compliment. Felix Salinger may have been the owner/operator of one of the fastest growing cable networks in the country, but Tor was one of the few people who knew that everything Felix had learned about business he'd learned while fleecing tourists in Europe when he'd been a young man, and Danny had been his tutor. In fact, Tor would be hard pressed to find a single person living in the Salinger residence who wasn't quite adept at breaking a law or two, including Grace, who was their grease man—a balletic, clever thief with no fear of heights, enclosed spaces, or being groped by sad reporters who were pathetically grateful for someone making sure he was okay.

"I try," he said modestly. He did, too. Breaking the law with the Salingers had gotten him some really amazing and important stories. That summer they'd brought down an entire police department that was hiding spousal abuse and murder. He was proud of being able to bring that caper home.

"We have a very small favor to ask of you," Molly said. "Stirling, show him."

Stirling Christopher very gravely pulled a toy out of his pocket. Tor stared at the toy and then at Stirling. The sober young man was absolute poetry with computers—Tor had thought he was decent at tracking down facts, but Stirling was *amazing* and could code on the fly, plant spyware, and use monitors like extensions of his own cerebral cortex. He also designed sets for a local theater company, because that was Stirling and Molly's jam.

What Stirling did *not* do was fiddle-fart around with Legos.

"What's this?" Tor asked. Then he frowned and took the toy Stirling offered him. "Wait. Is this *me*?"

"Yes!" Molly squealed, clapping. "See? It's a little guy who looks like you! It's our present to Grace. We're all going to hide our little doppelgangers *really well*, and then Grace is going to find them as his Christmas present."

Tor smiled at her in bemusement. He'd had the misfortune—or good fortune, depending on his mood at the time—to arrive at the Salinger mansion right before Christmas. He'd gotten to watch as the group of con men, hackers, and thieves became joyous children overnight, working hard to delight each other, not with money—most of them had plenty—but with thoughtfulness and kindness. Tor wasn't sure if it was because Josh's chemo was going well and it seemed like he might recover from the vicious bout of leukemia he'd been fighting, or if being together as a group for the first time was just a heady, enchanting drug, but the mood around the mansion had been effervescent with plans and presents and joy. Tor wasn't, he knew, even the only rescue in the mansion this Christmas. Sometime in that hazy, sleepless first week, there'd been a new addition. Since then, solemn Stirling had been keeping company with the company's forger, a waiflike, terminally shy young man with sober blue eyes that he hid behind glasses.

Torrance was looking forward to finding out more about young Etienne. Tor liked Stirling, and the idea that two quiet, introverted people could find their centers in the Salinger hurricane appealed to him. Now that he'd caught up from most of the work he'd left hanging when he had his little… uhm, moment, he was ready to attend some of the dinners in the Salinger home, maybe stay for some of the games (often poker, which was a favorite), and generally participate in the merriment he'd sensed going on around him but hadn't heard or engaged in.

"So that's my present to him?" Tor asked suspiciously. "Hiding this little guy?"

"You may want to get him something to open too," Stirling said flatly. "He will love this present the most, but if he doesn't get any packages under the tree, he'll be hurt."

Tor remembered the prickly thief's irritable comfort and thought that, as unlikely as that sounded, it might actually be true.

"God forbid," he said lightly, and he heard a touch of Felix in his voice. It made him proud.

"So," Molly said impertinently, joining him sitting cross-legged on the bed while Stirling took the chair and moved it forward. "Are you staying here for Christmas? Are you going to be here tonight?"

Tor smiled slightly. "Yes," he said. "I mean, I need to go work in my apartment a little. I know you all have something you're dealing with for young Tienne, but yes. Felix, Danny, and Julia invited me to stay and play with them and to block out some time after Christmas as well, and…." He shrugged.

"You look tired," Molly said soberly. "You *should* take it easy for a bit."

"Besides," Stirling said, "hanging out with us almost always gets a story dropped in your lap. It's like a working vacation."

Tor grinned at him. "For me, *every* vacation is a working vacation."

Molly chuckled and patted his knee. "Then you need to hang out and make sure you get some rest while you can." She darted her eyes around the room. "Now where are you planning to hide the little guy? It's got to be somewhere good because Grace breaks into everybody's room while we're sleeping anyway."

Tor's eyes went wide. "I hadn't known that was a regular occurrence."

Stirling grimaced. "I think he just likes to check on us."

Tor remembered a Labrador retriever he'd had as a kid who stuck his cold, wet nose into every bed, counting every human under his watch before he curled up in the kitchen. Could they possibly mean Grace was like that?

Naw.

"Is this the same guy who steals my wallet every time I walk through the door?" Six times out of ten, Tor at least saw him leaving, but those other four times….

"It's a sign of affection," Molly said seriously, nodding. "Now tell us what you're looking into?"

Tor gave a slight smile. "Well, I've got a couple of stories working. One that I'll be wrapping up next week is about contractors who screw their clients and run. It's pretty intense. I mean, it sounds small, but if you've saved for years to update your bathroom—and not just cosmetic, like to fix dry rot and stuff—and your contractor stiffs you...."

"That's awful," Molly said soberly. "What can be done with that one?"

Tor grimaced. "That one's tough. Mostly what we can do is run a series of very public stings. The city's building commissioner is very much on the take, so nothing legal ever happens, but if someone makes a big stink about it on YouTube, the clients have enough fuel for a very public lawsuit." With a grunt he dragged his hands through his coiffed hair, feeling the gel breaking and trying not to sigh about it. He was known for being well-dressed at every turn, but apparently he had other things to worry about now.

"Lawsuits are hard," Stirling said. "People have to hire lawyers. They have to prove their claims. There are court costs if they lose."

Torrance nodded. "Yeah. I've got my most recent sting to post next week, but when this vacation is over, I've got to figure out some way to fix it permanently."

Stirling and Molly looked at each other and then nodded.

"We'll help," Stirling said, like that was a given.

"Not *now*," Molly clarified, contrite. "I'm sorry but, you know. Christmas. New guy here. Danny, Felix, and Julia have something cooking, and Josh is finally better. Just...." She bit her lip.

"It's fine to take some time off from being Robin Hood," Tor said, laughing. "In fact, I plan to be with you on all that after next week. But yeah." He nodded, and his job—which had become overwhelming and painful, with every thought of it leading to that fetid back alley and a dead teenager—was suddenly exciting and doable again. "I think maybe I *will* ask for the family's help when we get back."

"Yay!" Molly gave him a high five, and he refrained from wincing. Molly was like Josh: a Jane of all trades. She was passable on the computer, a first-rate thief, a phenomenal shill, and an amazing con woman, but she was also as strong as Hunter and Chuck, and he hoped she hadn't snapped his wrist.

"I'm glad you approve," he said, and his chest warmed a little. "I'll do some more research in my spare time."

THAT WAS the plan, and it was a good one. But there was always a wrinkle.

In this case the wrinkle was the mystery "vacation" that everybody had told him to clear his calendar for. It turned out to be the Caribbean cruise of his frozen-toed Chicago-winter dreams, and while there was a mission—and the possibility of a story—there was also lots of promised sun, clubbing, and lying out on a rather splendid yacht belonging to Josh's long-lost relative on his biological father's side who was determined to buy his way into Josh's mother's heart.

It was everything a vacationing reporter could want. Investigating the mysterious deaths of Stirling and Molly's adoptive parents? He was there for it. Looking into gambling debts of their profligate, coldhearted adoptive brother? Absolutely. And on top of it, there was sleeping in the sun and hanging out in the shade with a group of people who had made it very clear they *liked* him. They wanted him to be with them while they did exciting, mysterious things. It was like having an invitation to go on a camping trip with favorite cousins, except this time with a guarantee that they wouldn't break his best toy or torment him with bugs.

Growing up in a conservative family with lots of extended branches had *not* done Torrance Grayson any favors.

As the meeting in the den announcing the vacation plans broke up, Tor found himself wandering next to Hunter up the stairs to the front room.

"You're looking better." Grace's boyfriend spent a lot of energy being nondescript and dangerous—and using as few words as possible. Tor took that as the compliment it was.

"Thank you," he said, fighting back a yawn. Ugh. Still tired, though. Suddenly they couldn't be in the Caribbean soon enough.

"You staying the night?"

"Yeah. I've got to go back to my apartment tomorrow to put some more stuff in order, but by the week before Christmas I should be here for the whole von Trapp family *thing* Felix, Danny, and Julia have planned."

To his surprise, Hunter's quiet face with the granite jaw split into an almost delighted grin.

"Awesome. It wouldn't be the same if you weren't with us. Speaking of which...." Hunter raised his eyebrows a couple of times. "You up for poker?"

Tor opened his mouth to say, "Oh my God, *yes*!" but found himself yawning instead. "Oh God," he managed through his second yawn. "I have no idea why this is happening!"

Hunter chuckled. "Go to bed. There will be lots of other games, believe me."

Tor nodded, grateful, and then, to his surprise, his stomach growled. He'd discovered, after his first week of sleeping off the bender, that he'd lost nearly fifteen pounds. Usually one to document every morsel he ate—the better to fit into the slick suits he wore on camera—he'd been lifting his usual diet restrictions a tad because he didn't have enough money to get refitted for his entire wardrobe.

And also because he loved carbs, and denying himself was one of the hardest parts of his job.

"But first," he said decisively, "I'm going to go to the kitchen to get a snack. Think Phyllis would mind?"

Hunter shook his head. "Naw, she lives to feed us. Or at least to have her staff feed us." He shrugged. "I think she *really* likes having a staff to order around."

Phyllis was the Salinger's housekeeper, who, Tor was pretty sure, had originally taken the job so she could study philosophy and live somewhere with a bathroom and running water. But she'd had the job since Josh was born. She'd known who Danny was to Felix and had watched the relationship thrive, fracture, and then more recently repair itself. She'd watched Josh grow up and, in the last few months, had been as terrified as the rest of them that he wouldn't recover from his illness and all that promise would be cut short. While everybody in the family had two jobs—Grace was a dancer *and* a grease man, Felix ran his company *and* the various family capers, Julia played society doyen while keeping the pulse of the wildly diverse and talented members of the crew—Phyllis had one.

Keep everything running, even when the family was afraid it was falling apart.

She did it with panache. And with food.

And, now that the mansion was constantly full of people, with staff.

As Tor neared the vast kitchen, passing the counter that doubled as a pass-through when they were having big dinners and heading for the big refrigerators that were tucked out of sight of the living room, he was surprised to see one member of the staff still working.

Midsized, like Torrance himself, with curly black hair, enormous sloe eyes, and a little bit of a *schmutz-stache* starting in deference to the late hour, Torrance had seen this kid working in the kitchen a lot in the past two weeks. Now he was finishing up with dishes from the dessert table that had been laid in the downstairs den while they'd planned their Caribbean adventure, and at the same time, keeping his eye on a timer set on one of the three shiny chrome stoves. As Torrance entered, he heard a beeping and looked to see that one of the ovens had preheated, and he couldn't hide his surprise.

"You're baking already?" he asked, and felt bad as the young man—Marco, he was pretty sure—whirled and took out his earbuds.

"I'm sorry?"

"Nothing," Tor said sheepishly. "I was just, you know, impressed. There were lots of desserts leftover from the meeting. I didn't think you'd need to be working on cookies quite so soon."

His answer was a blinding white smile in an olive-skinned face. "Oh! This?" He nodded toward the stove and a pan of something on the stovetop covered with a clean dish towel. "This is for Dr. Morgan. He's got a soft spot for my chocolate cream cheese muffins. I usually bake them in the morning, but now that *he's* fallen in love with them, *everybody* loves them. I thought I'd work on an extra batch now so we don't run out."

Tor had to chuckle. Yeah, everybody loved Danny, aka Benjamin Morgan. Unbidden came that moment in the bathtub when Tor had sobbed into the man's chest, soaking him in dirty bathwater, unable to stop. Danny hadn't left him, hadn't even moved to keep his shirt dry. Tor was pretty sure he'd had to change into some of Tor's clothes before they left to avoid walking into the freezing sleet while soaking wet.

"He's worth it," Tor said soberly. "And I'm certainly not here to steal his muffins."

"Then what can I do for you, Mr. Grayson?" young Marco asked, and Tor was tempted to say "Nothing" and then flee this dimly lit kitchen and the odd intimacy it threw over him and this industrious baker.

But his stomach gurgled again, and he gave an embarrassed smile. "Uhm, nothing with sugar," he said, surprising himself. "Do you have any leftovers?"

Dinner, if he remembered, had been London broil disks, served family style with a choice of mushroom Bordeaux sauce or garlic butter, along with steamed broccoli and some sort of magical mashed potato that he couldn't get out of his mind.

His baker chuckled. "I can get you a small plate. Here—sit at the island, and I'll have a snack for you in a minute, okay?" He winked. "Normally, Phyllis doesn't mind when people rifle through the fridge, but two of the three big muscly guys tend to raid the place like locusts. She's started hiding little snack-sized leftover portions in the back specifically for everybody else."

Tor laughed softly. "So which big muscly guy *doesn't* raid the place like a locust?"

"Mm.... Carl," Marco said, nodding his head in approval. "The big Viking guy who just moved in with the Salinger's mechanic, Michael."

"Wow. You do know everybody here," Tor said, impressed. "Yeah, Carl worries about his weight, because I think once you get that close to forty, metabolism stops being your friend."

"So my father tells me," he replied, shooing Tor to a stool at the island. The timer on the stove beeped again, and he paused to put his pan of muffins into the oven before moving toward the refrigerator with purpose. "'Marco,' he likes to say, putting his hands in the front of his pants like this," and Marco mimed a man of portly proportions adjusting himself in his too-tight waistband. "'Marco, be careful. I know you like to cook, and you do the family proud with your nonna's recipes, but I'm telling you. Every man in this family leads with his belt buckle. Don't be like us. Be better.'"

Marco erupted into chuckles as he finished his imitation, and Tor had to smile in return.

"But you cook and bake so well!" Tor protested. "How are you supposed to resist?"

Marco winked. "Tiny bites," he said wisely. "If something is delicious, one or two tiny bites will stay with you for a long time." Then he grimaced. "And if it's crap, you don't have so much to spit out."

It was Tor's turn to laugh, and he found himself utterly charmed with Marco, a quiet, industrious treasure in this hurricane house of brilliant criminals.

"Hold on," Marco murmured as Tor chuckled. He was bent double in the middle refrigerator, moving food containers neatly aside. "Hold on... yes! I knew we had some extra portions!"

And with that he pulled out a small brightly colored plastic container, neatly split into three compartments. The container had a clear top with pinprick holes in it, and Marco looked over his shoulder. "Mushroom Bordeaux or garlic butter?"

"Bordeaux," Tor said, his eyes going to half-mast just thinking about it.

"Excellent!" And with that, Marco trickled a teeny bit of water onto the lid before shaking the container slightly to make sure the water got in. "The steam helps make it fresh when we reheat it," he said before putting the meal into the microwave.

"That's impressive," Tor said, feeling a little bit sentimental over Marco's care. "I really can't thank you enough."

Marco shrugged. "It's nothing," he said, and a companionable silence fell over the kitchen.

Tor was just thinking that he'd really lucked out meeting Marco this evening when he noticed the young man was staring at him intently, almost uncomfortably so, before shaking his head and muttering to himself.

Oh, this was no good. Besides being almost angelically beautiful, with the raven's wing hair and the big black-rimmed brown eyes, Marco had proved to be a pleasant companion in the quiet of the kitchen. Tor hoped he hadn't done anything to offend the young man; a little alarm sounded in his head that if he was going to spend the next month with the Salingers, he'd better not insult their best cook!

"Marco?" Tor asked after a fraught moment. "Have I done anything to offend you?"

Marco sighed. Glancing around the kitchen, he sighed again, as though the immaculate state of things—and the two timers progressing nicely without him—had left him with nothing to hide behind. The microwave dinged, and he startled and then threw an almost guilty look at Tor before going to get his snack.

"You don't have to plate it!" Tor told him and then grunted as he saw it was too late. Marco had arranged everything nicely, and then he set it down on the counter, complete with a place mat and silverware rolled in a napkin.

"Thank you," he said, breathing in the steam lightly. "I appreciate it. I just, uhm, wish I knew what you were thinking about just now. I suddenly felt guilty about something that I didn't know I'd done."

Marco grimaced, looked at the timer on the oven that held the chocolate cream cheese muffins, and then back at Tor.

"You… you do the exposés on YouTube, don't you?" he said, and Tor stopped with his fork nearly to his mouth to gape at him.

"I'm sorry?"

"No… no, I'm sorry. I… you're eating. And you're a friend of Dr. Morgan and Mr. Salinger's, which means you're on the level. It's just… oh my God, take that bite!"

Without a word Tor shoved the mashed potatoes and London broil into his mouth. He was going to chew rudely, but then the flavors hit him all at once and he sighed a little, the startlement leaching from his body with every carb-filled molecule.

He swallowed, feeling far more blissed out than he had on quarts of Jim Beam, and took a deep breath, hoping to start again. "Okay," he said. "I'm going to take another bite, and you're going to figure out what you want to talk about." He made a show of glancing around the kitchen. "Just you and me here, kid. I swear I won't bite your head off, okay?"

Marco nodded, and to Tor's surprise he didn't merely *swallow*, he *gulped*. "Okay," he said in a small voice. "Just… please don't get mad."

"I won't," Tor said, hoping he could keep the promise. "But you need to tell me what's wrong before we can see if I can fix it."

Marco nodded. "It's my uncle Flory," he said with a miserable sigh. "He has a construction company. It's... well, half my cousins are employed by it, and the ones who don't work construction work design or reception. It's a big deal, you know?"

Tor nodded, but inside, alarm bells were going off. Oh no. Oh no. He *did* know. He could see where this was going from a thousand miles away, but he'd promised. And Marco was such a sweet guy! The least Tor could do was hear him out.

"I know," he said at last. "Keep going."

"So, this morning my uncle Flory gets a notice. His company is getting sued." Marco gave him a sharp, almost accusing look. "You probably know this—Flory Gallo and Sons—don't lie to me and say you don't know."

Tor's heart sank. "I know," he said. "But I don't know *you* or your family's side of the story. So tell me."

"So the lawsuit says that Flory Gallo and Sons got caught in a contracting scam. They'd been hired for a bathroom and kitchen renovation, and the result was a disaster. They sent pictures. There was a portajohn in the basement and a stove that was so badly ventilated it would kill people and holes in the floors—it was a *disaster.* I mean, we all stared at the pictures and we're losing our minds because who does that? And then we realized that *they thought we had.* Or at least my uncle's company had done it. That *we* were the disaster. And we looked through the papers and realized that they had proof. They had receipts from our receipt books—that we hadn't printed out. They had signatures from our employees—that we'd never hired. They had plans filed by my uncle—but the signatures didn't match. And then there was the kicker."

That accusing look was leveled at Tor again, and he had to fight not to throw up his London broil.

"Me," he said through a raw throat.

"You," Marco said, almost apologetically. "They said that the great Tor Grayson had run a sting on the company, and we were going to be exposed for the frauds we are."

We. It hadn't escaped Tor's attention that Marco kept saying "we." This wasn't just his family—Tor had "family" all over the Midwest, most of whom he'd ignore if he passed them in the grocery store. This was *family* the way Felix and Danny were family. This was Marco's anchor to the world, and yes, Tor had been planning to go to the editing board tomorrow morning and cut their family business to confetti.

Torrance sighed and sat back, wiping his mouth and gazing mournfully at the rest of the leftovers, which he could no longer eat. Oh God. What was he supposed to say?

"Is it true?" It came out of his mouth before he could stop it, and he cursed himself. Of course it was true. He had receipts, pictures, plans from the county registrar, firsthand accounts from suppliers—mounds and mounds of evidence that Flory Gallo and Sons was as crooked as a New Jersey mob boss. He'd tried to interview the head of the company—Florian Gallo—but had gotten the brush-off, and none of the employees would talk to him. But then that wasn't unusual. Nobody liked a snitch.

"Is what true?" Marco asked, something like hurt in his voice. "Is my family full of crooks and cheats?"

"No," Tor retorted. "And by the way, I tried to interview your family. You know that, right? I called the numbers the family gave me, I visited jobsites—"

"And we didn't know who you were and who you were representing!" Marco retorted. "Or at least my uncle Flory didn't. I didn't know about any of this until this morning."

"But how am I supposed to know there's another side of the story if nobody will *tell* me their side of the story?" Torrance snapped. "I *tried*, do you understand that? I triple checked my facts, I made *multiple* attempts to track somebody down from the company because I don't like persecuting innocent people. Do you think I don't *know* how much power the internet wields? *Nobody would talk to me*, and now you're telling me I'm about to go live with a story that's all crap? You're *blaming* me for that when I've got at least five hours of footage of your uncle's company blowing me off?"

His voice had risen, and it was echoing in the kitchen in spite of Marco's frantic arm waves to shush him.

"You said you wouldn't get angry!" he protested in a whisper, and Torrance glared at him.

"Well, you *didn't* say you were going to suddenly speak for a group of people I worked my *ass* off to talk to weeks ago when I was putting this story together."

Marco subsided and managed to look embarrassed and defensive at the same time. "Well, they're talking now," he said after a moment. "Will you listen?"

Tor groaned and sank his head into his hands, every bit of the exhaustion he'd come here to recover from sinking into his bones.

"Sure," he said after a moment. "I would have listened before." He swallowed. "Well, not two weeks ago. Two weeks ago I was...."

"Sick," Marco said with confidence. "Mr. Felix told us."

Tor shrugged. A sad little part of him said he would have liked to tell Marco the truth about that, but not now. Because Marco, the sweet guy who was making muffins, wasn't the only guy he was talking to. Apparently now he was talking to Marco *Gallo*, nephew to a guy Tor'd been about to prove was one of Chicago's crooked residential contractors.

"Yeah," he said. "I was sick. And honestly? I was going to wrap up the exposé and download it and then go on vacation. I've got another story I can run with instead while I talk to your uncle, but…." His voice shook, and so did the hand he brought up to his mouth. "Marco, I-I really need to start that vacation."

Suddenly Marco's eyes, which had grown so hard and bright when he'd been vehemently protesting his family's innocence, softened. "I'm so sorry," he said. "Please—please eat."

"No—"

"Yes. Please. I… if you can come see me tomorrow at ten, after breakfast is cleared, we can talk. I can get my uncle on the phone. We can discuss. Is that okay? Can you… can you promise not to run with that story until my uncle has a chance to talk to you? At least hear him out?"

Torrance nodded. "Yeah," he said. "Sure. I'll text Phil and have him table the contractor story." He remembered what he'd been saying to Stirling and Molly that afternoon. "I was going to follow up on more bogus contractors after Christmas. We can push it off until then, at least."

Marco brightened. "Thank you," he said softly. "A thousand times thank you." And then he frowned a little—but not with anger. With concern. "But eat," he ordered. "Please. Please. I… I was enjoying our conversation," he confessed almost shyly. "I would hate to have it end in anger."

A month ago, Tor would have refused. He would have gathered his dignity in both hands and gone off to his bedroom to start editing and reviewing his story and tracking down the roots of the thing to see where he might have gotten it wrong.

But God, he was so tired. And he'd promised Phil, promised Danny—promised *everybody*—that he wouldn't push so hard for a little while.

And maybe not pushing so hard was accepting an olive branch from a baker in a kitchen after hours.

"I was enjoying it too," he confessed, picking up his fork again. He gave Marco a tired, if sincere, smile. "Now tell me about your family."

Marco did.

Surprise Guest

"No, HE hasn't left yet," Phyllis reassured Marco. "And yes, all your duties are done. You can always go knock on his door, you know—now that everybody's fed, you're a guest."

Marco grimaced. "That doesn't feel right," he told the older woman with the graying frizz of curls.

Phyllis rolled her eyes and leaned against the counter. "This isn't *Downton Abbey*, Marco. The Salingers don't hire servants—they hire staff, and then they respect us enough to let us do our jobs."

"Maybe," he said. "But I don't see *you* invited to any of their secret downstairs confabs."

Phyllis laughed outright. "Because I'd rather serve cookies. What you *also* don't see is Julia and me talking about the plan while we're doing yoga in the mornings, or Danny and me on the treadmill afterwards, or Felix having me sit down so he can run something by me when he's in his office. I may not be going to the confab, but I definitely know what's doing."

"But aren't they going on vacation?" Marco complained. "In the Caribbean? *Without* you?"

Phyllis laughed some more. "I hate the beach. I hate the sand. The idea of putting on a swimsuit in front of the entire family gives me hives. No. They asked me, and I asked *them* if I could take my own vacation in France. Two weeks in Paris—not exactly in the spring, but I *like* the snow. And I am fine going to the Louvre without crowds. Also, there's a tour of the birthplaces of French philosophers in January." She gave a happy sigh. "Voltaire, Sartre, Beauvoir, Descartes—I don't care what their philosophy *was*, I want to see the place that spawned it!"

Marco was forced to smile with her—she really did look rapturous, and his original assumption—that she'd been left behind while the family went to party without her—had irritated him no end. It was, in fact, part of the reason he'd let down his guard enough to talk to Torrance Grayson the night before.

Part of it.

The other part had been that Torrance Grayson had seemed so... approachable. So human. It would have been one thing if he'd come in and thrown his weight around and acted like his fame and notoriety on the internet won him some special favor or something. Marco might have just thrown a cold plastic container at him with a fork and told him to knock himself out. But he'd been kind and had smiled, apologized for bothering Marco at his job when—as Phyllis reminded the kitchen and cleaning staff repeatedly—the people living in the mansion *were* their jobs, and had generally kept that civil contract between client and server with what seemed to be sincere politeness.

And when Marco had felt his temper slipping, had been *dying* to know how this slightly built, *tired*-looking man had managed to make such a heinous misjudgment, Torrance Grayson had listened.

Which was more than Marco's uncle Flory was threatening to do at the moment.

His phone buzzed in his pocket, and he murmured, "Excuse me," to Phyllis before pulling it out.

He's being stubborn, his cousin Camille had typed in. *He says he can't stay until 10:30.* Camille was Flory's receptionist and the scheduler for the construction teams. She literally made the calendar, so he'd gone to her for help the minute Torrance had gone to bed the night before, his body sagging with weariness but his small snack plate licked clean.

If I'm bringing in the guy who can make or break his business, he'd better stay until 11! Marco typed back frantically. *Torrance is listening— he's going to back out now?*

He's claiming he's got a meeting with clients at a site, but Frankie says that's BS.... I think he's scared.

Of what? Marco's stomach went cold, and he remembered his staunch and passionate defense of his family the night before. *Cammie, he's not part of this, is he?*

NO. Camille's response was immediate, but there were little thought bubbles continuing… *but I think he knows what this is about and he doesn't want to tell us.*

Well, tough. I've got the guy who could make or break the company primed to hear our story—if you have to tie him to the furniture, make him wait until 11!

He hit Send with undue force, grumbling to himself, and a low chuckle penetrated his irritation. With a little squeak he fumbled his phone, his adrenaline spiking as he pictured it hitting the tile floor and splintering the screen. His relief when a hand came out and caught it was matched only with his embarrassment when he realized who it was.

"Oh my God," he muttered. "Sorry."

Torrance Grayson was there, neatly dressed in black jeans, black boots, and a tight cream-colored cable-knit sweater. "No sorry. Just glad I could save it for you. Intense conversation?"

Marco scowled. "My uncle Flory is being obstinate," he muttered, embarrassed. "Cammie and Frankie—my cousins—are trying to keep him from taking off, and they're pissed. I mean, it's *their* company too, you know?"

Torrance nodded. "Yeah, I get it. People our age tend to forget, but not everybody likes to be on video. Let's go see him, and if he's not there, maybe Frankie and Cammie can shed enough light on the subject to at least get a start on things."

Marco nodded unhappily. "That's really kind of you. I just… I mean, you're putting yourself out. I got upset last night, but I pay attention. I know this is your livelihood too."

Tor gave him a crooked smile. "Yeah, but my livelihood goes down the tubes if I put out a shitty story. Let's try to make sure I'm using my platform to be as truthful as I can, okay?"

"Okay." Marco let out a sigh. "Thank you."

"Hey!" Phyllis interrupted. "You two—before you go out into that mess, you need the essentials." And with that she pushed two enormous travel mugs of chocolate-laced coffee into their hands, and a small insulated bag that was throwing steam off from its seams into Marco's other hand. "Give those a few minutes to cool down," she advised. "They're hotter than the surface of the sun."

Marco looked from the bag to the mugs—all of which had been prepared while he'd been texting his family—with profound gratitude. "Phyllis, if I wasn't gay, I'd marry you," he said with a hint of reverence in his voice.

She cackled. "In this house, I get that a *lot*. Marco, I'd love to see you back here at four to prep for dinner," she said, "but I understand if you'll be late."

"I'll get him back on time," Tor said with a quiet smile. "I promise, Phyllis—I may need to drag him to the city to get more clothes and to close up the apartment, but I promised Danny and Felix I'd be under their roof until we take off."

Phyllis's gaze went fond and gentle, and she patted Tor's cheek. "Blessed boy. You do that. I want you here so we can fatten you up, okay?"

"Yes, ma'am," he responded, and while his eyes were twinkling, Marco got the feeling he was taking her very seriously.

She kissed his cheek. "Now drive safe," she said, and away they went, stopping in the foyer for their heavy jackets and pulling the hats out of the pockets before they even opened the door.

"Felix loaned me Danny's SUV," Tor said, tossing the keys in the air.

"Don't you have a vehicle?" Marco asked, appreciating the beauty of the vast front yard, even covered in snow. Two pairs of boot prints could be seen along the side of the drive, untouched by the wheels of the vehicles that had already come and gone that day, and Marco wondered who had taken an early morning walk and then thought he might know. Benjamin Morgan—more commonly referred to as "Uncle Danny"—had taken the house's other Christmas rescue out into the predawn cold, and Marco wasn't sure what they'd said, but they'd both been quietly luminous when they returned. His attention went back to Tor, who was playing with the key fob, and then the SUV, which had been pulled in front of the house already, turned over, the lights coming on as the engine began to purr.

"I do!" Tor said, lighting up as he headed for the driver's side. "But it's in the garage at my apartment building, and it's a Mazda Miata. Great gas mileage but crap in the snow and ice." There was a pause as they both hoisted themselves into the SUV and buckled in. Marco noted with a little sigh of pleasure that the seats were warmed, and then Tor continued.

"Besides—Felix is always trying to repay me, I guess. Spoil me for being loyal to him back in March. Telling him no, I wouldn't borrow his vehicle, seemed churlish, you know?"

Marco chuckled, sort of liking Torrance Grayson's almost sheepish explanation. The private man Marco had glimpsed in his last month of working for the Salingers was very different from his public persona.

"My father is always giving me cash," Marco told him, snorting softly. "I've got a small apartment, my rent's paid up, and cooking for the Salingers is an absolute dream job, believe me. But every time I go to my parents' place for dinner—and we're talking once a week—my father tries to stuff a bunch of twenties in my back pocket. 'Here you go, Marco, so you never have to worry, okay?'"

He fell into his father's second-generation immigrant accent naturally, knowing it could have been *his* accent if he'd stayed in the old family neighborhood and worked the family business.

"And do you?" Tor asked. "Have to worry, I mean?"

"Not since I graduated from chef school," Marco said with a shrug. "I put the money in savings."

"For what?" And there was no disguising the curiosity in his voice. Marco smiled slightly and realized he had no reason, really, not to indulge in his own hopes and dreams for a moment.

"Well, one of two things," he said, and he realized he was absolutely bubbling with excitement about telling somebody. "The first is obvious— my own restaurant or pastry shop. I mean, every chef wants one, right?"

"Of course," Tor said, tipping his head.

"But I'm still sort of torn about that. I mean, the hours are horrendous, the stress is off the charts, and I saw this in school, you know? It becomes all about the politics and the schmoozing, and not so much about the food."

"And you like it to be about the food," Tor said, prompting him.

"Well, *yeah*. I mean—" He let out a breath. "—I started cooking in my grandmother's kitchen. The woman wouldn't have known a recipe if it had bit her on the ginormous backside. But God, she could cook. She taught me spaghetti sauce by throwing all these fresh ingredients into a pot, adding some sugar, voila! She had me do the same, and I added a little chili powder, a few jalapenos and some spicy sausage, and suddenly the family thinks I invented food. My grandmother was *delighted*. She turned me loose on her other recipes, and for a few years, we played the game of Marco or Noni? And when she got older and started getting sick and forgetful, I sort of took over. When I graduated from high school, the whole family sent me to chef school. Like everybody. My father, my uncles—Uncle Flory's company paid my tuition for four years, so I could get a humanities education too. And now once or twice a month, when I go home, I cook for the whole family and try out recipes and stuff. And the whole family celebrates with food—and they celebrate *me* and *my food*." He paused for a moment, not sure how he could sum all this up.

"You want what you do to be important," Torrance Grayson said softly. "So when you make a special recipe or go out of your way to do something spectacular, it makes people feel good, like it did when you were a kid."

"*Yes!*" Marco crowed, ecstatic that somebody got it. "I don't want it to be about how many stars I get, or if the right person tastes my food and doesn't spit it out. I want... you know. Families to come eat at my place because the last time they had my sauce, it made their son's graduation a celebration."

"That sounds amazing," Torrance said. "Why can't you do that, again?"

"Hours, overhead, politics," Marco summed up shortly. "Also, I'm really good at pastries, and I don't know which one I want to open yet. A restaurant or a pastry shop. So there's that."

Torrance laughed throatily, like he enjoyed Marco's dilemma. "What's the other thing you want to save up for?" he asked.

"Well, the thing is, I *love* my job right now. Phyllis lets me plan menus and order everybody around. I mean, five days a week, we cook for at least ten people, often twenty, and it's almost like having a very tiny restaurant in which I'm only making one very cool thing a night. It's exciting without being stressful, and Felix knows *everybody*. I've probably cooked for more celebrities in the past three months than would come through my door if I set up shop in the Loop and sent out invitations. So all the ways a chef's ego gets stroked, believe me, it's happening right now, and I sort of want to enjoy it without health inspections and overhead and bills, right?"

"Absolutely," Tor agreed. "So what's your other plan?"

"Mmm…," Marco hummed. "I want to take a sort of food tour of Europe. You see them on BBC or the cooking channels all the time, right? I want to look up all of the greatest places to eat and to go stay in the cities for a few days and see where they shop and have a dinner there. For an entire month, I want to do nothing but taste other people's cooking when they're at the top of their game. Selfish, I know," he said, but then he nodded enthusiastically. "But *so* worth it. I figure that if I start to get burned out, I'll start planning that trip. *That* trip would fill up my soul. After a month of that, I could cook for the rest of my life."

"Wow," Torrance said, piloting the SUV through the streets of Glencoe to the interstate. "Just… just *wow*. That's impressive."

"What is?" Marco asked, suddenly embarrassed.

"The scope and breadth of those dreams!" Torrance told him, laughing. "I'm—wow. You're so passionate. It's amazing. I barely eat, and I could listen to you talk about food for hours. Damn." He shrugged, but he was grinning and looking sincere, so Marco figured he'd take him at his word.

"You know where we're going, right?" he asked, suddenly remembering that he hadn't given directions.

"Yeah, down this interstate, out by that little airstrip?"

"Yes!" Marco was surprised. "How did you know?"

"Easy," Torrance told him dryly. "I came out here more than once. I told you. Five hours of footage." With a jerk of his chin he indicated the iPad he'd put on top of their winter coats on the bench seat of the vehicle. "I really did try to talk to your family."

Marco grunted, the excitement of talking to a companion as much fun as Torrance Grayson fading as he remembered what they were doing.

"God," he muttered. "I don't know what got into Uncle Flory."

"We'll find out," Tor murmured. "In the meantime…." He paused and lifted his mug from the holder and took an obviously satisfying swig of coffee. "Pass the croissants, Marco. We've got at least forty-five minutes once we hit the on-ramp—traffic's a bear today."

FLORY GALLO and Sons Contracting looked like a lot of construction companies. There was an office building that consisted of a double-wide trailer which sat in the center of warehouses, machinery, and towing equipment. The snows had come thick and fast in the beginning of December, so a lot of that machinery was tucked under lean-tos and ports, but the snow had been cleared from all paths, so it was obvious the company was still active in spite of the inclement weather.

"Pull up under the carport by the ramp up to the office," Marco directed. "The snow's coming down again, and I think Frankie clears the pathway, like, once an hour. That way Mr. Salinger's nice car won't get spattered."

"Good thinking," Tor said appreciatively. He did as Marco told him and turned off the car. The cold was immediately apparent, but Tor held his hand up before they could gather their coats. "Look," he said soberly. "I want to listen to everything your family has to say—but I think it's important that they see the footage *I* have first so we know where to start. If this is somebody from your uncle's company, and he doesn't realize they've been doing shoddy work, we can post him saying he'll address the issue."

Marco swallowed and nodded. "I can't think of any other explanation," he said miserably. It had occurred to him on the drive over, as Torrance had continued to talk to him kindly, genuinely interested in his family, in his schooling, in his dreams, that this wasn't a man who wanted to hurt people. If Torrance Grayson had a reason to think Flory's company was up to no good, his evidence must have seemed legit.

"I can think of two," Torrance said, surprising him. "And if your uncle Flory is the guy you've been telling me about, the other explanation is going to take a lot of untangling."

Marco nodded. "Look. I… I can't see my uncle's company doing what you say they did. I can't. But I need to say thank you. For listening to me last night. For coming out here and trying again to listen. I don't know what the explanation is for this—but I know Flory's a good guy. The best. I wouldn't be doing my duty as family if I didn't try to protect him."

"I get it," Tor said, a slight smile on his face. "Believe it or not, that's why I walked away from Felix's cable show. Somebody was making false accusations about Felix, and I just couldn't watch everything he'd put together come tumbling down. When I struck out on my own, I made a promise to myself that I was never going to be that guy—I wasn't going to be the guy who chose clicks or sponsors over the truth. So here I am, making sure that's not what's going to happen. But I've got no guarantees I even know what the truth is. Are you ready?"

Marco nodded, shivering as the cold seeped in. "Ready or not, we're freezing our asses off," he said grimly. "Let's go."

Together they bundled up against the snow. Then Tor grabbed his tablet and they were rolling out.

The heat from the office hit them like a wall as soon as they walked in, and Marco found himself undoing the snaps to his outerwear in a hurry.

His cousin Camille was on her knees in front of a filing cabinet, her black hair a sprayed cloud over her head, tethered to earth with a bright red-and-green scarf, as she shoved files in with speed, accuracy, and force. "Don't forget to wipe your boots off!" Camille hollered, and Marco stopped in midstride before tugging Tor back to the cast-iron scraper and the thick mat designed especially for people with snow and mud on their boots.

After some scraping, the two of them were back in the office, shivering because they'd unsnapped their coats before going back outside, but hey, at least they weren't tracking mud.

"We're all clean now, Camille," Marco called. "Are you happy?"

"Hey—I just cleaned in here," Camille told them both, heaving her round figure to her feet and adjusting her wool skirt and festive sweater with a few deft tugs. There was a bigger desk near the door with *Florian Gallo* etched onto the brass nameplate, but judging by the files piled on Camille's desk, as well as the various carts with *other* files and receipt books piled on them *next* to Camille's desk, it was pretty clear who was doing all the work.

"Did you find Uncle Flory?" Marco asked, stripping his coat off and hanging it on the coatrack before taking Torrance's. He noticed that while his own coat was a lined peacoat, Torrance wore a slick, well-insulated parka cut tight enough to restrict his breathing, and Marco wondered if Torrance ever let himself not be buttoned down.

Even sneaking a snack in the kitchen the night before, he'd been all professionalism, dark hair gelled, blue eyes alert—he'd even been wearing a suit. He had an arresting face, with wide cheekbones and a square jaw that seemed to add weight to his pixie-thin figure. A hundred years ago, he might have been described as "dapper," but those cheekbones…. It would take a lot of laugh lines and crow's-feet to make him look older than twenty-five. And today, in black jeans and a sweater, he was just as arresting—just as handsome.

"Finding's relative," Camille replied, pulling Marco away from his almost swoony appraisal of Torrance Grayson's coat. *It smells good,* a little voice in his head whispered, and he had to tell it to stop that. So a guy listened to his hopes and dreams during a forty-five-minute car ride—it wasn't a marriage proposal! "Frankie has a tracker on his phone, and we know where Flory is. We just don't know why."

"Where is he?" Marco asked, appalled.

"Industrial corridors of the city proper." Marco's cousin Frankie answered the question while emerging from the back of the trailer. A hallway down that way led to individual offices, restrooms, and a break area with big couches that lent themselves to naps when inclement weather stopped a job in midtrack.

"Seriously?" Marco asked, surprised. "Is he visiting a vendor?"

"I have no idea," Frankie said in disgust. "There's a lot of buildings that way, and the phone tracker only narrows it down to the block. The block he's on has fabrics and furniture, so it could be, but…." Frankie shrugged, and Marco grimaced at his handsome, sloe-eyed cousin. Frankie was about ten years older than Marco, slender, with pale brown hair and a slightly crooked nose. He was never without company, male or female, and Marco had always marveled at how easily Frankie handled the family pressure to settle down. Right now, though, he looked anything but settled.

"You guys told him what this was about?" Marco asked, although he knew they had. They were the ones who had called *him* the day before, when they'd gotten the letter about the lawsuit.

"I swear to Christ we did," Camille told him, holding her fingers up like a Girl Scout. "Marco, he was all excited about meeting with you this morning, and then he got a phone call—not even on the landline in here, but on his cell while he was doing equipment checks outside. Got a call, and suddenly he couldn't get out of here fast enough." She shook her head. "It was weird." Then she turned to Torrance, her eyes pleading. "I don't suppose there's any chance you'd talk to *us*?" she asked.

"Off the record?" Frankie asked. "Our brothers are all out on jobs, but they asked too. You wouldn't want to tell us what… what made you think this company that did such shitty work was ours? I'm… I mean, I'm baffled." He shook his head, looking hurt and outraged and miserable. "My old man, he spent our entire lives beating a work ethic into our thick heads. Not, like, physically!" he hastened to add. "Just… you know. Don't do shitty work. People depended on us. Our quality was important. The idea that you've got a story that shows this company—like, *my family's company*, being assholes—that's awful. I couldn't sleep all last night. There's gotta be an explanation. If nothing else, I need to see the workers who did this so I can drive them out of the business, am I right?"

"I hear you," Torrance said. "Okay, then. Are you needed up here, or do you want to go somewhere private? The footage I'm going to show you is proprietary, and I don't want anybody but you folks to see it."

Camille waved her hand. "Oh, we're on the tail end of our season. I think we've only got two jobs out at the moment, and they'll be done and inspected by Friday. We don't come back to work until the middle of January."

Torrance nodded. "Do all contractors do that?"

"Naw," Frankie told him. "But Dad, as soon as he started making enough money that he wasn't panicked all the time, that was the route he took. He works us hard during the summer, 'cause that's when people are doing their renovations, but he flat out closes the place down over Christmas. Some of the guys, they pick up their own contracts, but between the snow and the holidays? Forgettaboutit."

"I hear you," Torrance murmured, nodding. "I'm doing the same thing, in fact, so whatever we learn today, I'm going to have to leave it alone and come back to it. I texted my assistant—we're going to quick edit another story we had ready. It's not as hard-hitting as this one, but if you can prove to me that this isn't you, I'm going to need to do a *lot* more research about what really went down."

Camille and Frankie both nodded soberly, and then Camille set the door to ring should someone enter, and Frankie gestured them down the hall to the break room.

Torrance immediately sat and started pulling stuff up on his tablet while Camille poured coffee and served up a plate of cookies.

"We're good, Cammie," Marco told her. "Phyllis wouldn't let us out of the house without provisions."

In response, Camille set the cookies down in front of him—his favorite, his aunt Marie's homemade Milanos—and pinched his cheek. "You're so cute, you know that? Thinking you only need one sweet a day, thinking that's enough coffee. I could just eat you up, but I'd die of sugar shock."

And then she flounced over to the stuffed chair and sat primly, her wool skirt still covering the tops of her long, warm boots. Camille had wide hips and a blousy figure, but she dressed like every straight man in Illinois only *wished* he was looking at her ass. She was never short a date on a Friday night, although Marco had a feeling she was thinking about settling down.

"Do I get a cookie?" Frankie asked, snatching three from the plate.

"You're gonna get fat, and then nobody's gonna want to blow you," Camille shot back, unimpressed.

"You're my *sister*," Frankie complained. "What a fuckin' mouth!"

"You should hear him whine if he goes too long high and dry," Camille told Marco, confidential-like, and Torrance caught Marco's eyes and winked. "He's not like you, Marco—you're a monk. As far as we know, you don't *have* a sex life!"

Marco wished fervently that he could be swallowed by this heinously uncomfortable and appallingly orange-and-green ugly break room couch. "I keep my private life private," he defended weakly, and Camille guffawed.

"No dates, no boyfriend—don't think your mother don't talk to mine. She's worried it'll shrivel up and fall off."

Tor let a muffled snort sneak out, and Marco resisted the urge to put his hand over his face. "Is there poison in these?" he asked, picking up a Milano. "Please tell me there's poison."

"Oh, as if. My mother *loves* us. The only one *she's* gonna poison is Dad if he doesn't get his ass down here to defend his company." She let out a worried huff, and the family nose-in-the-business banter subsided. "Are you ready yet, Mr. Grayson, because I feel like we need more cookies."

Marco patted her arm, and she squeezed his hand.

"I'm ready," Torrance said. "Okay, first thing I'm going to show you is the worksite. Camille, you saw the address on the papers, right?"

"Oh yeah, we did," she muttered. "Wasn't in any of our records."

"Okay, then, that's something," Torrance said. He flipped the tablet toward Frankie, Camille, and Marco as they sat, and touched the screen.

Marco had to admit—the site was a *mess*. The portajohn was *in the basement*, which no self-respecting contractor would do, and the work on the kitchen installations—yeesh!

"Holy fucknuggets," Frankie muttered, watching the camera pan over unrepaired holes in the floor, cabinet doors that had been left hanging off their hinges, and a ventilation system that would either set fire to or suffocate anybody who lived in the house. "If my team left a site looking like that, I'd kill them. I'd buy a gun, learn how to shoot, and kill them dead. This is disgusting. Oh my God—I need my sandbag so I can beat something up!" He made a couple of impressive air punches that had Torrance jerking back in startlement. Frankie may have been built slender, but he worked his ass off—even his air punches hit hard.

"There's more," Torrance told them, and Marco's heart sank.

Torrance came on screen then, doing a "tweener," as Marco had heard him call it, when he narrated something the camera was going to show. He was illustrating where he'd hidden cameras in the house to keep track of the contactors when they came back for what was supposed to be a walk-through inspection in what was, essentially, an unusable, unlivable jobsite.

"That's good," Frankie said approvingly. "That camera in the kitchen *should* catch them fixing all that shit on the floor and doing the tile—if they don't even address the cabinets, you know something's wrong."

"What about downstairs?" Camille asked. "What do you have down there?"

Torrance grimaced in distaste. "Well, the best place to put the camera in the basement turned out to be the outside of the portajohn because there's an ambient light in the roof of the john." He shook his head. "Let's say that one of our two bad actors here had a *very* unfortunate meeting with the portajohn, and the speakers on the camera caught every moment."

There was a general groan, and Marco squeezed his eyes shut in sympathy. "I'm so sorry," he murmured.

"Just another editing session in the life of a glamourous journalist," Torrance said dryly. "But the shots we got from that camera got some great conversation—some that you need to hear." He grinned unexpectedly. "That's the job too. You gotta sort through a lot of shit for the real gold."

Camille and Frankie roared with laughter, and Marco chuckled. For a guy who was here because Marco had unloaded on him in the kitchen the night before, he was proving surprisingly charming. Surprisingly human. Marco took a deep breath as Torrance leaned over the table for a moment, hoping surreptitiously to get another hit of his smells—soap, antiperspirant, aftershave. Whatever it all was, it was making Marco's chest buzz, and contrary to what Camille and Frankie thought about him living like a monk, the truth was he knew what sex was, and he knew his weakness.

A delicious smell made him want to devour something.

"Okay, here's the conversation *without* the editing I used for the segment. I'm just going to let it play. When it's done, you can tell me if you recognize the two men on the screen." Torrance was gazing at everybody in the room soberly. "Remember, we have receipts and invoices done on company stationery, and I can let you look at copies of that too. But in the meantime, watch the convo and tell me what you think."

Marco nodded tensely, knowing Camille and Frankie were doing the same, and Torrance hit Play.

They were in the dank basement again, with the portajohn sitting front and center like a stench-ridden blue Tardis. There were some sounds off camera, and a burly, *over*muscled man with a blue watch cap, beige eyebrows, and almost no neck, who was wearing a bright blue T-shirt with the company logo on it entered, throwing rubbish from the floor haphazardly into a big plastic bucket. Even as they watched, he ignored things like nails and tools and stuck to broken shards of wood.

"The hell are you doing?" The voice was also off camera at first. "We don't need to clean up!"

"The old man would have a fit," the big guy grumbled, throwing more wood into the bucket. "I gotta."

"The old man doesn't care!" The other guy came in, wearing the same shirt and a red baseball cap with the same logo. This man was smaller, both in height and weight, presenting as very midsized. Average. Brownish hair, hazel eyes, a few crooked teeth, but nothing too eye-catching. The eye would skate over this guy any day of the week.

Marco thought that they *could* have employed this man and nobody would have noticed.

"But it's not safe," said the giant. "There's nails on the floor and shit. And hammers—those are expensive."

"Well, pick up the tools!" And the smaller man started doing that, throwing them into what sounded like a toolbox off camera. As the metal objects clattered and banged to their destination, Marco, Frankie, and Camille all winced.

"That's no way to treat a tool," Frankie muttered. "Dad would filet this asshole with a pry bar."

"Sh!" hissed Camille, because they were talking again.

"Is the kitchen done?" the big guy asked, and the little guy snorted.

"That was harder than I thought. I think we should get out of here before the people get here. We can just invoice them and sue if they don't pay."

"But Cheezer, people could get hurt. Flory says you gotta do it right!" The whine in the big guy's voice was unmistakable. Not smart enough to know better or wanting his pay? Marco wasn't sure which.

"We're doing what the *boss* wanted," Cheezer (must be a nickname!) told him sharply. "Off books. It's fine. I mean, it looks a little rough, but it's not gonna blow back on us."

"But Mr. Flory'll get mad!" the big guy said, trying to make a stand.

"Who *cares* what Florian Gallo thinks!" Cheezer snapped. "Who gives a crap? We're not doing this job for him, we're doing it for—"

At that moment there was a clatter down the basement stairs and the camera angle changed. This must have been edited footage, Marco realized, switching to Torrance's cameraman's point of view.

Torrance was suddenly front and center, although his attention was on the two men in the basement, staring at the camera like possums about to meet their maker.

"I'm Torrance Grayson of *City Live*," he said. "You sent an email to the owners of this house saying the job would be done tomorrow. Are you aware that we've had the state inspector out, and not only are you out of compliance, but if the problems in this house aren't fixed, the house will be condemned?"

"Cheezer!" the big man cried, obviously frightened.

"Out of here, Clyde!" Cheezer yelled, and for a moment, the image became chaos as the two men quite literally shoved their way past Torrance and his cameraman as they stood at the foot of the stairs. Torrance fell backward and to the side, and while the camera was held at the cameraman's side, it gave a fractured view of a hand coming out to give an assist to get him back on his feet.

"Fucking. Ouch." Torrance cradled his wrist for a moment, grimacing.

"Are you going to have a bruise?" his cameraman asked, and to his credit, he sounded legitimately worried.

"No place that's gonna show up on film!" Torrance cracked with a wince. "Think we can catch those bozos?"

"No," said the cameraman, "but let's check the video we got from the planted cameras and see what we get."

With that, the picture went black, and Torrance closed the tablet.

The silence in the room was thick, and then Camille sighed. "Can I see the receipts?" she asked politely, and she sounded thoughtful, not angry.

Torrance pulled up pictures on the tablet, then handed it to her so she could scroll through. "Okay," she mumbled. "Okay, these look like ours, sort of."

"Sort of?" Torrance asked, alert.

"Here," she said, handing him the tablet. "Let me go get our registers and our stationery. It's gonna be like one of those kids' games, the kind where you compare pictures, you know?"

Torrance nodded, smiling slightly. "Yeah. I remember those. Go get them and we'll play spot the differences. But what about the guys?"

Frankie grunted, and so did Camille.

"The guys," Frankie said after a minute, "are where it gets complicated."

Marco stared at him. "Those were our guys?" he asked, his voice squeaking.

"No!" Frankie retorted. "I told you—it's complicated!"

"It's not that complicated," Camille said, rolling her eyes. "The big guy? Clyde?"

"Yeah?" Torrance asked, with what Marco felt like was a massive quantity of patience.

"He worked for us for a couple of years. Sweet guy. His father—a *very* elderly man—would bring him here every day, and Clyde would pick up the jobsites. A lot like he was doing there, by the way."

"Except our guys don't leave tools around like that," Frankie muttered.

"And our guys sweep nails up too," Camille added, like this was obvious. "But Clyde's only job—you remember."

"Picking up wood scraps to sell to the guy who makes sawdust," Frankie confirmed. "Yeah, I remember. He was good at it," he said to Torrance. "I mean, obviously not that bright, and built like a frickin' *bear.* Every now and then we'd ask him to help us haul stuff. But not often because he couldn't think on his feet, you know?"

Torrance shook his head. "You're going to need to explain," he apologized.

"Well, lifting stuff and hauling it around takes a certain…." Frankie grappled with the idea. "Athletic intelligence, I guess you'd say. If a load shifts, you've got to figure out what to do next. If someone is walking nearby, you've got to, you know, not head for them in a straight line and almost take their skulls off when they try to dodge the giant pipe on your shoulders. It's just that all the things that make a site safe take some thinking, and that wasn't Clyde's strongpoint, you see?"

"I get it now," Torrance said, nodding. "Do you think he was learning-disabled? This clip here is the only place we hear him speak, and it was a tough call to make. We used a lot of clips of Cheezer talking—and of his face—because we didn't want to put Clyde on the spot if that was the case."

"We suspected something," Frankie said, nodding. He gave a slight pained smile. "The T-shirt he's wearing was definitely one of ours when he was working here."

"Why did he stop?"

Camille—who had left briefly to grab the promised paperwork—returned in time for the question. "His father passed," she said.

"I didn't know that," Frankie told her. "Aww, Dad knew the guy. What happened to him?"

She made a face that showed all her teeth and curled her upper lip. "That Cheezer guy showed up one day—you were out on a job. Clyde was in the passenger seat, and it was sad. He waved at me like he always did, and then Cheezer snapped at him and came inside and told me I needed to cut Clyde his last check because he wasn't working here no more."

"What did you do?" Torrance asked.

"Well, I went into an office to try to get Flory, and by the time I got hold of him and he said to delay the guy, Cheezer was driving away with Clyde—and his personnel file, by the way." She snorted. "I couldn't get hold of him after that, except to send him his last check."

"Oh!" Torrance said suddenly, and Marco looked at him, seeing the expression of someone who had just put a couple things together.

"Whatever that's about," Camille said, "here. Here's the stationery. Now see? Here's our invoices. Both copies have the company letterhead, but if you check the ones in your story?" She nodded at Torrance for his permission for her to touch the tablet. "See?" She enlarged the picture. "The logo is fuzzy here. We use a good printer—the image is crystal clear. This looks like an old-fashioned copy of a copy. Not even on a good machine. You see?"

"I do," Torrance murmured. "Anything else?"

"Yeah. See these signatures?" She enlarged the picture so they could see "Florian Gallo" written in big, florid, clear letters on every page.

"Yeah," Torrance said, nodding.

"This is Dad's *real* signature." Camille showed him an invoice that had just been signed—and dated—that morning. "See how different it is?"

Marco knew the signature like the back of his hand. It had graced a lot of his education and housing checks. "Uncle Flory has the neatest handwriting," he said.

"Old-school," Torrance murmured. "Got it."

Camille plopped on the chair again and regarded him. "So?" she asked. "What do you think?"

Torrance grimaced. "Well, I think it's a good thing I decided not to run the story. But I think a couple of other things too."

And then he leaned forward, putting his weight on his elbows, and started putting the pieces together.

When he was done, he sat back and listened to their reactions, and while Camille and Frankie were vocal—and not shy with the questions—Marco had to admit it.

He didn't think Torrance Grayson was wrong.

Hiatuses and Hand Grenades

"ARE THEY going to be okay?" Torrance asked Marco as they were driving away.

"Yeah," Marco said, his handsome face with the aquiline nose and the clear brow still set into thoughtful lines. "Yeah. I think it's going to be deciding what to do with the information that's going to be hard."

"Well, let me know what they want *me* to do," Torrance said. "I'm willing to take the case further, investigate it down to the ground, but...." He let that hang, because that was the hard part right there.

Some of the discrepancies were easy to spot.

When Cheezer had come to collect Clyde's last check and made off with his personnel file, he'd obviously made off with copies of the stationery as well, and then had clumsily copied the logo for invoices and receipts. That was an easy deduction. As was figuring he'd stolen a T-shirt from the lockers in the back of the office. Six months ago, Cheezer had walked off with the trappings of a successful contracting business and had obviously gotten busy booking gigs of his own.

That was worrisome. For one thing, Clyde needed some intervention and protection, and setting the police on Cheezer didn't guarantee that would happen.

But that wasn't the most worrisome thing.

The *real* problem, Torrance had noticed, was that they had a boss—and obviously not Florian Gallo.

When Torrance had first seen the film, working with all of the trappings of Flory Gallo and Sons, the obvious interpretation had been that Flory Gallo was "the old man."

But given that all that evidence had been contradicted, when Cheezer said, "We're not working for Flory Gallo, we're working for—" had been the worst possible time for Tor to come downstairs. He needed to know the name of that boss—the real boss—the one who *wasn't* Florian Gallo.

Someone who could not just hurt Clyde if he wanted to, but who could put a hurt on Flory Gallo and Sons by insisting Flory's company had been behind who-knows-how-many bogus, dangerous jobsites and scams. Flory could very well lose his company—and possibly his freedom—if they walked into an investigation and exposé without knowing who "the old man" really was.

And while Torrance was never afraid of exposing the truth, he was *very* aware that it could have dire consequences for innocent bystanders.

Marco's family needed to talk.

But first they needed to think, which was apparently what Marco was doing as Torrance piloted Danny's posh vehicle into the city.

When the thoughtful silence dragged on too long, Torrance hit the presets on the stereo, grateful when an alt-rock station came up—probably Danny's influence, because Torrance had the feeling Felix was an NPR man.

Outbreak Monkey started to play "Empty Room," and Torrance was caught, as always, by the musicality and desolation in the lyrics. He started to hum along, surprised when Marco joined him.

"God, I love that song," Marco said softly when it had ended and the announcer came on.

"Me too. One of Blake Manning's, actually—he started writing more, and the band really embraced his sound." Outbreak Monkey had really started to hit when Tor was in high school—he still followed the band religiously, unabashedly reading everything he could find about them.

"I was in high school when Mackey Sanders came out," Marco said dreamily, the thoughts so closely echoing Tor's that he wondered if the younger man could read his mind. "He probably has no idea what that meant to a gay kid in Illinois. None. But God—I already liked the music. I used all my allowance to buy their first CD." He let out a chuckle. "Now I stream everything they put out."

"Not *everything*," Torrance said smugly.

"Oh?"

Tor cackled, loving the covetousness in the young man's voice. "I...." He blushed. This was not exactly on the up-and-up. "I *bootlegged* their last concert when they were in Chicago." He kept his eyes on the road because traffic was tricky, but he allowed himself a self-indulgent little shrug. "I couldn't help it. I'd seen them in concert before, and it's... it's *amazing*. I had to capture it. Not to sell it, mind you, but just to...." He'd downloaded it to his tablet, and during his first week recovering from his bender, when he'd felt queasy every minute of every day and tearful all the seconds in between, that recording had been the thing that had pulled him through. He'd had a moment of weakness—he knew to ask for help now, so the moment didn't become a lifetime of it. But Mackey James Sanders—*all* the guys in the band—had admitted to having their problems with drugs. With alcohol. With sadness. If they could recover, he could learn the strategies to help himself not fall into that trap, of thinking the hole he'd spent a week in would save him.

"To live it?" Marco asked delicately, and Tor realized his cackle had subsided to a thoughtful silence.

"To let it save me," he said, voice quiet. "That recording…." He swallowed, remembering that Marco didn't know. Nobody knew. The household staff had been told he'd been sick—caught a wicked virus, needed help recovering. Everybody else in the Salinger home knew how to keep a secret like it was locked in a vault, never to show its face again.

He had to finish that sentence, though. "Man, when I was sick, it was my only reason to wake up."

"Can I pull it up?" Marco asked, reaching for the tablet in the back.

"Let me," Torrance said hurriedly. He'd taken pictures that horrible day, the day he'd found Jancy Halston. The idea of Marco stumbling on those made his marrow run cold. "Wait until we get to my apartment." He paused. "Thanks for being okay about making this a day trip," he added. "My assistant was so good about helping us catch up when I was out. I don't want to make him do all the work for a segment we were supposed to have weeks to finish up."

"No worries," Marco mumbled. "You… what you're doing for my family. Offering to help find out who set them up. It's really nice. You didn't have to do any of this—hear us out, put off airing the bit, offer to help—all of it. It's above and beyond."

Torrance shook his head. "You don't understand," he said. "This, what I'm doing for your family, this *is* the job."

Marco grimaced. "You did your due diligence," he protested. "You showed us the time you'd logged trying to get hold of Flory. I don't know why he'd been avoiding you—I don't. I know those guys weren't his employees, but I don't know why he's been running so hard from this. It's *not* your fault."

Sweet kid, Torrance thought fondly. Too bad he doesn't get it. "Look, kid. Do you remember the big scandal last March, when somebody accused Felix Salinger of impropriety?"

Marco nodded, and even from the corner of his eye, Torrance could tell he looked deeply uncomfortable. "Yeah. That was… I mean, I didn't work for the Salingers then, but I remember feeling so let down, you know? He always presented as one of the good guys."

"He's always *been* one of the good guys," Torrance told him, meaning it. "But that moment, of somebody smearing his good name across the internet, across the broadcast waves, for a million people, that's *all* they're ever going to see of him."

"But didn't they catch that woman?" Marco asked, sounding confused. "I mean, dead to rights. She fell apart on broadcast TV."

"But what's easier to believe?" Torrance asked. "An elaborate scam, or what *Joey for Breakfast* or whatever has to say on the radio the next morning? Yes, Felix's good-guy karma has stepped up for the most part. But he was lucky—and he had help. So much planning went into getting his accuser to confess. You will never know. My microphone and camera? They can be *seriously* misused if I am not careful. We've got an entire major network that has poisoned a generation and really fucked it up. They're not even news. They get away with what they say because judges rule that no sane person could take them seriously, but plenty of *insane* people are taking what they put out in the world and running with it. If I'm going to represent what I say as the truth, Marco, it had damned well better *be* the truth. If I run with this story now, knowing what I know, not just about your family but about Clyde, who seems to have been drafted by some sort of crime family as muscle, well, nobody would charge me with a crime, because look at the insanity that I have to contend with. But they *should*. It should *be* a crime to misrepresent facts intentionally for money or fame or to watch the world burn. So if the world isn't going to hold me to account, *I* need to hold me to account. The minute you told me about your family, that story was getting killed until I had more info."

He took a breath and realized he'd been soapboxing. The silence settled between them, thick and thoughtful. *Way to go. Kill that kid's respect for me but good.*

"*You're* a really good person," Marco said, his voice full of admiration.

"No I'm not," Torrance muttered, Jancy Halston's face burning the back of his retina.

"Yeah, you are," Marco said. "You... you're amazing."

Torrance tried to beat back the warmth the words set off in his stomach. "I just don't like to misinform," he muttered. "That shouldn't be a special quality in a journalist. It's worse for the world that I can think of so many examples of journalists who suck."

"That guy who thinks tanning his balls is manly?" Marco suggested. "That guy has got to go."

Torrance had to work hard to keep his eyes on the road, but that didn't stop him from laughing, mouth open, unable to even hold his hand over his face as the laugh burst out from him. "Oh my God," he chortled.

"Yeah. Thank God you're not him," Marco said seriously. "I mean, I like the Salingers for a lot of reasons, but one of my favorite reasons is that my cooking is never going to be squandered on assholes like *that*."

Torrance chuckled again. "Amen," he said. Then, "Oh—there's our exit. Hold on to your butt. Traffic becomes a competitive barbarian sport here."

"Into battle, captain!" Marco called, and Torrance had to spend all his attention on the road.

A RATHER frantic half hour later and they were in Tor's apartment, with his oh-thank-God state-of-the-art editing computer and his files—because sometimes he needed to see things on paper, that's why—and his kitchen, so Marco could make more coffee.

"This is sad," Marco said, poking around the kitchen while Tor got busy at his computer.

"I was sort of really busy before I got sick," Tor mumbled. His friends had done a great job cleaning the place up, right down to the new couch and area rug that Felix had ordered. The couch was a sort of distressed burgundy denim that Tor was *really* taken with, but then, Felix had always had exquisite taste.

"Your cereal is moving," Marco told him, absolute disdain in his voice.

"Burn that," Tor muttered, cheeks flushing.

"Way ahead of you." There were some more sounds in the kitchen, and a few "*hmm*s," and then a grunt as Marco found the coffee. "Okay. No. I'm not making this. It's over a month old, and your coffee maker smells like a police station. The cooking gods would take away my license. I'm going out. Where's the nearest store?"

Torrance looked up at him blankly, his brain temporarily shorted out from its editing trance into the real world.

"I fried all your circuits talking about food, didn't I?" Marco surmised. "Uhm...."

"Yeah. Okay. You do what you gotta. I'm going to get some supplies."

Oh. Wait. Suddenly Torrance could think again. "Not too much—like I said, I'm going to stay with the family over Christmas vacation, and then we're going on...." He grimaced, because the details of the vacation were, well, sort of a Salinger family secret. They were planning to investigate the deaths of Stirling and Molly's adopted parents, and while their mantra was "Do no harm," their credo was "Rules are for people who would do harm."

Torrance believed in the truth, and he believed in doing good—as long as his story was solid, he had no problem with that whatsoever.

But Felix, Danny, and Julia had also done their best not to drag innocent civilians into their off-the-books projects, and that included people like Marco.

"A vacation," Marco said dryly, interjecting himself into Torrance's ethical dilemma. "Go ahead and call it a vacation, and we'll just forget the little top-secret Felix meetings you all have with no staff allowed."

Tor gave him a lopsided smile, glad Marco thought it was Felix-work related. "We're super grateful for the cookies. I think that's the only thing that gets Grace downstairs." He paused, then added, "And Chuck, although I think Chuck is game for anything."

Marco chuckled. "I don't even want to know what Chuck does for the network. Hunter either. Whenever he and Hunter go away for a couple of days, they come back with singe marks or bruises and this look like German shepherds in the back of a pickup truck. It's a good thing they're not dating each other. That breakup could blow up Chicago."

It was Tor's turn to chuckle. Chuck was a munitions and transportation expert, but so far his gift had been at *preventing* explosions. And Hunter was a mercenary soldier. Retired. The mercenary part, not the soldiering part. "You're not far wrong," he said. "And I think their current partners are in it for the long haul, so Chicago is safe."

"Good to know," Marco said with mock seriousness that might not have been so "mock" if he knew the truth. "Also, someone needs to keep Grace in check."

Tor remembered that grumpy presence coiled up on the other side of his bed, telling him with thinly disguised impatience that bad dreams weren't a sign of weakness and for God's sake just shut up and take comfort. "I think," he said thoughtfully, "that Grace is more a danger to himself than anyone else."

"Fair," Marco conceded. "Here—let me run to the store for some long-term things. Applesauce is good for months. Crackers. Tins of soup. It will bruise my soul a little, but there's an outstanding deli around the corner, and that will make up for the crap, and I can get some coffee that isn't—" He shuddered. "—whatever that shit is in your suspiciously empty garbage can."

Tor gave him a grateful glance, then frowned. "What do you mean, 'suspiciously empty'? You know I haven't been here!"

Marco shook his head. "This whole place looks like it's been visited by an ubermaid. Like it was annihilated and then completely revamped.

The couch and the rug are new, the bathroom is lemony fresh. It's... it's highly suspicious."

Torrance grimaced. "You should have been an investigative journalist," he muttered. "But I was sick—"

"So you said," Marco said dryly.

"I mean, *really* sick. Danny and Felix sort of came and got me, and the rest of the team, erm, group, sort of cleaned up." He sighed. "Yes, that means the couch and the rug, because I hadn't moved from either one for about a week, and they're rich and so that's what they do."

Marco was still staring at him with skepticism in his eyes. "For a week?"

"Yes," Tor told him stonily.

"Sick."

"Yes."

"Covid?"

Oh geez. "No."

"Stomach flu?"

"Sort of." Well, throwing up *had* been involved.

"C'mon, Tor, is it really worth all this hassle to not tell me what happened?"

Tor scowled and barely bit off the obvious retort that it wasn't the young man's business. Except Marco and his family were currently trusting Tor with *their business*—their livelihoods—and they should know who he was.

But of all people, Tor knew it didn't always work like that. Sometimes a struggle with drugs or alcohol could be spun—Outbreak Monkey had done it honestly. But Torrance Grayson wasn't a rock star. He wasn't a politician. He was a journalist, and his integrity had to remain unassailable.

But this kid was looking at him gently, with a raised eyebrow, and....

"I won't tell anyone," Marco promised.

"Sure you won't," Tor muttered.

Very deliberately, Marco crossed his arms over his chest and stood, feet apart, obstinate and determined.

"Why?" Tor demanded. "Why's it so important to you? I was sick. Why can't you let that stand?"

"Good question," Marco said, adjusting his body language, making it less aggressive. One predatory step at a time he started to advance to where Tor sat at his desk table in the corner of the apartment. Tor had swiveled the chair so he was facing the rest of the front room/kitchen space so Marco didn't have to stare at his back, but normally he had the option of gazing across the river out the old-fashioned sash windows.

He, uhm, sort of wished he was looking at the view of a snow-crusted Chicago now.

Marco, with the sweet eyes and the blinding smile, seemed very... determined... as he drew near, and Tor—who spent his life in front of people, in front of a camera, in front of the *world*—was suddenly as nervous as a first grader in the school play.

"Do you have an answer?" Tor asked as Marco got quite close to him, bending over the chair, in fact, and resting his hands on the padded arms.

Marco nodded slightly. "You smell good," he said softly. "Your smell, in your winter coat. It was delicious." He put his nose to the hollow of Tor's shoulder and breathed in gently. "Like vanilla and oak." He inhaled again. "And the only time your... your smell gets off, gets sweaty and weird, is when you talk about being sick."

Tor gaped at him. "You have a superpower?" he asked, absolutely astonished.

Marco chuckled, low and appealing. "Sure. I smell handsome men to see if they're lying. Guess what it gets me."

"Probably not laid," Tor snapped, feeling vulnerable. To his surprise, Marco tilted his head back and laughed, the long, appealing line of his throat close enough to lick. Or nibble. Or stroke.

Oh God. Suddenly Tor knew where this was going, and he felt stupid because it had just occurred to him.

"Marco," he began, his "it's okay, sweetheart, but this isn't going to work out" tone primly in place.

Marco met his eyes with an amused look, and the gentle condescension died a not-so-gentle death.

"What?" Marco asked throatily.

"This...." It came out a squeak, and he cleared his throat and tried again. "This isn't wise," he whispered.

"Mm...." Marco feathered a kiss along his temple, and Tor's pulse skyrocketed in his throat, his chest, his—omg *groin*?

"Seriously, I work seventy hours a week, and I'm only at the Salingers now because I was—" He swallowed.

"Sick," Marco prompted.

"Sick," Tor whispered, grabbing hold of the lie like a lifeline.

"So you've said." God, the little shit was laughing at him.

"Please?" he whispered. "Can we please just—"

Marco's lips on his were whisper soft at first, a promise, and Tor sucked in a harsh breath, his brain doing a quick countdown of how long it had been since he'd been kissed.

One year, six months, twenty-one days, six hours....

God, he couldn't even remember *who* it had been, but he could remember how *long* it had been. The nearly forgotten hunger swept over him, and he groaned, opening his mouth, allowing Marco in.

Marco invaded, tongue exploring, hands cupping Tor's cheeks, the kiss openmouthed, inviting intimacy, and Tor responded, taking more, offering a tentative exploration of his own in return.

Marco pulled away then—not brutally, but teasingly. "You like that?" he murmured.

Tor made a needy sound and then hated himself.

Marco straightened up and wiped the corners of Tor's mouth with his thumb. "Honesty," Marco said softly. "I like honesty."

And with that, he kissed Tor's forehead and backed away before grabbing his peacoat from the coatrack and heading down the hallway, closing the door gently as he left.

Tor groaned and thunked his forehead on his desk. Oh, he had *not* anticipated this.

"WHAT'S UP *your* ass?" Grace asked that night. "You're usually better at poker than this."

Tor glared at him balefully and threw his cards into the center of the dining room table, wishing for a drink.

This is why you don't drink anymore, a little voice in his head cautioned, and Tor had to admit, the temptation to drink himself stupid to avoid the consequences of drinking himself stupid was pretty strong.

"He's right," Chuck said, pulling in the chips in an extravagant gesture that made Tor want to hit him with a few. "You're usually such a neat player—no frills, no bragging, just a solid hand. What gives?"

At that moment, there was a bustling from the kitchen and a cleared throat. "Are you all good for the night?" came a familiar voice. Tor stiffened, but he didn't look up.

"Lots of cookies, right?" Grace said, absolutely unrepentant.

"Absolutely," Marco told him, and Tor didn't have to look to know he had his usual amused smile aimed at the tawny-eyed, ethereal thief. "Especially for you."

"Coffee?" Hunter asked. "And no, don't go brew more if there's not. I'm just checking."

Tor glanced up to catch Marco's grin. "There is," he said. "As well as fruit cups for late-night snacking, extra muffins, and cold cuts in the fridge on the left. We got you covered, guys."

"Thanks, Marco," Lucius, Chuck's boyfriend, said, his voice almost as smooth as Felix's. While Chuck was a big, sprawling auburn-haired cowboy, Lucius was a cosmopolitan businessman, even wearing a chic white turtleneck and slacks. "You and Phyllis take very good care of us. I understand you're one of the staff members we're losing for Christmas Eve and Christmas?"

"My family would never forgive me," Marco said. "But don't worry. I'll be here two days later, and I'll be on the catering staff for the big New Year's Eve party."

"And then you all go on vacation like us, right?"

Tor glanced at Grace and saw that the look he was aiming at Marco was wide-eyed and, well, friendly. This mattered. He wanted Marco to have a vacation.

"Yes," Marco said, and there was a solid moment of quiet, long enough to make Tor glance up to see if something had happened to interrupt him.

But no, he was staring at Tor, waiting for him to make eye contact—as he *hadn't* for pretty much the rest of the afternoon while Tor had wrapped up his work and then driven them quietly back to the mansion. The first thing Tor had done after Marco had gone for groceries was pull up the Outbreak Monkey concert on his tablet. When Marco got back, he'd gestured to the tablet, knowing that for a good two hours, Marco would be engrossed while he finished up. And that had set the tone. When they'd arrived back at the mansion, Tor had managed to thank Marco for his time, to tell him he'd be working on his family's dilemma after the trip, and to scuttle back into the house and up to his room, all without making eye contact.

A kiss. A stupid kiss. And he had barely been able to pull his head out of it long enough to do his fucking job. He was glad Phillip was okay with changing the story up—and didn't mind doing a little catch-up editing for some Christmas money—or Tor would be down a story he counted on for revenue and shit out of luck.

And now he was actually meeting Marco's eyes, and the gentle reproof he saw in them made him wish for alcohol all over again.

"I'll be here after your vacation," Marco said, directly to Tor. "I like working here. I'm not going anywhere."

Tor swallowed, and a strangled "Good," slipped out before he could stop it.

"You think so?" Marco asked, tilting his head.

"Yeah," Tor answered helplessly, drowning in his eyes.

"Good."

Marco broke the contact and smiled prettily at everybody at the table, including Hunter and Carl, who had sat silently through the conversation, before turning and heading for the kitchen, removing his apron and whistling as he grabbed his coat and headed outside, probably catching a ride with somebody to the apartment he'd told Tor he rented near the mansion. Tor turned his attention forcibly away from the closed door and back to his companions at the poker table… and realized they were all focusing on *him*.

"What?" he asked defensively.

"Holy UST, Batman," Carl said, his powerful Viking's body giving his voice a resonance Tor had never appreciated until now.

"What's that mean?" Tor asked, feeling plaintive and out of the loop.

"It's short for Unresolved Sexual Tension," Grace said. "It's that thing he and Michael had until they got all sexed up and cow-eyed over each other."

Carl gave an almost swoony smile, likely thinking about his adorable mechanic boyfriend. Michael had left that morning to go visit his ex-wife and their children, and while the stoic man hadn't said anything as emotionally obvious as "I miss him," seeing that expression on his classically handsome face told Tor everything he needed to know.

"We had some of that," Carl admitted. He gave Tor a level gaze. "But none of that crackling irritation. No, Tor and Marco—they've got some serious sparks."

"Et tu, Carl?" Tor asked, and Carl gave him a sympathetic look.

"Your poker game was very…."

"Sad," Hunter said shortly. "It was sad and pathetic, and so were you, until Marco walked in and threw you a bone."

"You guys…," Tor said, and heard it as the whine that it was. With a groan, he thunked his head on the table. "It's complicated," he mumbled, knowing they could probably not hear.

Except Grace. Grace could hear because Grace just would.

"Is it complicated because you're still in love with Josh? I thought you were friends. I could have *sworn* that's what you said to him the other night. That you were friends. That it was okay. Tell me it's not complicated because of that. Because it's doomed."

Tor's eyes went wide in the shelter of his arms on the table. "Wow," he said, not sure where to start.

"My God," Hunter said to Grace, wonder in his voice. "You're like… like a one-man wrecking ball."

"And you love me," Grace replied without any irony whatsoever. "But talk to us, TV man. You're not still thirsting for some boss's son, are you?"

"I hate you," Tor said limply, without passion. "I mean that. And no. No, I'm not still…." His voice trailed off as he realized this could be true. "I'm not still thirsting for Josh."

A collective sigh blew across the table, and Tor sat up, glaring at them all. "And thank you for your confidence, I might add."

"Aw, son," Chuck said, his green eyes far more sympathetic than Tor would have imagined. "It's not that we don't like you, it's only that—"

"Josh has a thing for cops," Grace told him bluntly. "Which is weird. But you're not a cop, and you look like more of a bottom—"

"Grace!" Hunter cried, clearly mortified.

"Oh please," Grace said, yawning and showing all his pointy teeth as though bored. "You're all thinking it."

"I'm a top!" Tor protested, and the laughter around the table quickly disabused him of any dominance he might have imagined he had. "I'm not a top?"

"Of course you are," Lucius said soothingly. He had the same tone of voice a friend might have while assuring their other friend that they could sing. Or dance. Or act. When obviously they could not. "You're just—"

"Too pretty," Carl said diplomatically.

"Yes!" Grace chimed in, as though unaware Tor could hear him grabbing at straws. "Josh has to be the prettiest. It's a rule." He nodded like a bobblehead doll, and Tor closed his eyes.

"You all suck," he said distinctly.

"We do," Hunter agreed, "and no, Grace, not because we're all gay. We suck because we've lost sight of the core idea here."

"And what's that?" Tor's head was starting to throb.

"What in the hell did you do to that kid to make him pity you?" Hunter asked, and speaking of pity, he had none.

Tor fought the temptation to bury his head in his arms again. "He's not buying the sick story," he told them, broken down by the day and by the inescapable fact that the quietly dangerous, flat-eyed Hunter was absolutely dead-on. Pity. *That* had been the look in Marco's eyes. It had been what he'd stared at Tor with when he'd come back with the groceries to find the tablet set up to entertain him like a child. It had been the look in his eyes as Tor had given him the brush-off when they'd gotten out of the SUV in front of the mansion.

And it absolutely had been what he'd been giving Tor as Marco said good night to a man too scared to even glance at him.

Pity.

Fucking Jesus.

"Oh."

They all said it, and Tor searched the face of every man at the table.

"Oh what?" he asked, at a loss.

"You're a consummate storyteller, Gray," Carl said, using his nickname—his last name—like only a friend would. "You... you spin a perfect yarn. You take all the complicated strands that make up a story and weave them into a cohesive whole with such ease."

Tor fought a smile. "Are you my friend or my announcer?"

"I'm your friend," Carl said, the sobriety that marked the man on full display. "And I'm trying to say you're a storyteller. What you're not...." He paused, and everybody nodded like they could see where this was going when Tor couldn't.

"Is what?" Tor prompted.

"A liar," they all said in unison, and Tor stared at them.

"What?"

"You should tell him," Grace said. "If he doesn't suck entirely, he'll understand."

"I can't," Tor told him miserably. "I'm... I pulled a story for him. For his family. I'm researching it for them because there's more to it. They... they *trust* me, do you get it? They can't know what a fuckup I am!"

"Is that what you think?" Carl asked, his voice dropping quietly. "That you're a fuckup?"

The dining room was a really lovely space. The table was big and rectangular, one long side up against a wall with a bench seat. Hard to get out of, but there was lots of room. The cream-colored carpet and pale wood gave the impression of leisure and casualness. There was a Picasso clock on the wall above the table, and the area on the other side of the table was open, with colorful paintings on the opposite wall—warm cityscapes, mostly, because Chicago was everybody's mistress. It wasn't the greatest place for playing poker, but there was another game going on in the small "foyer room" that had a coffee table the perfect width.

But with Carl's quiet voice, the understanding implied by his words, all that space became a vault, sitting on top of Tor's shoulders, crushing his lungs.

"Can we not?" he begged, suddenly seeing how this innocent poker game, during which only two people (Grace and Chuck) had been unrepentantly cheating, had suddenly become the group therapy session he'd never wanted to have.

"I think we must," Hunter said, gathering all the cards. "Grace, the ones up your sleeve?"

"I'm not—"

"Chuck, the ones in your socks?" Chuck was wearing short sleeves to prove he was a manly man in Chicago in December.

"I thought I was being subtle," Chuck said in mock hurt. But with a few deft motions that Tor knew for certain *he* wouldn't have detected, he produced the cards.

"Grace?" Hunter prompted again.

"How do you know *mine* aren't in my pants?" Grace leered.

"Because you're wearing yoga pants so tight we can tell you're not circumcised," Hunter said dryly, and to Tor's surprise, Grace's naturally golden skin darkened to two red crescents at his high cheekbones.

"You cheated," Grace said, but the words had a hollow quality to them that told Tor he was fighting legitimate embarrassment.

"Yes, precious, I did," Hunter said. "But not at poker. Now give me your cards."

Hunter was gazing at his lover with a level, steely, gray-eyed steadiness that was probably the only thing that made him and the chimerical Grace a couple.

"Nobody look," Grace said sulkily, and Tor closed his eyes without question. He opened them when he heard Hunter shuffling and peered around to realize that the others had taken the request seriously too. It hit him—not for the first time—that this group of people understood accepting a person, even someone like Grace, brilliant, impulsive, terrifying, for all the good parts while understanding that the bad parts were there too.

"Can we filet Grayson like a fish now?" Grace asked, his cheeks still red.

"No," Carl told him, voice absolutely unyielding. "We can poke him gently." He sighed. "You're not a fuckup, Torrance."

"I—"

Carl held his hand up, forestalling any protests. "I think… I think every human being holds a roster in their heads. A list of transgressions that they think they can never be forgiven for. You were drunk for a week. *I* was drunk for years. And even when I *wasn't* having a three-scotch dinner, I still wasn't living my best life. I mean—" He shrugged and winked across the table. "—I was sober when I slept with Chuck way back when."

"Not my finest moment either," Chuck said apologetically. "And alcohol isn't my drug."

"Yeah, Danger Mouse, we know what your drug is," Lucius said with affection. "It's why you can't drive my vehicles anymore."

"But you'll let him fly your planes," Grace prodded. "How smart is that?"

"Back to the subject," Carl said grimly. "My bad for bringing it up. But you get what we're saying, Tor—"

"He asked me the day before," Torrance said, so surprised that when it came out, he almost clapped his hand over his mouth.

"Marco?" Carl asked, puzzled.

"No." Tor shook his head. "Hugh Halston. He... he called me up the afternoon before I found... I found his daughter. I-I was in the middle of editing. So close, you know? Just let me finish this one thing. I'll make a few calls. I'll get back to you tomorrow. Let me know if she shows up. I was as bad as the cops. I thought she would show up. Just a stupid kid, getting lost in the big city. Ninety-nine percent of the time, they show up." His voice grew thick with self-hatred. "I-I fell asleep at my desk, and I woke up at two in the morning and went to bed. She was dead behind a dumpster, and I went to bed! Her father—he was one of my college professors, and he's the sweetest man, and I just... I went to *sleep*—"

He took a deep breath then, trying to get hold of himself before he lost it in front of all these flat-eyed mercenaries, cons, and thieves.

And then he felt himself lifted onto Carl's lap like a little kid and wrapped up in his arms as he cried again, fucking *again*, for Jancy Anne Halston.

He finally took another cleansing breath and peeked out from under Carl's enormous bicep, figuring all the guys would be gone.

They weren't. Instead, they were gathered closer to him, Grace curled up at his feet like a kitten.

"It wasn't your fault," Grace said.

"I know—"

"No, you don't." Grace looked around. "We all get super noble about helping people, but brother, you get to sleep. There's so much bad shit in the world. We're only people."

"I... she was all alone in the cold," he whispered, knowing that was wrong, knowing she had died the day before, probably almost immediately upon taking the pills. But she'd been Hugh's daughter, and while he hadn't known her, he'd known the sort of hole she'd leave in her father's heart.

"And you are going to carry that pain for a long time," Hunter said. "I've got my own pain like that. There wasn't a thing I could do to stop it, but dead is dead, and it's not fair. And you—you reacted to it because you're human. And you were tired. I know that kind of tiredness too."

Tor nodded. "God, you're huge," he muttered to Carl. "Does it ever occur to you that you're larger than life?"

"I work out," Carl said modestly.

"Gah!" Grace said unexpectedly. "I was going to make a dirty joke, but I *can't*, because your boyfriend is *so sweet* I'd have to shower for a week to get off the shame."

"Aw, Grace," Carl murmured. "Thank you. That's kind."

"Look at him," Chuck said affectionately. "All you had to do is mention Michael and he gets all gooey."

"Unless his boyfriend is hanging out of a modified truck window with a crossbow," Tor said snottily, because he'd been there for that.

"They're perfect for each other," Lucius said, sounding smug. "It's adorable. Anyway"—and his voice grew sober—"Torrance, you don't have anything to be ashamed about. If this young man is worth your worry, he'll forgive you for being human." Lucius gave Chuck a fond look. "It comes with the relationship territory."

"I'm not ready for a relationship," Tor muttered, feeling like a coward.

"Wait until after Christmas," Carl pronounced, lifting him up like a rag doll and returning him to his own seat. "After this trip to the Caribbean, you'll come rolling in all tan and healthy, and maybe you'll feel stronger about things."

Tor nodded, wiping his face on his shoulder, and thought that was probably a good strategy.

But also pretty sure he couldn't follow it.

Gentle Touches

MARCO WATCHED as most of the household left for the day. He'd caught bursts of conversation about a trip to go shopping at the Art Institute and some sort of "job" for most of the men, *regular* shopping from Molly and Julia, accompanied by Josh's uncle Leon, who was so obviously infatuated with Julia that a bystander could practically smell the pheromones.

It wasn't until everybody was gone that he glanced up and realized Tor was there, looking freshly showered and still tired—but a happy sort of tired.

"Hey," Marco said, keeping his voice friendly. "You missed everybody else."

Tor nodded. "They were going Christmas shopping and running errands. I sort of already have Christmas presents for everybody. I took advantage of the wake pool to get some swimming in once everybody had left the gym."

The Salingers had an actual gym out beyond the garden and the outdoor pool in the back of the property. Complete with machines, free weights, a dancing platform, a wake pool, and a Jacuzzi. Marco had noticed that the place got hard use—enough to employ a part-time custodian for the gym alone. Not for the first time, he wondered if Felix Salinger was *squandering* his money or simply *using* it proportionally, because if he was doing *that*, he was *really* good at making money.

"It apparently knocked you out," Marco said softly. "You want some protein after that?"

"Please," Tor said, giving one of those quiet smiles that didn't seem to fit in that outrageously handsome face. "An omelet would be great if you've got stuff."

"All premade," Marco told him. "Sit right there."

He went to work happily, glad he and the other household staff had worked at pre-chopping ingredients for the next few days. In no time at all he had a sauté pan working with a light, fluffy disc of whipped eggs in the center, and cheese, tomatoes, chives, and ham in the middle of that. Tor watched him, not making any conversation, but seemingly content to simply sit at the counter and be.

When Marco got back to him with the plated omelet and a place setting, Tor smiled, asked for some orange juice to wash it all down, and began to eat.

Marco felt the pull of the man, even quiet like this, as low-key as a human could possibly be, and drew up a stool next to him before grabbing a couple of chocolate muffins, warm from the stove, and setting them next to a dish of shaved butter.

"I didn't know that was standard with an omelet," Tor chided him.

"Only for you," Marco said, keeping his voice gentle.

"Hm." Tor ate quietly for a moment, and Marco was racking his brains for an "in" to the conversation.

Tor saved him the trouble.

"I wasn't sick," he said. "You're right."

"Oh?" Marco's eyes shot open. He'd been going to leave it be, give the man time to think about it, but apparently that wasn't Tor's style.

"I was drunk," Tor said brutally. He gave a bitter smile when Marco's eyes got even bigger. "Yeah. Not something you want the guy in charge to admit, is it."

"Depends," Marco said, his heart pounding in his ears like he'd had an actual shock. "Why? Why were you drunk?"

Tor shook his head. "Not now," he all but begged. "Please. I-I talked about it last night with my friends, and...." He rubbed his chest. "Still raw. It... I'm not strong enough to have that conversation twice in the same day."

Marco barely refrained from growling, unreasonably jealous that Tor's friends had been the ones to share his burden and he was left out.

"Then why tell me now?" Marco asked.

"Because I like you," Tor said with a crooked grin. "I mean... I'm getting over a long case of 'he'll never love me back' with someone else, but I think I could like you quite a lot."

"But...?" Marco heard it, and it sent his heart in a death spiral to his feet.

"But not right now. Not with Christmas bearing down on us at a thousand miles an hour. Not with this latest project"—there was only the slightest hesitation before "project"—"which is sort of a gift for Stirling and Molly, and the reason we're all going to the Caribbean. Let me have... have normal a little. Let me find my feet. The Salingers promised me sanctuary here. Kindness. I need that so I can get strong enough to deal with all of...." He rubbed his chest again. "This."

Marco nodded, his own heart aching a little too.

"It's not a no," Tor said softly.

Marco gave him a hesitant smile. "Are you sure?"

"Very sure." Tor covered Marco's hand as it rested on the table. "I'm asking for time. We don't have to spend the time pretending the other person doesn't exist. We don't even have to pretend we never kissed. We just have to not force anything. The rest will come, or it won't, but I need to be strong for it, or it won't be my best. Do you understand?"

Marco did. "It's important?" he asked, lacing their fingers together. "That it be your best?"

Tor tilted his head in sort of a shrug. "I'm not great with relationships," he admitted. "I'm usually too driven. The story, the promotion, the next thing."

"I get that," Marco said, and saw Tor's surprise. "Cooking for a living is pretty intense. I told you that. The hours suck. The odds of a restaurant surviving are slim. I wanted to get out of school, and then I worked at one of those scary competitive restaurants for a year—and my family was *not* happy about that. But it doesn't leave a lot of time. I've only been here for a couple of months, but I'm starting to see that the pace is different. There's room now." He winked. "And a *very* nice-looking man who smells *really* amazing did something nice for me and my family, and I thought I'd take advantage."

Tor took a thoughtful bite of his omelet. When he'd swallowed—after closing his eyes blissfully and humming a little—he said, "Please... please don't base your feelings for me on what I can do for your family," and Marco caught his breath. Oh, that had been *Marco's* bad.

"Only that you're trying," Marco said softly. "It... it just seemed like a decent thing to do."

Tor shrugged. "I try," he said, but he sounded so disheartened. He'd said he didn't want to talk about it, so Marco didn't. Instead, he rubbed the back of Tor's hand gently with his thumb and let the man finish his omelet in peace.

When Tor was done, he insisted on splitting a muffin.

"What are you up to today?" Marco asked, and a smile flirted at the edges of Tor's mouth.

"Some research, I think, on other people who might have been scammed by the guys in the video," he said heavily. "Finishing presents if I have time."

"Do presents," Marco told him soberly, remembering the phone conversation he'd had the night before. "Sleep. Let Frankie and Camille ask around. They're all fired up. By the time you get back from vacation, they should have part of your work done for you, and you can put it all together."

"I don't want to—" Tor interrupted himself with a yawn. "—make them do my job!" he tried to protest, and it was Marco's turn to rub his chest.

Impulsively he bent to where Tor sat and kissed his cheek. "Rest," he ordered. "Please. You held the story. Give us some time to build you a new one. You said go slow. Go easy. That means on yourself too."

"A nap sounds so decadent." Tor laughed, and then he yawned again.

"Well, I happen to know that the downstairs den, with its giant television and all the pillows on the floor, is going to be empty for quite some time," Marco said pertly. "You go watch some television, and when I'm done for the morning, I may join you." He usually had the middle of the day to himself. Quite often, he'd use the gym, since it was offered, and since his apartment was a bus stop away, he often caught his own nap at home between shopping, catching up on TV, tending to everyday business.

Tor's next smile was almost shy. "I'd like that," he said.

AN HOUR later, after turning the kitchen over to the woman who did shopping and dinner prep, Marco ventured down into the den. He'd only been there in the past to bring cookies—sort of a tradition—for what Marco could only think of as "strategy meetings." The staff was never let in while they were going on, so he had no idea what the strategy was *for*. He assumed it was some sort of work for Felix's cable network, but he couldn't think of any other way to describe them, and it didn't help that he'd spotted Hunter and Chuck taking position at the base of the stairs like sentinels as he and the other servers had left. Phyllis kept the place stocked in between times, which was another red flag to the staff, because Phyllis was a very capable head housekeeper, but she was also very okay without doing a lot of housework herself.

But Marco had asked, and Phyllis had told him that she had no problem with the staff going where they'd been invited. As far as Marco had seen, the people who stayed at the Salinger mansion weren't the type to take advantage. There were no stories of women being groped—although it helped that most of the men were gay—but Marco himself had never, not once, felt so much as a shiver of impropriety working there.

It was why he'd been the one to kiss Torrance Grayson the day before. He was pretty sure, unless he'd made his move, it would have taken an eternity for Torrance to kiss him first.

Marco could go for a lot longer on the hope of a second kiss.

The den itself *sounded* imposing, but upon first glance, it was just a large basement room decorated for the *many* Chicago sports teams. Hockey, basketball, baseball, football—there was a wall color and giant decal for all of them. In the back of the room sat a wet bar, which Marco had cause to know held no alcohol. More than one member of the Salinger mob was in recovery, but Marco had never asked specifics. Instead of expensive gin- or oak-aged scotch, the bar held juices, sparkling water, a hot chocolate and espresso machine, and a soda gun with a myriad of choices, all of it kept antiseptically clean. In front of the bar was furniture: a couple of couches, one of which had seen better days, a few stuffed chairs, a mass of beanbag pillows on the floor, and a stack of regular pillows and throws in an open shelf against the wall. Marco knew that the younger people in the household would sit down here for hours watching movies or sports games, or even playing video games when the mood suited them. Since Josh Salinger had recovered enough to move about the house, this had become one of his favorite places to lounge.

And there were, of course, coffee tables to hold the drinks and the cookies, and stools up against the bar.

It *looked* like an average entertainment cage except for two things.

One was that it could have easily sat thirty people, and even Marco's parents' family room wasn't that big.

The other was that the "entertainment" system had state-of-the-art computer hookups, multiple screens, and its own Wi-Fi server. Marco couldn't prove it—and wouldn't even know how—but he was pretty sure that Stirling, the mansion's "computer genius" in a place *full* of hackers, could access the Dark Web, track down users, and destroy hard drives with just his phone and the hookups provided by their "entertainment" system.

Seeing Torrance Grayson asleep on the firmest of the couches with a pillow under his head and a fluffy blanket pulled up to his chin while *The Owl House* played on the big screen, was almost laugh worthy.

Except for how peaceful he looked and the fact that he was watching a kid's show—had it set to stream from episode one on—and how tight he'd drawn the blanket up to his chin.

Marco sighed and sat down at Tor's feet, picking up the remote control as he did.

The TV wasn't very loud, so Marco looked for an old movie—Cary Grant old—and settled on *His Girl Friday*, one of his mother's favorites. He'd nearly immersed himself in Cary Grant's frenetic performance—and Rosalind Russell's sultry voice—when Tor began to shiver, whimpering a little.

Marco slid his hand along Tor's calf and murmured, "It's okay. I'm here."

"Marco?" His voice—usually modulated and specific—was muzzy and blurred.

"Yeah."

"I can't see you."

Marco laughed a little and got up, making Tor lift himself so Marco could sit back down and let Tor's head fall on his lap.

"Better?" he asked.

"Nice," Tor mumbled. Then, "Don't go."

Marco smoothed his hair back, noticing it had grown long. He'd never seen it *not* high and tight and professional. "I'll stay until I have to go back on shift."

"Thanks."

And then he was asleep.

Marco joined him, leaning against a cushion and completely losing consciousness. Phyllis came and woke him before he had to go help with dinner prep, and his lap was warm and his legs numb from not moving. Tor was still on his lap, drooling faintly onto the pillow under his head.

"I hate to move you two," she murmured. "Do you need help?"

"Naw," Marco told her. "But go up the stairs quick. I don't want him to know people saw."

"Sure," she said, like she knew something he didn't. Marco wriggled out from under Tor and stood and stretched. Before he left, he bent down and kissed Tor's forehead, surprised when Tor's eyes fluttered open.

"You can go for the lips," he said, a little more lucid than he had been earlier.

"When I kiss you again, I want you awake for it," Marco said, but that didn't stop him from bending down and giving him a tender, brief brushing of lips that made him yearn for more.

Then he was gone, leaving Tor to struggle to wake up on his own. He'd been planning to shop for his apartment, but Phyllis had no problem giving him leftovers. He'd been thinking about calling Camille and Frankie to see if they'd gotten hold of Uncle Flory, but he figured they'd contact him when they had.

The fact was he whistled softly as he took the carpeted stairs two at a time, absolutely pleased with the way he'd spent his day.

AS CHRISTMAS neared and things got more and more frantic, Marco had less and less private time to spend with Tor, but that didn't mean he didn't have *any*.

They watched television together in the den if everybody else was gone, or sometimes Marco went up to Tor's room, with those fanciful paintings of cats, and simply read while Tor edited on his computer.

"I thought you weren't working," Marco had chided the first time he'd done this.

"Christmas presents for the family," Torrance said.

"Video?" Marco asked, frowning.

"Outtakes." Torrance grinned at him, a spark of devilment in his eyes, and he turned his computer so Marco could see it.

On the screen, Marco could see Chuck, big hands gripping a steering wheel, eyes narrowed in concentration. A sound of panic came from off-screen, and then Chuck said, very seriously, "Tor, if you cannot keep your freakouts from messing with my groove, we're going to end up a grease spot on the macadam."

Marco let out a surprised guffaw, and the picture changed. It was still Chuck, but now he had his arms crossed and a stern look on his face as he stood behind Lucius Broadstone. Lucius was talking to a group of what appeared to be politicians, as well as employees of his own business, about how he ran a shelter for battered women. Suddenly, while Lucius was speaking so articulately, Chuck made eye contact with someone behind the camera—probably Tor—and then his eyes flew to the left.

With a stunningly quick leftward leap, Chuck grabbed somebody—oh my God, was it a *policeman*?—by the ear and hauled him back to where Lucius was holding court.

There was motion off camera, and then Chuck grinned at the lens and gave Torrance a thumbs-up, like a little kid.

There were other moments. Some didn't have Chuck on the camera at all but featured Torrance talking about something—often something dangerous—that Marco assumed Chuck had done.

"Outtakes," Tor said happily, pulling the computer toward him. "I've been working on them since the murder bird thing in Napa. At first it was for my own collection. Nobody here wants their face in the press, and I honor that. But then it was because I thought *they'd* like to see the outtakes. And then, when I told Felix and Danny I'd be here for Christmas, I thought, 'Aha! I have the perfect thing!'"

Marco laughed. "I've got to ask—why does everybody call him Danny or Uncle Danny, and not Benjamin or Ben?"

Tor's face grew carefully neutral. "His middle name is Daniel," he said, and just like that, Marco knew that wasn't the truth.

"You're lying," he said quizzically. "Why would you lie about that?"

Tor winked. "I wouldn't," he said with a smile. "Do you want to see Hunter's?"

Marco let himself be led to a different topic—and an amazing video of Hunter stopping purse snatchers with nothing more than his intimidating gray-eyed smile—but inside, he filed it away with things he'd noticed about the people at the Salinger mansion: They called themselves a crew, their "den" meetings happened in a place with state-of-the-art electronics, *everybody* could not only play poker but cheat at it, Hunter really *was* scary, Chuck apparently could blow shit up, and Benjamin Morgan was not "Uncle Danny's" real name.

CHRISTMAS CONTINUED to hurtle toward them at lightning speed. Marco had to give up his afternoons watching cartoons—or watching Tor's videos—in order to take care of his own Christmas needs. He told Tor about them in the mornings, though, either after the mass workout session (which fascinated Marco—he'd never seen a group as dedicated to working out together as the people in the mansion. It was like they all had a purpose in the gym, and he couldn't figure out what it was) or after a quiet lunch. Tor wasn't there 100 percent of the time either, and sometimes he went into the city with one of the others for "work."

And Marco didn't know whose work.

He was beginning to wonder if the Salinger family was its own branch of the mob.

The thought hit him two days before Christmas, and he shook his head. That was ridiculous. Felix's income stream was very well documented, for one thing. His stock trades were legendary—even Marco's father knew when the man made a killing in the market—and he owned an entire, very successful cable network. Not just a struggling station, a *network*, which won scads of news and programming awards as well as humanitarian notices. Nobody as *public* as Felix Salinger could be a criminal.

Right?

But the family was so... odd. The game they played where they lifted each other's wallets, for instance—Marco couldn't explain that. The fact that everybody's present to Grace was hiding a Lego guy somewhere impossible to find. Marco had listened to the whispered conversations. These people had secret compartments in their luggage that *still* weren't safe from Josh Salinger's irritating best friend.

The fact was that, besides Felix, who ran his company, Benjamin Morgan—Uncle Danny—who was an art docent, and Tor, of course, Marco didn't know what any of the people at the mansion *did*. He gathered some of them had their own money, and he knew Grace and Molly performed on the regular, but they chose to hang out in Glencoe, which was absolutely baffling. As was the presence of Leon di Rossi, who was supposedly Josh Salinger's uncle, related by blood, but *not* related, apparently, to Felix, Josh's father, or Julia, his mother. Hopefully not to Julia—the European tycoon appeared to have a stunning crush on her.

Thing after thing after thing struck Marco as odd, but until his family struggled desperately to get his uncle Flory to actually *talk to them* about Torrance Grayson's tape and why those two guys were pretending to work for him, he hadn't realized how easy it would be to suspect someone you respected and cared about of working outside the law.

"I swear to God, Marco," Camille said to him over the phone the last day the company was open until mid-January. "He had me buy for and organize the Christmas party, and he showed up long enough to give out bonuses and cut the cake, and he disappeared. And Dad, he ain't lookin' so good. He's lost weight. He looks tired. I mean, your friend, he did us a good turn by holding back that story, but... but I'm starting to worry about whether or not we did the right thing by asking him, you know?"

"But Cammie," Marco said, hating the thought of his uncle Flory engaged in something illegal, "you *know* your dad. He's not... he's not a connected guy. Wasn't he, like, *Switzerland* when the mob moved in?"

"He was!" Cammie's voice rose. "He was scared for a while when me and Frankie were in high school. You remember when we all got shipped off to some sort of summer camp? All three family's worth of kids, showing up in a place in the Catskills none of us had even heard of. You remember that?"

Marco blinked. "Yeah," he said, "I do. May and Gianni were *pissed.*" His older brother and sister had both been having first romances that year, while Marco—ten at the time—was starting to realize his brother's *Sports Illustrated* calendar did absolutely nothing for him. "I mean, it worked out for *me*, because I got that crush on the camp counselor, and all of you, like, defended my honor, and nobody messed with me, but I didn't think that's why we were there!"

Camille laughed a little. Marco was the youngest of sixteen cousins— the baby. On the one hand, he had no privacy and never would have any privacy, and if he ever did own a family restaurant, he had a much older brother and at least three cousins who would be dishwashers and staff because they couldn't hold down jobs.

But on the other hand, he'd never have to be alone.

"I only know 'cause I'm sneaky," Camille said. "You know that about me. That's why we're close." And they were. Camille was the next youngest cousin to Marco, and she had four brothers, including Frankie. She wasn't great in a fistfight—the only way she'd survived her rough-and-tumble brothers was by having the dirt on them. They couldn't rough her up for tattling if she had blackmail for bigger transgressions.

"What do you mean?" Marco asked. He heard Camille take a bite of something on the other end of the line and assumed it was cake, because Camille wore stretchy bodices and cotton bras and did not give two shits if she was a size twelve or a size twenty. It was one of the many things Marco loved about her. If nothing else, Cammie always ate his food.

"Well, I happened to be playing under my parents' bed," she said with zero shame, "when they had a rip-roaring fight."

"Your parents?" he asked dumbly.

"My parents."

"Uncle Flory and Aunt Marie?"

"The very same. I shit you not. I know—it's gotta be bad when they're fighting. I've never seen a blowout like this. Dad wanted to pick the whole family up and move—both his brothers, their families, the works—and Mom was like, 'You can't do that to us, Flory. This is our neighborhood.' And Dad—God, I'll never forget it. He said, 'These guys don't take prisoners, Marie,' and she said, 'Well, you got three weeks to work it out. I got the kids booked at summer camp. Everybody's paying. Your brothers will be there for every meeting.' They chilled after that, and then, thank fuck, the guys came banging in the house asking for a snack. Otherwise I might have heard my parents having makeup sex, and then you woulda had to kill me."

"Thank God you avoided *that*," Marco said, thinking about his own parents having their own version and how scarred for life *he* would be.

"I'm telling you. Anyway, I think Dad dealt with the mob trying to weasel in on his business back when we were kids, but lately something changed. I don't think he wants us to know it changed—he's still trying to protect us. But Marco, I don't know what we're going to do about that lawsuit. I know your guy—"

"He's not my guy."

She stopped, and he heard a long inhale, as though through a straw. "Hah. Really. Because I didn't mean anything by that, but when you say he's not like it's the most important thing in the world, I think maybe I should have."

Sneaky, he thought dismally. Make that sneaky and *smart*.

"We're not talking about it right now," he told her, although he and Tor had probably talked—and exchanged sweet, tantalizing kisses—every day since their conversation over muffins and an omelet. He could *feel* Tor wanting more, but also, in a thick, palpable wave, he could feel that he'd been telling the truth about being tired. Needing rest. Wanting time.

And as Marco became aware—truly aware—of the oddities in the Salinger mansion, he thought that time and some space was probably in order.

But that didn't mean he wasn't dreaming of more than kisses, more than sweet moments holding hands, more than quiet conversations, every time he went to sleep in his empty apartment.

"Well, you're going to have to talk about it sometime," she said practically, "especially if we uncover something about Dad that we might not like. 'Cause the guy who's not your guy treated us decent. It's our job to do the same for him."

"I hear you," Marco said with a sigh. "But all that can wait until the family gets back from vacation. We've got Christmas first, and the Salingers have a New Year's Eve blowout—I'll be lucky if I get a breath."

"Well, you get as many breaths as you can. I'll see you Christmas Eve for the family shindig, and you, me, and Frankie can talk more. Maybe we can even talk about how to be sneaky, 'cause I gotta tell you, Dad usually has a sort of ritual about locking up the office every Christmas, and he hasn't done that. I'm tempted to put a voice-activated tape recorder in his office to see what we pick up."

Marco blinked slowly. "I don't even know where you'd get one of those—"

"One of what?"

Marco almost dropped the phone. He'd called Cammie from the kitchen after it had emptied out for the afternoon, and he hadn't even been aware of Phyllis coming in with trays of scattered dishes from the kitchen table.

"A voice-activated tape recorder," he blurted, surprised into telling the absolute truth.

She "*hmm*d." "Give me ten minutes," she said, then strolled out of the room and into another part of the house.

"What's going on?" Camille asked curiously.

"I, uh, think my boss knows where to find a voice-activated tape recorder."

"Fucking *balls!*" Camille said, the frank adoration in her voice making Marco the slightest bit uneasy. "Can she really get one for you?"

"I don't—"

"Well, text me if she can. I'll come by your place tonight."

"I work tonight, remember?"

"Leave it on the counter. I'll use my key."

For the life of him, Marco couldn't remember how he could have been stupid enough to give this woman a key to his house.

"Sure," he said weakly. "But only if she finds one—"

"Got it!" Phyllis said excitedly, hustling back into the kitchen.

"That wasn't ten minutes," Marco said.

"Yeah, well, Julia knew where the secret stash was kept," Phyllis said with a shrug. "Here. Here's the device, here's the batteries. You need to replace them once a week, so I've got four, and you just put it in the bottom of a planter or something and change it out. See, it's got a USB port. Download it into your computer when you change the batteries and replace it. Easy peasy."

And with that, she put the tiny little spyware device in Marco's palm and strode away, probably to fix some other staff member's life.

"So?" Camille said, still on the phone and sounding vitally interested.

"So I'll leave it on my counter," Marco said, dazed. "It's fairly easy to use, but you have to change the batteries and download the conversations into your computer once a week."

"I'm on it," Camille told him. "Can do. So why do your bosses just have one of these laying around?" she asked.

"I've got nothing," he told her. "And I'm not sure I want to know."

She made a noncommittal sound. "Your guy, Torrance, has run some pretty awesome stories, Marco, and righted some really awful wrongs. I wouldn't get all judgy about the kind of help they give him."

Marco remembered how tired Torrance Grayson was, and how seemingly haunted by conscience, and was suddenly ashamed of his squeamishness. He of all people should know not to throw stones. His uncles worked in construction, and his father had sold his family restaurant when Marco was in high school. All three of them had experienced run-ins with the seedier parts of their industries, and it was almost impossible to come out of such meetings without a little mud on you. Sometimes the world was just stacked against an honest man.

"You're right," he told her. "I'll leave the recorder on my counter. If you have any questions, I'll ask Phyllis. How's that?"

"Perfect. I'll see you at the Christmas Eve shindig. Love you, baby."

"Love you, Cammie," he answered, not protesting when she pulled the "baby" epithet out. It was a cross he'd learned to bear.

They hung up, and Marco put the little device into the pocket of his slacks, his brain buzzing at a thousand miles a minute.

THE MORNING before Christmas Eve, Torrance once again came into the kitchen after the bulk of the Salingers had left, looking a little shy.

"What can I get you?" Marco asked. "Actually, sit and let me pick for once." He grinned. "I made biscuits this morning. No arguments about getting fat. A homemade sausage biscuit with a little syrup is a thing of beauty."

"You're an evil man, and I like it," Tor told him, hopping on his usual stool. Marco went about preparing his breakfast, and turned back with the plate, the setting, and some orange juice, pleased that Tor was so amenable.

When Marco finally came to sit next to him, he found a small package at his usual place.

"What's this?" he asked, genuinely surprised.

"I know it's dumb because we said no presents, but...." He shrugged. "Stirling got one for young Tienne, and I saw it when it came in. It was so pretty I had to get you one too." He grinned. "But then once I found the site, it had to have more color to it because, you know. You're you."

Marco smiled at him shyly, not sure what to say. "You bastard," he muttered. "We *said*—"

Tor leaned forward quickly and kissed his cheek. "I don't care. I don't care if you never get me a present. Looking forward to talking to you, to seeing you every day—you'll never know how important that's been for me these last three weeks. Please. It's such a small thing. Just say thank you and maybe wear it."

Marco grinned and opened the little tube of wrapping paper. What unrolled was soft, warm, and *bright*, done in sky blue and orange, a hand-knitted hat with an almost magical pattern wrapping around it.

"Wow," Marco said, enchanted in spite of himself. "Yeah. If I'd seen a website with these, I would have had to rethink my entire family."

"Right?" Tor took it from his hands and tugged it over Marco's ears. Marco closed his eyes and shivered, loving everything, from the bright colors to the softness of the wool. "It's dumb, it's unoriginal—"

"It's practical and perfect," Marco corrected, grasping Tor's hands as they hovered near his face.

Tor grinned and lowered their twined fingers. "Good." Then his gaze sharpened. "But you're thinking about something that's bothering you."

Marco dropped his eyes to their hands. "I, uh, got a voice-activated recorder for my cousin to put in Uncle Flory's office," he said. "Uhm, Phyllis got it from Julia."

"Oh!" Tor's voice was nothing more than interested. "Good idea. Did she tell you how to use it?"

Marco glared at him. "How does someone just *have* one of those?"

Tor's face did that careful neutrality thing again. "No idea." He released their fingers and turned toward his sausage biscuit while Marco let out a frustrated breath.

"You can tell me, you know," he said after a minute.

Tor gave him a sideways glance. "Can I?"

Marco endured his scrutiny for a long, uncomfortable moment. "*You're* a good guy," he said with conviction.

"I try. But so is everybody who lives here."

And Marco's expression must have given him away, because Tor sighed.

"Look, Marco, I like you. A lot. I bought a *hat* for you. But you have to ask yourself—if you think the people in this household are bad people, what are you doing working here?"

Marco swallowed. He *loved* working here. Everybody was respectful; nobody tried to hit on him when he was just doing his job. It was as though all the things that made him suspicious were coupled with other facts that made this place the perfect job.

"The people are nice," he said softly.

Tor nodded. "They really are."

Marco sighed. "And my uncle Flory is looking more and more guilty," he said unhappily.

"Give him the benefit of the doubt," Tor told him. "And while you're doing that, I need you to keep something in mind."

"Sure," Marco promised.

"You need to remember that while there's good and evil in the world, laws are neither. They're rules created by the fallible to be exploited by the unscrupulous and used to constrain the well-meaning. If laws made the law-abiding safe, people wouldn't need me to show them when they fail. Do you understand?"

Marco nodded slowly. "Things aren't always black or white."

"No," Tor agreed. "Nor even shades of gray. Even if you can see in technicolor—or can't see at all—there's always texture, taste, smell, and sound. It's complicated and messy, but rainbows are still good things."

Marco smiled a little. "True," he agreed. If nothing else they meant the sun was coming out.

"So give your uncle Flory a break," Tor prompted.

"I will." And the people in the Salinger mansion as well.

CHRISTMAS AT his parents' place, which was big enough to have become the family gathering place over the years, was always chaotic, but Marco loved his cousins, the entire loud, obnoxious, irritating bunch of them. He got mothered by Aunt Marie and Aunt Amelia, quizzed about his new job by his uncle Giuseppe (or Joe to the family, unless Aunt Amelia got mad), and fussed over by his parents and siblings. There were video game tournaments inside and two-hand touch football in the big backyard for adults and a perennial game of tag for the grandchildren. There was also a giant, mandatory, family-wide "white elephant" gift exchange for everyone over eighteen in the evening. The exchange had come about as a way for everyone not to go broke buying presents, so the gifts were both thoughtful, funny, and weird. A twenty-four pack of designer beers, a giant box of yarn, a year-long subscription to Disney+, or a signed set of romance books—all of them were wrapped and thrown into the center of the room and chosen blindly or competed over during a raucous two-hour drama that even the children, with their new toys and pajamas, watched eagerly.

Marco enjoyed every minute of it, even when he ended up giving the box of yarn he'd opened to his aunt Marie at the end of the game because she was the one who loved to knit. (He rather suspected she'd been the one to supply the gift, but he wasn't going to ask her.)

"Thanks, sweetness," she said, giving him a buss on the cheek. A padded, comfortable woman who often forgot to take her apron off after she'd been cooking and had never mastered the art of dyeing her graying hair black all the way to the roots, she was Camille's future, but Cammie didn't seem to mind. "Here, since it looks like someone already knitted you a pretty hat, I'll trade you the yarn for this." She held up the gift certificate for a high-end kitchen supply store that she'd ended up with. Camille had supplied *that* gift, probably with her mother in mind, but Marco took it gratefully.

"Thanks, Auntie," he told her. "I'll put this to good use." He couldn't help the smile that slipped out. "And a friend gave this hat to me."

"A *good* friend?" she asked archly.

"A pretty friend," he returned with a wink, because it was true—Torrance Grayson was definitely easy on the eyes—but also because the relationship was new. He wanted to keep their quiet meals and stolen kisses to himself.

She gave him a brief, sweet smile before her pleasantly worn face lapsed into thoughtfulness instead of her usual smiles.

"Anything wrong, Auntie?"

She gave him a perceptive glance. "I think you know," she murmured. "But Cammie and Frankie tell me they're looking into it. Your uncle Flory—he hasn't been okay this month. I'm…." Almost by instinct she searched out her husband, her true love as nobody had ever doubted, in the crowd. Marco followed her gaze and saw him sitting in the stuffed chair in the corner, near the stereo where Marco's father liked to listen to music—he was an avid Led Zeppelin fan—leaning forward to talk to one of the littlest children. The child—Emma, Marco's niece—smiled at her great-uncle Flory and without ceremony crawled into his lap, giving him the toy she'd been playing with. Flory wrapped an arm around the little girl and held the toy so she could yawn in his ear, pointing out its many features (Marco assumed) until she fell into an exhausted doze.

While Marie and Marco watched, Flory kissed Emma on the crown of her little head, a look of such profound weariness and care on his face that even if they hadn't suspected something in the first place, Marco would have worried anyway.

"See?" Auntie Marie demanded, and Marco "*hmm*ed."

"Yeah."

"What's wrong with him?" she asked, almost tearfully.

"We're trying to find out," he told her, remembering the voice-activated recorder that Cammie swore she'd planted and would be checking in the next week.

"Thank you," Marie whispered, leaning into him for a hug.

And that, right there, was the moment Marco really started to appreciate how much it *didn't* matter what was going on at the Salinger household. If someone there could help his uncle Flory and his family, he was not going to split hairs.

THE NEW Year's Eve bash arrived after Christmas, and Marco was so exhausted by prep and the holidays in general that he could have cried at the thought of a two-week vacation starting January. He and the staff ran themselves absolutely ragged pushing canapes and drinks—both alcoholic and non-alcoholic, served in different glassware—through the mansion as a staggering array of Chicago's richest, brightest, and most talented flowed through the doors.

Oddly enough, it was not the staff alone doing the work, Marco realized. Hunter, Molly, and Grace all came in caterer's uniforms like Marco's, while Michael, Carl, and Chuck helped out the valets. Marco didn't realize how *competent* everybody was and how seamlessly they blended into the staff dynamic at the mansion until Grace grabbed a plate of some of the best canapes and said, "I'm taking this to Josh's room for him, Stirling, and Tienne. Don't worry. I won't forget. I'll be back."

Marco nodded and said thank you before realizing that this was a *huge* help, because he wouldn't have been able to feed those three people otherwise, and that Grace had taken some of the strain that came with maintaining a separate quiet space for Josh Salinger's recovery, as well as his two *extremely* introverted friends.

"Damn," he muttered to himself, watching as Grace disappeared down the hallway, deftly avoiding any hands coming for the canapes.

"What?" Phyllis asked, bustling in from the tiny foyer room, which was jam-packed with people playing charades. "Is he giving you trouble?"

"No," Marco told her, stunned. "He just took a huge load off my back."

Phyllis's pleasantly round face relaxed into a smile. "He's a good boy at heart," she murmured.

"Well, even if he disappears for the rest of the night, he made sure Josh and his friends got fed, and I will make him whatever he desires for a month," Marco told her passionately and then went back to his job preparing the canapes that the others distributed.

He was so busy that he didn't even notice time passing until Phyllis thrust two glasses of sparkling cider into his hand and shoved him toward the open side of the kitchen. Marco was about to ask her what the hell she thought he was going to do with *those* when he spotted Tor, holding a finger to his lips and gesturing down the hallway, the almost secret route toward the back of the mansion.

They emerged out on the walkway through the garden to the gym, into the frigid night. There were a couple of propane heaters out back for the few cigar smokers at the party, and they probably kept Marco's lips from freezing together as soon as he hit the open air.

"What are we doing?" he asked, listening to the chaos coming from the ballroom behind them.

"Starting the New Year off right," Tor told him, voice husky. God, he looked good tonight. He was wearing a tailored blue velveteen tuxedo, of all things, tight to his body, his blue suede shoes so damned fashionable they hurt. He'd gotten his hair trimmed that week, and the past month of rest had put some meat on his bones, eased the shadows under his eyes, and given him some of the sparkle and shine Marco had seen on his videos back before September. He looked like the other young Chicago glitterati at the party, very comfortable with the rich and the famous.

But he was gazing at Marco with unfettered joy, no self-consciousness at all for being in private with the "help." His smile was blinding.

Inside, the countdown started at thirty, and Tor's eyes widened. "Here," he said, taking one of the glasses from Marco. "Are we ready?"

Absolutely enchanted by the moment, by the whimsy, Marco grinned back. "Fifteen," he said, and together they finished the countdown with the rest of the mansion.

"Five, four, three, two, one!"

"Happy New Year," Tor said softly, clinking their glasses.

"Happy New Year."

They both drank, and then Tor took the glasses and set them gently on a nearby table before turning and capturing Marco's cheeks between his palms and kissing him, the kind of joyous, openmouthed New Year's Eve kiss someone gave a lover when they wanted nothing more than to celebrate a new beginning with them.

Marco groaned and opened his mouth, taking over the kiss and plundering, rejoicing when Tor let out a breathy moan and dropped his hands to Marco's waist, letting Marco take his mouth again and again and again.

They might have kissed forever out there—they might have done more—but they were outside in a Chicago January night, and when Tor gave a violent shudder, Marco laughed softly and pulled away.

"We should go inside before the glasses shatter," he said, because that was a very real possibility in the cold.

"Yeah." Tor sighed regretfully. "Probably a good idea. I know the party's breaking up, but you're probably still cooking for a while."

"Till one," Marco told him, scooping up the glasses and dragging Tor reluctantly back into the fray. "And tomorrow's mostly cleanup, while I take it you all are packing."

"Yup. I got my summer clothes and closed out my apartment two days ago," Tor told him, giving one of those retroactive shudders as the warmth of the mansion welcomed them back into the hallway.

He and the others had also had a big strategy meeting, Marco knew, but he didn't say anything about it. Marco was beginning to realize that while yes, the people who moved in and out of the Salinger mansion were more than they appeared, any group of people who had more money than Marco could dream of who would voluntarily jump into catering and valet duty just to help were probably decent people.

At the very least, he was willing to trust.

"So," Marco said, the realization hitting him, "I won't see you for two more weeks, right?"

"Yeah." Tor caught his shoulder when they were deep into the hallway, right before it branched out to the bedrooms, the place no guests were allowed, not tonight. "As soon as I get back, Marco, as I promised. Your family will be front and center. I've done some of my own research on what your cousin told me, and you might need more than my help on this. Is that okay?"

Marco blinked, surprised. "Who would you ask?"

Tor chuckled and patted his cheek. "Oh, Marco. Just give me permission to share your story with my friends and you'll see."

Marco nodded. "Okay, do I know these friends?"

Tor threw his head back and laughed. "I hope so. Three of them helped your caterers tonight, and three more were on valet duty. And three of the others pay your check."

Marco gaped at him, and Tor snuck in another playful, happy kiss.

"I'm going to take that as a yes," he said happily. "Don't worry, Marco. We've got your back." He gave a regretful look down the corridor toward the ballroom and sighed. "But I need to go have Danny's back. He made me promise to be part of the schmoozers since Carl deserted him to go park cars."

And with that, he straightened his cuff, his tie, and his collar and disappeared down the hallway before Marco could wish him a happy vacation.

With a little laugh, Marco continued back to the kitchen where some more frantic activity—and exhausted cleanup—awaited. None of it daunted him, though, as he realized that the dawn of this new year might very well have been the most romantic moment of his life.

A WEEK later, Marco saw Tor on a story that would later be picked up by the AP newswire and aired on all the major networks, including Felix's. He was in the middle of a Caribbean jungle, wearing khakis, a madras shirt, and a tan, and interviewing an earnest young Interpol officer about stopping a massive gun operation that could be tied back to corrupt businessmen in Chicago.

In the background there were a lot of giant crates and the aftermath of some *very* big explosions. A medevac helicopter whap-whapped behind them as they spoke, and as Tor watched, appalled, he saw a man who looked very much like Benjamin Morgan getting loaded into the helicopter, a sling around his arm, before another man on a stretcher—the stoic Carl who had ditched out on a party to park cars with his boyfriend—joined him.

Also in the picture, running back and forth and doing useful things, he could see Hunter, Felix, Grace, and Chuck.

He even saw a flash of Molly's red hair.

Tor didn't name them—he called them "Good Samaritans" who had suffered minor injuries, and then the film cut to the businessmen getting arrested in their homes in Chicago in real time.

Marco stood, slack-jawed, in front of the computer Phyllis had turned on in the kitchen after what sounded like a frantic call from Julia, and took all this in.

Smuggled guns. Mobsters in Chicago. Torrance Grayson, Benjamin Morgan, the entire Salinger clan running around, involved, it appeared, on the side of the angels.

And that's when Marco got it. "Tell my friends." "Work on a project." "Look into a few things."

"Phyllis," he said, his voice dreamy, "who am I working for?"

"Best people in the world," she said with satisfaction. Then she grew grim. "But I hope Felix can be talked out of killing Danny. He really hates it when that man gets hurt."

Ice Man Waiteth

WHEN FELIX, Danny, and Julia had planned the trip to the Caribbean to find out what had happened to Stirling and Molly Christopher's parents, they had taken *nearly* everything into account.

Luxurious yacht, owned by Josh's uncle Leon? Check.

Hours and hours of background research, family meetings, deductive reasoning, fact-checking, and the occasional break-in to administrative offices that were none too friendly about sharing information? Check.

The various skills and specialties of their eclectic group of former con men, hackers, grifters, mercenaries, and thieves? Check.

So much good planning, so much good payoff. They'd even accounted for travel exhaustion, giving everybody a day and two nights in a luxury hotel to get used to the idea of solid ground again, those that liked nightlife and club dancing a chance to go out one last time, the sun-sensitive a chance to hide in the air conditioning, the sun-worshipping to lay out on the beach and simply bake, and the severe introverts a chance to huddle in their rooms and do quiet things that didn't require any human interaction at all, except for the human interaction Stirling and Tienne chose to have together.

Tor gathered from watching the two of them that there was a *lot* of *very* human interaction they chose to have together, and he was happy for Stirling, especially, who had been a good friend and a solid teammate in the past.

Of course, there were some things they *hadn't* accounted for too.

For example, they *hadn't* accounted for the wildly unpredictable Grace to veer off from what was supposed to be a harmless outing into imminent danger for himself and Michael, Carl's boyfriend.

They *hadn't* accounted for Danny getting injured in what was supposed to be a routine break-in to get access to some information authorities wouldn't even give Liam Craig, who was a legitimate member of a legitimate alphabet agency and who should have had access to anything he needed out of simple courtesy.

And they *hadn't* accounted for Carl catching a crappy knife in the shoulder when he'd been hauling ass in a Zodiac boat, trying to catch up with Michael and Grace as they'd been stowed away on the bad guy's cabin cruiser.

So, as Julia pointed out loudly and angrily during the second half of their trip—the half where two of their party were on forced bed rest to recover from injuries—having to utilize two *perfectly good* fake IDs on a Barbados hospital was *not expected*, and they were going to have to impose on Tienne, their forger and most reliable backstop man, for two more identities, and that had *not* been part of their plans!

Tor hadn't cared—he'd been riding the high of the story, thrown together on the fly. He'd been one of the party left behind on Martinique when Grace spotted the people they were pretty sure were responsible for Stirling and Molly's adoptive parents' deaths, and the chaos of the next twelve hours, of trying to scare up transportation, of putting all of the accrued information to use, of rounding up his cameramen in Chicago and siccing them on the businessmen who had given the orders for Fred and Stella Christopher's murders—all of it had been the adrenaline spiking, seat-of-the-pants sort of business Tor was used to pulling off with the Salinger crew, and it had been *exhilarating*. He'd gone on the vacation hoping for sun and sand and some clubbing and some sleeping—and he'd gotten all of that. But he'd also gotten twenty-four hours of mile-a-minute thrill ride, and *that* had fired his blood too.

By the time they'd all spent some time in the hotel—and he, Carl, and Michael had spent some time out by the pool, warming their bones to keep them sustained through the winter in Chicago—he'd felt rejuvenated, excited, *reborn*.

And he'd also felt… incomplete.

The first thing he'd wanted to do after that thrill ride of taking a helicopter out to the tiny island that had been used to store all the illegal guns and throwing his story together on the fly—quite literally—was sit down and have a quiet moment with Marco while he told him everything that had gone down that day. Everything from Molly's badass hands-on fighting skills to Michael's cheerful dismantling of the gunrunner's home base to Carl and Danny's injured heroics needed telling, but none of that went into the story. The bad guys got front and center—as they should have—so they could go to jail when everything fell out. But Tor knew the *real* story, and Marco knew all the players, and wouldn't Marco love to hear how the people he saw every day, the people he fed, the people whose company he enjoyed, went out into the world and did amazing things?

It was like living with superheroes, and Tor wanted to share that world with someone.

With the young man whose black-fringed brown eyes seemed to follow him wherever he went.

"I'm sorry my company's so onerous, my boy," Danny told him on the flight home.

Tor gave him a wink and clinked his orange juice glass with Danny's, letting him know Tor hadn't forsaken him entirely. They were in one of the two private planes they'd engaged to fly the party and luggage back and forth from the States, and Tor sighed and wriggled into the leather upholstery, thinking it would suck the next time he had to fly on his own dime. He was a slightly sized man, but as small as he was, coach was still getting more and more lemming-sized by the day.

"Your company's amazing, as always," Tor told him, which was true. He gave Felix a glance as he dozed in the seat next to Danny's, and smiled. "But it looks like you've tuckered Felix out."

Danny gave his husband a fond glance—but one that was tinged with tiredness as well. "He's been a neurotic mess," Danny said baldly, keeping his voice low. "One little gunshot wound, some running around on a little island, and he thinks I'm ready for the little thief's retirement home."

Danny Mitchell, aka Benjamin Morgan, aka Uncle Danny, was one of the most legendary thieves of all time. Nothing—not mistreated artwork, not culturally appropriated rubies, and not pretty baubles belonging to the patently undeserving—was safe from his charm and skill. The ten years he'd spent apart from Felix had only increased his cachet. And his legend. But Tor could see in that one glance that Danny would give it all up to know Felix would be forever by his side.

Danny caught Tor's glance, and his own eyes sharpened with perception. "I asked you how you were doing a few moments ago, and you got lost in the answer. Can I assume, perhaps, you got lost in a certain pair of fathomless brown eyes?"

Wildfire raced under Tor's skin as he realized Danny knew *exactly* who Tor was thinking about.

"He has a job for me," Tor said. "Involving his family. I've been doing some poking around into it, Danny, and I think I may need your help on this one."

Danny's smile—offset by a couple of crooked teeth in the front but made magical by his slanted hazel Peter Pan eyes—seemed to light up the plane.

"Really? A job? So soon?" Those eyes darted to Felix. "How delightful," he said in complete sincerity. "Tell me about it."

Tor nodded, excited about the prospect of doing just that, before he sobered. "But Danny, we're going to need his help on this. We'll probably need to bring a couple of members of his family in. You'll see when I explain, but—"

Danny nodded soberly. "Talk to him," he said. "See how much he *wants* to know."

Tor nodded, not sure where he stood there. "He's such a good kid," he said, but they both knew that was a double-edged sword. Unbidden, their eyes strayed to Josh, who was fast asleep between Grace and Liam Craig, their Interpol friend.

Grace and Josh had been best friends since practically the cradle, of course, although Grace might have been curled up with Hunter if Hunter hadn't been flying the plane. That wasn't a given. Josh and Grace's friendship, their brotherhood, was so thick that any significant other would have to accommodate their bond. Like twins in the womb, sometimes they had to be in their own little space if they were to exist outside of it with someone else.

But Josh and Liam had seemed to forge their own space during the trip. Tor doubted they'd become lovers—in fact, they probably had mostly become friends after having the occasional "Oh, it's *you*," moment in the past. But watching Liam's casual arm around Josh's shoulders while Grace practically lay in his lap made Tor realize that Josh had *always* been destined for somebody else.

Tor would have squirmed under the weight of the two of them, but Liam looked like he could take it in stride.

Which was fortunate, because Josh and Grace were *not* good kids. Both of them had been breaking the rules, and often the law, since the third grade. By their tweens they'd been breaking and entering—mostly for good causes, Tor understood, but still, laws were really more suggestions than rules to the two of them and always would be. Grace was a stunning thief—Tor couldn't even look at him without checking for his wallet. After their little adventure in Napa, Tor had needed to call Josh from the street in front of his apartment building from a stranger's cell phone to make Grace return his wallet, phone, and *keys*, all of which Grace had pocketed on the drive from the airport.

And Josh wasn't much better. Before he'd gotten sick, Tor had needed to censor not one but *two* stories about mysterious masked strangers—Josh and Grace—BASE jumping from the top of Chicago buildings. The thing that few people knew about those jumps was that *many* layers of security had needed to be breached for the two of them to even get to the jump point, and while Grace *may* have been able to breach some of them by sheer stealth, it had taken Josh—and Josh's fine brain—to pull the entire caper off without a hitch and without being identified.

Josh may have been a *great* person, whose heart was driven by kindness and altruism and whose actions were dictated by a very active conscience, but he was not, all things considered, a "good kid."

Marco *was* a "good kid." Tor had seen the rising awareness in Marco's eyes. He'd seen the realization that these "nice people" that he worked for weren't entirely… *conventional.*

Seriously, who just had a small military-grade voice-activated recorder in their junk drawer?

But if Torrance Grayson, independent reporter, was going to research what he *thought* was going on with Marco's family, Tor was going to have to utilize his "research team," and that meant letting Marco in on the secret, however much of it he hadn't guessed for himself.

It would mean letting Marco in *period.*

Danny moved restlessly, breaking the thoughtful silence. "Tor?" he said delicately.

"Yes?"

"He can still be a good kid—and a lover—if you decide not to bring him in all the way."

Tor's eyes widened. "Wow."

Danny gave him a droll look. "Exactly how clueless do you think we are? Seriously. On a scale of one to ten, one being you two carrying on a quiet courtship in the kitchen with nobody noticing and ten being paying retail, where do we rank on the 'my family doesn't notice or care,' scale."

Tor's eyes narrowed now. "My real family didn't know I was gay even after my brother cleaned out the attic," he said grimly.

"And what was in the attic?"

"My coveted collection of Yaoi, a sleeping bag, and a box of tissues."

Danny brought his hand up to his mouth so quickly, he had to suppress a wince when he jerked his injured shoulder too hard. "What did you tell them?"

"Nothing. I said, 'Huh, that's weird, I wonder how long that's been there.'"

Danny's snort was a thing of beauty. "How long did they buy that?"

Tor chuffed out a breath of satisfaction. "Until I graduated from high school and told them about the full ride to State. My dad had expected me to help him with the business, but…." He looked away, trying to keep his bitterness from making this story angry instead of funny.

Danny proved that he was *never* on the clueless scale. "Outspoken against gay rights?" he asked softly.

"Violently," Tor said, swallowing against the hurt. "I came home from graduation, ate cake, hugged all my aunts and uncles, and when they'd left, I packed my car. Mom and Dad came out to ask me what I was doing, and I told them I'd secured an apartment and a job in the city and I started the next day."

Danny let out a low whistle. "That's… that's clean, friend. I won't lie. That's a clean break."

Tor nodded, knowing the word he was avoiding was "cold." But cold was how he'd felt—how he still felt—remembering that moment.

"Mom started crying," he said, remembering that. "I hugged her, knowing it was the last hug I was going to get from her for a while, if ever, and stepped back. And I said, 'You guys, that gay porn in the attic was mine. You spent months telling everybody how a disgusting baby-raping pervert must have lived in your house. Mom got a priest to bless the place. I'm gay. And now I know exactly how you feel about me.'"

Danny sucked air in through his teeth. "They didn't bother to deny it?"

Tor shook his head sadly. "Nope. They just stood on the lawn and let me go. I've lived out and proud ever since… until…." He let out a breath, not realizing that this was the truth until right now.

"Until Felix told you a secret about me," Danny said, voice aching with sympathy. "And you kept it. I'm sorry."

"Don't be." Unexpectedly, Tor's throat tightened. "I… families are vaults full of secrets. Full of stories. Some of my best segments have been families coming clean about long-ago sins. But… but until Felix trusted me with the secret of Danny Mitchell, of his *real* true love, the person who wasn't Julia, I hadn't realized how much I missed being a part of that. Every time you called me for a story, I felt like I was… I was in a real family."

"You *are*," Danny said softly.

"I didn't believe that, though," Tor said, his voice breaking a little. "I didn't. I thought, 'Oh yeah—they're using me. I'm convenient.' Because you all did the groundwork without me and then presented me with the story. And I was okay with that, really. I got to pretend. And then…." He wiped at his cheek irritably. "God, I'm a fucking watering pot. But I woke up after that… that horrible week, and you all were there. And you've let me be your nephew or your…."

"Little brother," Danny murmured.

"And now I look at Marco, and I want him." He let out a broken laugh, remembering that cold, magical kiss on the back porch on New Year's Eve. "I do. I would really like to see what Marco and I could do together. But if he can't accept my family, I need to hold out for someone who can."

Danny's hand on his was unexpected—but comforting. "And I'm going to hold out hope that you can have your twinkie and eat him too," he said, his words so ribald that now it was Tor's turn to hold first one hand over his mouth and then both as he tried to keep the laughter in.

"It wasn't that funny." Danny chuckled unexpectedly.

Tor grinned behind his hands and then leaned in, his voice so tight with humor and tears that it squeaked. "I think he's a top!"

That broke them. Both of them. Felix snorted himself awake as they threw their heads back and howled with laughter.

THE LUXURY jet was nice—in fact it was *amazing*—but it was still travel. By the time the SUVs pulled into the Salinger driveway, to be moved into the garage by staff, everybody inside was exhausted, hungry, cranky, and trying *very* hard not to take it out on their fellow passengers.

It helped that Felix reminded everybody that the contents of their luggage would show up in their rooms cleaned and folded sometime in the next two days—something they'd all known beforehand so anything they'd needed had been in their carry-ons, as had their winter wear, which had been stored on the planes themselves while they'd been in the Caribbean.

Still, the group of people who staggered into the foyer of the mansion and disbursed, some to shower or sleep before eating and some to raid the kitchen first, were frayed to their last nerve.

Tor saw Marco in the kitchen, supervising hot sandwiches and soup for all the cold-shocked vacationers, and smiled to himself but stayed in the hallway, heading for his room and the shower he'd called dibs on while Chuck, Hunter, Felix, and Michael had been talking about food. On his way he watched Tienne and Stirling cut through the kitchen toward the downstairs den—Stirling's room was attached, although very few people knew that because they usually kept it locked when there was company in the mansion. Both of them had the haunted look of people who needed *quiet alone time right now*.

Josh was so tired he was nearly staggering, and as Tor glanced around the hallway to find someone to help him, he saw Hunter scooping the younger man up in his arms and heard Liam Craig protest.

"That's my job, mate!" Liam's London's East End showed in his voice.

"Hush, you," Hunter said, "or I'll call Chuck and have him carry *you*."

Liam, who had curly dark brown hair, dark blue eyes, and enough zinc oxide to coat a truck on his peeling nose, gave a bark of unexpected laughter. "Ouch! For the kill, yeah?"

"Yeah," Hunter said with good-natured sincerity. "You go to your room and shower, and I'll go dump Sleeping Beauty here on his clean sheets."

Tor half expected Josh to protest, but as Hunter rounded the corner to the staircase, he realized that Josh Salinger, who had been invaluable as their hacker during the maneuver with Gunrunner's Island, as everybody had been calling it, had fallen fast asleep.

Tor thought he might be next as he emerged from the steamy bathroom half an hour later, dressed in sweats, a hoodie, and, thank God, chafe-free underwear. He stopped in his room to drop his travel-stained clothes in the hamper and was surprised to find Marco there with a tray, complete with hot chocolate, a hot roast beef panini, and rich bacon, potato, and jalapeno soup.

Tor's knees gave a definite wobble as the aroma of Marco's cooking hit him. He dumped his clothes in the hamper and gave the tray on his desk a look of pure desire.

"I *want* that," he said, and Marco laughed a little and stepped aside, holding the chair for Tor and letting him get settled.

Tor glanced shyly up at him before he tucked into the food. "Special treatment?" he said, hoping it was true.

"Yeah." Marco leaned over and kissed him softly, engaging his lips with promise. "Two weeks didn't used to be so long. I missed you."

Tor beamed up at him. "I missed you too," he said. He grew a little embarrassed. "I kept wanting to text you, but… but there was so much unsaid, and I—"

"Eat first," Marco urged him, moving to the corner for the padded wooden bedroom chair. While Tor devoured his first bite of sandwich, Marco moved the chair to the desk so he could sit kitty-corner and they could bump knees.

Tor swallowed the sandwich and went for the soup, making sounds of pure bliss as he tasted. "Jalapeno, bacon, and potato soup," he said in wonder. "It's amazing. God, is this a family recipe or—"

"My own invention," Marco said humbly. "What's this?"

Tor had reached into his pocket and pulled out his phone. "Well, like I said, I wanted to text you, but I wasn't sure where we were and… anyway. Every time I saw something amazing, I took a picture, and then I captioned it, like I would if…." His face grew warm, and it wasn't the jalapenos. "If we were… a thing. For real. Anyway, I saved them all and then edited them on my phone, added a soundtrack and….” He shrugged, trying to make it casual. “If you like it, I’ll email it to you.”

The smile he got in return was as luminous as the sunset over Martinique.

“You saved this? For me?” Marco asked, sounding as though nobody had ever done something personal like this for him before.

“Yeah,” Tor admitted through a bite of sandwich. He swallowed and tried not to be an oaf. “I, uh, missed you. I told you that.”

Marco’s eyes got bright. “I missed you too,” he said softly. “I came back to work early so I could cook for the staff, but really I just… I wanted to imagine you there, in the kitchen, when I was done. Phyllis said I was crazy, but if I’m taking vacation time off, I want…. I mean, next time maybe I can go with you.” He gave a hesitant smile. “Although I don’t know how much help I’d be bringing down gunrunners.”

Tor grimaced, hiding his face, embarrassed as he hadn’t been since losing his virginity in college. “You saw that, did you?” he asked, playing for time.

“All of Chicago saw that,” Marco retorted. “But I didn’t realize Phyllis was getting undoctored feed until nobody I knew called to ask me why Benjamin Morgan and Felix Salinger were running through the jungle taking down criminals. I guess Phyllis has some sort of special privileges?”

Tor nodded. “Yeah. Julia asked me to send the footage to Phyllis first so she could call Danny and yell. I guess Phyllis was too busy telling him how brave he was for it to make an impact, and Julia was… well, not furious, because she loves Phyllis, you know that, but… frustrated.” He nodded vigorously. “Julia was very *frustrated* that Danny got hurt and Felix didn’t let her in on all the action on the island, and she was the only one yelling.”

Marco shook his head and stared. “Would… would she have been any help?” he asked, probably not as delicately as he should have.

Tor nodded. “Well, she said something about being out of practice, so honestly I have no idea what she’s capable of. Danny and Felix tend to treat her like she’s precious and—” He took a breath, not sure if he should voice things he knew about in confidence. “—I gather that wasn’t always the case with her father,” he said at last. Hiram Dormer’s brutality was a matter of public record; it was only logical for Marco to assume it had extended to his daughter. “But for this trip, her job was to communicate with the businessmen in Chicago while Josh was gathering information and helping me get my team in place. And like I said, she really wanted to be part of the action, particularly when Danny and Carl needed a doctor’s care at the end.”

He watched as Marco digested this information, and finally he gave a great big sigh, one that made Tor smile.

"Look, I-I don't know how to ask about any of this. I feel so stupid because I didn't notice the… the *anomalies* of this household until I started to get close to you. But once I started to see stuff, I couldn't *unsee* it. And then there was that film segment. As you say, unedited. But it leaves me with all sorts of questions, and… and… *where am I working?*"

Tor yawned and wiped his mouth, staring at the empty plate in front of him. The food and shower had revived him somewhat, and he thought he had the beginnings of the story in him before he crashed for good.

But first….

"Can I get another kiss?" he asked, cocking his head and trying to look cute. He knew he was handsome. You couldn't work on video without coldly assessing your appearance plusses and minuses, and he had a masculinely pleasing face, right down to the square chin and the hint of a divot.

But looking cute was another matter. Looking cute was playful, coy, and seductive all at the same time, and he was hoping….

Marco laughed a little and leaned forward to kiss him again, *promising* again, then pulling back before Tor could fall into the kiss and forget the subject.

Like he would.

"This is important," Marco said softly.

"I know," Tor agreed. "Particularly because if I'm going to get to the core of what's going on with your family, I'm probably going to need help from pretty much everyone who lives here, which means you have to be on board with your eyes open."

Marco nodded again, and Tor, to his embarrassment, yawned.

"But you have to hurry," Marco said. "I get it."

Tor shrugged and leaned back in his chair, stretching. "Okay," he said, his mind sorting information quickly, deciding on an angle for the story, trying to find the best way to explain how this place came to be. "I think I've got it. Are you ready?"

"Hit me," Marco said. "But make it quick. I can tell you're about ready to crash like everybody else. I gather it was a long trip."

"That's *another* story. Let's start with this one." At Marco's gesture to go on, he did. "Okay, so much of this is common knowledge among the Salingers and the people who live here, and if you know this, you'll understand how they came to be. You know the basic story, the one Felix and Benjamin Morgan shared on TV?"

Marco frowned. "That over twenty years ago, Felix and Dr. Morgan were knocking around Europe together as a couple. They had a spat, Felix hooked up with Julia, and although he and Dr. Morgan were very much in love, he married Julia to do the right thing. Felix and Julia divorced about five years ago. They both dated other people but were still so invested in their son, Josh, that everything was amicable, and then Dr. Morgan came back to town."

Tor let out a puff of laughter as he realized the giant gaps in the public story. "Yeah. That's what you were told. The real story is much more… human. And painful. Felix Salinger and Danny Mitchell were *con men* in Europe over twenty years ago. They spent their time fleecing tourists— mostly the rich, obnoxious ones, the kind who'd exploited Danny for years before he'd gotten away."

"Exploited?" Marco asked, eyes wide.

"I think once Danny got his feet under him, it got to be mutual," Tor said grimly. "Danny may not have a legitimate degree in anything, but he's one of the most brilliant, canny people I've ever met. But Danny and Felix were together, and they wanted to quit playing around, so they decided on one last big grift. Hiram Dormer—"

"Julia's father," Marco clarified.

"That's the fucker. He was well known in Rome at the time. He'd spawned and deserted almost an entire neighborhood of children on unwilling servant girls while he was squiring his daughter around, trying to auction her off to the highest bidder before he killed her himself in a fit of rage."

Marco recoiled. "That's… that's not a version in the press."

Tor knew his face was hard but didn't care. "But it's the truest version, nonetheless. Julia, Felix, and Danny have all confirmed it. And Felix and Danny wanted him to pay. So they sent Felix in to seduce Julia and steal from Hiram, but they didn't know the whole story yet. When Felix realized that not only was she in fear for her life on the daily, but also *pregnant* and therefore absolutely valueless to Hiram—"

"Oh God." Marco had paled. He obviously knew abuse statistics just like Tor did.

"Yes," Tor continued. "She was pregnant with Josh and smart enough after watching the criminals her father worked with to spot a con man. But she and Felix must have been human to each other while Felix was trying to infiltrate the household, because she asked for his help, and Felix asked Danny—who had always been their mastermind—and Danny came up with the plan."

"To marry off his lover?" Marco sounded appalled, but Tor shook his head.

"To spirit them away and out of Hiram's clutches before he could beat Julia to a pulp," Tor corrected. "The only thing that would give her autonomy was marriage to someone else. By the time Hiram caught up with them, Julia was very publicly pregnant, and they'd spent part of her trust from her mother on this mansion right here. Once they knew Hiram had bought the story and was well on the way to welcoming Felix to the family, Danny flew out to join them."

Marco's eyes grew huge. "Join them?"

Tor nodded soberly. "He, Felix, and Julia raised the baby together. Danny snuck in and out of the mansion and helped Felix study and acquire enough savvy to run the cable network like a pro. Together they treated acquiring wealth and social status like the biggest con of all, so they could back Julia Dormer-Salinger up when she needed it and give Josh a security in the world none of them had ever had. They traveled to Europe and knocked around there for a couple of years where nobody would ask questions. They taught Josh a zillion different languages and how to con for his supper." Tor laughed softly. "They did it for the game, I think. Felix and Danny. Julia too. By the time they'd all met, the world already felt… fixed, I guess. Like the deck was stacked against all of them. Pulling a scam on some awful old colonizer who was screwing over the house staff felt like their way of leveling the playing field."

He paused and saw Marco nod thoughtfully.

"They—all four of them—got very good."

Marco grunted, a quiet, ruminative sound. "What happened?"

"Danny…." Tor looked away. This part he knew more from Felix than from Danny, and it felt disloyal somehow, because Felix was so very self-recriminatory. "It's hard to be the invisible man. To have a family you can't talk about, a boy you think of as a son you can't take out to the park, a woman you regard as a sister who can't acknowledge you in public—"

"A lover who has to be seen with another person in the press and has to sell it," Marco said, as though remembering something.

"You saw them?" Tor asked. He had too—he'd grown up near Springfield.

"All the society papers," Marco murmured. "My mother used to call them Chicago's royal couple."

"Exactly," Tor said, glad he didn't have to explain. "When they got back from Europe, Felix had to suck up especially hard to Julia's father.

Their every step had to be accounted for because now that Josh was a part of their lives and such a bright little kid—"

And Marco wasn't stupid. "Hiram wanted him," he said.

Tor nodded. "One misstep. One wrong move and Hiram would have moved in to take the boy. So Danny became more invisible. He told me once he learned everything he needed to know about security systems by sneaking into this mansion. He and Felix would get the best systems to keep Hiram from spying on them, and if he wanted to see his family—"

"He had to sneak in," Marco deduced.

"Yeah. It took a toll. Danny started drinking and couldn't stop." He looked levelly into Marco's eyes and noted the quick inhale, the almost unconsciously bitten lip. Yes, Marco saw the tragedy here, of two lovers who had made promises and had given everything to keep them.

"So their reunion?" Marco asked. "The one where they took down the woman who was trying to blackmail Felix out of his station? How long had they really been apart?"

"Ten years."

Marco grimaced. "That's a long time."

Tor's smile held a glimmer of hope. "Yeah, but Danny wasn't really gone for all of it. I mean, to Felix and Julia he was, but remember all those thief skills?"

"Didn't he use them for stealing?" Marco asked, laughing like this was only natural.

"He doesn't like to talk about it," Tor said primly, although Danny totally enjoyed it when somebody else knew what he'd done, "but he kept current by sneaking back to Chicago to watch Josh grow up. He snuck into his plays, visited on his birthday and on holidays. Josh and Danny's relationship never really suffered. So when Felix was in need, Josh called."

"And Danny came." Marco bit his lip again and reached across to hold Tor's hands. "That's… that's amazing. Sweet even. But how did everybody else end up here?"

Tor chuckled. "Well, I ended up entangled when I offered to help Felix get his company back. That's when he told me the story, in fact, and I've been all in ever since. Carl and Danny had met during the separation. I gather Carl held quite a torch for a while, but while Danny may have had other lovers—"

"He only had one love," Marco filled in for him.

"Exactly." Tor felt a yawn coming on—a huge, body-shaking one—so he knew he had to get the rest of it out quickly or he'd simply settle his head down on his desk and fall asleep. Unlike Josh, he was not so insubstantial at this juncture that Marco could carry him to bed. "But the sacrifices they made for Josh were worth it. You've met the kid. He's—"

"Amazing," Marco agreed.

"And that's only the stuff you know," Tor told him. "He and Grace became friends with Stirling and Molly in middle school, when they were protecting Stirling from bullies. They moved on to college, and Josh met Hunter and Chuck. We met Chuck's boyfriend, Lucius, during a job, and I think that's everyone." Was it? He fought the urge to frown and count on his fingers.

"Michael and Tienne."

Crap. Tor gave half a laugh. "Michael's an old friend of Chuck's who had just been let out of prison for armed robbery—that he really didn't want to commit. Felix offered him the job of chief mechanic, and there you go." And then he yawned, so long and hard he felt his bones crack. "And Tienne's our forger. He was a kid when Danny met him during the separation. Danny wasn't in a position to foster him, so he sent the boy here for Felix and Julia to foster. The forging he learned at his father's knee, so that was blind luck."

Marco frowned. "Okay, look, you're tired. I can see that. But I've only got one more question before I let you get some sleep and I chew on this for a while."

Tor finally gave in and let another ginormous stretching yawn take over his body. "Shoot!" he said through his stretch, but Marco gestured him to finish. Finally the yawn let go, and Tor stood and moved to pull down the covers on the bed, knowing he was about done.

"Here," Marco murmured, suddenly there to help him onto the bed and then pull the covers up around his chin.

"You had a question?" Tor insisted, not wanting to lose the thread—or the closeness that the storytelling had brought them.

"Yeah," Marco said, sitting on the side of the bed. Without hesitation he began to smooth the hair back from Torrance's forehead. "Why did they all help during the party? One minute we were scrambling for waitstaff and valets and everybody was booked up, and the next, all the houseguests came out in the appropriate uniforms, ready to work. I understand they split their tips with everybody else too."

Torrance laughed softly. "Two reasons," he said, wanting to purr at Marco's gentle touch through his clean hair. "One, they like knowing their potential marks. Believe me, every guest had a new fact, a new secret, a new problem, recorded and filed away in somebody's brain on New Year's Eve. Julia and Felix use that information shamelessly, getting people to tilt their way in politics and fundraisers. Between the two of them, they've probably done more for LGBTQ rights in Chicago than entire presidential administrations."

Marco chuckled, although Tor hadn't been kidding. "And two?" he asked, sounding skeptical.

"Phyllis needed people, and she asked," Tor said simply. "I would have parked cars, but Danny and Felix begged me and Lucius to stay in the main room with Leon and be charming and available." And to keep an eye on Grace, to make sure he returned every wallet he palmed, but Marco was looking like he was on their side right now, and Tor didn't want to jinx it.

"Really?" Marco asked, still uncertain.

So Tor told the real truth. "They think it's fun," he said, letting some of his own puzzlement show through. "They play a game with Julia where they try to guess who's a good guy and who's a scumbag, and then they think of appropriate consequences for the scumbags. It's sort of cool. Like, if you ever wondered if someone *so awful* can go through life without comeuppance, they make you think that comeuppance is real."

He was babbling now, and he knew it, but he also knew it was the truth. Everybody who had put on a uniform on New Year's had dished and analyzed and crowed about that night, and sometimes it was the stuff they learned—or pocketed and returned—and sometimes it was an amazing save or a tray of glassware. It didn't matter. They'd done it because they'd enjoyed themselves and enjoyed being with each other as it had happened.

It was the same reason Tor showed up for dinners and strategy meetings. Because the Salinger family was unadulterated fun, and they all wanted to change the world.

"So?" Tor asked, as his eyes closed and Marco's movements grew slower.

"What do you want?" Marco asked softly.

"Is my family up to your standards?" he asked, suddenly needing the answer very much.

"I think your family is beyond my judgment," Marco told him, bending to kiss his temple. "But I also think I like them very much."

"Can you keep their secrets?" Tor asked, wanting to beg. "I trusted you with everybody. Do you understand?"

And he had. Everybody he cared about in the Salinger household, including Felix and Danny and Josh. Carl who had held him, Chuck who had carried him, Hunter who had given him advice, and Julia who had very carefully mothered him when he'd been sure he was beyond mothering at this point. All of them, *all* of them, could be irreparably destroyed by this lunchtime chat with Marco.

But Danny had told him to let Marco in.

"I won't tell anybody," Marco whispered. "Not even my cousins. I promise."

And Tor's eyes closed then for the duration, while inside he was begging, *But can you still care about me, knowing I'm in this up to my eyeballs?*

It was a question he'd really love to have answered—as soon as he woke up.

Landing and Flying

MARCO HAD just left Tor's room, the lunch tray in his arms, when Benjamin Morgan—Uncle Danny, as it was getting easier and easier to think of him as—got to the top of the landing and paused to yawn.

"Are you okay, sir?" Marco asked, thinking Dr. Morgan looked even more tired than Tor had, but then, the sling around his arm and the bandage at his shoulder might have had something to do with that.

"Oh yes," Dr. Morgan said. "Just, you know." He made a frustrated gesture to the sling. "My fault for being careless."

Marco thought back to Tor's stories. "I doubt very much you were careless," he said, catching Uncle Danny's eye.

Danny nodded slowly. "So our young reporter opened up to you, did he?"

Marco nodded. "I'll… I'll keep your secrets safe," he promised, suddenly sure that no matter what he did with his future—and he really did love working here—he could do absolutely nothing that would put the people he worked for under any scrutiny or in any danger.

Danny shrugged. "Safe or not safe," he said, "the important thing is that you don't break poor Torrance's heart. Do you understand?"

And that sealed it. That priority right there, of Tor's happiness over his own concerns, sealed Marco's loyalty forever.

"Completely," he said in all humbleness. "I would never do anything to hurt him or his family."

Danny gave him a faint smile. "Good. Then I think we'll get along very well." He let out a wistful smile. "Besides, my boy. I really do have a weakness for your muffins."

"Oh God, Danny." Felix's voice seemed to send an electric current through him. "Go to bed. You're wilting, for fuck's sake, and it's making me—" He yawned. "—tired," he said as he drew near to the landing.

"Of course," Danny murmured. "Just having a conversation with young Marco here. I think he's going to join the family."

Felix raised his eyebrows at Marco, who blushed. "That would be lovely," he said, nodding firmly. Then he gave Danny an exasperated look. "When we've all had some fucking sleep."

"Oh my God, Fox," Danny muttered, "it's like you turned into a nagging grandmother right in front of my eyes. Put on some costume earrings and a big banana slug of lipstick and I'll be right back on the Jersey shore in my youth."

"Oh, you wish," Felix retorted, taking Danny's good elbow with exquisite gentleness. "If you'd wanted a queen, you should have picked one up then. You had to go to Europe to find me."

"To *rescue* you," Danny shot back, so easily Marco knew this was an old and much-loved squabble. "That tourist would have pounded you."

Felix's laugh as they disappeared around the bend in the hallway to Felix's suite was absolutely carnal, leaving Marco under no illusions as to who had pounded whom.

Marco stared after them, still balancing the tray, and realized that, although he'd pretty much already given his word to Torrance Grayson, their little conversation had sealed the deal. It was cantankerous and cranky, but it was also the same bickering—minus the filthy innuendo—that he'd heard from his mother and father, from his aunts and uncles, his entire life.

It was the sort of quibbling that was only engaged in because it made conversation so much fun, made up of old personal jokes and new gentle insults, not with the aim of a winner or a loser, but with the aim of being the first person to make the other laugh. It wasn't the banter of people self-involved or cruel—it was the conversation of people who loved each other so much, they entertained each other with the simple task of going to bed.

It was the kind of relationship Marco had looked for his entire life—one that would rival the adults he'd seen and admired. If this was Torrance Grayson's family, Marco wanted in.

When he got down to the kitchen, he took care of the tray and set about tidying up. The ravenous hordes had descended, and Marco laughed quietly to himself at the thought of the junior cooks and assistants who had been absolutely certain they had enough food to last them a week packed away in the two giant refrigerators. The Salinger zest for food pretty much equaled their zest for life: bottomless.

He was about to claim his boots from the foyer and get dressed to walk to the bus when Phyllis caught his attention. "Do you have a minute before you go home?"

Marco nodded in surprise, particularly when she joined him in the foyer and put on boots and a parka that had been labeled "general use" for people who needed to make a quick trip outside but who had left their own gear in their bedrooms, or in the mudroom around back near the pool. Suitably dressed, she led him outside—but not through the front door.

"Wait," he said, following a little-used passageway that he'd always assumed led to a supply closet. "Where are we…. Oh."

The passageway ended in a small suite of rooms—*Phyllis's* suite of rooms, Marco saw, with a kitchenette, a living room, a door that probably led to a small bedroom, and a bathroom. It was *not* immaculately kept, much to his amusement. Instead it looked like what it was—the room of a quiet, bookish person who enjoyed cross-stitching, music, movies, and researching obscure topics when the mood struck her.

Why had they needed to put on their boots and jackets to…? Oh.

"Don't look at my undies," Phyllis ordered dryly, although the place wasn't *that* cluttered. Her meaning was clear, though. These were her private apartments, and very few people saw them.

"Wouldn't dream of it," Marco said as she cut to the sliding glass door on the far side of the living room. As she opened it, he saw that she had a small patio, cunningly masked by the east wing of the mansion, that was surrounded by a four-foot white privacy fence that led to the grounds of the house by way of a little gate.

The cold was so fierce that by the time they got through the little gate, Marco had remembered how to breathe again—opening his mouth slightly so his nostrils didn't stick together—and to be mindful that under the January snow, layers of ice might lurk.

Still he followed her through the gate and across the yard, and she kept going, leading him along a little path that led through a hedge off from the main house and not toward the gym in the backyard. He realized that while there was some wilderness back here, some "extensive grounds," not all of it tamed, he'd never really thought of the trees as more than a backdrop for the mansion.

"Phyllis, are you taking me somewhere to kill me?" he asked, mostly joking.

She laughed. "No, I'm showing you something new," she said. And then, only about twenty yards from the tree line, he saw it.

"Wow," he said, blinking in surprise. "How long has this been here?"

Phyllis cackled. "About twenty years," she said. "But it's been closed up for the last ten."

As the timing sank in, Phyllis led Marco past the fence of the little cottage, up the front stoop, and after producing a key from her pocket and fumbling with her gloves, through the front door.

The outside was simple—the lower half of the cottage was made of red brick, and the top half was white siding with green trim. Having worked for his uncle Flory over summers in high school, Marco could run his eyes over the joins, the gutters, and the window frames and see that the construction was sound, as was the brickwork over the chimney and the placement of the central heat and air appliance on the side of the building.

"Very nice," Marco said as they walked in, their footsteps ringing hollowly on what looked to be new tile floors. Peering through the foyer, he could see a large sitting room and a hallway leading to four doors. "Two bedrooms, a bathroom, and a laundry room at the back door?" he surmised, and Phyllis grinned.

"Got it in one," she said. "The fireplace is recently rebricked, the kitchen and bathroom retiled, and everything has a fresh coat of paint."

He'd noticed. It wasn't stark apartment white, either, but rather a crisp eggshell, something that looked very clean but was just a tad warmer. The ceiling was high and peaked softly with the roof, giving the impression of both snugness and space, and small touches—the carved railing separating the kitchen from the dining room, the indigo backsplash in the kitchen that matched the tile, the richness of the carpet—told him that this cottage had been built carefully, with love in mind.

"It's fantastic!" he said, meaning it. "Why are you showing it to me?"

"Well," Phyllis told him, a little smile playing at her mouth, "it was originally for, uhm, Dr. Morgan back in the day, before he left for Europe—"

"Uncle Danny," Marco said softly, suddenly seeing it. Danny couldn't always be in the house when Hiram Dormer was present, so they'd built a mother-in-law cottage to give him a landing place while he decided where and how to go somewhere else and how long he'd have to be gone. Suddenly the sadness of the place sank in, as well as the hope. This was Danny's way of being close to his family, and given that Felix had built it—probably with Julia's approval—it was also a way of saying, "please stay."

Danny probably hated it, Marco thought, looking around, but Felix probably thought of it as a place of hope.

"Yeah," Phyllis said softly. "He wanted the place razed, I think, but Felix had it renovated. Said he thought it was a place made for second chances."

Marco kept the hurt sound deep in his chest, and Phyllis kept going.

"Anyway, I was doing household accounts the other night, because I'd had enough of vacation and I was bored. And it occurred to me that you were ready for a raise. However, Felix and Danny just had this place refurbished, and Julia asked me if there was anybody I wanted to offer it to. I figure that the cost of rent taken off your expenses, to have this place rent free—"

"Is a way better raise than I could imagine," Marco breathed, looking around appreciatively. This was no prefab cracker-box apartment. For better or worse, this place had a history—and love was part of it. "It could eat my apartment in one gulp and have the one next to it for dessert."

Phyllis chuckled. "Well, yes. We… well, there's a slight caveat in that sometimes we need a guest lodging, so we might ask if you can put someone up in your guest room from time to time, but we'd throw in the same maid service the rest of the house gets, plus maintenance for the privilege. What do you say?"

Marco thought about his small one-bedroom apartment in downtown Glencoe and shuddered. He'd grown up three suburbs closer to Chicago, where the vibe was more urban—and more old-school. The opulence of Glencoe was newer, but it meant the affordable housing didn't have quite so much character.

"I could move in?" he asked, thinking about Torrance's stories, about how deep he was already in with a group of people who had a loose association with the law. "Uhm, who would I have to put up in my guest room?"

Phyllis laughed and shrugged. "Who wouldn't you? Right now, we're thinking young Mr. Craig should visit more often. He's currently sleeping in Danny's den because it's the last room in the house. When Carl and Michael go back to their house—probably in the morning—he'll move into Carl's old room, but see, that's the thing. We don't really know when the mansion is going to fill up, and while some of our folks have places in the city, and Danny even has a city apartment that he keeps, we do like to be able to offer hospitality as needed." Her expression grew canny. "And just as a word to the wise? If we ever put somebody up in a hotel room instead of offering them a room? You don't want them in our house anyway."

Marco nodded, taking the advice at face value and not laughing at all. After Torrance's story, he realized that protecting the family meant everything to these people, and putting him up on their property included him.

And that gave him the same sort of obligations he had to his own extended family.

It was scary, on the one hand, because his own extended family was huge—part of his life and his heart as not many other things could be. That sort of obligation with the Salingers was not something he took lightly, and while he realized he was on the entry level of familyhood here, he also couldn't forget the video footage Phyllis had shown him.

"You know what we're asking you," she said now, eyes level as he took in the generosity and the strings that were attached, even if Danny and Felix wouldn't want there to be.

"I do."

"Do you want us to simply adjust your pay?"

It was a fair question, and the fact that she asked him determined it for him.

"No," he said, a smile pushing at the corners of his mouth. It didn't take much effort to free it. "No, I'm in. I'll move my stuff in this weekend and sublet my apartment. I'll…." He did a turn around the cottage, loving its size, its dimensions, its coziness, its general sturdy quality. "It will be worth it to pay rent a little while longer so I don't have to commute."

"Excellent," Phyllis said, grinning.

Spontaneously, Marco hugged her, and she squeezed him tight, much like his mother would. "Welcome to the family, my boy. I think you're really going to love it here."

THAT NIGHT he called Cammie, partly to get her to put out the all-call to move him into his new digs and partly because he wanted to find out where she was on operation Bug Uncle Flory. (Cammie had tried calling it "BUF," but Marco and Frankie had pretty much downvoted that idea.)

"Well, first of all," she said, sounding tired but excited, "kudos to you on your new promotion to houseboy—"

"It's free rent," he said, rolling his eyes. "I mean, you know how much that is a month."

"I hear you. Next thing you know, you'll be able to afford a vehicle and parking."

"The place has a garage," he said. It was tiny, one car only, attached to the side of the cottage, but anywhere near Chicago, covered parking was gold.

"Ooh-la-la." She laughed. "Fancy. I'll call up Cousin Edgar's car dealership. Let's see if we can get you a small SUV or something for cheap."

"I need to get out of my old apartment and find someone to sublet it first," he warned.

"Pfft. I got six people who'd love an affordable flop in Glencoe off the top of my head. You got no worries here, Marco. You leave the whole thing to me and it'll be fine. Now you want to hear about that other thing?"

"Yeah," he said, all honesty. "I really fuckin' do, Cammie. Did you see your dad on Christmas?"

"Yeah," she said with a sigh.

"He sounded just…."

"Sad," she murmured. "Yeah. We all saw it. It's why Frankie distracted Dad while I grabbed the bug, changed out the battery, and uploaded the conversations. Me and Frankie listened to them last night over two bottles of wine and a pepperoni pie, and I gotta tell you, Marco, it's—"

"Bad?" he asked softly.

"Yeah." She sighed. "Okay. So I'm putting a file together to send to you of all the convos I recorded that seem to be significant. I put the most significant on the top, and I put them in order, so, you know, you can put together the puzzle like we did. You listen to this shit for us and talk to your friends, and you tell me what you think, okay?"

"Talk to my friends?" Marco asked warily.

"Yeah. Your media boyfriend, the people he works with—your bosses, right? I mean, we all saw the video feed, kid. Your guy, he's got some serious sources if he's picking up stories on international gunrunners and hooking them to local corrupt businessmen."

"He claims he was on vacation," Marco said, practicing keeping his voice empty.

Cammie snorted. "Sure. Yeah. I don't believe that. And frankly I don't care. Listen to the tapes, Marco—get some advice from Mr. TV News Personality and then get back to me. Please?" She sighed. "Me and Frankie can only do so much."

"I hear you," he said softly. "I'll call you after I talk to Tor."

There was a moment's pause on the line. "So did you get a hello kiss? After he was gone for two weeks?"

Marco smiled softly to himself. "He made me a travelogue while he was gone. I, uh, was going to watch it again after I hung up with you."

"Aww, that's super fucking romantic, kid. This guy—he's like Bruce fucking Wayne or something, right?"

"Clark Kent was the news reporter," Marco said. And Torrance *did* have that sort of pure quality to him. He *could* be a superhero only in it for the altruism.

"Wait a minute," Cammie said, mock suspicion in her voice. "If your new boyfriend is Clark Kent, does that mean you're living in Justice League headquarters?" She laughed then at her own joke, and Marco made a noncommittal noise in response.

"Marco?" she said after a moment.

"Sure," he finally answered weakly.

"*Marco?*"

"Look," he said, absolutely intent on keeping the Salinger secret but knowing his cousin wouldn't be able to stop bugging him, either. And Cammie could keep her mouth shut—he knew that too. "Tor's got some sources he's going to talk to. I just don't want to compromise his sources, okay? I don't want to talk about them, I don't want you to talk about them. You saw that footage about Gunrunner's Island. That's what he did while *on vacation.* I'm just saying that this isn't *Real Housewives of the Chicago Suburbs,* okay?"

"Yeah, yeah," she started, but by the time the sentence ended it had lost some of its spice. "I get it, Marco. I do. We're talking to serious people because whatever's going on with Dad, it's serious. No clown-car stuff. No hopping into Frankie's truck and saying, 'Get in, losers, we're gonna fight.' This shit is real. Sorry I gave you a hard time, okay?"

"No worries," Marco murmured, glad—so glad—that Cammie seemed to get it. "Let me listen to the recordings and talk to Tor tomorrow." He chuckled a little. "If anybody's moving tomorrow. Man, I've never seen a group of people so wiped out."

"I thought they were all on vacation," she said. "What were they doing, by the way, when your boy did his hero piece on the gunrunners?"

"Some of them helped," he said vaguely, partly because he *was* a little vague on that part. "I'm not really sure how, but I get the feeling Felix Salinger is sort of a sponsor of his work."

"*That's* something that doesn't make the society pages," Cammie said, sounding surprised.

"Yeah. Did I tell you that most of the younger set in the mansion turned out to help with catering and parking? They were good at it too." Whew. This sounded like dishing, but it was general knowledge. Hey, he could do this!

"Why'd they do that?" she asked, legitimately curious.

"They had fun doing it." He shrugged. "It's like, you know, going to a buddy's house to rearrange his DVDs. If it was *your* collection—"

"Forgettaboutit," she said, hamming up the bogus accent. "Yeah, I get that. I used to go clean my girlfriend's room. It was great. I left, and I could imagine it clean for *months.*"

"Yeah, this was something like that, I think. If they had to do it to make a living, not so much fun. But they were doing it to help Phyllis, so, you know...."

"No big deal. But also, really fuckin' human. Nice. And they're letting you stay in the old gardener's cottage. Gotta tell you, Marco, when you went away to school, I was thinking, 'Wow. He's either going to disappear into a restaurant, never to be heard from again, or he's going to end up working fast food and being a bitter old man.' But you really landed. I mean, I'm not hating getting to see you at holidays, right?"

He chuckled, and they went back to a breakdown of Christmas—apparently Cammie was still a little steamed that Marco got the gift certificate to the specialty kitchenware place *and* her mother was making Marco a sweater out of the yarn in the box.

"Well, if you'd learn to knit or crochet or whatever she does," he told her, "she'd probably buy you yarn to have company."

He thought she'd laugh at that, but she grew thoughtful instead. They continued the conversation, but he was wondering how long it would be before *Cammie* was the one making sweaters and scarves and stuff, because she wanted an excuse to talk to her mother.

Sweet, he thought after hanging up. He looked around his tiny apartment, at the walls that had no posters and the kitchen that was barely big enough to boil water and keep veggies fresh, and thought about where he'd be moving by the end of the week. Kindness came in so many forms. He wondered how much he'd have to give back to deserve a fraction of what he'd been given.

THE NEXT morning, people were up, surprisingly, and working out before breakfast, so Marco was kept on his toes. By the time Tor came in, later than the others as usual, looking refreshed from his swim, Marco had cleaned the kitchen and whipped the remaining omelet ingredients into a simple quiche, which was almost done.

"Smells heavenly," Tor murmured, cradling his coffee to his chest.

"It does, right?" Marco said excitedly. "I love experimenting with leftovers. I mean, a well-stocked refrigerator is great, but have you ever made something delicious with ingredients you didn't know you had?"

Tor laughed softly, and Marco grinned. His dating life had been full of people who didn't get the joke—and dating chefs was often the worst. So literal. It was great when someone got you.

"Can I ask you a question?" he asked, pouring his own cup of coffee and grabbing a fresh lemon poppy seed muffin for them to split while the quiche finished baking.

"Sure," Tor said, his eyes on the muffin in a sort of mute agony. "I told myself I was, uhm, going to go back on my diet today."

Marco stared at him. "Seriously?"

"Seriously. The holidays are over, vacation is over…." He patted his flat stomach. "It's time for good boys to eat sensibly."

Marco scowled. "Go find a scale," he ordered. "There's one in the hallway bathroom."

"What?" Torrance asked, setting down his coffee.

"I'll concede to no muffin if you go get on a scale and tell me how much weight you've gained. I mean, I'm all for eating sensibly. I make egg white and spinach omelets for Felix and Carl, I've gone gluten free and vegetarian for Josh, and I had trays of halal and kosher canapes for New Year's. You go get on a scale, then come back and tell me there's a legitimate reason to not share a muffin with me, and I am all over that." Marco scowled. "But until I see some sort of objective proof that you can't eat the muffin that is *literally* making your mouth water, I'm not buying it."

While he'd been speaking, he'd been slicing the oven-steaming muffin in half and putting a thin curl of butter on each half before he set them on a plate.

With a sigh, Tor held out his hand for the plate.

"You're not going to get on the scale?" Marco asked sweetly.

"Yeah, I will," Tor told him, looking a little hunted. "But I'll eat the muffin first."

"Fair." Marco handed the plate over. "Now for my question."

"Shoot," Tor said.

"How come you don't exercise with everybody else? It's almost a religion with this household."

Tor bit into the muffin, hiding a faint, almost erotic moan as he chewed and swallowed. When he was done, he said, "Exercise is usually pretty meditative for me. And anonymous too. I go running through the park or along the river, or I swim at the Y. I communicate a *lot* in my job. Working out is the one place I don't have to communicate." He rolled his eyes faintly. "As long as these people are together, they don't stop talking. It works better for me if I go after the rush."

Marco nodded and repeated, "Fair." He gave a self-conscious shrug. "I just, you know, wanted to make sure."

"Sure of what?"

"Sure they weren't excluding you for any reason."

Tor shook his head. "No, baby—they've done sort of the opposite. It's all good." He winked and then swallowed his next bite of muffin. "Now," he said, looking eager, "about your case…. Do you have any new information for me?"

Marco nodded and stood to pull the quiche from the oven. "I'll be right back with the recordings Cammie made. I think there's some good stuff."

Group Think

AN HOUR later Tor was listening to the files Marco's cousin had recorded for the umpteenth time, his brow furrowed in concentration, his fingers scrabbling on the keyboard of the tablet to make a transcript. They were still in the kitchen, and he suspected Marco had pushed more than one piece of quiche on him, as well as some juice, while he made notes and put together a timeline and tried to mesh what Marco's uncle Flory was saying with what Tor knew was true.

He was deep into it, only peripherally aware that Marco was doing the prep for the lunch and night menus while he worked, when he felt a tap on his shoulder. He turned his head and was surprised to see Josh Salinger there with a game smile that was so close to his old pre-illness pixilated grin that Tor wanted to clutch his heart.

He'd let go of his crush, but God he was glad this kid was going to be okay.

"Whatcha doin'?" Josh asked, sitting on the chair Marco had vacated. But while Marco's presence had made Tor feel warm and a little tingly, Josh was simply reassuring. Josh pointed to his earbuds. "What's playing?"

"Ooh!" said a voice behind Tor. "Let me listen!" And that's when Tor realized somebody had snatched his earbuds right as the audio files began to play.

"Grace!" he protested. "Grace, those are priv—"

"Oh wow, Josh. Someone's getting blackmailed by mobsters. It's bad."

"What?" said Marco, and Tor heard the clatter of what was probably his chef's knife. "Tor, is that what this sounds like to you?"

Tor grunted, the conversation playing itself in his head without the benefit of the earbuds.

"You need to let me take care of the boy," said Marco's uncle Flory. "I promised his father. No, I don't have any compensation. I don't care if he's thirty-five. He's a kid! He's not a functional adult! But if you keep using my company as a front, I'll go bankrupt. I'm already losing business. No, you don't understand. There's a reporter who's about ready to smear me all over the internet as a con artist. There are lawsuits breathing down my neck. You have got to stop using my name with your operation or I'm not the only one who's going down!"

A sound followed then, like the plastic ring of a handset getting slammed down on the pedestal, reminding everybody who heard that not *every* phone was a smart phone.

There was a click as the next file started, and then, "No, I'm not threatening you. Because I'd get my ass handed to me on a platter if I was. I'm telling you that I'm one guy with a small company, and you are going to lose me as an asset if you don't pull your team out and stop making him break the law. No, it's not me saying it, it's common fucking sense. What do you think, Eppie? You can go around fucking people's houses up and grabbing their cash and nobody's going to say boo to a mouse? This is a bad plan. Just give me the kid and let me rebuild what's left of my business, and you go pick on somebody else, okay? No, I'm not going to inform on you. Because I don't want to die, that's why! No, don't hang up! Don't hang up! I'm not being taped. I'm not, I swear!"

There was a sigh then, and the click of the receiver being set down, and it was obvious the person on the other end of the line *had* hung up.

That wasn't the last phone call, several more followed, but Tor could tell Grace had gotten to the worst one when Grace tapped Josh on the shoulder and turned anguished eyes to him.

"We're taking this job," Grace said without preamble. His beautiful amber eyes were red-rimmed, and his voice was almost squeaking with rage. Tor wanted to protest that he'd been going to put the whole story together for them, show them the work like they did with all the other jobs, when Josh showed him what loyalty and leadership looked like.

"Okay," Josh said, not batting an eyelash. "Let me listen too."

"Fine. I'm going to go get Stirling and Molly while you listen. We're doing a run today, okay? You promise?" Grace was already halfway out the door.

"I promise," Josh said, nodding. "Do we need Hunter or Chuck?"

"They're doing anti-gunrunner things." Grace grunted, then brightened. "Carl! He and Michael went home after breakfast, but Carl's good for muscle. I'll call him. You stay there, recovery boy. I'll be back. Don't worry. I'll get the people, you make the plan, it will all be good."

And with that Grace pressed the earbuds into Josh's hands and practically danced away, leaving Tor gaping.

"You don't have to—" he said, but Josh shushed him.

"I'm listening," he said, and Tor winced because he knew what Josh would hear toward the end, and it still broke his heart.

"But it's Christmas, Eppie! I promised the boy he could come be with my family for Christmas. We were gonna visit his parents' grave. I got him new boots! Man, I just want to take the kid home, that's all. Is it so awful to let him go? He's your pawn, but he's no good on a jobsite, not the way you got him working. I could give that kid a family! But can I at least see him? I promised him…. No. No! Fuck you, Eppie, don't tell him that! Aww Jesus, no…."

This time after the click, the recording hadn't gone dead after fifteen seconds. The faint sound of sobbing had continued for a good two minutes before a door had closed, and there'd been silence until the audio clicked off.

Josh listened to that damning conversation and turned to Tor.

"Okay," he said. "You've got an hour to get your ducks in a row and then meet us downstairs." He raised his voice. "Marco, did you hear that? This is your uncle, Tor said?"

Marco, who had been trying to work, turned toward him. "Yes," he confirmed. "My uncle Florian. He owns a contracting business."

Josh nodded, jaw squared, eyes narrowed. "Okay, let Tor walk us through the rest. He knows how we lay shit out. In the meantime"—he turned to Tor—"can you text Stirling the phone number and time stamp for those? He can find out who was calling and where from by the time we meet."

Tor nodded, realizing that oh hell, yes. They were doing this. Just that fast, helping Marco's family was a go.

"Anything else?" he asked.

"Do we have the identity of the young man—the one with the disability—that Florian is so concerned about?"

"His first name is Clyde," Marco said. "But I can call my cousin to find out more."

"Can she meet us in an hour?" Josh asked frankly.

Marco didn't even think about it. "For her father? Anything."

Josh grinned. "My kind of girl. Okay. Do we know anything else about this?"

"I've got the names of people who were defrauded by Clyde and the guy handling him," Tor said, pulling up the list of people who had made complaints when he'd put together the first story.

"Send it to me," Josh said. "I'll use the prep time looking them up. Anything else?"

"Video footage from the exposé I was going to do," Tor told him, his face heating at the thought of what he'd almost let go out on the air.

"Fair," Josh said, nodding. "Can you give us the raw footage and not the edited stuff without Clyde?"

Tor stared at him. "How did you know I edited that out?"

Josh stared back. "Because you're one of us. You know what's not right. Jeez, have some faith in my family, okay?"

Tor couldn't hold in the beaming smile that wanted to slip out. "Oh, I do," he said. "I've got one more thing you might want."

Josh made a gimme gesture. "Yes...?"

"I've got an address I tracked down from Flory's phone the first time I met with Marco's family. He'd dodged out on the meeting, but his son, Frankie, traced it. I ran the location, but I only got the first layer of info. It's in the garment district, and it's zoned as a factory."

Josh nodded thoughtfully. "Okay, then. We've got all we need—"

"Cookies," said Molly, coming down the stairs from her room, obviously responding to the text. "Marco, if you have some, I'll plate them. It won't be a jam session without them."

"Muffins too?" Marco asked shyly.

"Awesome." Molly winked at him, gathered her tatty old sweater around her tightly, and shook the ends of her curly red hair from the messy bun on top of her head out of her eyes. Belatedly Tor realized that everybody—Josh, Grace, Molly, and probably Stirling and Carl as well—was wearing their hanging-around-the-house clothes, the ones with holes and stretched necklines and broken zippers, that probably should have been thrown out but just felt *so* good.

And they were all ready to get down to business and work, because Grace had listened to a desperate man beg a monster to be kind to an innocent person.

He wanted to cry.

This hadn't been the family he'd been born to, but he liked to think they were the one destined to be his all along.

HALF AN hour later, Julia wandered into the kitchen, freshly showered and still looking tired. She went immediately to the fruit bowl, sighed softly when she recovered a ripe green apple, and peered about at Tor, Josh, and Stirling, who were all hard at work. Tor had done this sort of thing with them before; Josh and Stirling were a perfect match when it came to researching and being on the computer. As Tor strung together a timeline and a presentation, Stirling was digging up new information about the stuff they *did* know, and Josh was using his spot-on intuition to find out more about the areas in which they were totally blind and to come up with more things they needed to know to take action.

But Tor wasn't aware how synchronized they were until Julia parked herself across from Josh at the island and stared at him until he looked up.

"Whatcha doing there, son?" she said, and if she hadn't used Josh's exact verbiage from when Josh had come out to bother Tor, Tor might have missed the shrewdness—and the worry—in her eyes. They were supposed to be resting, he reminded himself, feeling wretched, and Josh was still weak.

"Helping Marco's uncle Flory," Josh answered, face as bright and open as any child's as he hid absolutely nothing from his mother.

"Helping Marco's uncle Flory do *what*?" she asked, her eyes drifting—as though randomly—from Josh to Stirling to Tor.

"Help an old friend's son," Josh said, and Tor's eyes flickered to Josh, because obviously the boy had narrowed down exactly who Clyde was to Flory Gallo.

Julia's eyes narrowed, and it became clear that she was not buying any evasive maneuvering on her son's part. "Help an old friend's son do *what*?" she asked, her eyes steely and blue.

Josh gave a snort of annoyance and glared up at his mother. "Look, Mom, we're going to have a meeting downstairs in half an hour with everyone available. You are welcome to join us, but if you want the intel to be complete, you're going to have to trust me here, okay?"

"Who's we?" she asked, unyielding.

"Grace, Tor, Carl, Stirling, Molly, Tienne—right, Stirling?"

Stirling glanced up from his computer but kept his eyes on Josh. "Yes, Tienne wants in," he said, before giving Julia a brief apologetic smile and focusing back on what he'd been working on.

"Marco," Josh continued, "and Michael if he's not working, but I think he is."

The sound his mother made was *not* encouraging, and Tor realized that the sweet little ponytail and worn pink sweats were like camouflage, disguising the fact that "Mrs. Josh's Mom," as Grace called her, could be a *very* dangerous woman.

"Hunter and Chuck," she said unequivocally.

"They're doing errands for the dads," Josh responded.

"We'll just see about that," she muttered, pulling her phone out. "Liam."

"No."

Julia's eyebrows, impeccably shaped, arched to her hairline. "No?" she asked, with the inflection of a supervillain.

"No," Josh returned, like just anybody contradicted his mother.

"Explain," she ordered, and Josh was not that much of a fool.

"American politics," he said grimly. "Interpol has no jurisdiction with this. Liam could lose his job. I don't even want him to know about it. It's one thing when he's got a dog in the fight—we can't hurt him and he can help us. But this could hurt him, and I say no."

"That's sweet of you, boy" came the unmistakable accent from the hallway, where Liam had apparently been lurking. "But seems to me I've got four more days of vacation here, and as it turns out, I've not seen much of your lovely city. So what are you going to show me today?"

And Josh's iron façade—which hadn't chipped when confronting his mother—seemed to melt, leaving a vulnerable, still-healing young man who was very much hoping for good news from his oncologist for a full remission in the next week.

"Liam," he said, face twisted in apparent pain. "Isn't there some way you could sit this one out? I mean, after gunrunners, this is going to be small-time, you think?"

"But what if it's not?" Liam asked, sauntering up to the island to wedge himself between Josh and Stirling. Stirling didn't even give him a sideways look, but Josh—Josh scowled up at him as though searching for words that would make him go away.

"Not what? Small-time?" Josh asked, flailing.

"That's right. What if a street-smart cop is exactly what you need?" Liam's smile held more than a touch of swagger, and Tor had learned to appreciate the young officer on the trip to the Caribbean. Besides being good company—and a good sport—he was also pretty handy to have around. His contacts at Interpol, at the very least, had proved invaluable.

"I have contacts in the police department," Josh said with dignity, and Tor wasn't sure if he was talking about his ex-boyfriend or his unrequited crush, Nick Denning, but whoever it was, they didn't pass muster with Liam.

"Not while I'm in town, mate," Liam said, and the thing was, he sounded cheerful and not at all possessive. Tor would have been surprised if Liam and Josh had so much as kissed in the time they'd known each other, but the words—and Liam's oh-so-subtle shoulder bump—were unmistakable.

Liam *would* be somebody to Josh Salinger, unless Josh was very active about saying no.

The mix of emotions on Josh's fine-boned face came from a variety of places—confusion, kindness, exasperation—but "No" was not among them.

Josh huffed out a breath. "Fine," he said, glaring at everybody. "But if you want this presentation to be ready by the time Marco's cousins get here, you need to leave us alone. We're working here!"

"We're having company?" Julia complained, aghast. "I'm not presentable for company!"

"It's okay, Miss Julia," Marco said hurriedly, finally coming from the edges of the conversation where he'd been listening. "It's only my family. You don't have to impress them."

Julia gave him a dark look. "Torrance?"

"Yes, ma'am," he said quickly, not wanting to be on her shit list, unlike apparently everybody else.

"Smack your young man on the back of the head for me."

"Ma'am?" Tor asked, surprised into questioning her orders.

She arched an angry eyebrow, and he reached over to the counter and did what she said.

"Tor!" Marco hissed as Julia stalked off. "What was that for?"

"Were you not paying attention?" he hissed back. "For God's sake, Marco, don't piss that woman off!"

"Right," Marco said, and finally it sounded like he got it. "I totally understand."

And then the kitchen lapsed into silence again as everybody got back to work.

ROUGHLY FORTY-FIVE minutes later—which they used to full advantage, researching and sharing quietly while Tor built the timeline— there was a tentative knock on the door.

Phyllis answered, and moments later she ushered in Camille and Frankie, who were dressed in their work clothes and looking *very* uncertain.

They brightened a little when they saw Marco, and Camille hugged him nervously, although he tried to distance himself because his apron still had a little bit of lunch on it.

"Are you sure we're supposed to be here?" she asked, and Tor bumped shoulders with Josh so he could address her uncertainty.

"Yes," Josh said. "I told him to ask you here. Tor let us listen to your audio files, the ones of your father talking. Given the information Torrance and Marco both gave us, we've got a better idea of who and what we're dealing with and maybe some plans for how to fix it. Your father seems like a decent man. We'd like to help him out."

Cammie glanced at Marco, who smiled encouragingly. "Superman indeed," she said with a sniff.

"The Justice League at the very least," Josh told her with a wink.

Molly, Grace, and Carl, Tor noted, were in the dining room, trying very patiently to teach Tienne, Stirling's boyfriend, how to cheat at poker. Unlike so many things, because Tienne really was very bright, this lesson didn't seem to be sticking, and Tor took it as a sign of personal growth on Grace's part that he wasn't actively climbing the walls and getting into the ventilation through the light fixtures.

"Guys?" he said. "This is Marco's family. Do you want to get them settled downstairs with refreshments while we finalize some stuff?"

"Josh," Molly said seriously.

"I know."

"Do you want me to—"

"Please," Josh said with a sigh. "Yes, it is time to go get my mother."

Liam, who hadn't left Josh's side since he'd arrived—who had, in fact, pulled out his phone and had been working on something of his own—gave a little grunt and bumped Josh's shoulder.

"I need to finish talking to Tor," Josh said. "Stirling and I have to—"

Tor chuckled when he realized Josh had read Liam's mind without a single word. "I've got it, Josh. Send me that last thing you were looking at and then go with her. Your mom will be happier if she knows you're bringing her in voluntarily."

"I just don't want her to worry," he said plaintively.

Liam leaned close and murmured something into his ear. Tor couldn't hear—although they weren't sitting that far apart—but whatever it was, it made him blotch, the color like a red flag against his pale skin.

"Fine," he muttered with little grace, before pressing a couple of buttons quickly, sighing, and hopping off the kitchen stool, ostensibly to go alert his mother. Unfortunately, the blush drained from his face immediately, and he swore, wobbling on his feet as he stood.

"See?" Liam said softly.

"Can't you go home?" Josh complained, voice bitter. "I… I really hate that you've only seen me puking and fainting since we've met."

"Only happened a couple of times on the ship," Liam said breezily, wrapping his arm around Josh's waist. "You're fine. Molly-girl, go get Julia, but—" He glanced around. "—we don't have to tell her about this, do we?"

Whereas Tor originally would have said, "Are you kidding? Nobody keeps secrets from Julia Salinger in her own home!" at this moment he saw thoughtful nods—and a lot of speculation.

When everybody nodded, Tor was about to ask what in the hell was *that*, but Josh was speaking even as Liam was snagging his laptop and helping him toward the stairs to the basement den.

"What are you doing? You can't ask them to keep that secret!"

"I'm not," Liam said, sounding as patient as Grace had when teaching Tienne about poker. "I'm asking you to tell your mother like a grown-up that you respect her rules."

"Fine," Josh grumbled. "Just get me downstairs and let me sit before I puke. God, cancer is a fucking drag."

It was as bitter as they'd ever heard him, and Liam's response made Torrance proud.

"We know it is, my boy. That's why we're going to drag you out of it, right?"

"Thanks."

They all heard Josh sigh then, but nobody remarked on it. Instead they gathered their stuff and filed quietly downstairs. As Camille and Frankie brought up the rear, Tor heard Camille murmur, "Is he going to be okay?" to her cousin.

"Yeah," Marco said softly. "He's in remission, but they got in from that trip last night, and he's chafing. I get the feeling nothing kept him down before, and he's learning his limitations."

"Should he really be doing this?" she asked, her voice compassionate, and Tor caught Marco's questioning glance in his direction.

Tor thought about that long-ago discussion he and Josh had, the one that had Tor falling far and fast and hard. How intense the young man could be about his moral duty, about helping people, about using his gifts for the best. And about how many gifts he possessed—not one of them having to do with fortune.

"He wouldn't want to do anything else," Tor replied truthfully. "But that's why there's so many of us. To back him up."

Marco and Molly had already set the refreshment table up in the den, and Grace made a point of steering Frankie and Camille to the couch that didn't sag in the middle. Josh sat in the center of the room at the console connected to the big-screen monitor that dominated the far wall. Tienne sat behind the wet bar and smiled shyly, pushing his glasses up his nose and flipping his long blond hair out of his eyes as Marco's cousins took in the room.

"Bar service?" Camille asked with a smile.

"No alcohol," Tienne said earnestly, his voice faintly accented from a boyhood spent speaking French, among other languages. "But they've got pomegranate juice, and it's delicious."

"I love pomegranate juice," Camille said, clearly surprised. "I'll take a—"

"Flagon," Josh said, glancing up from his seat at the media console. "A large flagon. Ice?" he asked.

"Yeah," she replied, grinning.

"Oui." Tienne gave a shy smile and started to pour the rich red juice into an enormous mug—and yes, there was ice. "We also have coffee and hot chocolate." He paused and blinked. "And an espresso machine, but only Michael knows how it works, and I'm afraid he's not here."

"I can work it," Marco offered. "Frankie?"

"Coffee sounds awesome," Frankie said, rolling his eyes. "We all know you're fancy, Marco, but don't you have better things to do?"

Tor caught Josh's raised eyebrow at Marco, as expressive as his mother's, before Marco went to work on a caramel latte for his cousin. While he was doing that, Josh nodded Tor over to the media center.

"Do you want to walk everybody through?" he asked. "It's your gig."

Tor swallowed. "Honestly?" he asked.

"Yeah."

"I'd rather you do it. I want to hear it all the way through. I'm better at catching problems or errors that way. It's how I edit."

Josh nodded. "Fair. Okay, let me just pull up—aww. *Mom!*"

Julia arrived, nicely dressed in slacks and a twinset, both in January blue, which Tor was well aware held a very different tint than Christmas blue. At her side strode the brutally elegant Leon di Rossi, the man who had loaned his yacht—and his trading expertise—to their latest caper discovering the gunrunners, Josh's uncle on his father's side. And his mother's charming suitor. Di Rossi was wearing a pair of casual slacks and a cashmere sweater over his collared shirt, and neither of them looked as snuggly and casual as the rest of the group.

But then, royalty wasn't supposed to blend in.

Together they descended the staircase into the rowdily painted sports-themed den and introduced themselves to Marco's cousins while Marco tried to pretend that he was just the help.

"Latte, Mr. di Rossi?" Marco asked greenly after he'd handed Frankie his own mug.

"That would be wonderful, Marco," Leon replied smoothly. "But please let me make my own. You should be with your family. Miss Julia?"

"I'd love one," she said, giving him a charming smile. "Do you get artistic with the cream at the top?"

"Would you like me to draw a little heart?" he asked, the savage planes of his face practically melting with his smile.

"I dare you," she said, and Josh made a mock gagging motion.

"Be nice," Tor murmured, thinking that yes, watching your mother flirt with your father's brother might be a bit much on a recovering boy's constitution.

"It's a good thing he doesn't suck," Josh muttered back. "If he was horrible, somebody would wake up with the Chinese Triad's art collection, wondering what happened to his life."

Tor snort-laughed into the back of his hand while Josh shook his head in disgust.

"Did I miss something?" Liam asked, cradling his own mug of plain coffee.

"Me being spiteful and petty," Josh told him, and Liam chuckled.

"Must have been spectacular. Is anybody going to rescue your boy there from barkeep duty, or should I go booty-bump him out so Leon can show off to your mother?"

They both looked at Tor.

"We, uhm," Tor mumbled. "Uhm… we're not quite, uhm—"

"Oh dear God," Josh muttered, at the same time Liam said, "Sweet Jaysus."

Tor glared at them. "I've been trying to take my time," he said. "You know, romance?"

Josh glared back. "Romance is great, Torrance, but he's awesome, and you don't want to let him get away."

"Pot, meet kettle," Liam chided gently.

Josh shot him a filthy look. "That's. Different." He growled it out from between his teeth and then took a deep breath and yawned. "Goddammit. And time is marching on." He leaned back so he could get everybody's attention. "Folks, if I could have everybody settle down, find a seat—" He blinked, and Tor realized that Carl had settled himself back against the bar near the base of the stairs, arms crossed. This was usually the place taken by Chuck and Hunter, who acted as sentinels when they were running meetings like this, and Tor watched Josh reassess.

"Except you, Carl," Josh added belatedly. "You're good where you are. But everyone else, we're going to want to be ready to run reconnaissance tomorrow at the latest, so I need you up to speed now."

"Recon?" Tor asked, surprised. "So soon?"

"It's time sensitive," Josh said, his pixieish face set in sober lines. "You heard those phone calls. We can't let this go on any longer than necessary."

And Torrance realized once again that he was with people who took this shit seriously. It was a good feeling, in fact, because he'd promised

Marco they could help, and for the first time since he'd said those words, he felt them in his stomach. He had people to back him up.

"So some of you may know some of this," Josh said, looking to Frankie, Cammie, and Marco, who had all gathered on the good couch, while Grace, Stirling, Tienne, and Molly puppy-dog piled on the one with the bad springs that they all refused to give up. Sometime during the presentation, Tor was sure, at least two of those people would sort of roll off the couch and onto the pillows, leaving two of the people on the couch now smushed together in the middle. He'd been that guy, and he had the back twinges to prove it.

"But I don't think any of you knows all of it," Josh continued, "because Stirling, Tor, and I have done some work this morning, and we've got pieces everyone needs to know. Are we all ready?"

There were general murmurs of assent.

"Stirling, you logged in for emergency info?"

"Always," the young man said without looking up.

"Then let's begin." Josh took a breath, and Liam, who had sunk into the chair on the other side of him, patted his shoulder reassuringly, which was when it hit Tor. Josh had done this on occasion, but with Uncle Danny present. This really was his first time on his own.

"Okay, so this," Josh said, "is Marco's uncle Flory, and Camille and Frankie's father." With that he pulled up a picture of an older man, in his early sixties, with slicked-back salt-and-pepper hair and laugh lines in the corners of his brown eyes and bracketing his mouth. The photo had been cropped from a newspaper article about breaking ground on a library, and he was wearing a ceremonial hard hat and one of the T-shirts Torrance had seen in the manager's office at Flory Gallo and Sons. "He has six children, four grandchildren, and runs a successful business that employs three of his sons and one of his daughters. There you are, Cammie—don't you look pretty." And with that, he pulled up a series of pictures featuring Marco's family when the company had been in the news.

"Lookit you," Camille said, "doing your homework."

"We try," Josh told her, inclining his head modestly. "So these are nice people, and until recently the business was clean, well thought of, and had an excellent reputation. About two years ago, they hired this man, Clyde Staunton."

The picture he pulled up was a still from Torrance's original piece, one of the ones Tor had edited out.

"He is, by all reports, a gentle giant with a developmental disability, who loved his father—this man here—with all his heart." Another picture came up, this one of an older man, in his seventies, holding Clyde's hand.

"This is Frank Staunton, who passed away in early June of this past year without leaving a will or a care provision for Clyde."

"Can Clyde care for himself?" Julia asked, her concern immediate.

"From what Stirling could gather," Josh told her, "Frank had initiated induction into an adult care facility. It wasn't great, but it was clean, and Clyde would be cared for. Unfortunately he passed before he could finish signing the papers, and Clyde—who had been a faithful employee at Flory Gallo and Sons—dropped off the map."

Tor heard the collective gasp in the room, and while Josh set up the next slide, he took a glimpse around to see that the others were, for lack of a better word, absolutely entranced.

This, he thought with satisfaction, was why he fit so well with this family. Because this man that they'd never met before *mattered*. Because something had gone wrong, and everybody there wanted to do something. And they hadn't even gotten to the part where it affected Marco's family.

"So," Josh said, looking at everybody, "that's what happened six months ago. Back in the beginning of December, Torrance here was doing a story about contractor scams." Josh turned to him. "I really think you're going to have to do this part," he said apologetically, and Tor nodded.

It *had* been his story in the first place.

"Okay," he said. "So I won't play the clip for you—Frankie, Cammie, and Marco have already seen it." Josh had pulled up the video showing the destroyed basement, portajohn and all. "The scam was people would make a good-faith down payment on contracting services, and a couple of guys in Flory Gallo and Sons T-shirts would come around, destroy their homes in the name of doing work, and then vamoose, taking the final payment and leaving destruction in their wake. I'd gotten at least four complaints, including one from someone who hadn't paid yet." He sighed. "I'd done my due diligence, guys. I tried to get hold of Flory several times—"

"He knew the way to the manager's office," Camille said. "Apparently Dad had his best guys scare Torrance here away."

"The scammer guys were slick," Tor said, still feeling guilty. "They'd made copies of the company stationery, they wore company uniforms, and they were using company receipts, complete with check routing numbers, for payment. I was about to do an exposé on this company and use it as an example for *all* the contracting companies that are screwing people over when Marco here approached me. The last victims of the scam contractors had filed suit on Flory's company, and Cammie and Frankie finally knew something was wrong."

"And that's when Dad dropped off the map," Frankie said glumly. "That was about two weeks before Christmas, right, Torrance?"

"It was indeed," Tor agreed. "So their office was closing up, and we were working on another project. But while we were gone, Camille here had done a very smart thing."

"I planted a bug on my father," she said with an intonation that said she'd never live down the shame. "Frankie and I listened to the audio files, and I gave them to Marco last night."

"And that brings us to today," Tor said, looking at Josh. "And Josh knows the rest."

Josh sighed. "Really?"

"What?"

"Never mind." Josh made eye contact with the rest of the room. "What Torrance is conveniently not telling you is that his video gave us a whole lot of information, including information he edited because he's a stand-up guy. The two guys perpetrating the cons were this man—" Josh showed a still of a smaller, balder, more weaselly looking guy. "—Jeter Stoya, commonly known as Cheezer, who while having mob affiliations, has yet to be a part of any one group. He's like some guy you grab by the nape of the neck for your side. The other guy we already know."

Josh had done his homework with this one, getting several pictures of Clyde, including one from a collective of citizens with disabilities. Tor was reasonably sure he didn't have the kind of facial recognition software Josh had used to pull those photos, but then, most police stations didn't either.

"Here's Clyde when he's *not* downstairs in a fetid basement," Josh continued. "Now before Torrance left, he told Camille and Frankie not to do more than record their father's phone calls, and for good reason." He glanced at Torrance, who realized that he had to step up this time.

"Cheezer—erm, Jeter—spoke more than once of having a big boss. Given the way the cons were pulled, and how few people I could find who would actually risk exposure by testifying or filing suit, I had the uneasy feeling the big boss could be… you know." He gave a shrug. "A *really* big boss. One of the last things I did before Christmas was run the location of Marco's uncle Flory when he was supposed to be meeting with me. I found him in this building."

Josh pulled up a satellite photo of a large steel-and-concrete factory eyesore in the middle of the industrial area of South Side. "It's zoned as a garment factory," Josh said. "I've captured a couple of satellite photos that show fabric going in and clothing coming out, so I think that part at least is legit."

"Who is it leased to?" Julia asked curiously.

"We're getting there," Josh said, giving his mother a nod. "Trust me, Mom, I've learned from the best."

"The most dramatic," she said tartly, and he gave her a wink.

"I'll leave that to Torrance," he said. "Although he seems to be playing dead *today*. Danny always said he's the best front man he's ever seen."

"I'm a *reporter*," Tor said, irritated, "not a showman."

There was sort of a stunned silence around the room. Then, tentatively, Marco said, "Uhm, Torrance? What do you think a reporter *does*?"

Torrance opened his mouth to argue. The entire reason he'd left his job with the cable network was because of performative bullshit—he refused to scream his virtue signal into the camera. It hit him then, hard, that since he'd left the station, he'd been focused on hard-hitting, socially conscious, important stories. Stories meant to help people—like Marco's family—find ways to cope against a world in which the odds were more and more frequently stacked against them.

But unless he was working for Josh and his family, when the chyron could read anything from "Gunrunners of the Caribbean" to "Murder Birds Discovered in Napa Valley," that joy of pulling people into an entirely new world had been missing.

Torrance remembered that moment standing in front of the dead teenager and the feeling that he'd been freezing to death for months and his heart had only now felt the cold. Was that because he'd forgotten how much he'd loved what he did for a living? How fabulous it was to have a platform that could help fix the world? Or even, sometimes, how much joy he got when he had an audience in the palm of his hand and he was pulling them into a story they'd never imagined before. When he'd been a cub reporter, just starting out with Felix's network, he'd been the one guy who'd never chafed at puff pieces, who had always loved going to the new restaurant opening or meeting the artist who had amazed the citizens of his or her home country and was in the process of starting an entirely new conversation about art in Tor's hometown.

When had he begun thinking that unless it was tragic, it wasn't worth telling? Because most of the stories he pulled in via Josh and his family had a real-life happy ending and a lesson people could take into their own lives about helping those happen.

"You're right," he said to Marco, giving a thoughtful smile. "I'll have to remember that more often." He winked. "The showmanship is half the fun."

"I'm betting we can do something about that," Josh said, and there was a sort of happy determination in his voice, as though he'd had an idea but wasn't ready to share it yet. "But onward with Clyde Staunton. What you're about to hear is part of one of the audio files that Camille supplied us with, and I think it helps us get to the heart of the problem."

With a few taps on the keyboard, he called up the file, the monitor running under Clyde's picture.

"What do you think, Eppie? You can go around fucking people's houses up and grabbing their cash and nobody's going to say boo to a mouse? This is a bad plan. Just give me the kid and let me rebuild what's left of my business, and go pick on somebody else, okay?"

There was a collective intake of breath, even though many of the people in the room had heard the clip before.

"So yes," Josh said. "This is Marco's uncle Flory, and there's a lot more where this came from. What we can gather from this is that Flory Gallo had some sort of promise or verbal contract with Clyde's father to look out for the man after his father passed away. Before Flory could make good on that, Cheezer showed up at the manager's office with Clyde in tow and arranged to have Clyde's last check sent to this same address in the garment district. While he was there, he stole the stationery and receipt book and uniforms to start his own scam business with Florian Gallo as the patsy. And given what we listened to this morning, the person in charge has been using Clyde as a hostage—and as a patsy—to keep Flory from talking to anybody. Torrance, his kids, the police. Anybody that could help Flory has been completely cut off, and what's left is Flory begging to get custody of Clyde while Cheezer and 'Eppie' wreck his business and reputation."

"Aww, man," Camille all but moaned. "Dad! Why didn't you say anything?"

"I might know," Frankie said. "But first, do we know who this Eppie is?"

"We do," Josh said. He turned to Stirling. "Were you successful?"

Stirling nodded. "Sent," he said tersely, and Tor realized that Josh really *had* been working to the wire.

"Alrighty, then." A picture appeared on the screen, this one taken from a society magazine, and it featured a family sitting in a truly gaudy monstrosity of a room—leopard print and zebra stripe seemed to be the rule of thumb, and gold was a common color, right down to the shiny gold frames around the plaques that bore real leopard and zebra heads in the background. The color scheme and grotesqueness of the room was so strident that it was hard to spot the humans—dressed in gold-and-black camouflage satin and silk—sitting in the foreground on a couch, facing the camera.

"That," Julia said in horror, "is one of the most offensive things I've ever seen."

"Not as offensive as the headline," Tor said dryly, knowing that "The Doyenne of Good Taste" would go down as the most ironic title in history.

"Wait," Julia muttered. "I *know* her. That's Hepzibah Coulter-King—her father, Gregg, struck it big in oil in the Midwest, and she brought all that money to Chicago to start her own fashion empire." She made a pained sound. "Or something," she finished weakly, obviously almost overcome by all of that gold and black.

"And that's where the 'Eppie' comes from," Josh said. "I had to look up where that nickname might stem from, and the name Hepzibah helped us mine through all the shell companies that held the title for the garment factory." He pulled up other pictures of Hepzibah, a petite blond woman whose taste—or lack of it—could be seen in platform heels while traversing city streets and extravagant silk zebra-patterned piazza pants paired with gold-lamé bikini tops for theater debuts. She often had her three children—and the nanny who wrangled them—in tow, while her husband, who managed their foreign interests, frequently in countries that held interests in pretty much anything awful, was absent. Fur trading, blood diamonds, Saudi oil companies—Byron King had his fingers in all of it, while his wife pursued her "fashion" empire at home.

"This," Josh said as everybody absorbed the media on the screen, "is the mob boss who is blackmailing Flory Gallo."

"But why?" Camille asked, sounding legitimately baffled. "I mean, look at her. She's got all the money and power in the world. Her husband's making a fortune betraying his country. Why would she put so much energy into abusing a disabled man? It's… it's sick!"

"And from what I can gather," Josh said, "that's part of her MO. Originally most of her clothes were made in India and the Philippines, until she got busted for running not just sweatshops, but sweatshops that exploited the disabled population in particular. She sent emissaries to institutions and promised that the workers would live in a halfway house and earn a living wage."

The next photo on the screen was of a filthy basement floor, covered with pallets of blankets, with buckets in the open filled with waste. Rats could be seen in the darkened corners, and a group of bewildered, dirt-covered humans, male and female, were being given food by humanitarian workers. The headline was simple and to the point: "Hepzibah Coulter's Secret Shame."

"And hanging's too good for her," Grace said, reflecting the horror of everybody in the room. "But it'll do."

"She paid some fines," Josh said grimly. "Nothing stuck. But she wasn't allowed to keep factories in those countries anymore, and she had to move her operation here. Consequently she lost a *lot* of money, and it appears her husband and father were no longer willing to foot the bill."

The photo of the atrociously styled room came up again, and Josh used his mouse to circle the two men behind her. One was corpulent, older, with an obvious black toupee under a cowboy hat. He was the only person in the picture not styled in gold and black—his boxy American suit sported a basic red-and-blue striped tie and appeared styled purposely to make him look dumpier.

Unexpectedly Carl made a sound of dismay. "Ugh."

"You see it now," Molly said as though they were having an old conversation.

"Yes, I see it," he muttered.

"And you admit you should start getting them tailored and European cut, am I right?"

"Molly," he whined plaintively.

"Say it, Carl. Say it, or I'm going to save this picture and show it to you whenever you wear that polyester mass-made crap to a function."

"I was working as a valet!" he protested.

"And the real valets almost kicked you out for trying to steal cars," she told him crossly. "Remember?"

His next words were a complete sign of concession. "Yes, I understand."

"Thank you."

"Thank God," Josh said. "Carl, I didn't want to say anything, but I can give you the name of Felix's tailor. But moving on—this is Eppie's father, Gregg Coulter, and after he got his start in oil, he supplemented his income on… anyone? Anyone?" He looked directly at Frankie as he said it.

"On development deals that were *famous* for not paying their employees," Frankie said grimly. "And he was *great* at paying off the right politician or policeman or inspector to get out of trouble when it came to bite him in the ass."

"Wait a minute," Marco said, obviously catching on. "I know this story—*he* was the guy who tried to pressure Uncle Flory and Uncle Joe into working for him, but they said no."

"Oh my God!" Camille muttered. "Mom and Dad's one argument. Frankie, this is the guy?"

"Yes, he is," Frankie said. "This is the guy. And Dad and Uncle Joe barely escaped his clutches. I think they made like Switzerland. They told Coulter they wouldn't do any of his deals, but they wouldn't bid on any of the land he had earmarked, either. They managed to walk a fine line until…." Frankie frowned. "Until about five years ago, I think, when Coulter stopped working land deals and became the NRA's favorite congressman." He cocked his head and stared at Josh. "So his daughter picked up his playbook and started working the same scams?"

Tor, who had been as fascinated by the information on Hepzibah as the rest of the room, was able to answer this. "Different scams," he said authoritatively. "After you guys asked me to pull the story, I started doing a deep dive into reported scams across Illinois and adjoining states. Flory Gallo was the most local, but there were seven or eight other companies that were charged with the same kinds of scam. Before I left for vacation, I got hold of two of them," he said, nodding at Marco, "and they... well, they avoided me at first, but after I talked to their employees and told them that Johnny Law was getting close and they might want to talk, they told me similar stories, of company owners who had been straight shooters their entire lives until the last couple of months."

"But you couldn't contact the company owner," Josh said thoughtfully. "We could use that somehow...." He shook himself. "So that's how she's making her money," he said. "Volume. And if she's using her father's playbook, she's obviously using the chapter on her father's old grudges and adding a dash of blackmail to the mix. She's going after small businesses. They don't have a lot of free cash, but if she taps their customers and blackmails the businesses to stay quiet, she can trade on their reputations to make more money. As long as the contractors *appear* to be working, she can cash the check."

"And don't forget she's exploiting vulnerable people," Grace said, hurt and angry.

"And practicing generally shitty behavior," Josh added. "I mean, look at them."

That picture again, Hepzibah in the center, her husband, wearing a gold lamé suit with a black tie but seeming remote and alien and unassociated with the crimes of fashion that surrounded him, and her father—a carbuncle on the ass of humanity if there ever was one—ranged behind the couch where she sat.

One of her children huddled at her feet, reaching for her as she ignored him gold onesie and all, and the other two were ranged on either side of her on the couch, looking plastic and compliant while wearing gold skirts and black sweaters with gold Peter Pan collars peeking out.

The children in particular had the appearance of people who had never had a kind word sent their way—not from their parents, at any rate—and a look of... of *neediness*, of *hunger* in their eyes as they gazed at their mother in supposed adoration.

"She's a black hole," Julia said. "I know her—not personally, but I know women like her. All of the money, all of the adoration, all of the good fortune in the world cannot make up for whatever her father broke in her as a child. She's like a cracked seal in a space station, and the howling emptiness of space will suck in whatever lies in her range and path."

As a whole, everybody in the room shuddered.

"And the fate of Clyde Staunton and Flory Gallo is apparently in her hands," Josh said.

Around them, Torrance could feel the air congeal, and the icy hardness of the world outside seeped into this warm, cozy den.

"We need to fix this," he said, not willing to just report the story this time, not when Hepzibah Coulter-King had gotten away with so much, slipping through the media's grasp like a water moccasin through a bayou.

"And *that*," Josh said, meeting the eyes of everybody in the room, "is where we begin."

There was some muttering then, some clarifying of details, some discussion—Josh had made his pronouncement at the perfect time. People were getting restless, and there was motion as people excused themselves to the restroom or got another drink. Grace disappeared and came back with a pomegranate apple juice for Josh, complete with a goofy reusable straw.

Josh grinned at him and booped him on the nose with it, like they were children instead of adults, and Grace grinned back.

"Lucky you're still in recovery. Be careful. One day you're going to be all perfect and healthy and shit, and you'll have to watch out for my loogies."

Josh groaned but still took a sip of juice. "Oh my God, are you twelve? I can't believe you have a perfectly functional relationship with a reasonable adult. How's that work, anyway?"

"First," Grace said grandly, "I have to change out of my Sanrio underwear!"

Josh guffawed, and Stirling glanced up from his computer monitor. "You're laughing like you didn't get him a complete set for Christmas."

"A different pair for each day of the week," Josh confirmed. Then he winked at Grace. "Because we all know telling time isn't your strongpoint."

Grace gave his best friend, his heart's blood brother, an impudent grin before sobering. "Clyde," he said, and Tor watched the thief, the dancer, the constant pain in the ass become the angel who had climbed into Tor's bed as a comforter and for no other reason.

"Yes, Angel," Josh said softly, taking Grace's hand without self-consciousness. "We'll save him. Why else are we us?"

Grace nodded and smiled, like that made perfect sense. "Thanks, Recovery Boy. I wonder sometimes." Grace's voice started to wobble, and Josh gave him a gentle push to the arm.

"Go get me a cookie," he said softly, "so I have the strength to go on."

"You've got a plan?" Grace pleaded.

"I think we can come up with one," Josh said. "Now go."

Grace nodded and bebopped away, like that terrible, tender moment of extreme empathy for a stranger had never existed.

"God, he's a surprise," Torrance said softly, watching him go.

"Not to me," Josh said, giving Tor a glance. "And not, I suspect, to Hunter."

"Well, bless you both," Torrance told him. "That kid deserves people who get him. So much heart that nobody else would see."

Josh laughed softly. "Particularly not his marks—but we won't mention them."

Tor's eyes grew large. "Wait, Frankie and Camille?"

Josh shook his head and blew out a breath. "Naw, he wouldn't steal from civilians... I think."

Tor nodded, not believing him. "Marco?" he called, and Marco was there at his shoulder as though he were a guardian angel waiting to appear.

"Yeah?"

"Look, don't, uhm, read too much into this, but maybe check Cammie and Frankie before they leave and make sure they have their, uhm, phones, wallets, keys... you know. Just casual-like."

Marco laughed softly. "Grace already stole them and then dropped them back into their pockets. Don't worry. They have no idea. Does he do that to everybody?"

Tor let out a breath. "I think it's sort of a rite of passage for anybody who gets to come down to the den. Uhm, maybe double-check before they leave. He... he's upset, and that doesn't always work out for him."

Marco sobered. "He took Clyde's situation really hard, didn't he?"

Torrance nodded, turning his head to watch the young thief gently tease Tienne about his bartending skills before palming enough cookies to feed an army. On his way back through the room, he deposited one in Stirling's hand, one in Molly's, and one in Carl's—to his apparent immense dismay.

"Grace," Carl said sternly, "the holidays are over—"

Tor couldn't see Grace's expression, but it must have been unusual because Carl started shoving the cookie in his mouth with undue haste.

"Ith delithiouth," he mumbled. "Thanth, Gwathe."

Marco sighed. "I don't understand that young man," he said, "but I think he's capable of great goodness and great mischief, both at the same time."

"Oh, I think you understand him just fine," Torrance said with a weak chuckle.

Marco's hand on his shoulder suddenly dominated his attention, filled him with warmth and ease and a surprising amount of bubbles, sparkling like cider or champagne.

"You—all of you—are amazing," Marco said, almost whispering the words in Torrance's ear. "I had no idea what I was setting in motion when I asked you for help."

Torrance gazed into those amazing, fathomless eyes, and what came out of his mouth next was unplanned and completely true. "I'd... I'd do about anything if it made you look at me like that."

Those sloe eyes lit up, and Marco bent close enough for his lips to brush Tor's ear. "I'm moving into the guest cottage on the property this weekend. Do you want to come to my apartment tonight and... help me pack?"

Torrance stared at him in surprise. "That's a euphemism, right?" he asked, making sure. "I mean, don't get me wrong here. I'd put stuff in boxes if you needed me to, but—"

The kiss was almost chaste, given where they were, but it carried with it banked heat, the promise of wildfire and conflagration.

"I don't need help putting things in boxes," Marco whispered. "Bring a change of clothes and a toothbrush."

Tor would have followed him to the Arctic Circle with less.

"Sure," he said, breath deserting him. "I can do that. After dinner. I'll—"

Next to him, Josh cleared his throat loudly enough to catch the attention of the entire room.

"All right, everybody—we've had snacks and refreshment and hit the head. It's time to come up with a plan. I've got some ideas, but I need everybody's help on this one, so hear me out."

Marco pulled away and moved back to his place behind the couch where Camille and Frankie sat, but not before giving Torrance a brief kiss on the forehead.

I'm going to his house to pack! Torrance thought, and then Josh really got rolling and his attention was needed elsewhere.

Teamwork

"YOU LOOK pleased with yourself," Cammie murmured as Marco leaned over the back of the couch.

"I'm going to do unspeakable things to that man tonight," Marco told her without shame.

Cammie chuckled. "That's my boy," she said softly. "Watching him like this is pretty sexy—not gonna lie."

Marco sobered. "But that depends on what the plan's going to be. The last time this group went and 'did something about it,' we had a gunshot wound, a knife wound, and a whole lot of sunburnt noses."

"Noticed the noses," Cammie said, nodding to Molly Christopher, who was curled up at her brother's feet. A natural, exuberant redhead, Molly's Caribbean tan was already peeling. Marco thought a little sadly that whatever mysteries the group had answered for Stirling and Molly, the two of them seemed subdued and sad. He noticed that the others were giving Molly lots of passing touches, and although Stirling was not a hugger, Grace had been excruciatingly polite to him over the past two days.

"And the damage," Frankie said softly.

Before Marco could answer that, Josh was at it again with the big screen.

"Okay, guys, I'm putting up an outline here, and I want you to talk about it for a minute and then start helping me beef it up a little. The way I see it, we have three things we need to do."

On the screen, the words *Save Clyde and any other exploited workers* showed up in big, bold white font against a black background. Josh turned toward Frankie, Cammie, and Marco. "I know this isn't the priority you were probably hoping for," he said apologetically. "But if it's a choice between leaving our vulnerable citizens in the hands of monsters like Hepzibah and saving businesses…." He bit his lip. "But that doesn't mean we're not planning for you guys too."

Underneath the first caption, the words *Expose the con and exonerate the ruined businesses* appeared.

On the couch in front of him, he heard Frankie and Cammie let out breaths they'd been holding.

"That's fair," Frankie said, the words simple and accepting. "That's Dad's priority too. Help Clyde first, fix the business second. May not be the easy choice, but I get it."

"Yeah," Cammie said. "My mother would never forgive me if we helped Dad but left that poor guy stuck in some awful place being yelled at by a guy named Cheezer."

There was some quiet laughter, and Josh let out a relieved sigh. "Thanks, guys. Let's see what we can do to make both those things happen." Then he tapped on the keyboard again, and everybody in the room made a little hum, a feral, dark sound of approval.

Fuck Hepzibah Coulter and her shitty family so hard their eyeballs are found in a field in Kansas.

Josh looked over his shoulder again, and Torrance did too.

Everybody in the room—including Danny, Felix, Chuck, and Hunter, who had all ghosted silently down the stairs, probably when Marco had been promising Torrance a night of passion and pleasure—were now ranged behind the couches. Danny was showing Felix something on his phone. Possibly the work they'd all presented in the last hour because Josh had sent it to them, and Chuck and Hunter were doing the same.

Grace took advantage of the moment to slide next to Hunter and press sinuously against him, probably searching for comfort. Marco hoped mightily he found it, because Grace's pain at Clyde's distress had been heart-wrenching to see.

"I like this plan, son," Danny said, eyes narrowed. "I think we need to talk about how to implement it and meet again tomorrow." He smiled at Cammie and Frankie. "Has anybody invited you to dinner after this? You're welcome to stay."

Cammie nodded. "Is Marco cooking? I could eat."

The thought of getting to the kitchen, creating food, while all of this swam around his busy brain, made Marco almost weak with relief.

"Good," Danny told Camille. "Josh, do you want to come up with teams now, or do you want to wait to see who's got a plan?"

"We put all this together this morning, Uncle Danny," Josh said, and the more Marco heard it, the more it sounded like it fit. "Give us the night to start planning. This is going to be a doozy, yanno?"

"Oh, I do." Danny smiled at everybody. "All right, then, children. How about everybody adjourns to their corners for the next couple of hours, and then we meet for dinner." He paused, and his phone buzzed. "Marco, Phyllis says you're not obligated to cook tonight—"

Marco sprang up from his crouch behind his cousins. "Oh no," he said. "I really think better while I'm cooking."

Danny chuckled. "A thing I completely understand, although I think Felix and Julia would forcibly bar me from the kitchen for the sake of all involved. If that's so, you should probably go upstairs in a few moments. I think she needs you."

Marco gave an uncertain look toward his cousins, but Danny waved him back down.

"And don't worry, my boy, we don't actually eat *people*. They'll be fine. Trust us." He made an exaggerated gesture toward himself with just a hint of smarm, and Marco chuckled.

"Okay, Mr. Morgan. Thank you so much." Marco did what was asked and stayed put, although he'd started to appreciate Danny's way of not ordering—simply suggesting what was logical and waiting for input.

"Thank you for trusting us," Danny said kindly. Molly stood then, prompted by a glance from Julia, and turned toward Frankie and Camille.

"Do you guys want to come with me to the upstairs TV room? There's an hour or two before dinner, and I'd like to pick your brains about your father's business. Stirling, do you and Tienne want to come with us?"

"I'll come with you, Molly girl," Chuck intervened. "I think Danny's going to need Stirling, am I right?"

Danny nodded. "I'm afraid your visit will have to wait," Danny said to Stirling, whose expression of relief might have been unflattering had Marco's cousins seen it, but even Marco recognized it as an introvert's fear of being stuck with new people for social interaction. "We're going to need you here."

Tor went to stand up to join them—bless his heart—but Danny shook his head, and he sat down.

"Give us a moment, yes?" As they left, Danny turned toward Grace and Hunter. "Grace?"

"Danny, they've got a mentally disabled guy, and they're keeping him away from people who love him, and it's not fair—"

"I understand, precious," Danny said, his voice gentler than Marco had ever heard it. "But I need my best minds in the room right now. Usually that's you, no matter how much you deny it. I need to know if you're up to helping."

Grace straightened and nodded. "Yes, Uncle Danny," he said with uncharacteristic humility. "I can pull my shit together for this."

Danny's eyes grew shiny, and Marco had a thought: All the people in the mansion—Chuck and Hunter, who looked like enforcers, Stirling the hacker, Tienne, who freely admitted to being a forger—they weren't their jobs here any more than he was "the cook." They were Felix and Danny's *children*. Of course Josh was theirs—and Julia's—in the way parts of a person's soul were bound to the rest of them, hearts and minds included. But that didn't mean this vast mansion of people, including Torrance, were disposable or simply "coworkers." They were family, very much the same way his uncles and aunts and cousins were family. Marco and Cammie were especially close—he'd often joked that he'd trade her for one of his sisters any day. This was the same, he realized. This family had been handpicked, and it was no less precious for that.

"I know you can," Danny said softly. "You listen to me, Dylan Li, our Grace—there is nothing you can't do, and all sorts of marvelous things you *can* that you haven't even tried yet. And not because you're a freaking genius, but because your heart is possibly smarter than your brain. Someday you'll believe me." He took a deep breath. "Felix, anything to add before we get down to it?"

Felix had stood there, seemingly tranquil, while Danny was dealing with people, but in the meantime, he'd had his phone out, fingers flying, and now he glanced up.

"I have some information on Hepzibah's holdings, where her properties are now and what they're zoned for. Once we start working on the plan, it will come in handy."

Josh grinned at his father. "Show-off," he said.

Then, surprisingly, Liam spoke up. He'd sat quietly during the presentation, so good at making himself invisible that Marco had literally forgotten he was there.

He held up his own phone and said, "I've put out some feelers to the intelligence community for her henchmen. You know for sure she didn't set up those sweatshops without brokers for labor. She may have used the same sources or the same techniques this time. It can help."

Josh's look at Liam was more like exasperation. "That's fabulous. Don't you have to go home, like, tomorrow?"

"No," Liam said pertly. "Now I'm working. I can stay as long as I want if it involves nailing Hepzibah Coulter on slavery charges."

Josh glanced around uncomfortably and dropped his voice. "I thought we agreed…."

Liam shook his head. "No, mate, you agreed that we'd talk about us later, when you were recovered. That has nothing to do with me working with your family business, does it?"

If Marco had been Liam? He would have backed up a few steps. But Josh's glare didn't appear to singe anything—eyebrows, peeling nose, or even Liam's freckled cheeks. Instead, the young Interpol officer glared at Josh Salinger in turn and booped him on the nose, much as Josh had booped Grace.

It had the same result as booping a German shepherd. Josh looked confused, shook his head, and went determinedly back to what he'd been doing.

"So," he said to his parents, "did I leave anything out?"

"Only us," Felix said dryly. "Was there any reason you chose not to wait until we were here?"

Josh swallowed defensively. "I, uhm, you know." He gave an ingratiating smile and suppressed a yawn, and Marco remembered that he was supposed to be *resting*. "Didn't want to be left out again."

"Oh, for fuck's sake," Liam muttered, but Danny and Felix glared back.

"Would you have been okay running through the jungle?" Felix asked shortly. "Because it wasn't a picnic for *me*, but it would have been less so if I'd needed to carry you." He snorted. "It was bad enough with Danny and Carl wounded. No, son, you were far more help back at overwatch this time."

Josh made an exasperated growl, and unexpectedly, it was Grace who stopped what looked to be an impending collision.

"Besides," he said, as though he'd been in the conversation the entire time. "It's my fault, remember? We had a plan, and I ruined it. So don't yell at them and go take a nap."

And like he'd been waiting for that cue, Josh yawned, and then yawned two more times, and when he was in the middle of saying, "Grace, I hate you," he yawned again.

There was a brief chuckle, and then Julia said, "Danny, hurry up with what you were saying, and then Josh can take his nap and we can all go do our assignments."

Danny nodded. "Josh's breakdown was spot on, but the one thing he left out was that this is going to take a variety of cons, and most of the players *can't be us*." He glared meaningfully at the core family. "People, we're dealing with politicians, and they *live here*. Like it or not, we're big fish in this little pond, and we are recognizable." He gave a significant glance toward Julia. "And some of us have made a name for ourselves in the area of fucking with the immorally rich. This can't smell like us, my children. Grace, that includes you. Hunter, Chuck, Carl—they're background guys, and they're good at it, but Grace, your parents are a big deal, and your adorable little puss has been on a lot of society pages. Thieving in a black balaclava, yes. Even a little bit of valet or waitstaff work, yes. But you absolutely can't confront the douchebag squad as Dylan Li, son of the outrageously rich Li family, do you understand?"

Then he looked at Torrance. "You, my boy, are our one exception. You're our front man. You're giving us a press pass to take on the rich and famous and to rope the masses where we need them to go. I know you're probably thinking one *huge* story here, but I want you to think about how to break this down, much like Josh did. A story on exploited, vulnerable workers to start with, and then another one on grifters using legitimate companies as a front to take advantage of innocent consumers, and then a third on sweatshops, and then hit the vulnerable workers again. We want this woman's reputation *savaged* before we even say her name."

Marco glanced at Torrance curiously—everything about the man Marco was coming to care for seemed to scream independent and group resistant, and here Danny was, practically dictating his course of action.

To Marco's surprise, every suggestion hit Torrance like a little shot of evil. His smile practically curled, like the Grinch's, and the expression he turned toward Danny was one of luminous retribution.

"Good shit, Danny," he said, his voice breathless. Marco could see a spark inside him—one that had been lit that morning as he and Josh worked side by side—but this proposition seemed to fan it to flame.

For his part, Benjamin Morgan nodded, seeming equally inspired. "You'll do us all proud," he said, and then his eyes fell on Marco, and Marco tried not to quail. These complete strangers were moving mountains to try to help his family, and Marco could only hope to be worthy.

"Don't look so frightened, sweet boy," Danny said kindly. "The reason I asked you to stay is to ask about your family. Your two cousins appear very committed, and for all the reasons I just gave, I need to know how far they'll be willing to go. Do you think they'll be willing to help here? I understand if they wouldn't. We're going up against some very powerful people. And if we ask them to do anything they're uncomfortable with, they need to feel free to say no. But that said, I'm going to need you to sound them out. Ask them how much they're willing to do, and ask them if they have any ideas while you're at it." Danny glanced around the room. "We're not proud here. We'll take all the help we can get."

Marco nodded thoughtfully and then gave a ghost of a smile. "My family," he said slowly, "is very much ride or die. This is for my uncle Flory, and he's fighting for a friend's kid. I mean, I know Clyde is an adult, but he apparently was Clyde's father's friend, and that means something to us." He glanced around. "Like family means something to you guys, I think. I'm in it—to my eyeballs. Ride or die. Ask me anything. Let me ask Cammie and Frankie, but if I know them at all, they'll be with me." His mouth twisted. "If we get busted, we'd appreciate adjoining cells," he added, "although I'd rather not bunk with Frankie. He's got terrible foot fungus."

"Good," Danny said on an appreciative smile. "Very good. Not the fungus but the commitment. And you may want to put this to some other members of your family, but it's not necessary." He paused and shrugged. "It's only that their presence here—and yours—indicates a, uhm, similar sort of family constitution," he said carefully. "You've already seen how upset *we* get if we think we're being left out."

Marco glanced at Josh and then Julia. "I'm, uhm, getting the idea," he replied. There was a buzz in his pocket, and he jumped before checking his phone. "Uhm, speaking of family?"

"Is Phyllis threatening Felix's life again?" Danny asked, earning himself an indignant look from his husband.

"Me? You're the one who can't seem to shut up!"

Danny grinned impudently. "You just like to stand there and look imposing. We know you, Fox."

"She does sort of need me," Marco apologized. "But I can talk after dinner."

Felix and Danny met eyes. "Perhaps ask Phyllis if you can eat at the big table tonight with the rest of us," Felix said. "Very often, amazing things happen when we talk shop over dinner, and since you're in on the family secret, there's no reason to exile you to the kitchen, is there?"

"Room?" Marco asked uneasily, not sure if the long banquet table could take another person.

Felix snorted. "Would you believe that thing sections out, and we've got another section in storage? Don't worry, Marco. You make enough food and we'll be able to eat family style, yes?"

"Yes." Marco grinned. "Thanks, Felix. Thanks, Uncle, erm, Dr., erm…."

"Uncle Danny is fine," Danny said, smiling. He glanced at Felix. "You know, I really thought I'd hate that, but it's grown on me."

Felix gave him an unimpressed look, and then Marco's pocket buzzed again and he *really* had to run.

MARCO HADN'T lied—he did his best thinking in the kitchen, and he was used to cooking family style and adjusting for numbers. It was starting to dawn on him how the Salingers had so many big family-style dinners with different guests every so often. They weren't just a makeshift family—or a very odd business. They were a combination of both of them with, he suspected, some off-the-books activities thrown in.

He threw himself into chopping, sautéing, braising, and plating with all of his heart, ordering the kitchen staff in a crisp, no bullshit style that he still worked to keep respectful. He'd *worked* in the high-stress, diva-chef environments; his one vow was to never create that for himself.

And given the way Josh had presented the breakdown of what they knew and what needed to be done, inviting everybody's input and utilizing their gifts, he had the feeling that no diva chefs would be tolerated in their kitchen, much less their home.

Good. He really liked it here.

By the time dinner was done and only the plating and the setting the table remained, Phyllis bustled in and told him to go change.

He indicated his standard polo and slacks, which, although he wore an apron faithfully, couldn't escape stains.

"Go up to Torrance's room," she said softly. "I think Danny gave him some of Josh's old clothes from before he got sick. They should fit. Don't worry. You don't have to be fancy, but all the kids changed, and Tor didn't want you to be uncomfortable."

"Thank you," Marco murmured, seeing the kindness in this. "Are you sure you don't need me to help?"

She shook her head. "No worries, Marco. You earned your keep today. It's fine."

He laughed softly, grateful that she seemed to read his mind, and then he left, hanging up his apron on the rack and hurrying down the hallway toward the bedrooms.

Tor had left his door open, and Marco found him dressed in a button-down with a tie, contemplating a sweater over the top.

He was freshly showered and tan and relaxed and happy, and Marco suddenly wanted… oh, he wanted.

He came up behind Tor as Tor adjusted his tie in the mirror and put his hands on his hips, lining himself along Torrance's backside and breathing in the hollow of his neck.

"God, you smell good."

Tor chuckled and turned, and Marco danced backward before he could do the same.

"What?" Tor laughed. "Don't you smell good too?"

"I smell like *dinner*," Marco complained. "And that doesn't mean I don't smell *great*, but chicken fajitas do not make a sexy cologne."

Tor tilted his head back then and belly laughed, and Marco stared, suddenly besotted and more than a little bit in love.

"What?" Tor asked.

Marco shook his head. "Later," he murmured. "Later. Right now let me shower, and then we can make it on time for dinner. Phyllis said I had fifteen minutes, which barely gives me time to get the smell of fajita marinade off my hands."

"Understood," Torrance murmured, showing him the clothes he'd picked out—a pair of slacks, a button-down, and a richly colored brown-and-rust sweater that looked very much like something Marco would have chosen for himself. "And we share a bathroom with Chuck, but he told me he wouldn't need the extra shower, so it's all yours." With that he gestured toward the door, and Marco nodded gratefully.

"Awesome. Back in a flash!"

Showering was one big tease. Tor was so close, and he was clean and scrubbed and looked glamorous and smelled *amazing*, and Marco— ooh, Marco wanted him so badly. In his entire life, he'd never desired a man more, and the little world of food service could be very intense in its connections and liaisons. Marco had tried to shy away from most of that. There was a lot of drama in hooking up with your fellow soldiers of the kitchen, and he'd been there to cook and to learn. That didn't mean he hadn't crushed a *lot* and made out some more, but he'd never, ever, seen or spoken to a man who called to him so consistently, day after day.

Their quiet kisses in the kitchen after breakfast had left Marco yearning and needy when Tor had been gone, and Marco was so ready to put an end to that now.

And a beginning to what they could be, now that there were no more secrets between them.

He was fast but thorough in the shower, grateful for the expensive soap and the exfoliating soap bag because it meant he could clean himself up for real.

When he went home that night, with Torrance in tow, he didn't want to stop and fiddle with things like showers and soap. He wanted to ravish Tor's mouth and touch all his skin and remember what all the shouting was about—and make Torrance Grayson do a whole lot of it while he was at it.

So he emerged from the shower with clean hair and clean creases, pink and sweet, and only a little self-conscious about putting on someone else's clothes.

That turned out to be a perfect fit.

Tor had hung them up in the bathroom while Marco had been showering, and they were fresh and wrinkle free by the time he emerged. He slid into a new pair of briefs, right out of the bag, and the rest of the ensemble, marveling at how much more substantial Josh Salinger had once been. Marco could swear he had forty pounds on the young man, and he was only an inch or so taller.

"What?" Torrance asked as he emerged from the bathroom. "Here's some loafers of mine—they should fit. What's that look?"

Marco shook his head and ran his hand down the fine cashmere of the sweater. "I'm just... you know. Glad Josh is getting better. That he'll be able to fit into this again someday. I mean, you know. I saw him getting sicker and then saw the family excited that he was in remission, but I.... Until today I never really saw who he truly was to everybody."

"Yeah," Tor said, coming up to adjust Marco's cuffs. It was such an easy, intimate thing to do that Marco's chest practically opened up with sweetness. "Josh Salinger is pretty special."

There was something in his tone—something wistful. "Did you and he ever...?" Oh God. How was Marco supposed to compete with *that*?

Torrance shook his head. "No... no." He gave a sheepish little smile. "But he was my 'never been' for a while. I... it's hard to explain."

Marco snorted. "No, it's not. I mean, that guy? Healthy, happy, leading people into adventures? Man, he probably had men eating out of his hand."

Torrance grimaced. "Never the right one," he said. "But Liam.... Liam's a wild card. Josh has a thing for law enforcement, and Liam seems like the kind of guy—"

Marco kissed him, softly, because he didn't want to get them all mussed after they'd just spent some time getting all pretty. "The kind of guy who would ask to go slow, day after day, so when it really did happen, it wouldn't be a mistake," he said, kissing Tor on both cheeks before pulling away.

Tor gave him a hesitant smile. "Was that... did that work for you?" he asked, biting his lip.

"It made me hungry for you," Marco said huskily. "And then you went on vacation, and it made me *starving*. Now come on. My cousins are downstairs, and if we both miss dinner, I'll have to change my name and move to another state to escape the jumbo ration of razzing they'll be dishing out."

Tor laughed and led the way out of the room, pausing to close the door out of habit. Marco took that opportunity to grab his hand, holding it down the stairs and through the hallway so they entered as a couple to a cacophony of catcalls and "You go, guys!" and "Woo-hoo, Torrance, way to go!" as they entered the dining room.

Yeah, they both blushed, but Marco made a point of holding Torrance's chair as he sat down, and the ruckus settled as he took his own seat.

And that must have been the signal—he knew from his own days in the kitchen that there was usually a lookout—because that's when the servers came trooping in bearing big platters of fajita fixings and warmers full of tortillas.

LIFE ON this side of the table was a lot of fun; Marco could admit it. Everybody was complimentary of the food—and not just because the cook was sitting right there—but it was more than that.

The dinner conversation was… well, chaotic, but once Marco caught the rhythm and realized that anybody could join in if they could get a word in edgewise, he was game.

"Hey, Marco," Grace called from a couple seats down and across. "These little chicken wrap things are delicious! Me likey. I could eat until I can't fit in ventilation shafts anymore."

"They're fajitas, Grace," his boyfriend corrected, and Marco shot Hunter a grateful look because he hadn't wanted to do that. "And you know it."

Grace gave him a sideways glance. "That's what you say, but I can go into any Thai place in the city, and they'll give me big sheets of lettuce—"

"Leaves," Hunter corrected, obviously trying not to smile.

"*Tortillas* of lettuce, and then they'll give me a delicious chicken and vegetable mixture to put into those tortillas—"

"Leaves."

"—of lettuce, and I will wrap them up into a delicious little roll that I can put into my face with my fingers." Grace demonstrated by popping the last of his fajita into his mouth. "So what's the difference between them?"

"Lettuce," Josh said dryly from the other end of the table, and in response, Grace pointed to the bowl of shredded lettuce next to him that had been used to dress his fajita.

"Spices," Camille said from next to Marco, and he stared at her in surprise because she sounded as absolutely into Grace's madness as the rest of the family was.

"But spices get traded!" Grace said proudly. "Etienne, you lived in all the places. What did the streets of Morocco smell like?"

"Spices," Tienne said softly from next to Stirling. His face was pink, Marco noticed, as though he didn't speak in the group often, and he realized Grace had pulled him in on purpose.

"But were they the same *kind* of spices?" Molly asked.

"Well, that's what spice traders are for!" Grace practically crowed.

"Unless we're in the *Star Wars* universe," Stirling said, lobbing a conversational grenade with complacency. "Then it's all about drugs."

"Are you saying Han Solo was a drug runner?" Molly asked in outrage.

Stirling gave his sister a level look. "And he shot first."

"But did that space meth taste good on chicken in a tortilla?" Chuck asked. "That's all I want to know."

"Ooh," Carl's boyfriend, Michael, cackled. "I'm telling Lucius that you're a junkie for fajitas!"

Carl regarded his boyfriend—who had apparently arrived while Marco was changing—with affection. "He's only a space-meth junkie if he needs that fajita to function," he said, partly as though he was making sure and partly as though he was backing up his buddy.

Michael—smallish, with longish brown hair and wide brown eyes—squinted at Carl skeptically. "Lookit the size of that man's biceps, Carl. He's using *something* to function!"

Chuck cackled and flexed as he sat at the table. "This body is powered by space-meth fajitas!"

"And the workout room has the gas fumes to prove it," Molly retorted acerbically.

"But in the *Dune* universe," Tienne said carefully, "spice was the medium for interstellar transport. So if we're using the word inclusively, spice is both the fuel for the gas and it is the gas itself!"

"Ooh," said Hunter, for once not the grown-up of the children, "does that mean interstellar travel smells like farts?"

The table groaned, and Julia gave a wince. "Children," she said with exaggerated patience. "Do we have to add 'space-meth gas' to the list of things we can't talk about?"

"You all have a list, do you?" Liam asked, delight written all over his face. "What are some of the topics?"

Josh snickered into the back of his hand when Danny pulled out his phone. "*Ahem*—"

"Danny…," Julia said helplessly.

"Limburger cheese juggernauts, the location of the devil's anus—"

That one brought a chortle from the assembled diners, as well as a "Please don't" from Felix.

"How to assemble a penis after a firecracker accident—"

"Oh my God!" Camille and Molly both shouted.

"How many sperm are in a rabbit's ejaculation—"

"Sorry," Carl muttered. "That one's my bad."

"Which led to how many rabbits have to fuck to get a bridge of rabbits to the moon—"

Grace grinned proudly. "That was me."

"And then we have 'Could Josh ride a murder bird to Mordor while he's still in chemo?'"

"That was Stirling's," Josh said, eyes threatening dire retribution as Stirling grinned.

"The ever-lengthening list of things we'd like to do to rapists, pedophiles, and men who vote about women's bodies in congress."

"I've got some shit to add to that," Molly said seriously, and Julia nodded as though willing to let that one slide.

"And that brings us to page two," Danny said, putting his phone down for a moment before glancing at Julia. "Am I adding space-meth fajita gas to the list, dearest?"

Julia sighed, appearing bewildered. "Honestly, Danny, I can't tell anymore if it's better or worse."

"Let's leave it off for now," Danny said judiciously. "We'll just—" He glanced up at the table. "—reiterate that the ban on gas of any sort that's not petroleum based or related to a case, remains."

There were some general nods, and then Grace said, "Han Solo only shot first because he knew Greedo was an assassin."

And the conversation was on again—loud, rambling, sometimes gross, and often profane. The people at the table bounced from topic to topic, and the only limit on who spoke was on who could get in there the quickest with their zinger.

Everybody quieted down a little as the kitchen staff came in to fetch the trays, and Marco smiled at his friends and coworkers, who spoke easily back to him and the rest of the diners.

"Did I make enough for you all?" he asked Tess, who was picking up his plate.

"Plenty, Marco, as always," Tess said. "What's it like at the big table?" She grinned at Tor, who winked back.

"*Loud*," Marco said, laughing softly. "And fun. I'm starting to see why they eat so much—their brains probably burn calories while they sleep!"

She laughed too and said, "Do you know if we're eating dessert here or downstairs tonight?"

Marco shook his head and shrugged, but Felix had heard her. With a sidelong glance at Josh, who was tired and peaked, he answered for Marco.

"We'll be having dessert up here, Tess," he said softly, giving his son a look with a raised eyebrow when Josh made a sound of dissent.

"Tomorrow, Dr. Morgan and I have business in the city to attend, but I assume everybody else will work on our current project during the day, and we can reconvene tomorrow night. Is that good for everybody?"

There was general assent, but Marco couldn't have been the only one who saw Felix lean over and say softly, "And you can get some rest," to Josh.

Josh yawned and nodded sheepishly. "Understood," he said. "Dessert first?" Then he yawned again.

"I'll bring it to your room," Liam said, standing.

"But—"

"No arguments, mate," Liam replied, eyes all concern. "I've got selfish reasons of my own invested in getting you well."

And with that, he took Josh by the elbow, helped him up, and guided him gently from the dining room as everybody else bid him good night.

Marco's eyes lingered, though, worried because Josh had taxed himself for Marco's sake, and he felt bad, so Marco was the one who watched as Josh swayed on his feet. Liam caught him and swept him up, back and arms flexing underneath his sweater as he carried the young man with surprising strength up the stairs toward his room.

He met Tor's eyes for a moment and saw the concern there, too, and said, "Mr. Salinger, I think Cammie and Frankie have family obligations tomorrow. Can we meet in three days? It will give everybody a little more time, right?"

Felix turned grateful eyes toward him. "That sounds like a better plan, Marco. Thank you."

Then Danny elbowed him and murmured something, bobbing his chin toward where Grace was currently balancing a fork on each one of his fingers.

Felix nodded and caught Hunter's eye, and Hunter swept all the forks off in one swift move, directing Grace's attention toward the head of the table where the grown-ups sat.

"Grace?" Felix said, making sure Grace was making eye contact.

"Yes, Mr. Josh's Dad."

"You need to not go haring off into the wild yonder, do you understand? I know you were upset at hearing about Clyde—it hurt all of us—so you need to not—"

Grace shifted on his chair, and his eyes went left and right again. "I'm not!" he said, but his voice rose at the end, like a child's.

Danny let out a sigh. "Grace," he said softly. "Think. If you find out where Clyde is and swoop in to get him, and he's safe, what happens to all the other people *with* Clyde who are being abused and exploited? Can you guarantee *their* safety?"

Grace looked uncomfortable. "I wasn't going to—"

"And Grace," Julia added, watching as Grace's eyes flew to her face in agony. "Think about this—unless we pull this off, Hepzibah Coulter isn't going to *quit*. She's going to move her resources around, change their locations, change their names. What does that tell you?"

Grace wasn't stupid, Marco had figured that out very quickly. "If we fuck up a rescue, we'll have to find them again, and it will take longer and be harder, and it might not work the second time."

Julia nodded soberly. "We're all as appalled by this as you are. But we need Josh's brain, and that means we need to give him time to rest. You can help by doing everything he asks you, and by *not running off by yourself*. Do you understand?"

Grace swallowed, and to Marco it looked like surrender.

"Yes, Mrs. Josh's Mom. I promise. All courses of action will be Josh-sanctioned. It's fine. Whatever."

She smiled a little. "We love you, Dylan Li. We need to trust you to honor that."

Grace rolled his eyes, but two spots of color appeared on his cheeks. "Yes, ma'am."

Hunter wrapped his arm around Grace's shoulder and mouthed "Thank you" to the three parents at the head of the table.

Julia, Danny, and Felix all inclined their heads, nodding soberly, and then dessert was served.

Rest and Real

TOR DROVE them to Marco's apartment, glad for both their sakes that by car it was a ten-minute drive. Chicago in January was a shitty time to be out at night—the cold and icy conditions didn't fuck around.

Marco directed him to the parking spot he didn't use, and Tor parked, listening to the engine idle for a moment. Marco hadn't said much after dinner. They'd lingered an appropriate time, seen Cammie and Frankie off and fielded their sincere thank-yous with promises to pass the sentiment on and call them for the next meeting. Then they'd gone back to the dining room table, where everyone else was finishing up with coffee or chocolate or one last cookie.

"Anybody playing poker?" Chuck asked. "Or can I go sext my boyfriend?" Lucius had left early that morning to run his own business in Springfield, and Chuck was obviously feeling the loss.

He waited for a moment until Carl said, "I'm bushed. I suggest we all rest up and meet tomorrow to work out and go from there."

Michael gave him an arch look. "Don't you have work to do?"

Carl shrugged. "I can do it all by laptop at the moment. You?"

Michael sighed. "Sadly, all our vehicles need all my attention. *I* will be up to my elbows in grease until I get home."

"Then I'll be there with a bath," Carl said, smiling into his lover's eyes. He broke the spell reluctantly and said, "I think Marco had the right idea. We pitch ideas, we fiddlefuck around, we meet again with some solid ideas." He yawned and stretched, wincing as he overreached his recently wounded shoulder. "And we remember that three days ago, we were all on a beach, recovering from a helluva ride."

Tor took that as his cue to run up to his room and grab the bag he'd packed while Marco had been in the shower, coming back in time to follow Carl and Michael out the door.

Felix took him aside as Phyllis was pressing leftovers into Carl's and Marco's hands and murmured, "You up to this?"

Tor smiled, his eyes a little bright. "If I'm not up to *this*," he said, "I'll never be okay again."

Felix nodded approvingly. "Just remember if things break, we're here. And if they go great, we're here." He grimaced. "Just, uhm, try not to go nuclear if they break, because Danny *really* enjoys that young man's cooking."

Tor laughed softly and, on impulse, hugged his former boss and mentor, a man who had become his family and friend. "I'll do you all right, I promise," he said, and for a moment, he ached for the family who had never given him the opportunity to make that promise. They'd missed out, he thought. Being a part of a relationship based on respect, caring—it was worth it, whether it involved a lover or a friend or a de facto older brother.

But now, as the night settled around them, he wondered if Marco was having second thoughts. He'd been so quiet on the drive over, staring out into the dark thoughtfully as though something was weighing on him.

"We don't have to," Tor blurted into the quiet. "I mean… you know, I was looking cute there for a minute, but now that you've seen what we talk about at dinner—"

Marco shot him a glare of impatience. "If you back out now I'll never make you breakfast again. Phyllis will be all, 'But Marco, you cooked breakfast for the rest of the household,' and I'll be, 'I don't know, Phyllis, I was just two blocks away when he wandered into the kitchen all sad and regretful and horny.'"

Torrance gave an amused snort. "And I would be all three," he conceded, then sobered. "You're just… I don't know, far away."

"I was thinking about Grace," Marco said, surprising him.

"Gra—"

"And Josh. And Liam. And Stirling and Tienne and Hunter and Chuck and Molly, bless her, and Carl and Michael—but first about Grace and Josh. What happened that made everybody so worried about Grace? That made Josh so desperate to please him, to help him do something good, that he'd push himself so hard. Why—why did he need to be told to rest, and why did Grace need to be told not to run into the wild blue yonder?"

Tor sighed. "The Caribbean," he said, content to let the engine idle for another moment. The minute he shut off the engine, the cold wouldn't merely seep into the vehicle, it would *slam*. "Danny had just been wounded, shot in the shoulder. It was only a flesh wound, really, but scary, and half the group was back on the yacht, resting with him. The other half of us were out on Martinique, shopping and clubbing and watching the sunset."

"Watching the sunset?" Marco asked, turning to gaze at him for the first time.

"I sent you the video," Tor said, his cheeks burning. "Do you remember the sunset?"

"You were thinking about me," Marco murmured. "I do remember."

Tor gave him a shy smile. "Yes. Anyway, we passed some people speaking Serbian, and nobody noticed but Grace and Hunter."

Marco frowned. "You said some people got left behind," he remembered.

"Yes," Tor said. "That's… well, it's one way to look at it."

Marco stared at him, eyes large. "And the other way?"

"Grace took off to follow them, smuggled aboard their cabin cruiser, and Michael and Carl saw him. Michael said—and this is a quote, I understand—'Somebody's got to look out for that boy' and joined him. The ensuing clusterfuck would need a map and colored pins to explain, but by the time it was done and I arrived, the people who had gotten to the island first had taken out twenty-four guards—you heard that right, we made Hunter count—as well as destroyed a stately old mansion and blown up most of the gunrunner's stash."

Marco gasped. "And you…?"

"I was taking live video feed from a computer on the island and waking people up in Chicago to coordinate the story that hit the AP wires, and I was doing it from a tiny helicopter that held four people but was really only big enough for two."

"You could have been *killed*."

But he couldn't have Marco thinking that Tor had been the hero. "I was *fine*. The rest of the group did the rough stuff this time, although sometimes I'm more heavily involved. They like to call me their face man. I think in old con terms it means the guy who ropes people into the con, who goes out and charms people into spending their money. In the case of the Salingers, I'm the public face of all the dirt they dig up helping people. But…." He let out a breath and a little bit of that bitterness and answered the original question. "But the thing is, I think there's something a little bit… broken, in all of us. I don't want to talk about anybody's histories, but I know enough about all of them to know we were all, at one time or another, thrown out of the idea that 'normal' is good. We understand chaos. And Grace is brilliant. In so many ways. He's a world-class dancer—I mean *world class*. People come from all over the world to study with him, and he's completely oblivious. But he's also a world-class thief, and *nobody* knows about that because he's *that good*. And Grace… I think he's pretty sure the only way he can have love is to steal it. He's getting better. I think the island scared him because Carl got hurt, and Carl's one of the people Grace can't let get hurt, but… but he's still…." Tor felt disloyal saying this about the angel who had kept watch over him.

"A little broken," Marco said softly. "Like all of you."

Tor smiled crookedly. "Like me." He let that sink in. "I could just drop you off, you know, and go back to the—"

Marco didn't let him finish. Without warning he hit the ignition button and killed the engine, and then he grabbed the key fob off the console and slid out of the passenger seat, letting the frigid air into the SUV.

"Oh my God," Tor gasped, because he hadn't been ready, and the carport was no protection at all.

"Move your ass," Marco ordered. "Carefully. The ice will kill you if you rush. Follow me."

Well, that was an answer, Tor thought with a smile, and before he could remind Marco to lock the car, he heard the beep of the security system and figured maybe Marco really did know what he was doing.

HE WASN'T surprised by the tiny one-bedroom apartment—he'd lived in his share coming up through college, before he got his break with Felix—but he was surprised by its bareness. No posters, no tchotchkes, only shiny blue enamel pots in the kitchen to give away somebody wonderful lived there.

The furniture was handsome, though: sturdy wooden end tables and a gently scuffed leather couch and chair. The area rug was bright and cheerful, making Tor think that it wasn't that Marco didn't care about his surroundings.

"No posters, I know," Marco said, wrinkling his nose. "I got a bunch of pictures framed while we were on vacation, but—" He shrugged, indicating the frames in the corner. "And I'm moving this weekend anyway." He paused. "Did I tell you where?"

Tor shook his head, divesting himself of his coat and shoes in the foyer as Marco had. The heat had clicked on the moment they'd entered, and he was beyond grateful.

"No. Where?"

Marco's grin was brilliant. "There's a mother-in-law cottage on the mansion's property. Phyllis offered it to me yesterday. It's nice—I mean, *nice*— and I get maid service if I offer my guest room to people if they need it."

Tor grinned back. "That's awesome!" He felt his cheeks color. "It means, uhm, I can visit."

He hadn't moved far from the entryway, and he was abruptly conscious that this was where things got awkward.

Marco seemed to feel it too. He moved, suddenly in Tor's space, those amazingly pretty eyes wide and predatory, his nearness as mesmerizing as it had been all along.

Tor swallowed, wondering when sex had gotten so big, so meaningful. "It's been a while," he confessed.

"Me too," Marco murmured, moving just a little bit closer. "You wanted to take it slow so it would mean something."

They were close enough now that their lips almost touched, and he could feel Marco's breath along his cheek. "Does it?" Tor asked.

He thought of Marco, of his quiet humor, of his fierce family loyalty, of his surprisingly autocratic streak and the way he worked quietly, doggedly, to get his way. Of his patience. Every day they'd been gone, Tor had thought about him, and now it was as though his body came alive, lunging out of the quiet cage of "wait" into the greedy jungle of "now."

"A lot," Marco murmured. "Our families—yours and mine—we're loyal people. I can't see this happening and us not being loyal to each other."

Tor's eyelids fluttered closed. "That," he murmured, "is damned sexy."

"Just wait." Marco placed a butterfly kiss on each lid. "There's more."

Then his mouth was on Torrance's, carnal, demanding, uncompromising. Tor found himself backed up against the door to the apartment, feet spread to brace himself, hands rucked up underneath Marco's sweater as he struggled to touch skin.

Marco tore his mouth away and worked to master his own breathing. "Bed," he said.

Tor was going to say something arch, like "No seduction?" but it was perfectly obvious that the last month and a half had been seduction, and now they were both well and truly seduced.

What remained was consummation, and their need had grown urgent, explosive over the long courtship, and their choices had become to either be consumed in flames of desire or to explode.

It was close.

Marco grabbed his hand and dragged him through the apartment, slamming the bedroom door behind him after they entered. Before Tor could look around, the kiss was on again, both of them tugging at each other's clothes, palming revealed bits of skin, never able to keep up with where they wanted to kiss, to touch, to stroke, next.

Finally they were naked, standing breathlessly by the bed, and Tor stared at Marco's fine, long body in the lamplight, loving the lithe muscles, the sturdy thighs, even the soft tummy that probably came with loving his own food enough to sit down with Tor and eat muffins every morning.

Marco extended a strong, long-fingered hand to Tor's abdomen, tracing the taut muscles. "You could cut diamonds with those abs," he said, almost accusingly.

Tor grinned. "Complaints?"

Marco shrugged, allowing his hand to drop lower, tracing the bikini line where Tor shaved conscientiously. "You can too share a muffin with me every morning," he said mildly.

Tor lowered his own hand to Marco's hip, loving the soft skin, the tiny tummy. "I might get one of these," he whispered, wanting badly to know it was okay.

"Do you mind mine?" Marco grinned, dimples popping in his cheeks, and Tor's heart stuttered, knowing that this man—young as he looked, *sweet* as he looked, was just fine with *how* he looked.

"I love it all," Tor said thoughtlessly, dropping his own hand almost to the danger zone. Marco didn't shave, and his chest was surprisingly furry, with a bold happy trail leading to a barely trimmed garden. And jutting from that garden was a… oh, wow. A thick and mighty column of flesh, with a wide head and a rapidly disappearing foreskin. "You—you are absolutely, positively you."

"I know," Marco said, tossing his head back in a classic preen. His breath caught, though, when Tor raised his hand to explore Marco's chest, to tease a nipple, to knead a pectoral. He moved closer, trapping Tor's hand against his heart. "I think we're both avoiding the real question here, though."

"Which is?" Tor's entire body was on fire, burning with the need to be closer, to touch more, to stroke, to be stroked, to—

"Which one of us you think is going to top," Marco whispered in his ear. Then he turned Tor around by the shoulders and gave him a gentle shove so he fell on the bed face-first.

Tor scrambled to his hands and knees and turned his head, laughing at the sudden playfulness. "You think that's you? Oh… oh…."

Marco draped himself along Tor's back, letting Tor feel all the lines of his body, and Tor's knees went out from under him, leaving him arching his hips and thrusting against the comforter.

"Yes," Marco murmured, nibbling Tor's ear, kissing along his neck. "That's me."

"Why—oh!" Marco had smoothed a hand along his backside and then palmed the inside of his thighs, spreading them a little, opening him up. The air, hitting his pucker, sent shivers down his spine. "Why on my stomach?" he breathed.

"Oh, I'll have you on your back," Marco whispered, kissing his way down Tor's spine. "But you're busy."

"Busy?" Tor gasped. Marco's hands were separating, tickling, reaching underneath him and… "Oh wow!" Grasping his cock, adjusting it so it lay hard and flat between Tor's abdomen and the bed.

"You *think* you want to top." Marco had kept moving slowly downward and was now perched, knees between Tor's, hands framing Tor's hips, his lips trailing along the small of Tor's back. "You keep reaching to touch, to twiddle, to arouse."

"You don't like that?" Tor moaned. Marco had spread his asscheeks in earnest, and they were apparently going to start on Target X, and Tor's cock was *aching* as it ground up against his abdomen.

"I'll love it," Marco whispered, breathing softly on his hole. "Later. When you know who's boss."

And with that, he licked, and Tor was helpless, burying his face into the covers and moaning.

He'd never started here before, he thought almost frantically as he pulled his knees under him. His body felt like it had been hurtled into the stratosphere when he'd expected a few stairs to travel. It didn't matter. His nipples were buzzing, his cock was buzzing, his taint was buzzing, his *asshole was buzzing*. Without conscious thought he lowered his shoulders, reached behind him and spread his cheeks, begging Marco to do whatever he wanted, for as long as he needed.

Marco's chuckle vibrated against all his sensitive places, and he knew his quick and easy surrender had been noted.

A pause followed, and then a little plastic *snick* while Tor tried to get his brain in place, to ask questions, to insist on rolling over, to reclaim some power in this situation, and then—oh God, Marco took him up on his invitation and slid a lubed finger where he'd have begged for one to go if he had any words left.

"Oh God," he moaned, hands dropping as he lay there and shook, his body being invaded, stretched, prepped, and generally taken over by the deceptively sweet-looking man currently fingerfucking him into the mattress.

"Oh, this is a dilemma," Marco murmured, biting Tor's cheek gently, with enough of a snap to make Tor groan again. "Because you look *delicious*. *Amazing* like this. And I could just take you and fuck you and you would be helpless and melty and mine."

His words made Tor's cock ache, made him shake, made him moan, and Tor couldn't give him any alternative plans, any ideas, any suggestions because Marco, doing all the thinking for him, taking him out of his busy brain, making love to him aggressively, without apology, was everything he'd needed in a lover but hadn't known how to ask for.

"But then," Marco murmured, adjusting himself on the bed so one hand could reach under Tor's body and grasp his cock, "it feels like I'm missing something." He thrust another finger into Tor's ass at the same time he stroked Tor's dripping cock. "Another meal course. Because as much as I adore eating, I *love* a good cocktail." He punctuated this with a deeper thrust into Tor's body and a stronger stroke to his cock. "What do *you* think, Tor?"

Tor answered, the word muffled by the covers, and Marco fucked him and stroked him again.

"What was that?" Marco taunted, continuing with his fingers, continuing with his fist.

Tor tried the word again, his entire body shaking. He was at the gates of orgasm so quickly his brain couldn't keep up, his *words* couldn't keep up, and he tried again and again, while Marco tormented him, stroking him, fucking him with two fingers, but not… not….

"*Everything*," he finally mewled. "*Fuck me, suck me, everything!*"

Marco removed his fingers, let go of Tor's cock, and for a moment, Tor wanted to sob, his body trembling with want, with desire, with arousal, and suddenly deserted in its moment of need.

"Anything," Marco murmured into his ear. "Anything and everything you want."

And then he positioned himself and thrust inside, stretching Tor even farther, making him cry out with pleasure, with the welcome bite of pain. Marco's cock wasn't small, and it wasn't thin, and it battered into Tor's body, breaking down any last resistance.

"Good?" Marco breathed when he was all the way seated.

"So good," Tor rasped. "More. Please. More."

"Great."

What followed was the most basic, animalistic fuck Tor had ever had, Marco's cock rocketing inside him, pulling out aggressively, his hips snapping hard to get back to where he belonged. And for the first time in his life, Tor's only job in bed was to be pleasured, to be pummeled and fucked and destroyed, and his noises, already unfettered from the surprise rim job, were breathless, incoherent pleas to do more and more and—oh God.

"Coming," he gasped, surprised, as his body simply surrendered, convulsed without warning, gave in to being owned, to being possessed and taken. "God, coming! Don't stop—"

Marco gave his own cry, pressing his hand to the center of Tor's back, hips rabbiting, hard thighs slapping against the backs of Tor's thighs, his cock *fucking, fucking, fucking*—

Tor's orgasm stole his breath, stole his voice, took over his muscles, shorted out his brain, and pulled the world in tight around the focus of his pleasure, his asshole, where he and Marco were joined.

And then it exploded outward as Marco collapsed over him, hips stuttering as he came hotly, spent himself wetly and without shame inside Tor's willing body.

Tor's cock spat come against his stomach, and his muscles all relaxed at the same time, leaving him facedown, debauched, covered in semen, and wanting very much to clench Marco inside him for the rest of eternity.

Marco joined him, both of them lying half-diagonally across the bed, their breathing filling up the confines of the modest room. "How you doing?" he asked, sounding smug and triumphant and proud.

"I'm ruined," Torrance confessed, not even tempted to twitch his fingers to see if his nerve endings still worked. "I can't move. Your family is going to have to wrap me in this comforter like a burrito and throw me into the cottage like furniture."

Marco's low chuckle warmed him, as did his quick kiss on Tor's shoulder. "I'll move you myself before then. Nobody gets to see you naked but me."

"I'd say cavemen leave me cold, but apparently that's not true." Tor gave a short, bewildered laugh. "Who knew?"

"Hey," Marco murmured, kissing him again. "Don't sound so lost. You didn't know you needed that."

"How did you?" Torrance asked, turning his head to the side so he could see Marco's eyes.

Marco pushed Tor's sweaty hair from his face. "Just knew," he said with a shrug. "You... you do a good job of running your own business, taking all these hard-hitting stories, creating regular content. I've spent hours on your website, watching your segments—it was how I spent my vacation."

"And?" Tor needed to hear this man praise him.

"You're great," Marco murmured. "You know it. But...." He bit his lip, like somebody did if they had a critique they didn't want to share.

"What?"

"I started to be able to tell, you know? When you were working for Felix and the household. I could tell by your smile. I could tell by how passionate you got even if it looked like a fluff piece. I could just tell. And

I thought of all our kisses, and how much you seemed to need me to start them, to finish them, to take them over. And I thought, 'He's smart. And he's independent. But he's dying for somebody to remind him what's important.' I gotta tell you, I fantasized about us together a *lot* while you were gone." He gave a wicked grin. "This comforter has been well laundered, so don't even worry about coming all over it. I've got another one in the closet."

Tor groaned, embarrassed, but Marco kept going.

"Every time I thought about us together the first time, it came down to me telling you that it was okay. You were in good hands." He gave a lazy smile. "And the thought of doing it the way we just did it made me hard *every* damned time."

Tor chuckled and could suddenly move enough to give Marco an almost chaste kiss on the cheek. Marco pecked him in return and motioned for him to stay where he was.

"I'll be back in a sec."

He disappeared into the bathroom—Torrance assumed for a washcloth because wasn't that etiquette? Top had cleanup? It wasn't until he heard Marco gargling that he laughed outright.

"What?" Marco demanded, coming back into the bedroom with a washcloth like Tor had first thought.

"I just… gargling." He couldn't even get himself to talk about where Marco's tongue had been, but he'd been damned glad he'd washed *all* the places, using the detachable showerhead with impunity.

"It's like champagne between chocolate and strawberries," Marco said wickedly, and Tor must have been more out of it than he thought because that stumped him.

"What's strawberries?" he asked, feeling stupid.

But Marco just laughed and washed him off, and then, after getting him to roll over, he washed him off again. But when he was done, he paused for a moment, taking in the sight of Torrance on the bed, regarding him soberly as he wiped off Tor's abdomen, his thighs—his not-quite-deflated cock. When everything was clean, Marco lowered his head and pulled Tor's cockhead into his mouth slowly, lingeringly, gently enough to outweigh any post-orgasmic tenderness Tor might have had.

He took his time pulling back, savoring, and then plied his tongue at the slit, tasting, Tor realized, a tiny droplet of precome that had already gathered there.

Tor shivered, a little chilly but more aroused, and he pushed up on his elbows, trying to get his feet back under him. His control.

Marco grinned at him. "Strawberries," he said, nodding, and Tor had no choice but to grin. "But you're getting cold. Here, get under the covers, and I'll be right back."

Tor did, scrambling because Marco was right, and because it was something simple he could manage, and Marco came back with a bottle of water and the rinsed-out washcloth—and two T-shirts and flannel pajama bottoms he'd pulled out of his own drawer.

"What are those for?" Tor asked, laughing. "I brought clothes!"

"I know," Marco said, shivering and burrowing under the comforter next to him. "But it's colder in the living room, and I didn't want to wander around there naked."

Tor grunted and shivered a little more, welcoming Marco into the cocoon of warmth by wrapping his arms and legs around his body. "But you turned out the lights and brought me a bottle of water," he said dryly.

Marco smiled slyly up at him. "I want you in my clothes," he said baldly. "I… I… you think that was a new experience for *you*, but the truth is, that was amazing for me too. I want you to remember me. To smell me on your skin. To think about me at odd times during the day. For this little bit of time here, you're mine."

"Oh," Torrance murmured, and then he kissed Marco because he had no argument to that. No argument for the courtesy, for the possession, even the knowledge that yes, he would put on Marco's clothes when he got up to use the bathroom.

After.

Their bodies were rubbing together as they warmed, and Tor, already a little drifty from being taken so masterfully, found that his erection wasn't going away. Marco quickly took over the kiss, rolling on top of him and wedging himself between Tor's legs while he went on another adventure quest of Tor's body—this time from the front.

Tor slid his palms down Marco's back, along his biceps, while Marco nibbled his way down Tor's neck and ended up at his chest, at his nipples.

"Don't I get—ah!" Marco began to suckle and lave, and Tor had nothing to grab but Marco's hair while he began to arch rhythmically up against Marco's groin. "I want to explore—oh God!" Marco switched to the other nipple, and Tor had to work hard to hold on to his mind.

"Please," he breathed, and Marco released his latch on the nipple to look up and meet Tor's eyes.

"No," he whispered. "Unless you can tell me you want me to stop, I'm going to take over this time too." He bent down and flickered his tongue at the aroused and aching flesh, and Tor gasped. "Do you want me to stop?" Marco taunted.

"No… don't stop," Tor moaned. "Next time?"

Marco released him again and gazed up into his face. "Someday," he said judiciously.

"I'm not going to—ah! God!" Because Marco's clever tongue was relentless, and Tor's hips would *not* stop rutting.

"What?" Marco teased. "You're not going to what?"

"Run away!" Tor managed, but he was not reassured by Marco's smoky-eyed regard over his body.

"You've been running since we met," Marco told him levelly. "And I've caught you. And you're going to have to do some damned fast talking to get me to let you go."

And with that he captured the nipple he'd left alone for a moment, the one cooled by the air and aching, and suckled on it some more before teasing it gently with his teeth. Tor knotted his fingers in Marco's hair and tugged and released in rhythm, his body already surrendered, even if his brain was still having delusions of taking control.

"No talking," he mumbled. "Oh God… but… but I need…."

"I know what you need," Marco whispered, kissing his way down Tor's waxed chest, down his naked abdomen, to his cock in its trimmed garden. "You need this."

And with that, he pulled Torrance into his mouth, all of him, to the back of his throat, one swallow.

Tor cried out, spreading his legs and massaging Marco's scalp through his hair. Marco kept up the suction, pulling back and pushing forward, slowly, rhythmically, squeezing Tor's base with his fingers, plying his tongue on the head, and Tor could do nothing but cup the back of Marco's head, feeling unbearably lewd, wanton, and needy.

His cock ached and wept with the need to come.

His asshole ached with the need to be taken.

His entire body quaked, on Red Alert: Orgasm Imminent just that quickly again.

"Oh God," he groaned. "Please!"

He wasn't sure when Marco accessed the lubricant, but he knew the fingers that entered him were slick once more, probing gently around his rim, making sure he was ready for this rodeo again.

But fuck ready—he was gibbering, out of his mind, unable to make words or even think about what came next.

Now! Now! Now!

Suddenly Marco pulled back, keeping his fingers right where they were. "Don't come," he ordered. "Not yet."

Tor's entire body relaxed at the command, and while he still shook with need, with invasion and pressure, a part of him had gone limp, floaty, and content, knowing that he didn't have to come yet, knowing Marco would take care of everything.

"Okay," he murmured, his fingers losing some of their tension, his shoulders melting back into the bed.

"Good," Marco whispered, and then he slowed down, teasing Tor's cock a little more, teasing his entrance, rubbing his taint to find out if *that* was sensitive, gently using his tongue and the slightest edge of teeth to tease Tor's frenulum, to see what that would do. Tor let out sounds with every new experience, but no words, no description. His brain was free, floating as his body responded, and his body was gleeful, accepting every new sensation as its due.

Without warning, his cock spurted a blast of precome, and Tor found himself shaking *hard*, sweating, fighting climax with every sinew.

"Just wait," Marco whispered, swallowing and wiping his mouth on his shoulder. He pulled his fingers away, wiping them on the already stained comforter, and moved up the bed, covering Tor's body with his own and placing gentle kisses on Tor's sweaty forehead, his wet cheeks, his chin.

"You're doing so good," he said, lips touching Tor's ear. "Trying so hard to please me. I'm going to fuck you now, and as soon as I'm inside, you can come any time, okay?"

"Yes," Tor whispered back. "Thank you."

"Wait for it...." Marco positioned himself, and this time as he entered, Tor's sensitized entrance felt everything—the flared head, thicker with foreskin, the wide shaft, long and veined, as it slid through his ring. Thrust, thrust... all the way in, and suddenly Tor's entire body unfurled, not in climax but in... oh God. Contentment.

"I need you inside me," he all but sobbed, and it wasn't until Marco kissed his briny cheeks again that he realized he'd been weeping freely, so caught in the moment he'd lost control and hadn't known it.

"I know you do," Marco told him, pulling back slowly and thrusting forward just as slow. "You need me inside you all the time, not only my body, but my heart."

"Oh God...." Because Marco's heart hadn't been the thing that had hit his nerve bundle, *just so*, and Tor raised his legs and his hips, feet in the air, not caring, doing anything, *anything* to feel that again.

"Say you need me," Marco urged, thrusting forward again, and Tor was his.

"I need you," he moaned.

"Say it again!" And this time Marco snapped his hips forward harder, and Tor screamed, the pleasure crashing through his bloodstream in a violent collision, destroying everything he'd ever known about sex and climax in one massive come.

"*I need you!*" he cried, and then orgasm swept through his body, obliterating every defense, every inhibition, every wall Tor had ever erected between himself and another man when locked in this most intimate of dances.

Marco was still fucking him, eyes closed, head thrown back, the cords of his neck standing out in exertion, and Torrance—Torrance's body convulsed again, his muscles completely out of his control, his orgasm riding him as effectively as Marco's cock as he ejaculated again and again and again.

When Marco finally heaved forward and let out a keening cry of his own release, the shock of his second spill of come sent Tor into one more aftershock before Marco collapsed, hips still rabbiting, on Tor's shaking body.

MANY, MANY minutes later—Tor assumed he'd lost time somewhere in the subby, floaty aftermath of what he and Marco had just done—Marco was wiping him down again and helping him into pajamas.

"No underwear?" Tor slurred.

"We may have one more go in us," Marco assured him.

Tor nodded and leaned his head on Marco's shoulder as Marco pulled the bottoms around his hips and then let him sit down again.

"I'm crying," Tor mumbled. "Why am I crying?"

"You're crying," Marco laughed softly, "because you needed domination in bed more than any man I've ever been with. How'd it feel to let go and let me take over?"

"Like I've never had sex before," Tor said, his throat raw. "Why is that?"

"Because I think you've been very self-contained," Marco told him. After a quick little shimmy of his own into pajamas, he laid a clean towel over the wet spot and slid into bed next to Tor, arranging them so Tor's head was on his shoulder.

"Self-*reliant*," Tor corrected, because that at least he could do. "Until this last year, it was only me."

"Mmm." Marco kissed the top of his head. "I figured. You didn't take me home to meet your mother and father. You took me home to meet your real family."

"You were there already," Tor said, and then giggled. "It's true!"

Marco nodded indulgently, although he hadn't argued. "It is. I meant tonight. It's why I dressed up for dinner, right? It was my first time there as family."

"You were already family," Tor mumbled. "I was the outlier. They only call me in at the end, usually. Assume I'm too busy with my own stuff."

"You are!" Marco laughed. "I'm surprised how much you do!"

"Exhausting." Tor hadn't admitted that to anybody before, although Carl and the others had guessed—as had Marco. But the fact that being alone, doing it all himself—yes, Phil was his employee and helped, and Phil was a great guy, but being the guy in charge was different. He remembered when he'd started working for Felix and had worked with a producer. Had enjoyed it, actually. "I miss having a boss. I… the Salingers call me in, and I'll drop any story I'm doing to come help. Felix was a good mentor. Is still a good mentor." Felix had been the one to make a list for him, had resourced all of the techniques that had worked for other independent journalists. Everything from posting regularly to how to get sponsors to monetize his YouTube channel—all of it had been Felix's idea.

"Have you told him that?" Marco asked softly.

"Yeah. But not about wanting a boss again." He grimaced. "I made such a big deal about it. About liking my independence. Doing it on my own. Truth was I just wanted a chance to work with everyone else. Can't do that for the news station." He sighed.

"Is that why you spent a week drunk?" Marco asked, and Tor blessed the floatiness, the disconnection, because that memory, it had no power to hurt him now that he was in Marco's arms.

"No," he murmured, eyes closed. "I was drunk because Jancy Anne Halston wouldn't stop haunting me," he said. "Poor kid. Horrible name. Good father. Old friend." He sighed, blessing this subspace thing because this story was so hard to tell. "Bad end. Found her behind a dumpster. She was fifteen. I got drunk for a week and couldn't forget her face."

He heard Marco's caught breath. "Oh, baby," he said softly. "Why would you hide that from me? You needed all the hugs you could get."

"'Cause I didn't stop it from it from happening," Tor said sadly. "Put off finding her. Thought her father would. She was already dead, but she spent a night out in the cold alone."

"Wasn't your fault," Marco whispered. "I'm so sorry. I'm so sorry."

And like his words were a magic curtain suddenly ripped away, Tor was right back in his own body again and crying one last time, completely and cathartically, for Jancy Anne Halston and the limits of fragile human beings.

Puzzles and Plans

"FRENCH TOAST—WAIT! No! Monte Cristo?" Chuck practically purred. "Oh wow, Marco. You should take Tor to your place more often!"

Marco tried—unsuccessfully—not to preen. "I hadn't made it for you before," he said primly. "I thought you were due."

"I will be due for a calorie diary if you serve this more than once a month." Carl sighed blissfully. "It will be so worth it." Since Michael needed to work on Felix's SUV that day, he'd dropped Carl off at the Salingers' so Felix could drive his and Carl wouldn't be without transportation.

And also, Marco surmised, because Carl would be working on his own job as an insurance investigator that day, as well as mining the information they needed for their silent war on Hepzibah Coulter.

Marco gave him a satisfied smile, not bothering to comment on the sly remarks about Torrance. He figured there were no secrets since Tor had left with him openly and come back that morning to research first and then use the pool.

"I'm sure Michael looks forward to having more of you to love," Molly said, giving him a sideways hug. Marco noticed that Molly seemed to fit easily into the group of men, and they, in turn, treated her like a much-beloved younger sister. It was as though she found safety in the group, although there was also something very… dangerous about Molly. She was like Grace—her heart was big and open, and she was a fearless performer in her own right, he knew that, but she was also wary. With family, she relaxed and hugged and sat in laps and snuggled. On New Year's Eve, when she'd been dressed as waitstaff, Marco would have been *very* cautious about approaching her in any way save, "I'm sorry, could I get another canape?"

"Michael has enough of me to love," Carl told her dryly. "Every time I think I'm fit, I end up in a situation where I regret every last ounce. I still think I could have dodged that knife if I'd been a little bit smaller."

"You're fine," Hunter said, after his own blissful swallow of Monte Cristo in syrup. "Chuck, tell him he's fine."

"He's not my type," Chuck deadpanned, "but he's quite fit. Also, the knife in Martinique had nothing to do with weight or even reflexes. It had to do with you keeping the boat steady so the three of us weren't jumping into the ocean. If you'd dodged the knife, you might have killed us all—don't forget that. You literally took one for the team."

Carl grunted. "You are making that sound way more heroic than it really was. I was single-minded, that's all."

"Well, Michael was aboard their ship," Molly said. "But we've seen you in action, Carl. You would have done the same thing if it had only been Grace."

Carl gave them a beleaguered look. "Fine. Yes. I would have taken the damned knife. I just…." He stared longingly at the Monte Cristo still on his plate. "It's taking so long to heal," he muttered pathetically, and Marco watched as he used his off hand to cut himself a bite.

Dangerous, he thought, some of his good feeling from the night before dissipating. What these people did was dangerous. Uncle Danny had been babying *his* shoulder that morning before he'd left for work with Felix, and while Marco had smiled at Felix's smugness as he cut Danny's ham into bite-sized pieces, Tor's confession, delivered in subspace, had been unspooling again in his brain. They played for keeps. All of them. All the games, all the flirting and the laughter, the raucous dinner table, and all of it was played out in the very real world, and they were going to play this dangerous game for *him*. For *his* family. And if it hadn't been for Clyde Staunton, he would have just blurted out, right then and there, for them to stop.

"Eat your french toast, Carl," he ordered gently. "It was well earned."

"Besides," Hunter said, "aren't you guys getting a dog? I mean, yeah, the elliptical will keep you in shape, but so will running a dog back and forth between your house and this place, because those things have a *lot* of go."

"Unless you choose a basset hound," Molly said. "You're not going to, are you?" She regarded him worriedly. "Those dogs are really overbred, and so are bulldogs. It's really hard on their bodies."

Carl snorted. "I assumed we'd go into the shelter and choose whatever Michael fell in love with. I'm expecting it to have one eye and be the dog equivalent of two-hundred-and-seven years old."

There was a general chuckle around the table. "I'm going the other way with that bet," Chuck said. "It will probably be their most destructive animal in ages, and its primary function will be to eat your house." He smiled. "Which is fine. I'm pretty handy, and Marco knows contractors. We'll keep you in tables, cabinets, and stairway rails as long as you don't break that boy's heart."

Carl cackled. "And thus spake the voice of doom," he said, nodding. "You possibly have predicted my future."

General laughter followed, and then Marco produced the next plate of Monte Cristo. "Who's next?" he asked and then frowned. "What about Grace? Or Josh or Liam?" Stirling and Tienne had already eaten and gone back to Stirling's room—which was *their* room now. Tienne had said something about, "I have ideas," and Stirling had said, "I need to research," and they'd gone. But the others hadn't yet shown up after their workout, and Marco had made enough stuffed french toast for the lot of them.

"I'm here," Liam said, jogging into the kitchen from the hallway. "I'll take a tray up for them."

"What's up?" Chuck asked, eyebrows raised. Then he sighed in exasperation. "Overdid it, didn't he?"

Liam grimaced. "You mean that little dance-off this morning, designed to show us all that Josh was completely fine and didn't need the rest?"

Molly snorted. "When he realizes how easy Grace and I were taking it on him, he's gonna be pissed."

"Dance-off?" Marco asked. It sounded like innocuous fun—but then, so did much of what these people did.

"They've been dancing together since middle school," Hunter said. "Grace is world class, but Molly and Josh aren't far behind."

Molly snorted. "I'm chorus line at best. But we have fun. One of us will do a move and challenge the others to improve on it. We've been playing the game forever, but—" She shook her head. "—Josh keeps pushing to show he's better, and…." She shrugged. "It's going to be a while."

"Well, he's too tired to move," Liam said grimly, "and Grace is upstairs giving him grief so he doesn't get out of bed until I'm back. Anyway, he'll be working from his room for the rest of the day, and I'm going to assume we'll all be on our own." He glanced at Marco. "Tor still working out?"

"Yes," Marco said, quickly gathering enough for a couple of trays. One of them had what he and Phyllis had started to call the "Josh special" on it. Melon and oatmeal, the good old-fashioned mushy stuff, nothing steel-cut about it. When he'd been at the height of his chemo, it had been the only thing that he could—maybe—keep down.

At that moment Phyllis strode in. She took one look at the trays—and at Liam—and her slight smile turned into a hard line of pressed lips. "I was going to tell you to start breakfast for Julia and Leon, who are in the dining room, but I'll do that. You help Liam up with the food." She sighed. "Should I tell Julia?" she asked, and there was a terrible silence in the room.

Even to Marco, the thought of not telling Julia about something that impacted her son sounded like blasphemy.

But Liam didn't seem to see it that way. "Just tell her he's working in his room," he said judiciously. "Grace and I are with him. It's no worries." He took a look at the tray Marco was building. "And between you and me, son, put some of that french toast thing on his plate. If I present him with oatmeal right now, he's likely to throw the whole thing at me head."

The others let out a relieved sigh. This *wasn't* chemo, Marco could almost hear them thinking. This was recovery. It was exhaustion for the things that used to come second nature, but it wasn't sickness again.

"He'll be fine," Chuck murmured, almost to himself.

Liam turned toward him, compassion in his eyes. "Yeah, yeah. No worries. Naught to worry 'is ma over, aye?"

They all nodded mutely, but as Marco followed Liam out of the kitchen and down the hallway, he could swear he heard Chuck say, "We'll know something's *really* wrong when Liam stops speaking English altogether."

"That was English?" Hunter said, completely serious. "Are you *sure*?"

"I'd ask him," Molly answered, "but if he lapses into full cockney, I'm lost."

Marco and Liam rounded the last corner to the stairway, and Marco heard Liam snort softly in the front.

"Guess the accent got a bit thick," he said, just loud enough for Marco to hear.

"It was so close to American English," Marco said apologetically. "*So* close."

Liam chuckled, but it came out strained. "Do you know what Josh and Grace do for fun?" he asked as Marco made it up to the landing.

"Hack the Pentagon?" Marco said, only partway kidding.

"Good guess, but that's Stirling's gig. These two—I've got footage, yeah? They go BASE jumping off buildings in Chicago. Those suits that open up like a flyin' squirrel's and send them swirling the air currents trying to avoid traffic. You see those idiots that do that?"

"It's terrifying," Marco had to agree, thinking now he knew who'd done that and made the news the year before, and Liam paused before taking the turn in the corridor that would lead to Josh's room.

"It is," he said, his expression troubled and yet resigned. "But there's nothing for it. Can't take the trouble out of the boy without taking the joy, right?"

And there was Tor, in his arms again, weeping himself clean over somebody else's sins.

"Right," Marco agreed, not even sure what he was agreeing to.

Liam took the remaining few steps, then knocked on the door and announced room service. Grace was the one who greeted them, taking them into Josh's suite, which was bigger than the guest rooms, but not so big it took up the entire wing of the house. Marco looked around curiously, noting the queen-sized bed in the corner, under the window, and a solid oak pedestal with matching end tables and desk. The foreground of the room was dominated by a comfortable den-style couch and two recliners in front of a wide-screen TV—not a wall-dominating wide-screen like the one in the den downstairs, but the standard wide-screen that was found in most American living rooms, hooked up to all the gaming stations, all neatly arranged in the cabinet under the set.

The decorations were young—but not cheap. Framed prints of ballets that Grace had danced in—Marco could see his name in the credits—and shows that Josh had probably acted in, although he wasn't always the lead, mixed with bands that Marco enjoyed too, and a few memorable framed art prints that looked to be *very* high quality, including a Renoir that had its own lighting and apparently a temperature-controlled, museum-quality safety-glass frame that was so brilliant Marco could swear he saw the brushstrokes.

"Grace, what's for breakfast?" Josh asked from his place on the bed, legs crossed, laptop in front of him. He glanced up and grimaced. "Sorry, Marco, I didn't mean to pull you out of the kitchen. I'm sorry. I should have gone down and got my own, but—"

"But you fell getting out of the shower, you idiot," Grace told him without embarrassment. "Which would be sad and pathetic, but I'm over it. Sit until it won't happen again. Eat. Sustain life. Give me orders. I'm bored."

"You want orders?" Josh asked sweetly. He took a deep breath and grimaced. "Okay, I've got some orders. Go research the kinds of locks and securities used by most warehouses. None of it is delicate and smart, but a lot of it is *muscular*. You might need more than the standard gear, but you still have to be ready for heat and light sensors, deal?"

Grace perked up, his sullenness melting away. "What *sorts* of warehouses?" he asked cagily.

Josh gave him one of those looks among friends that meant "Stop screwing around, moron," and blew out a breath. "Look—every sweatshop she's ever owned, complete with slave labor, has depended on a workforce locked in the basement of her property. We need to *check first* to see which of her properties is housing her sweatshops. Then we'll need to run a con—or an exposé—on her teams that go out and pretend to work for other contractors. Then we need to *con her*, getting her to commit all her money to something so we can take her for everything she owns right before we throw her to the legal wolves."

"Why?" Marco asked. "I mean, not that she's a good person, but why are you robbing her first?"

Josh glanced at him in surprise. "Well, for one thing, to reimburse her victims, because what they'll get from the courts is bullshit. But for another, to make sure she doesn't have the capital to throw at a thousand lawyers. We want her to *overcommit*. Maybe spend some of her father's or husband's money too so we can implicate *them* and *really* piss them off. I mean, there's no *promise* we can win the trifecta on this one, but I don't want her buying a fancy trial lawyer and a judge out of this."

Grace let out an evil chuckle. "I want that chair in the magazine," he said. "The ugly one covered in fake zebra."

Josh wrinkled his nose. "What for?"

Grace shrugged. "So when Carl and Michael get a dog, we let the dog sleep on it and pretend it's suffocating Hepzibah witch lady in her sleep." His eyes went to half-mast with dreamy anticipation. "That'll be great."

Josh's eyes grew really wide. "Just, uhm, never co-opt any of *my* furniture, okay?"

Grace sniffed and glanced around the room. "None of this shit is tacky enough for that fate. It's got to be *really* ugly for furniture to figure into my revenge fantasies."

They both nodded, completely simpatico.

"And that shit was *really* ugly," Josh agreed. "I get it."

Marco busied himself setting the tray up on a rack next to Josh's bed, and Josh squinted at him as though trying to remember something.

"Oh!" he said after a moment, the confusion on his face clearing. "How's Tor?"

Marco felt heat creep up into his cheeks. "Good," he mumbled, trying to remind himself that he'd expected this at some point. These people *cared* about Torrance, and if you cared about somebody, you grilled their new lovers *unmercifully*.

"Don't sell yourself short," Grace said critically. "You're cute. I'm betting Tor's *great* right now, but what Josh meant was, how are *you guys*?"

Marco gave him a flat look. "I can translate friend-speak," he said.

"But can you speak it?" Grace asked, eyes growing mutinous, and Marco took a breath, remembering what he'd *just thought* about family and friends.

"Sorry," he said, meaning it. "I'm just… you know. We did… we had a really nice—" That was dumb. "We really enjoyed ourselves." That was also weak sauce. "I…."

He glanced up and met three sets of patient eyes, waiting for him to get his shit together.

"It was perfect," he said at last, smiling a little. "Hopefully as perfect as he deserves. You'll have to forgive me. I keep trying, but it's harder than it should be, getting used to the idea that you're all family. I know Cammie and Frankie are going to grill Tor like you're grilling me, because you want to make sure the person *we* picked isn't going to hurt us. But the lot of you are... you know."

"Overwhelming," Liam said. "We get it. Let's have it sit with 'as perfect as he deserves,' and you're off the hook."

"Oh my God!" Grace said suddenly, and they all glanced at him to see him swallow the first bite of Monte Cristo from his tray. "Josh, eat this! It's heaven!" He took another bite and swallowed, humming in his throat like somebody who lived to serenade his food. "It's a good thing you want to treat our friend right," he said, humming again. "Because it would really suck to have to fire someone who can cook this good because he was a douche."

Marco laughed. "I promise," he said, and this was *easy* to say, "that I would never, ever risk Tor's feelings by being a douche."

"Goolb," Josh said, his mouth full of Monte Cristo. He swallowed and let out a breath. "Because *that* is the food I've been dying to eat since July."

Marco grinned. "I'll remember that," he said. He sobered. "And don't worry—I'll remember to treat your friend right."

"Good," Josh said, taking another bite. "And thanks, by the way. I was half-afraid I'd end up with oatmeal again."

Liam winked, and Marco shot him a quick grin. "And with that," he said regretfully, "I should go downstairs and help Phyllis."

They all nodded, and then Josh said, "If you get a chance, come up when you're on break and I'll run you through what we've got. If you could quiz Frankie and Cammie about some stuff, I think we might be getting near a plan."

Marco's grin went full throttle. "That's good news. I can do that," he said. "Thank you."

And then he absolutely had to go or Phyllis would filet him when he got back down.

WHEN TORRANCE wandered into the kitchen, less than an hour later, he looked tired but happy.

"Good workout?" Marco asked, moving to fix him a plate.

"Great workout," Tor said, and then, a little panicky, "but Monte Cristo?"

Marco regarded him levelly, reminding him without words of that moment of intimacy, revealing their bodies in the lamplight, and Tor's granite-cut abdomen.

Tor's cheeks colored. "A small portion, please," he asked humbly, and Marco gave him a smug smile.

"Wow," Tor muttered, mostly to himself, "I had no idea that bottom was a way of life."

"It's not with most people," Marco said happily. "I think you've needed someone to step in and care for you for a while."

Tor shook his head, refuting that, Marco thought, in one last-ditch bid for independence.

"I was fully grown when I left home," he said sullenly.

"You're not fully grown *now*," Marco told him. "I mean, you've got the posh apartment and the slick clothes, but that doesn't mean you don't need a keeper."

Tor raised an eyebrow. "That's ridiculous," he said, pulling his dignity back on. "I was just fine a—"

Marco kissed him before he could say it. He didn't want to hear how great Torrance had been doing alone when Marco was absolutely certain the man would do so much better with Marco in his life.

And that's where they were when Julia bustled in like a snow flurry, full of enough energy to level a city, Leon di Rossi a quiet, baffled shadow behind her.

"Pardon, gentlemen," she said with no compunction whatsoever. "Torrance? What sort of clothes do you have here at the moment? Anything in a day-formal flavor?"

Torrance had pulled back from the kiss and was blinking rapidly, as though trying hard to orient himself to the here and now. "Off-white wool suit with a winter-blue shirt?" he asked.

Julia made an appreciative moue. "With your black boots?"

"Yes, ma'am," he said. "Why?"

"Because I put out feelers with my friends last night, and there is a fundraising event at Kemper Lake's Country Club in two hours. I have it on good authority that Hepzibah Coulter-King and her mother, Traci Coulter, will be in attendance."

"Ooh...." Torrance nodded. "The possibilities are endless. Do we have a plan?"

Julia tapped her lower lip with a manicured finger. "I think…." In a moment she'd straightened. "Torrance, I think you'll escort Molly, Chuck will escort me, Grace will do catering, Hunter will do parking lot surveillance, Stirling will work the hyperbolic mic in the van, and Josh and Carl will be here on overwatch. What say you?"

"I can't escort you?" Leon asked, sounding genuinely hurt, and she turned to him, her own look of bafflement in place. Leon was, Marco had often thought, one of the most brutally handsome men he'd ever seen, complete with a pointy bad-guy beard, a precise haircut, and lounging clothes that appeared to be made of silk and wool.

"Darling," she said, her head tilted. "This isn't a 'show off your beau in front of your friends moment.' Believe me, when I have one of those, you will be front and center. This is a job, and we all have our specialties."

Leon still looked hurt. "Don't you trust me to bow to your direction?" he asked, and Julia's blue eyes had gone wide and a little lost.

"I just…." She let out a breath and turned to Torrance as though he were her only ally.

Tor, obviously, was not buying into it. "You know," he said, "I'm going to go get into costume and alert the others. Any orders?"

She bit her lip. "Tell Molly to meet me in the panic room for hair and makeup in ten," she said decisively, before giving Leon a searching look. "And tell them that Leon will escort me and Chuck can be our friend along for the ride."

Leon's triumphant smile visibly brightened a white-tiled kitchen.

"Chuck can fill in when I'm absent," he said. Then he deflated a little. "When, of course, Felix and Danny aren't available."

"Well, darling," Julia said, obviously recovering some of her equilibrium, "I am a woman with responsibilities. Now come, we have very little time to be on the road."

They left, and Tor almost departed on their heels, but Marco stopped him.

"Not even a bite?" he said, feeling oddly hurt.

"A bite," Torrance teased gently, "or a kiss?"

Marco brightened. "I'll take a kiss," he said, because that was a no-brainer. Torrance took his mouth then, and Marco was reminded that as much as he needed Marco, he was also very used to being in the thick of it and making decisions on the fly.

When Torrance pulled away, his eyes were bright and sparkling, and Marco was suddenly *very* curious as to what was so exciting about a society luncheon. He'd catered quite a few of those and had always been of the opinion that his food was the most exciting part of the afternoon.

As though reading his mind, Tor said, "You know, once you're done down here, I bet you can go join Josh and the others in overwatch. Ask him if he's going to work from his room or the den."

"His room," Liam said, striding down the hallway. "And please, Marco, do join us. In fact, if you can pull in your cousin at the last minute, Josh got hold of the guest list. There's quite a few contractors and construction firms represented. Cammie might be able to give us some info."

"What are you doing?" Torrance asked curiously.

Liam scowled. "I've got phone calls scheduled with the people Hepzibah mortally offended in India and the Philippines." He cast a hunted look over his shoulder toward the bedrooms. "Besides, he's *supposed* to be resting today. Carl, Tienne, and I will be making sure your overwatch doesn't fall asleep in the middle of giving orders."

Torrance nodded. "Well, we've got a full day today." He winked at Marco. "I hope you're ready."

And with that, Tor and Liam disappeared down the hallway, leaving Marco to call his cousin and then hurry up with the rest of his morning. He'd be damned if he missed what was coming next!

Lunching with Crocodiles

"MOLLY," TORRANCE said gallantly, "if I wasn't gay, I would have married you by now."

Molly—dressed stunningly in a cream-colored wool tea-length dress with a blue belt that complemented Tor's shirt to perfection—threw her head back and laughed.

"If you weren't gay, the looks Marco's been giving you would have turned you that way," she said, and he could tell by the way she shook her head she was missing her waist-length ringlets. Julia—with some help from Phyllis and, oddly enough, from Grace, who had spent much of his life in the backstage of a theater—had swept Molly's hair back from her face and off her nape in a seemingly casual chignon.

"Lucky for us both they would have worked," Tor said, preening a little. The hunger on Marco's face had been mighty gratifying as they'd all waited in the foyer for Chuck and Leon to pull the vehicle around. Leon drove the large SUV, which held the people *actually* attending the luncheon, while Chuck took an unaccustomed seat in the back. Hunter drove the electronics van, with Stirling and Grace. Stirling would stay inside the van, working on surveillance with short-distance bugs and mics. Josh could manage overwatch—the coordinating of all the parties—from his room, with a little help, but if they were going to plant bugs on the spot, there needed to be somebody nearby.

In Torrance's ear, a voice in the nearly invisible bug he was wearing said, "Tell my sister to stop preening. The mic in her hair thingie keeps jostling around."

Torrance grimaced as Molly made a face. "You heard that?" he asked as both of them approached the entrance to the country club.

"Just once, he should be the one dressed up at one of these events," she murmured under her breath. "If I kept nagging him to look at the mark, he'd jump out of his suit and go running naked into the day."

"You can keep hoping for that," Stirling taunted over their earpieces, "but it's never gonna happen."

Tor and Molly met eyes and smirked, unable to answer him because at that moment they were approaching the entrance and Julia was presenting their—forged—bona fides.

"Tienne wants to know how the papers are doing," Josh said, him and Stirling both on the same frequency.

"Waiting," Tor sang softly into the speaker. Tienne was a brilliant artist in his own right, who painted original works that Felix and Danny quietly sold when he'd let them so they could get his art into the world. Tienne was *also* a brilliant forger, who had been able to study a computer scan of the invitation—and ask the bearer a couple of questions about paper quality and watermarks—and produce an exact copy in the hour and a half everybody had needed to prepare. Nobody asked what he was doing with exactly that kind of pricey card stock, just like nobody asked what he did with the eighty different passport covers representing nearly every corner of the globe.

The woman checking invitations didn't even bat an eyelash, and Julia, Chuck, and Leon entered in grand fashion, Julia locking elbows with each man at her side, followed by Tor and Molly, both of them smiling gaily at their gatekeeper as though they couldn't imagine anything grander on a Friday afternoon than to dress up in winter formal day wear and drink watered-down champagne.

"Oh goodness!" said the woman. "Torrance Grayson? I had no idea you were on the guest list. How wonderful!"

Tor grinned at her. "A fan?" he asked, genuinely touched.

"Well…." She grimaced. "Let's say I've seen some of your work. It—" She glanced around as though this was a well-kept secret. "—doesn't often show the wealthy in the best light. It would be *great* if you could see the good work we're doing here." She smiled prettily then, and he realized that she was young, with only the lightest bit of makeup. She had a round face and a plump bosom, and good will and good intentions practically radiated off her, and he had a sudden thought of Jancy Anne Halston.

The subtly cutting retort about the good works that cost $500 a plate died in his throat.

"I'll look with an open heart," he assured her, and she sent him a glance of supreme gratitude.

"Thank you," she said shyly. "That's all we can ask."

As he and Molly proceeded into the pleasantly decorated clubhouse, Josh said, "Marco wants you to know that was kind of you."

"She didn't make the world's problems," Tor said with a sigh, seeing Jancy Anne Halston in his mind's eye. "She's doing her best."

"A thing we must all remember," Julia said grimly, and as Torrance looked up to see who she'd seen, a praying mantis of a woman with banana-slug lips walked up to Julia, her countenance contorted into a smile.

"Julia!" said the woman, striding aggressively forward and grasping Julia's two hands in her own before air-kissing both cheeks. "So good to see you! I had no idea you were on the list of invitees."

"We had invitations," Julia purred. "Tracy Coulter, I want you to meet my friends—this is Charles Calder, fiancé to Lucius Broadstone, Leon di Rossi, who owns di Rossi Imports, Torrance Grayson of *Shades of Gray*, and Molly Christopher, lead actress in the upcoming version of *The Miser* for the Upswing Theater Company. Everybody, this is Tracy Coulter, the wife of Congressman Gregg Coulter. She organized this event. Say hello!"

"Oh my God, Mom," Josh's voice said in their ears, "you crashed the bad guy's party? You didn't tell me this was thrown by Hepzibah Coulter's family!"

"Hello, Mrs. Coulter," Torrance said smoothly. "So wonderful of you to invite us—we're awfully glad to be here."

Tracy Coulter's expression froze. "Torrance Grayson?" she asked woodenly. "Didn't you do that hit piece on poor Marion Kavanaugh?"

Torrance frowned. "You mean make her position on women's health care absolutely crystal clear?" he said, as though he hadn't corralled the woman in front of her club and told all of Chicago that she was waging a one-woman war on abortion rights.

"She was mortified!" Tracy Coulter said unhappily.

"Well, maybe if she's embarrassed to have that opinion, she should rethink it," Torrance responded. Then he gave his sweetest, most television-worthy smile. "I'm sure all *your* opinions would be welcome on my show, Mrs. Coulter. Right?"

"I'm sure they wouldn't," she replied with a hard look. "I'm not sure how you lot managed to finagle your way—"

"Torrance!" Tor turned his head quickly as a familiar voice penetrated his thoughts. "Oh, God, Torrance Grayson. I've been trying so hard to get hold of you. You have no idea how happy I am to see you today."

As though in a dream, Torrance turned toward a tall middle-aged figure whose shoulders were just beginning to hunch, and his heart lurched in his chest.

"Professor Halston?" he said, his voice laced with compassion. "What are you doing here?"

Professor Hugh Halston, Dean of Studies at Tor's old school, gave Tracy Coulter an almost embarrassed glance. "My wife asked to have a booth here—you see the tables? How each one features a different dish? Each table is fundraising for a cause and—" He swallowed, his brow wrinkled in grief. "—Michelle wanted to host a table fighting opioid addiction."

Tracy Coulter appeared distinctly uncomfortable, and Tor sent her a poisonous glare. This woman's husband was in the pockets of the pharmacy lobbyists, and Tor knew for a fact that the local police hated his guts because every time they started to make inroads on the crisis, Gregg Coulter proposed another law to make it harder.

Tracy Coulter had let Michelle Halston host the table to make her husband look good or Tor wasn't wearing his shiniest, most comfortable ass-kicking half boots.

"I would *love* to come speak to your wife," Tor said softly. He reached into his trousers and pulled out his phone. "If you like, I can do a brief spot with her, and we can really sell her cause."

"Don't forget to mention my name!" Tracy cried as Tor, Molly in tow, began to follow Halston away from the foyer and across the room.

"Oh, I won't," Tor shot back, and in his ear he heard a collection of snorts and relieved sighs.

They were *in*.

MARCO GAVE a sigh of relief as Torrance followed his old professor to the table representing his charity.

"My mom," Josh muttered.

"Titanium ovaries," Liam muttered succinctly, and Josh met his eyes and nodded fiercely. Marco remembered when he'd asked how much good Julia Salinger could *really* be in a tense situation, and he felt a little foolish now. Apparently she was made of Kevlar-coated stainless steel if she could swim in *that* shark pit and emerge unscathed.

Josh had put his and Stirling's computer feeds up on the big screen in his room, and Marco, Camille, Carl, Frankie, Phyllis, and Liam ranged about the recliners and the couch while Josh sat in the center, hunched over his keyboard. He'd set the sound feeds so that whenever he highlighted a camera shot they could hear that sound, and about the time Marco figured out how to listen to everybody at once without getting confused, he realized two things.

One was that *most* of the luncheon was arranged so that guests could visit the various white-clothed tables at their leisure and snack and chat and hopefully donate to the cause, tastefully represented somewhere nearby, whether on a small poster tripod or on brochures spread artfully on the tablecloths. Some of the causes weren't bad—Professor Halston's table sported a high-end rehab for opiate addiction. It wasn't exactly priced for the masses, but addiction sucked on every level, so Marco was on board.

He'd spotted a cancer ward for a children's hospital at one of the tables, and several scholarship programs. All in all, there were worse ways for the rich and bored to spend an afternoon.

Of course not every cause was one the Salinger house would have endorsed. Antiabortion was represented, as were parent groups that pushed for anti-LGBTQ laws, censorship, and book banning. Marco was busy scowling at the Parents for Purity table—which served hot dogs, of all things—when he heard Josh speak urgently into his mic.

"Grace, that's not what we're here for."

Grace's murmured voice could be heard clearly in the quiet room. "I'm a genius, Recovery Boy. I can multitask."

"Oh shit," Josh murmured, right when Carl said, "Hell no," and Liam snapped, "Fuckin' Jesus."

As they watched, Grace—dressed in the same waitstaff uniform as the other staff members, which he'd probably had to steal since they were all wearing blue waistcoats with their standard black slacks—bussed the anti-LGBTQ table. Every now and then, as he moved about, sinuous and graceful, Marco could hear gasps coming from the three Salingers in the room and—he was starting to realize—from the other people on coms.

"God, he's good," Stirling muttered.

"Don't tell him that," Josh muttered back. "He's already taking risks."

"Ooh!" Carl hummed. "Damn, that was close. I would have been so busted."

That was the first one Marco saw. While he'd been staring at all the other people in the highlighted section of screen, the people concentrating on Grace himself had apparently seen Grace lifting wallets and cell phones—at least three of each—and slipping them into his pockets. Josh and Stirling's feed was apparently wired directly into the security cameras in the country club, and as with most security cameras, there were holes.

"Down the hall to the left" came Stirling's voice. "Past the men's bathroom, one step, two… there, turn right."

"It's a closet!" Grace squeaked.

And then he disappeared from view.

But they could still hear his voice. "First phone," Grace murmured. "Stirling, you getting the clone?"

"Yup. Carl, you getting the intel?"

"Yup. Good call, Grace. The guy used the same picture on his Parents for Purity card that he did for his Grindr profile. Oooh… look at that."

"Ew," said Camille, who was peering over his shoulder.

"What's the problem?" Marco asked, leaning a little closer to the formidable Carl.

"His Grindr profile says 'the younger the better.'"

"Oh God," Camille muttered. "Think it gets worse than that?"

Carl "*hmm*ed." "I. Hope. Not," he said grimly. "But I'll be researching. Stirling, do we have the next one?"

"We do," Stirling said. "Grace, we've got people coming down the corridor. Hang tight for a couple of minutes."

"Can do," Grace whispered. "Do my marks suspect anything?"

Josh pulled up the feed from the front of the house, and they all swore. One of the men was starting to pat down his pockets, frowning, and it was going to be *much* harder for Grace to return a phone and a wallet someone knew was missing.

"Yes!" Josh hissed. Then he hit a button and spoke again. "Head's up, guys—we need a distraction for Grace!"

"For Grace to do what?" Julia asked, and while they could all see she was smiling graciously at Leon, her voice was frantic with worry.

"He pulled some wallets and phones. Chuck, your two o'clock—"

"Got him, Josh," Molly said, and she broke away from the party itself, like a woman with a purpose, and made her way to the table with Grace's mark. After a few strides, she turned her head and said loudly, but not crassly, "Oh look, Tor. It's your least favorite table!" before accidentally on purpose stumbling into the guy starting to pat down his pockets.

The jowly, middle-aged gentleman may have been a horrible human being, but he'd been raised in the age where women were helpless, and he immediately took his hands out of his pockets to keep Molly upright.

"So sorry," she said. "I'm just a mess on heels!" And with that she extended her leg to show off her sapphire-colored heeled half boots while she batted her eyes coquettishly at her rescuer.

The man made avuncular noises about what pretty shoes she had while Josh switched coms and whispered harshly, "Grace, you've got three people coming in each direction. Stay put." He hit another button and hissed, "Somebody get in there and help her. Believe us, this guy isn't as fascinated by Molly as he's pretending to be."

"It's like the girl is cursed," Julia said in astonishment, referring to the fact that they couldn't find a straight guy for Molly *anywhere*.

"Well, in this case the curse is working for her," Josh hissed. "Tor, what are you doing?"

"Hold up," Torrance whispered. "I've got an idea."

They looked over to where Tor stood, talking earnestly to the people at the table for the rehabilitation facility while holding his phone out and filming. He stood patiently, a kind smile on his face, while the middle-aged man spoke passionately about his daughter, and Marco had a sudden realization.

"Oh God," he murmured. "That's Professor Halston. See his name tag?"

"Oh dear," Julia said softly. Then, "Leon darling, could you go free Tor up?"

"How? Those people are getting some great publicity—"

"This is where we throw money at a problem, dearest," Julia said, steel in her voice. "Molly can't keep that man's attention for much longer, and I understand Grace is trapped somewhere with his wallet."

Leon's eyes went wide. "Next time," he said, his full mouth taking a firm line, "I get a com." And without another word, he strode over to where Torrance stood, one hand going for his wallet.

"Well, hell," Julia muttered. "Charles, that leaves you and me. Shall we go see what Tracy and Hepzibah are raising money for?"

"Prolife charter schools that believe in kitten-fur jackets," Chuck said, with an edge to his voice that indicated he might not be completely kidding.

"The society for the protection of straight white Christian males," Stirling muttered, as though it was a completely valid guess.

"Aren't those incel groups?" Hunter asked from his place in the valet lot, parking people's cars and snooping through their glove compartments. "Because I'd love to meet one."

"An incel?" Chuck asked. "Why?"

"A group of them," Hunter retorted, dropping something unwholesome-looking into the console storage compartment of a champagne-colored SUV. "I think we could have fun together."

Cammie leaned toward Marco and said, "His idea of fun sounds like it's got a whole lot of broken noses in it."

"And some concussions," Frankie added, admiration in his voice. "What's he putting in the cars?"

Carl was the one to answer. "Raw squid, I think." He checked something on his computer. "Since one of the tables is serving fried calamari, I think that's a good bet."

"This is a pretty polished operation," Camille said. "You guys do this a lot?"

Carl gave her a gentle smile. "It's one of Julia's favorite ways to shake out the cobwebs. I do miss the canapes from when I'm on escort duty."

Marco met Phyllis's eyes, and she nodded, texting something to Darcy, who did the shopping. Marco didn't even have to ask—he was pretty sure calamari and tempura were on the shopping list for that night.

But what was happening on screen in front of them was too riveting to ignore for long.

"Oh look," Josh said, glancing up from his feed. "Uncle Leon is writing a check."

As they watched, Leon di Rossi smoothly usurped Torrance's place as Torrance was filming the spot, pulling his checkbook out as he did so. With a concerned smile, he maneuvered the Halstons away from the rest of the crowd while Torrance Grayson, without warning, blossomed into the showman Marco had seen him become on his videos.

But only the ones he'd really loved.

The country club was designed as a half circle with a flat side, the flat side being the bank of windows that peered out over the snow-and-ice-covered golf course, which, Marco had to admit, looked absolutely lovely for something that had no use at the moment whatsoever. But the center of the circle—if there had been one—was a microphone stand, behind which a quartet of musicians was currently resting. Marco had heard music when their party had entered, so, lucky Torrance, he didn't have to butt into somebody's chamber music.

"Hello, hello, hello!" he said, his voice echoing through the PA system. "So good to be out this afternoon. Many, many thanks to Mrs. Tracy Coulter for inviting me!" He turned and gave her a bright smile and a cheery wave as she manned a table for....

"Oh God. The NRA," Carl muttered. "We're going to hell for this."

"But look! Hepzibah's with her!" Chuck said, a note of triumph in his voice, while in the front of the country club, Torrance kept talking.

"So I'm Torrance Grayson, independent reporter. I can see a lot of you know me." With that, he smiled at a table representing a prominent conservative politician who recently voted against free lunches for school children—a cause Tor had been quite vocal about in one of his casts. At his coquettish little moue, the table—mostly older white women—went from puckered lemons to blossoming roses.

"Oh my God," Marco said, gazing in awe at the expressions on the women's faces. "They are *melting* into his hand."

"And a wonderful young lady asked me as I entered if I was going to find the good being done here. Bless her heart, which I think is a good one. So I've got a challenge for you all. If you want to be featured in my next spot, meet me in that corner—" He indicated the far corner of the club. "—

and come answer the question, 'What good is my organization doing in the world?' And the best answer will get a feature in my show!"

There was a lot of excited chatter then as each table chose a representative to go earn some free publicity. And in the meantime, the hallway had cleared, and their mark had stopped checking his pockets.

Josh spoke into the com. "Grace, you can come out now. Replace the wallets. Then could you hit Tracy and Hepzibah Coulter's table next?"

"Can Stirling siphon all their money into a fund for widows and orphans?" Grace asked irritably.

"Let's wait to see how much their victims need," Josh said. "Widows and orphans get the leftovers. Right now, you're there for intel, remember?"

"Fuck," Grace muttered. "No, I did not remember. Thank you, Recovery Boy."

"I got your back, boo. Now Torrance is making a helluva ruckus out there for you. Use it."

"Roger that."

Josh wasn't overstating things. As Torrance swaggered through the club, using the window line as a pathway, a chattering gaggle of luxuriously clad women began to follow him like a peacock tail. Torrance had left the mic on the stand, but his natural projection made it easy to follow his progress as he charmed and cajoled them into getting into a straight line, one speaker per table.

Molly had disentangled herself from the bemused mark, and he was focused on Torrance as well, hunger in his eyes, as she made her way to his side to take his phone and act as his camerawoman while he drew the focus of the entire room his way.

Marco was so enthralled by his performance that he almost missed Grace returning and slipping the phones and wallets back into the pockets of his original marks. By the time he saw the gentleman with the icky dating profile patting his pocket and appearing *really* relieved, Julia was at Hepzibah Coulter's table, having a conversation that involved a *lot* of pointed teeth and some words that, Marco was sure, would cut like scalpels.

"Mrs. Salinger," Tracy Coulter said, her voice never losing its edge. "Were you thinking of giving to the NRA?"

"Only when they change the *R* to stand for Rainbow, I'm afraid," Julia said with a laugh that rasped like sand. "I was just swinging by to make sure Eppie is okay." She used the diminutive of Hepzibah's name, and Marco noticed that neither of the women seemed to notice.

"Smart, Julia," Carl murmured next to him, his fingers flying on the keyboard. "Most of her stuff is probably under Eppie."

"Okay?" Hepzibah asked. She looked, if anything, *more* garish than in her magazine layout picture. She was wearing silver lamé in deference to the luncheon's theme, but the fabric was less than optimum, seeming like a child's parka instead of the bodice to an expensive day dress. Her wool skirt was bright white, and the belt she wore with it navy. The skirt was cut in a clunky square that was probably meant to be avant-garde but instead made her very slim hips appear much wider. Her hair—streaked an ice blond—had been pulled back so severely from her face that Marco could see the thin spots from his place on the couch.

"Well, yes, dear," Julia said, her face set into kind lines. "That review of your spring line that just hit *Elle*? Brutal, darling. Completely unfair. I'm sure you can sue the judge for slander."

"*Elle?*" Hepzibah said blankly, her face assuming the stricken expression of someone who recently had her heart ripped out.

"*Vogue* too, Mom," Josh whispered. "*Vogue* called her 'trailer-trash billionaire with the sensibility of a color-blind wombat with a roll of tinsel.'"

Julia's eyes widened almost imperceptibly, while everybody in Josh's bedroom sucked in a pained breath.

"And the *Vogue* review was a farce, darling. We all know it," Julia told her, sugar dripping from her voice.

"Mother?" Hepzibah mewled. "Mother, look it up! See if she's telling the truth!"

Tracy had been minding a tablet set up on the table in front of her, probably to monitor donations, and in a moment she'd accessed the pages she'd been searching for.

"Oh, Eppie," Tracy said a moment later. "Honey, I'm so sorry."

"Mommy?" Hepzibah's voice was cracking, and as Tracy wrapped her arms around her distraught daughter's shoulders, Hepzibah began to sob. In any other group, Marco surmised, that might have brought comfort running from the corners, but here he saw several people actively glance away.

Which was fine, because they didn't see Chuck fiddling with the monitoring device in his pocket that had picked up on the password that Tracy had entered into the computer and was currently cloning all the cloud information it could get.

"You getting the intel?" Josh asked.

"Sure am," Stirling's voice came over the coms. "All we need is—oh. Thank you, Grace."

"Wait," Marco said. "What did Grace just do?"

Carl turned his head slightly. "You didn't see him lift Hepzibah's purse with her phone in it?"

Marco gave him a blank stare. "That is *uncanny*," he muttered.

"Oh my God," Camille and Frankie said in unison, and Marco turned to them both as they held their hands to their mouths.

"Josh!" Camille said. "That last screen you were looking at. The one where Hepzibah and her mother were crying because somebody said something mean about her clothes. Can you pull that up?"

"Yeah, right there?" Josh pulled the screen up again, although by this time the two women were mopping up their faces with tissues Julia had offered. Behind them, a big bruiser of a man in a fabulously cut suit was glaring at somebody off-screen, and Josh said, "Uh-oh. Hunter, Grace is coming out of the east service exit. He still has Hepzibah's purse, but there's a guy built like a tank with a broken nose who—oh, there he goes—is hot on his scrawny ass. I think he's going out the fire door instead. He may need an intervention."

"Goddammit," Hunter muttered, and Josh switched to an outside camera that featured an exterior shot of the building with a small door in a corner—and nothing else.

"Where'd he go?" Camille asked. "Your friend—shouldn't he be—"

"Whoamygod!" everybody in the room exclaimed.

The man Camille and Frankie had spotted suddenly burst out of the side door, with no Grace in sight, and as the door to the exit sprang back, Hunter, wearing a black balaclava over his head and face, seemed to drop out of the sky onto his head, fist cocked back.

By the time he'd borne their bruiser to the ground, Hunter had driven his fist into the guy's temple, and he was completely unconscious.

And then Hunter disappeared.

Not really. They all saw the blip on the film that ate up his figure. In fact, probably ate up the entire scene, but Marco realized that Hunter had made it easier by running flat-out in the camera's blind spot and using the man's dramatic entrance onto the frame as the perfect moment to attack.

"Wait," Frankie said. "Where's your little thief—oh. There he is. How'd he get back inside so fast?"

"Servants' entrance," Liam told him. "Josh used their prep time to download schematics. Grace has an eidetic memory, when he cares to use it. He ran back, gave Hepzibah's phone to Stirling, Hunter nailed his guy, and Stirling gave the phone back to Grace and then scrubbed the video." He shook his head. "I swear to God, I'm glad they're on the side of the angels. If I had to track these gits down for crimes, I'd be wasting my life."

"Technically," Camille whispered to Marco, "aren't they *doing* crimes?"

Marco shrugged. "But aren't they on the side of the angels?" he asked, and Cammie shrugged back.

Apparently so.

Breathlessly they watched as Josh pulled up the feed from inside the clubhouse, where Tor was wrapping it up with the last couple of "contestants" for a publicity spot on his channel. Julia, however, was still at the table with Hepzibah and Tracy, pulling tissues out of her clutch to comfort Hepzibah because "Eppie's" purse had somehow disappeared.

"Camille," Carl said urgently. "Give me details on the bruiser who's semiconscious in the snow."

"Jimmy Flat-Nose," Frankie said, when Camille struggled for a name. "I think it's Kaminsky. He works for Weurther's Contracting."

"A competitor?" Carl asked, starting another screen to Marco had no idea where.

"Dad's biggest." Frankie scowled. "They've been snapping up bids from under our nose all fall."

"But have they been doing it under their own name?" Carl murmured. "Hold on a sec. I have it here somewhere...."

They let Carl do magic and focused back on the screen again. Hepzibah was having herself another good old-fashioned ugly cry, while Tracy fruitlessly tried to comfort her. Julia stood politely nearby, and not even an eyelid flicker betrayed that she was waiting for Grace to return with Hepzibah's purse.

Which gave the people on the monitors unfettered access to Hepzibah's audio. "Money.... Mommy, the money. I can't... this will ruin... I owe so much!"

"Oh wow," Josh murmured. "Carl, Stirling, did you catch that?"

"The criminal owes people," Carl said. "Which means—"

"She probably owes other criminals," Stirling murmured. "Okay, that's my specialty. I'll pull that thread."

"He's very good," Tienne murmured, and Camille gave him one of the openmouthed smiles she'd give one of her nieces or nephews, the kind that said she saw and appreciated all that sweetness of heart.

"'Course he is," she murmured, patting Tienne's arm.

"Oh, look," Stirling's voice came through. "Guys, our enforcer is waking up. Grace, where are—oh."

As they continued to watch Julia's feed, Grace came cruising back, almost invisible, and dropped Hepzibah's purse on the floor by the table to be "found" later. "Grace," Josh said, "it's time for you to hoof it out to the second car. Hunter, where are you?"

"Delivering more fish," Hunter murmured into his coms.

"You got my back," Grace said happily.

"This'll be great, baby," Hunter told him. "It's freezing—nobody will smell a thing until the vehicle sits in a heated garage."

"It's like a signature," Grace said, sounding very earnest. "Every douchebag in Chicago will be afraid of douching in public in case the fish hits the car."

"That's lovely," Chuck murmured, still behind Julia's shoulder. "When can we bail?"

Julia barely suppressed a sigh and handed Tracy her last tiny tissue case, gesturing apologetically toward the next table. Tracy nodded, stricken and overwhelmed, and together Julia and Chuck made their way toward Leon, who was waiting patiently near Tor's old friend.

"Is he almost done?" Julia asked, batting her eyes prettily at Leon.

"Another half hour," Leon estimated. He cast a glance around the room and spotted a table with a children's hospital logo prominently displayed. "But in the meantime, I've donated to this place before, and they're offering brisket and asparagus sliders."

Julia batted her eyelashes. "I am feeling a bit peckish."

Leon offered his elbow. "Shall we?"

"Join us, Charles?" Julia asked, and he offered his elbow as well.

"My pleasure, Miss Julia."

The three of them sat and scanned the room desultorily for any other information while Grace quietly made his exit. The other van would change location to just beyond the parking lot so Grace could slip away unseen.

TOR AND Molly were the last to leave, a bevy of socialites waving a gay goodbye as they left.

As they neared the foyer, Torrance spotted the young woman who had so earnestly entreated him to try to find the good in the fundraising groups. She was slumped dispiritedly at the now-vacant registration table, scanning her phone.

"Goodbye," Tor said gently, offering a wave, and she gave him a look, complete with wobbly lower lip and wide, limpid eyes, one step away from a full meltdown. Tor and Molly glanced at each other and then approached while Molly pulled out her phone and texted briefly.

"Honey, what's wrong?" Torrance asked.

The girl held up her phone. "You interviewed people," she said, her voice fractured.

"Well, yes." Tor smiled, although in his heart, he knew what this was about. "Just like you asked me to. I asked people what good their causes did in the world."

She nodded. "And you let them talk."

"I did."

"And then you asked questions."

He and Molly glanced at each other. "That's my job, sweetheart. I'm a reporter."

She swallowed. "Their answers… weren't good."

Ah. "What do you mean?" he asked softly.

"Well, like my sister was with the prolife charity. You remember her?"

He did. Young and idealistic, she spoke passionately about "saving the babies from heartless women."

"I do. She had a good heart."

The girl nodded. "She does. She loves babies. But then you asked her if she knew what an unborn looked like at six weeks, and she didn't, and you gave her a… what was it?"

"A coffee bean," he said. Molly had slipped it into his hand before he'd done the interview.

"Is that true?"

"Yes, a six-week embryo is smaller than a coffee bean."

"And then you told her that the coffee bean could kill a woman if it was in the wrong place."

Tor nodded. "Yes, ma'am. Ectopic pregnancy."

"And doctors couldn't save a woman's life if the stringent abortion bills were passed."

"It's already come up in some states," he said softly. "That's true."

She nodded. "I know. I googled it." She held up her phone. "So I guess the other things you talked about were true."

"Yes, ma'am." He regarded her soberly.

"And the more my sister tried to explain, the stupider she looked."

Molly grimaced. "Not stupid, honey. Misinformed. There's a lot of misinformation out there right now."

The young woman nodded and wiped her face on a napkin. "And my sister wasn't the only one who looked stupid. A lot of the girls had their friends video their interviews—they were so proud. And a lot of them didn't see it. But most of those people you interviewed, they… they didn't look as smart as they thought they were."

Tor sucked air through his teeth. There'd been a lot of unconscious entitlement on the floor that day—a lot of harmful misinformation. Three-quarters of those interviews had been enough for him to lose hope in mankind completely.

Not all of them, though. "But some of them really did," he said softly. "The people who wanted new oncology equipment for the children's wing of the hospital? How'd they come out?"

"Really good," she said with a laugh. "And the people representing the rehab center were good." She swallowed and gave a soft smile. "And the place that repurposed prom dresses, gave kids with less money a chance to go to the prom—they were so pure."

"Honey," Molly said, crouching down by the young woman. "You're having trouble, aren't you? You want to do good work in the world, and you just found out that not every charity is really… charitable, didn't you?"

She nodded miserably. "I… I want to make a difference. Doesn't everybody?"

"They do," Molly said. "What you have to ask yourself is, 'Am I making someone else's life *better* or am I making *myself* look good?' Do you understand?"

The girl nodded slowly. "A lot of the loudest people are making themselves look good," she said, with dawning comprehension.

"They are indeed." Tor gave her a smile. "But think about this. You challenged me to find the good in that room, and there were some worthwhile causes that I'm going to put up on my channel because there *was* good in that room, and *you* believed in that. Don't despair because you're seeing some things in a new way. Hope, because now you know you can make change happen. You're really good at it, in fact."

She gave him a watery smile. "Thank you, Mr. Grayson," she whispered.

"Thank *you*—" He peered at the name badge she'd pinned to her dress. "—Belinda. You keep using your brain *and* your heart. You're going to do great things."

Molly's phone buzzed insistently. "And now we have to go," she said with a wink. Since she was closer, she offered a hug, and the girl gave it to her before Molly grabbed Tor's hand and ran through the foyer doors to the vehicle Chuck had waiting outside.

Good Trouble

"OH MY GOD," Camille murmured as Torrance and Molly came through the doors and Stirling killed the feeds. "That was a *rush*."

"Right?" Marco said back, his heart thundering in his throat. "I can't even believe they all did that!" He glanced over to where Josh and Carl were working and noticed Josh catching a yawn behind his hand. He caught Phyllis's eye and glanced at Josh again, and she nodded.

"Liam?" she said softly, and Liam saw the same thing.

"Give him a minute," he told her. "I think they're trying to consolidate information while it's all still fresh in their minds."

"Understood," she said and then got to her feet. "Marco, Cammie, Frankie? You want to help me take the lunch trays downstairs?"

Marco checked his watch and tried not to groan. He had about half an hour before he needed to start dinner prep. But then, as he followed Phyllis out the door, he looked behind him and saw Josh yawn into his hand again before slumping against Liam, seemingly without realizing it.

Cammie was right. It *had* been a rush. But none of it had been as easy as it appeared.

"Phyllis," Josh said through yet another yawn, "I might not make it down to dinner, okay? Send Grace and Stirling up with a tray, maybe? We can—"

"Tell everyone we'll have a mini-meeting at breakfast tomorrow," Liam interrupted, blowing his breath out in a huff. "And of course Grace and Stirling can come up with a tray, but no talking shop after four o'clock."

"Are you *high*?" Josh started to complain, obviously bristling.

And then he yawned *again*.

"God*dammit*!" he swore, and Carl closed his laptop and stood, following Liam's lead and gesturing imperiously for Josh to close his own, which he did reluctantly.

"Tienne," Carl said mildly—nobody spoke any way but mildly to the slender, elfin Tienne—"do us a favor and find something fun and not too serious on television for Josh to watch." He moved into Josh's space and tugged the laptop from Josh's reluctant grip. "Moderation," he said gently. "For everybody." Then *he* yawned. "I'm going to avail myself of my room and take my *own* nap."

Phyllis allowed the door to close, and Marco followed her downstairs.

"They do take care of each other, don't they?" Frankie asked.

"Family," Marco told him, and then yawned. "Seriously, I wouldn't mind my own nap."

"We need to take off anyway," Cammie said. "Dad can't miss us for much longer."

"You can nap downstairs," Phyllis told him. "But I'm thinking the sooner you move into the cottage, the better. Saturday and Sunday, right?"

"We'll be here with bells on!" Camille said. "And Frankie's big-ass truck."

"And your brother's," Frankie said. "Ozzie."

Marco nodded. Ozzie—the brother who most likely needed employment help, but also the brother most likely to be there with his truck or a casserole when needed.

"And then on Sunday night, I guess we're having the strategy meeting," Camille summed up. She patted Marco's arm. "So while we're hauling shit into your new digs, your peeps are going to be putting together a plan. Damn, Marco—it's like we sold you to Star Fleet or something. I cannot overstate how very cool your new job is."

Marco laughed. Mostly he couldn't argue.

TOR FOUND him, half an hour later, resting in the den where Phyllis had shooed him. Tor had changed into sweats and moccasins, but the smell of expensive wool and cologne still lingered, and Marco breathed him in as he sat on the couch and leaned his head on Marco's shoulder.

"Wow," Marco murmured, kissing his temple. "Just… wow."

"Yeah?" Tor asked slyly, and Marco had to laugh.

"Are you fishing for compliments?" he asked.

"No," Tor told him smugly. "'Cause we were *awesome*."

"Baby," Marco said, absolutely impressed, "I'm… *wow*."

"So much good stuff," Tor murmured happily. "It's going to be a hell of a strategy meeting."

"Mmm." Marco pulled him tighter. "Come home with me again tonight?"

"Yeah."

"Good. Nothing I saw today made me want you any less."

"Good," Torrance murmured. "Good."

They dozed then, both of them, until Phyllis came to wake Marco up for work. Once again Marco left Tor down there, covered with a blanket, fast asleep.

THE NEXT two days were a buzz of activity for Marco and his family—but as busy as they were, he had the feeling it was *nothing* compared to what the Salingers were doing. Chuck, Hunter, and Carl were deployed on various errands. In one case, the errand involved a rather shady part of town and a trip to a used car lot with Michael, Carl's boyfriend, to help them purchase an SUV that was a little battered but still sound.

All of this Marco noticed on the periphery. Torrance begged off helping with the move—he spent his time putting together the small ten-minute spots that Danny had suggested. The information they'd gotten at the luncheon had made everybody certain that the spots would be best released over the next two weeks. If nothing else, they wanted to get Clyde back to Marco's family as early as possible. From what Marco could see, *everybody* was pitching in to help Torrance get it done. Between editing, fact-checking, media research, and script writing, Marco would walk into the dining room and see six people bent over their computers and hear, "Tor needs some footage of the sweatshops in the Philippines," to be quickly answered by, "I've gotcha, mate—do you need some law enforcement comment too? I can secure some for you, rights granted."

"You're a lifesaver, Liam," Tor would answer. "Send me that stat."

And the hum of activity would resume, to be interrupted by the next request down the table.

Marco usually worked the weekends, particularly when the Salingers entertained, but Phyllis had given him the extra days off and pulled in some part-time staff who kept the lot of them well supplied with sandwiches, including the guys Marco tended to think of as "the away team"—Hunter and Chuck, and sometimes Danny, Carl, or Grace. (Basically the guys who could clear a kitchen in five minutes or less, except for Grace, who seemed to live on cookies and coffee and not much else.) Before Marco's newfound knowledge and intimacy with the family, he would have said they were spending the weekend doing business as usual, but now that he knew, he could feel the hum of suppressed excitement permeating the household.

And he could feel the worry knotting his stomach when the stakes they were playing for were made excruciatingly clear.

With his family's help, Marco had cleared out his apartment on Saturday and—after sleeping in Tor's room in the mansion that night—had unpacked and put together enough to be able to pull Tor into *his* room on Sunday night. He was looking forward to that and ready to shelve the rest of the unpacking to another day when he crunched his way through the snow and into the foyer. He divested himself of his jacket and boots and walked into the kitchen in the soft-soled slip-ons he kept at the coatrack for work, happy about helping with dinner before he changed to eat with the family.

What he found was chaos.

Julia stood at the island counter with a pad of white towels and a first-aid kit, cleaning Hunter's hands with antiseptic and giving him the tart side of her tongue.

Josh and Chuck were back against the refrigerators, sitting on Grace.

Sitting on him like he was a bench while he swore like a sailor, in at least three different languages.

"Hunter, I do believe you should have trusted a hospital to this," Julia was saying crossly while she applied butterfly bandages to the first of four split knuckles with exquisite care. "They could stitch these up in much more sterile conditions."

"They're fine, Julia," Hunter placated. "The guy was quick, is all. I got the wall and not his face."

"You fuckwads can let me up now!" Grace hollered.

"I don't know, Josh," Chuck said, grunting with suppressed effort. "Does he feel calm to you?"

"We'll let you up," Josh said through gritted teeth, "when you promise not to freak out!"

"*I'm not freaking out*!" Grace hollered. "I just need to kill someone! You understand. It's for the greater good."

"We're not that kind of outfit!" Danny snapped, striding into the kitchen with enough force to make Marco wonder if he hadn't grown taller. "Grace, you be still right now!"

There were a couple of loud deep breaths and finally a chastened, "Yes, Uncle Danny."

"Josh, you get off him first, and bend down to help him up. Chuck, if he can control himself once Josh gets up, you can get up too, but be ready to grab him and throw him outside if he starts to lose his shit."

"Right, Uncle Danny," Chuck said, eyebrows drawn into a dark frown. "He's bucking like a bronco."

"You've seen him dance," Danny said with a sniff. "Did you think he was made of feathers? Now, hold on, Grace. I'm going to check on Hunter first."

"He can't die," Grace said, sounding sniffly.

"Of course not, precious," Danny said patiently. "Nobody dies in Phyllis's kitchen. It's a rule."

Once the kitchen had calmed down a tad, he turned toward Hunter.

"How are you doing?" he asked softly.

"Feeling stupid," Hunter muttered. "Julia's right—I would have caused less trouble if I'd gone to the hospital and had them stitch me up before I came home."

Danny let out a breath and chuckled. "But you wanted to be home and feel safe, didn't you?" he asked kindly.

Hunter, oh he of the stalwart face and bearing, looked a little sheepish. "I admit it. I heard my knuckles crack on the wall, Danny. I really wanted to hold Grace after that." He turned sharply as Josh and Chuck assisted Grace to his feet and dusted him off. "As long as he wasn't completely psychotic, that is."

Grace nodded, all contrition. "I'm really much less stupid now," he said, like a recalcitrant schoolboy. "Can I go hug my boyfriend?"

Danny nodded. "Gently, precious. Julia is doing her best here, so you can't bump him too much."

Grace stood, and after giving Josh and Chuck wary looks, moved carefully into Hunter's space. Hunter used his free arm—the one with the hand that had already been bandaged—and wrapped his arm around Grace's shoulders.

"I'm fine," he said matter-of-factly.

"You're not supposed to get hurt," Grace whispered, burying his face into Hunter's shoulder.

"I know, baby. But you know better than that. This was a couple of security guards who moved a little faster than we anticipated. No big deal."

Grace nodded and simply stood, trembling, while Josh and Chuck stretched themselves out as though they'd just done a core workout.

"Rough?" Marco asked dryly, shooing them away from the refrigerators so he could make sure the meat for dinner was marinating.

"My stomach muscles are going to hurt for a week," Chuck muttered. "That kid's wiry, but he's *strong*." He eyeballed Josh. "You?"

Josh grunted. "He hardly even knew I was sitting on him. It's a good thing you were there or he would have beaten my fragile bones to powder."

"I would not," Grace snapped from the haven of Hunter's one-armed embrace. "I was fighting Chuck. I'd never hurt you."

Josh and Chuck exchanged patient glances. "I know you wouldn't have, moron," Josh said. "I'm just saying. I will *never* forget my vitamin supplements. I need to be strong enough to sit on you for real."

Grace gave a smug little grunt. "It'll never happen. You weren't that strong before you got sick, and you're not going to suddenly develop superpowers in the next six months. I'll be able to beat you at a dance-off for the rest of our lives."

"Ha!" Josh taunted. "I will beat you eventually. You'll get cocky, and then you'll get sloppy, and Molly and I will dance circles around you."

Grace stuck his nose in the air. "You tell good jokes, Recovery Boy. Keep laughing."

Josh got close enough to lean his head on Grace's shoulder briefly before he moved away. "Laughing my ass all the way out to the dining room, where I've got one last thing to do before dinner."

"Next time," Grace chided Hunter, "you'll let me come."

"That is a big no," Hunter replied with amazing speed. "No, sir, no, little buddy, hell no, holy shit no, no to the tenth power."

"So maybe," Grace said, with a straight face.

"Absolutely fucking not," Hunter told him with a definitive nod. "Danny?"

"We've made improvements to the panic room, Grace," Danny said. "It should only take you about fifteen minutes to break out, but in the meantime, he'd be well down the road, and you wouldn't even have access to the computer feed."

Grace let out a disconsolate sigh. "What happened?" he asked, and Marco was suddenly super grateful to be in the kitchen julienning steak, because he wanted to hear this too.

"It was so dumb," Chuck said. "We were checking out her properties—in this case, the one in the garment district where she's making her clothes. We've been there a couple of times before, so we thought we knew the guards' schedule, and we were halfway down the fence when a new set of guards came by." He blew out a breath. "We sort of had to knock them out before we could get out of there—the only way back was over the fence."

Danny's eyes grew large. "Well, is that the only way in *now*?"

They both nodded glumly, and Danny gave Grace a long-suffering look. "I hate to tell you two idiots this, but...."

"No." Hunter shook his head.

"Aw, Danny, no," Chuck begged, but Danny was merciless.

"You actually *do* need a world-class thief!" Danny said in frustration. "And he needs our two enforcers to keep him safe. Wait until Hunter's knuckles have healed a little and then go back—bring Grace and someone to sit in the van as overwatch. It can be Carl if you want, but yes. This isn't just a two-bruiser job. What were you thinking?"

Hunter grunted and turned away from Grace's furious reproof. "All our geeks have been working on the rest of the plan, Danny. We didn't want to disturb them."

"Well, better we lengthen our timeline by a day than you get hurt, do you understand me?"

Chuck and Hunter sighed. "Yes, Uncle Danny."

Then Danny turned to Grace. "And you, precious, will make your point much better if they don't have to sit on you as you scream your lungs out. Do you understand?"

Grace grinned. "I was right?"

"Oh God." Danny pinched the bridge of his nose.

"I was *right*!" Grace crowed, and Hunter and Chuck glared at Danny.

Danny glared back. "This," he said grimly, "is entirely your fault. You deal with it." He checked Julia's ministrations on Hunter's knuckles. "And you, as always, are doing an amazing job. Do you have the rest of it, dear one?"

Julia preened. "We're fine in here, Danny. Go help them put the presentation together."

"Of course."

The kitchen was a little calmer after that, but Marco was reminded, in startling scarlet detail, that the job the Salingers were doing for him and his family was *not* without its risks.

Including the risk to Torrance, who had been in Marco's bed for less than a week, but Marco was discovering to be harder and harder to live without.

Places, Everybody

PHILLIP WAS looking a mite ragged as Tor teleconferenced with him before dinner, but he also looked proud as hell.

"This?" he said, waving his hands at his screen—and at the five spots that they'd produced in record time. "This is a thing of beauty. This isn't just going to expose these fuckers—it's going to seep into the public consciousness one tiny little nugget at a time."

Tor grinned. "There's some good stuff there, right?"

"Oh yeah." Phil blew out a breath. "Tell me this won't be the last time we work together."

Torrance could see the tiny window reflecting back his own puzzlement. "Huh?"

"Well, you've obviously got a new production crew, Tor," Phil said, trying to muffle his own hurt, and Tor laughed.

"This is a onetime thing," he assured his friend. "No—this was… well, consider it synergy. Like the Gunrunner's Island thing. I was in the right place at the right time with a bunch of people who thought it would be fun to help. No." He sighed, remembering the crush of responsibilities that came from owning his own business. "As soon as the last one of these goes up, it'll be back to business as usual."

Phil sighed too. "You know what I miss?"

"Health and dental?" Torrance asked, because it had taken a chunk out of their revenue for sure. "The big full-service editing desk? Paid vacation?"

Phil nodded, putting his finger on his nose. "I do," he said seriously. "I… I mean, I wouldn't mind doing spots with you part-time, but boy, I wouldn't mind working for Felix again."

Torrance nodded. "Do you want me to put in a good word for you?" he asked. "Felix would take you back in a heartbeat."

"Well, yeah. But I'd like to keep working with you too."

Tor thought about it, thought about the pride that had kept him from giving in to Felix's entreaties to come back to work. Thought about Marco, taking the small, less famous road to a career he loved so he could have time to eat with his family once a week.

"Let me think about it," he said, giving a tired smile. "Maybe there's a compromise or something."

"If you mean compromise as in your own cable show, with your own production team," Felix Salinger said, sticking his head into Tor's bedroom to get his attention, "yes. Yes, I will compromise with that. Hello, Phillip. We need Torrance for dinner now. Nag him, won't you? I miss him at the station."

Phillip began to chuckle. "Oooh.... Daddy's so mad he's going to give you your own show."

Tor felt a little glow of hope, of happiness start in his chest. "We'll see," he said, but Phillip nodded knowingly.

"Yeah, wait until I tell my wife. She'll be thrilled. Peace!"

And with that he logged out of the conversation, and Torrance glared unconvincingly at Felix. "Who are you, Satan?"

Felix gave an evil cackle. "I don't know why you're so surprised. I've been trying to lure you back to the station since you left."

Tor nodded. "Yeah, but at first, I thought, 'Go back and do the same ole same ole? I wanna do something new!'"

"And you did." Felix nodded. "You did it amazingly well."

"And then I kept doing it with your family," Torrance laughed. "And it was... it was *amazing*."

Felix nodded again. "I won't argue."

"And now...." Tor bit his lip. "We could do a mix of formats, right? So I could be on the spot sometimes and offer commentary and have guest speakers and—"

Felix grinned. "It'll be great. Phillip in the booth with you, right? I've got the time slot and everything."

Torrance grimaced. "Can we... can we see how this goes first?" he asked. "The minispots leading to the big bust? I need this to go well."

Felix nodded. "Yeah. I get that. Not that I think you'll bollix this up or anything, but...."

"I just want to see it through," Tor said, feeling surprisingly earnest. He'd gone it alone because he thought that was his only option after he left the station. But now he really wanted to work with Felix again, especially now that he and the Salinger crew had done such great things together already.

"Fair. Now let's get downstairs for dinner." Felix scanned Tor's room for a moment before he turned away.

"What?" Tor asked him.

"Just wondering," Felix murmured, "if you want us to move the Chagall cats into Marco's apartment. You know, as the landlord, I'm saying you could probably get a real cat as well."

Tor felt a blush starting as they moved down the hallway. "Moving a little fast, you think?"

Felix snorted. "No, Gray—I don't. I've seen this coming since December. All those earnest discussions in the kitchen after we'd all worked out. My God, it's a good thing you don't carry government secrets."

Torrance glared at him. "But we've only… you know. Been… uhm…."

Felix turned to him, frowning. "You mean the sex thing?" he asked, for the first time in their acquaintance sounding more *dad* than any dad had a right to dad.

"Yes, the sex thing," Torrance muttered, although they'd slept in the same bed for the last three nights together, and Marco had… oh God. Mastered his body, heart, mind, and soul every damned night. Even the last one when they both should have been too exhausted to move. "Isn't there a rule? Six months of sex or something before cohabitation?"

Felix regarded him with pity. "So you keep the apartment in Chicago, the room in my place, and you sleep at Marco's three nights a week. I mean, I love you, Gray, and I don't mind supplementing your lavish lifestyle, but isn't this a bit grandiose, even for you?"

"I *really* don't want to give up the apartment in Chicago," he admitted. "It's so close to your office, and it's so nice when I stay in the city, and—"

Felix arched an eyebrow. "It doesn't mean you *can't* stay here," he said. "It just means, say, we can put Liam in your room instead of Danny's study."

"Isn't he going back to the UK?" Tor asked regretfully. He liked the young Interpol officer, and as much as he'd carried a torch for Josh, he thought Liam was a much better match.

"When we're done here," Felix said carefully. Then he gave a smile that was all teeth. "But we'll find a reason for him to come back here eventually."

Tor gave him a mild expression. "Interfering, Felix?"

Felix looked like he was going to play coy, but he grew sober as they got to the bottom of the stairs and followed the hallway to the dining room. "Living with someone isn't easy—even at the best of times," he said quietly. "But then, Danny and I haven't really had the best of times until this last year. It would be… quite wonderful, I think, if we could give Josh some of the freedom—the approval—we never had."

Torrance nodded, suddenly just as serious. "My little room has been quite the sanctuary," he said after a moment. "Can we keep it as is for a little while longer?" He sighed. "I mean, Marco hasn't even really unpacked."

"I'm just saying," Felix murmured, "make sure he leaves some room for your stuff. Those prints are Tienne reproductions, you know. First rate copies."

Tor clutched his chest. "And you're giving them to me?" he squeaked. Tienne could sell his forgeries for almost as much as the real paintings were worth—and that was when people knew they were reproductions.

"Consider them a housewarming gift," Felix said grandly. "No matter which home you decide on." They left the relative peace and quiet of the hallway and burst into the dining room. "Oh, Marco. Bacon-wrapped filet— you are *spoiling* me!"

"I like to watch Carl and Torrance try to stick to vegetables and then give in," Marco said with a straight face. "It's why I learned to cook."

"Dia*bolical*," Carl muttered, and as Torrance sat down next to Marco, the Salinger table talk commenced.

AN HOUR later, they were gathered down in the den, and Tor was amused to see two giant urns of coffee had been prepared and left, complete with cream and sugar stations, next to the cookies. Today's selection tended toward giant cookies with a little bit of crisp on the outside and a sweet squishy doughy middle.

Tor grabbed his snickerdoodle and his coffee and made his way to the console, since it was decided he and Josh would present.

"Ready?" he asked Josh, and Josh nodded grimly. The first thing they put up on the screen was a recap of their goals—because it was important.

Goal 1: Free and place the forced laborers
Goal 2: Exonerate the contractors implicated by the scam
Goal3: Expose the entire Coulter family and make them accountable

The family studied the goals for a moment, and Josh spoke into the silence.

"You can see that the last one has become more about the Coulter family than only about Hepzibah. Mom, do you want to elaborate?"

It had been Julia who had prompted the change.

"Watching Hepzibah come unglued on her mother the other day made me realize a couple of things," she said. "One—yes, she *is* so self-centered that her reviews are more important to her than human suffering, so she needs to be held accountable. But the other thing is that she alone did not create this mess. She's not *smart* enough to create this mess. Her mother enabled her, as did her father and her husband and even, I think, Mr. Flat-Nose. Felix, Danny, and I took it upon ourselves to view their spending habits and emails, and we found definite connections between the awful things Hepzibah has done, the awful things she was *told* to do, and the expectations thrust upon her. As the saying goes, vanity working on a weak mind can produce all sorts of mischief, and that's what happened here. Danny?"

"Agreed. But taking a congressman down can be harder than it should be." He grimaced. "The most we can do is expose him publicly and then hand over all our intel to the proper authorities. Anonymously, that is. But still, public opinion can be a *very* powerful weapon. And that's where Tor's spots come in. Tor—what do you think? Do your spots implicate the entire family?"

Torrance grimaced. "I may need to add some more footage," he said, rapidly sifting through his information. "But since I'm adding to the later spots, I don't have to do it before the first one's on the ground and running. I think we're good to go."

"Okay," Danny said. "That's good. Which order are the spots coming in?"

Tor held out his fingers and outlined his programming plan, starting with the abuse of the disabled and, with Felix's suggestions, ending with the family reaction to the scandal. That last one drew a shocked silence and some displeasure from the crowd. "You really want to give these people a platform?" Camille asked.

Torrance shook his head. "Here's the thing—you all remember the benefit luncheon, right?"

They all nodded.

"Well, when I aired those, I aired a chyron of actual cited statistics under the people talking. So, say, the people at the rehab facility got the cited statistic for how many spots there were in rehab clinics across the city versus how many people there were in need."

"Good one," Josh said. "That way people realize this cause is very necessary."

Torrance nodded. "Exactly. And for the girl spouting all the misinformation with the abortion statistics, I ran the actual procedures, plus the statistics of maternal complications brought about by the draconian laws enacted in some states. And the result…."

"Oh, she looked stupid," Molly said, nodding with satisfaction. "I mean… *really* stupid. She'll be the most hated girl in her dorm at college."

"Ouch," Stirling muttered.

"Women who vote against their best interest irritate me," Molly told him. "Fair."

"So you see," Tor intervened, "sometimes, showing the truth and the lie side by side can generate more understanding. I'm saying we get some video—edited, of course, to protect the victims—of the forced labor being liberated, and we air it side by side with Hepzibah Coulter saying some bullshit. And then, when her mother tries to cover for her—"

"We air the email quotes where she's telling her daughter that she needs to do what's necessary to not make her father angry," Grace said.

"And," Tor continued, nodding, "then we get her father and her husband denying everything, and we air it side by side with their text messages saying the people she's scamming deserve it and giving her pointers."

They all shuddered. The extent of the family's corruption had been detailed and boggling.

"There's only one problem with all of this," Josh said. "And it's all good stuff."

"What's that?" Tor asked.

"Timing," Danny said thoughtfully. "Timing and extra cameramen. I know you have a ride-or-die cameraman you've worked with before—would he be willing to do some work on this?"

"Absolutely," Tor said, knowing Phil would do it for free once he heard about the forced labor. "But I think we've got a couple of people here on the crew that I can train to do basic camerawork," he said. "Tienne?" He looked at Stirling's quiet boyfriend, who nodded excitedly. "Frankie?" Marco's cousin nodded too. "I've got enough equipment and handhelds that if we need to interview everybody at the same time, I think the cameraman there while the marks are taking questions from the crowd will be enough."

"I've got a lot of different aliases," Tienne said happily. "I could give Marco's cousin one too."

"I'll have a secret identity," Frankie said proudly. "Fuckin' awesome."

"Okay," Danny said, nodding. "Fair enough. So now that we've started with our third goal first, Josh, how about you walk us through the rest of it."

Josh grinned. "You'll be so proud, Uncle Danny," he said, and while the last few days had been exhausting for all of them—Josh especially—in that moment, as Josh began his slide show, he practically glowed.

THE PLAN, when it came down to it, was pretty simple—but like Danny said, it all depended on planning, timing, and media exposure.

Over the weekend, while part of their team had been putting together the media package, "the away team," as Marco called them, had been identifying the sites where the scam contractors were currently working, as well as where the forced labor was being housed—and taking video footage too.

"We got our best hit when Torrance tracked Marco's uncle to the factory in the garment district," Josh said. "Chuck and Hunter—" He gave them grim looks. "—got confirmation of armed guards this afternoon, and they also hooked Stirling up to some off-site cameras so we could scan the footage. The top three floors of the factory are used to make the ugliest clothing known to man. But the plans—filed at the county, by the way— say the basement has been fitted with a couple of bathrooms. We spent the last hour before dinner scanning off-site video at superspeed over the last few days. We saw…." He swallowed and sighed. "We've got footage," he said. "There's about thirty of them, some of them—maybe eighteen—big, so helpful with construction, but we've got footage of them leaving early in the morning, before the clothing workers get to the factory, and arriving late, after they've left. Their handlers all look a lot like Cheezer—low-level thugs and criminals, some of them armed." He frowned. "But… uniform. You see it once you see Cheezer in their ranks—and dressed in black jeans and black leather. I'd almost suspect mob muscle—even that Jimmy Flat-Nose guy—because I'm getting a real vibe off them. And very few of them besides Cheezer are popping facial recognition, so out of country too. Mostly they use physical violence and intimidation." His voice cracked a little. "The laborers don't have hats or gloves," he said, sounding impossibly young himself. "They're all too thin. And I'm betting the basement isn't heated. Anyway—" He let out a measured breath and looked at Liam, who nodded. "—we've got enough on film so that, if we can connect Hepzibah or any member of her family with those workers—and I think we can—we can nail them."

"So what's the play?" Hunter asked into the angry silence.

"The place is armed and well-guarded," Josh said. "As you two found out today. Danny's right, we need a thief. But a thief usually needs a way in." He hit a few keys on the keyboard. "And this is where I open the floor up to discussion."

Danny grunted. "Well, if this was anywhere else but our own backyard—and someplace half of us have just made a very public debut at that—I'd suggest a fake investor ploy. Hepzibah *must* be hungry for investors. Her company is about to take an ice bath, given the bad press on her latest line, and as Julia reports, she's terrified her father and husband are going to cut her off. If this was the old days—and we were in Europe—Fox and Julia would get themselves an invite to the business office and ask for a tour of the factory. Once they were in the factory, one of them would excuse themselves to use the can and let me in through a back door."

"One of them?" Molly asked suspiciously—although she was one of their best when it came to thinking on her feet.

Danny shrugged. "It would depend on the rapport, because you never know who's going to be the best bait. We once got access to a Renoir because one of the most famous bigots of Italy got a hard-on for Felix that could have cut glass. It's a crapshoot."

"Oh God," Josh moaned. "I so did not want to know that."

"But Danny's exploits you can hear about from dusk till dawn?" Felix asked, affronted.

"Uncle Danny's the fun dad," Grace told him, with that "duh!" tone that young adults could use. "You have no penis, Mr. Josh's Dad. Stop talking about it like you have one."

"I hate you, Grace," Josh muttered, banging his head softly against his desk.

"You love me, you have always loved me, and you'll love me until we go out together doing something stupid," Grace said, and the rote way he said it told Tor this was something they had agreed upon a long time ago.

Liam, who had made himself comfortable next to Josh as always, caught Tor's eye. "The scary thing," he said, loud enough for Tor to hear but still under the chaos that had erupted in the room, "is that they've made plans for this. 'Something stupid' is *not* a vague, amorphous something idi-fuckin'-otic. There are *specific* stupid things they've planned to do when they're ninety to make sure they go out together."

Tor knew his eyes grew large, and he felt his skin go clammy. "If you have any care at all for me," he said, thinking that he cared very much for Josh and had developed a real soft spot for Grace as well, "you will never show me that list."

"Only when I'm drunk, mate," Liam said seriously. "And even then I hope to forget it when I'm sober."

They both shuddered and clued back into the discussion that had continued to rage over their heads.

"*Enough*," Julia barked, cutting through the verbal mayhem. "As the final judge in this matter, *too many people* in this room have penises, and none of them should be using them to speak!"

There was a mass inhale while many pairs of male eyes—and two pairs belonging to females—widened with the eternal battle of laughing or not laughing.

Julia took a deep breath and settled herself. "So," she continued, as though she hadn't just issued the edict of the ages, "we've only got a couple of people in this room who qualify for the con." She looked at Marco, Frankie, and Camille. "Who's game?"

Tor glanced at them, surprised, and saw the same evil little smile on all three faces—it was the smile Marco used that first night when he'd said, "Oh, so you think you're topping?"

That smile.

"We're totally in," Marco said.

"I cannot wait," Camille said.

"Maybe I can take some film." Frankie smirked. "Two jobs in one!"

"Awesome," Josh said. "So the timeline is this. Tomorrow morning, Monday, Tor releases the first video—they usually take two days to get traction, right, Tor?"

"That's when eighty percent of my hits come," Tor affirmed.

"Right," Josh said. "So Tuesday afternoon, we have the tour of the factory to get Grace in place in the factory to free the workers—"

"We'll call it Operation Liberation," Grace said, sounding enchanted.

Josh shot him a look, but kept going. "So Wednesday morning we run Operation Liberation."

"Marco, I hope you're up to making coffee," Stirling muttered.

"For everyone but Josh," Grace said virtuously. "You sit out tonight's planning, Recovery Boy."

Josh grunted. "Please." He tapped his head. "It's all up here." Then he yawned. "But let's get through the basic plan tonight or it's all going to sleep with me. So we get Hepzibah to take that meeting on Tuesday—and that way we get Grace in place for Operation Liberation. He'll break in, find the worker's quarters, and prepare them for escape the next morning. Grace, you've done this before—"

"I'll need a warm coat, a woobie, a battery for my phone and my earbuds, and a pocket full of protein bars," Grace said, rubbing his hands together. "Check."

"Groovy," Josh said. "Don't tell us about your digestive troubles the next day. So we'll need the full team on Tuesday to break Grace into the factory, and we'll leave the van and the muscle in place to watch his back. Wednesday morning, Grace starts liberating people with the muscle to keep them safe, and while Team Liberation is doing that, led by me, the other half of us, directed by Torrance with Stirling, are going to be at our four main scammer sites. Wednesday, Tor drops the second video, the one about forced labor, including Operation Liberation." He paused. "Mom, you're in charge of having vans and school buses and relief stations, right? So we can get some crowd-sourced footage? And so… uhm, they're not alone, right?"

"Oh yes, darling," Julia murmured. "All in place."

"Great," Josh said. "That'll give Tor enough time to add the footage to his next spots, the ones that tie the whole crime family in with the scam."

Danny said, "Felix and I will work on having our cameramen in place with the Coulter-Kings before the video even drops. We can work at getting a crowd where necessary so we can get our key players while they're surprised and vulnerable."

"Hey," Grace said suspiciously. "You guys get all self-righteous about transparency, blah blah blah, and you can't run a scam, blah blah blah—"

Felix raised his eyebrows. "Well, yes—we can't pretend to be someone we're not, Dylan Li, but I think Torrance made it very clear where we stand on the entire Coulter family during your luncheon—and Julia has not been exactly silent. This isn't a scam—we don't need to be incognito. We'll be there as ourselves."

Grace grunted. "Righteous," he said. "I'm impressed."

"Well," Danny said with a completely straight face, "it's one of the perks of going straight. Josh?"

"Great," Josh said. "So Saturday, before everybody's forgotten about Operation Liberation because the news cycle is that stupidly short, Tor drops the video on construction scams. Monday, he drops the video on *the Coulter's* construction scams. He includes the connective tissue between the people released and the Coulters."

"Hey," Frankie said. "Is there any way my family could talk to the people whose names are being used? Like, Cammie and me, our cousins— we could go out and talk to the legit contractors getting their names smeared, have some stock questions? Is that too much to do?"

"No," Torrance said thoughtfully. "But do it *after* Operation Liberation. You guys have one chance to go in anonymously. After that, you're all on team enemy as far as the Coulters are concerned."

"Got it," Frankie said. "You set us up with questions, our little camera teams can go do that while you're doing your other stuff. Righteous."

"Dad would be so proud," Cammie said, smiling at her brother luminously. "You know, he always wanted you to go to college."

Frankie shrugged, looking pleased. "Yeah, but I always wanted to work with Pops. It'll be good to have him back in the office after this."

"Yeah." Camille sounded so incredibly wistful, and Tor found himself searching out Marco's eyes across the room, remembering what had prompted this in the first place.

"So that brings us to Wednesday again," Tor said, "when the Coulters will—hopefully with your help, Felix—be badgered into a press conference and we film the final spot and then edit it that night and release it the next morning."

"And then sleep for a fucking week!" Frankie moaned.

"Some of you," Molly said, laughing. "Stirling and I go back to work that Monday—Grace, aren't you starting rehearsal too?"

Grace yawned, all teeth. "Yes, and thanks to the last six months of shenanigans, I might actually have to practice."

"I'll think of you fondly from dreamland," Torrance said, and then, as though to make a point, he yawned.

"So," Molly said thoughtfully, "this timeline—locked in stone?"

"No," Torrance replied, knowing that the onus of it was on him. "I mean, we could go with five spots now, but we're anticipating lots of footage to edit in, so that's flexible."

"The one thing," Danny said, "that we *really* can't fuck up is—"

"Operation Liberation," Chuck said, and then grinned. "Y'all thought the rest of us fell asleep, didn't you?"

"Only some of us," Carl murmured, nodding at his boyfriend. Michael, who had been working his actual job of caring for the vehicles as well as helping everybody when he got to the Salinger mansion in the evening, was fast asleep on Carl's shoulder.

The whole room took a moment to go, "Aw…," and then Danny spoke again.

"Tomorrow, Camille, Marco, Frances—you're all here for breakfast so we can go over some things. I'm assuming Phyllis can get somebody else to make our muffins for us, because this is going to need your complete attention, Marco. And one more thing, children."

The whole room stopped to look toward him. "Once we've released the workers and the videos start dropping, *this entire household* needs to be on alert. During that week and a half while this is happening, we need to consider ourselves under siege. Hunter, Chuck, Carl—we will need our enforcement squad. When Michael shows up tomorrow, we're going to show him how to search for monitoring and explosive devices under our vehicles. The security in this mansion is top rated—that includes your new apartment, Marco. When you sign into your security pad, you are all synced up with us. Camille, Francis, you may want to consider sleeping over for a week and a half—yes, darlings, that does mean bring your pets if you have them. Until we get the *full amount* of information public, and the spotlight turns from Tor's news segments to the Coulters where it belongs, *their* bruisers are going to be taking us out. I'll make a list and have Josh send it to everybody." He took a breath. "This, people, is the biggest game we've played to date. Just because we're not on Gunrunner's Island doesn't mean the stakes aren't stupidly high. Do we understand?"

The whole room nodded soberly, and Frankie said, "Righteous," under his breath, one more time, sounding not cowed even a little tiny bit.

"Excellent," Danny said. "Josh, before we break up, can you take us through the plans of Hepzibah's factory? I want everybody thinking about it for as long as possible before we break Grace in."

"Roger that, Uncle Danny," Josh said, and he resumed the meeting.

WHEN THE meeting broke up about an hour later, Tor found Marco helping him to pack up his stuff before leading him to the foyer to put on his jacket and boots.

"Your place is ready?" Tor asked, trying to remember what day it was. The last two days had been a frantic, frenetic blur of assembling information and spitballing ideas. He'd known Marco was trying to move during that time, but the whole thing was very distant in his consciousness. He'd barely made it to his own bed the night before to fall in next to Marco, thinking they were too tired to do more than kiss until they fell asleep—until Marco had disabused him of that notion. He had the feeling that if they hadn't all been living in the same house, twenty people would have fallen asleep on Josh Salinger's floor in piles, like puppies, passing out where they sat.

"It is," Marco said, tightening Tor's jacket around his neck and pulling his hat out of his pocket for the walk through the snow.

"Are you sure you don't just want to sleep in my bed tonight?" Tor asked, thinking that the walk through the snow was going to be like a slap in the face.

"Yes," Marco murmured, before putting his lips next to Tor's ear. "You're going to get very loud tonight," he promised. "Breakfast isn't until ten tomorrow, and somebody else is cooking it. Tonight, we get to have glorious naked time in my new apartment before we go all James Bond on some very bad people. You okay with that?"

Torrance gathered himself for the cold and snorted. "James Bond is overselling it," he said, sure that was true.

Marco shook his head. "I am going to James Bond the *hell* out of you tonight."

Tor's entire body was starting to tingle, and he was suddenly looking forward to the slap of the night air.

It was slightly more than a slap, though. It was a breath-stealing beatdown with a frigid shiv. He was suddenly grateful for Marco's fussing before they'd stepped out of the house.

He and Marco trotted across the walkway, their boots crunching in the thin layer of snow that hadn't been shoveled off yet, their breath pluming out of them like smoke wishes into an indifferent diamond sky. The small copse of trees closed over them, protective as aunties, and Tor could feel the temperature drop again as they entered the small clearing where the house sat. They drew near the door, and he tried to control his shivers as Marco fumbled with the key.

Still, he lingered for a moment as the door opened behind him, so he could stare up at the night sky in wonder.

"C'mon," Marco murmured, tugging on his arm. "I know it's pretty, but there's parts of you I don't want to fall off."

Tor chuckled as he turned away from the vastness of the night sky, pleased to find the apartment was already warm and cozy.

"Ooh," he purred, stripping off his jacket and boots. "This is amazing."

"Timer," Marco said smugly. "Seriously, if I ever buy a house of my own, I want Felix and Danny to help me outfit it." He pointed to the security panel in the hallway that came with a small four-camera display showing each side of the house through a wide-angle lens placed on the corner. "Nothing like old criminals to make your house safe from actual dangerous thugs."

"Thugs?" Tor asked. "Is that who you think Coulter will send?"

Marco shrugged. "If Jimmy Flat-Nose is any indication, he and Hepzibah got all their security from the same Russian gangster slickness of Gunrunner's Island."

Tor let out another little laugh, this one sad. "You want to know a secret? One that we wanted to keep out of the press?"

Marco's eyebrows raised. "Sure. I mean, aren't *you* the press?"

Tor didn't laugh this time. "Part of being the press, I think, is being responsible about what needs to be reported. In this case, it's about the island."

"What about it? A tiny island with no name off the coast of Barbados, right?"

Tor shook his head and grabbed Marco's hand. "Walk and talk," he said with a little smile. "I want to see the rest of the cottage before we hit the bedroom."

"But we *will* see the bedroom?" Marco asked suspiciously.

Tor rolled his eyes. "After all the trouble you went to? Of course we will."

Marco's warm laughter steamed away the last of the chill of the starry night outside. Marco took him to the kitchen, which was now impressively outfitted with a lot of cooking equipment Tor had no idea what to do with, and said so, and then led him down the hall. "We're going to our bedroom—"

"Our bedroom?" Tor asked. "I thought it was your bedroom. I've got an apartment and a spare room in the mansion and—"

Marco stopped him with a kiss. "You are so cautious," he murmured. "Now tell me the big bad secret about Gunrunner's Island so I can make love to you until you scream and I see the guy who was *on* Gunrunner's Island in his khaki shorts and dress shirt, delivering the news in a tiny helicopter."

Tor took a moment to preen. "You noticed the dress shirt, right? We were totally unprepared for things to explode right then."

Marco kissed him again. "I noticed the shirt," he murmured. "It was dark blue, like your eyes. Now tell me your secret?"

"It's not mine, really," Tor said softly. "It's Stirling and Molly's. In fact, the *island* is Stirling and Molly's—it is *named* Stirling Molly."

Marco stared at him. "Oh my God. Seriously? They own an *island*?"

Tor nodded, not as bowled over about this fact now as he had been at the beginning. "Their adoptive parents bought it for them and then were killed when they made a trip to check it out. Our trip to the Caribbean was to see what had happened to them."

Marco's shocked excitement faded. "Oh wow," he murmured. "That's serious."

"Yeah." Tor thought about Molly and Stirling, who had worked as hard as everybody else, but who had also been quiet and subdued during the past week. The moment in the foyer of the gold club, when Molly had talked to that poor, disillusioned young debutante, had been the closest Tor had seen to the real irrepressible Molly since they'd come back from Gunrunner's Island. "And the thing is, Molly and Stirling got the answers they wanted—they did. But…." He grimaced.

"They've looked really sad this week," Marco filled in softly. "Stirling and Tienne have barely let go of each other's hands. Molly has spent the whole week sitting on Carl's or Chuck's laps."

"They're her favorite uncles," Tor admitted. "And Molly and Stirling had both lost so much, even before they were adopted. So this has been hard on them. I just want you to know that in case…." He grimaced, but he knew Marco would be able to finish the sentence.

"In case finding these answers about Uncle Flory doesn't fix all the things we thought it would," Marco murmured.

"Yeah." Tor shrugged. "You need to know—there's no guarantees the businesses that were used to defraud people will be able to build up their clientele or their trust. Your cousins haven't said anything, but I'm pretty sure their business isn't going to be the same when it comes back after this. So, you know—"

Marco shook his head. "No," he said softly. "This is what *you* need to know. What we're doing here—and it's a lot, I mean, *a lot*—but what we're doing here, it's bigger than Uncle Flory's business now. It's letting that kid, Clyde, out so he can have the good life his father wanted him to. It's letting the other workers out and getting them placed. It's letting people know that the businesses on the Coulters' hit list were being abused. And it's about not letting the Coulters get away with this. Everything they've done so Hepzibah could play at being an entrepreneur—this is not okay. There need to be consequences for this." Marco shrugged. "I know they may not see jail time. I know that this may be a huge scandal with no charges brought. Our justice system isn't great. But at least *we* did something to try to fix the world, just a little." He scowled at Tor. "What? What's that expression?"

Tor shrugged. "Something Danny's fond of saying. He says we're like the old trickster gods in a lot of the myths out there. The trickster gods were there to restore balance. Sometimes they tricked the people because the people weren't being mindful, and sometimes they tricked the gods because the gods were being pricks. Either way, there were agents of balance out there. That's what we are. We're… you know."

"Trickster gods," Marco said with a smile. Then his smile faded, and he drew Tor close, his breath fanning Tor's cheek. "What does that make me?"

"The trickster god's lover?" Tor said, savoring the warmth, the closeness, the way his chest felt now that he'd spoken frankly about his one worry before they began.

"Either that or his cook," Marco murmured. "We're going to go make love now," he promised. "And when we're done, you're going to know exactly whose bed you're going to be sleeping in from now on."

Tor was going to protest—he was. But then Marco kissed him in earnest, and it was like all the quiet conversation in the foyer and the kitchen and the hallway had warmed him up just enough to send him bursting into flames.

Marco mastered his mouth, swept his tongue inside, and bore Torrance back into the bedroom. Tor had been planning to look around—Marco promised to put his posters up, and Tor was all prepared to be a good boyfriend and compliment the décor.

But that's not what Marco wanted.

Marco wanted Tor in a raw, vital way that sang along his nerve endings and woke him from the near slumber he'd been in as their meeting had wrapped up.

With a little thrill, Tor realized the reason he'd told Marco about Stirling and Molly was so he knew, once and for all, that Marco saw him, saw *them* for what they were. Not perfect. Not magic. Not the solution to every problem. They could only do their human best to fix the world around them. But sometimes what they did could help.

And Marco apparently thought that was sexy, and that Tor was someone he wanted in his bed. Tor hadn't been able to save Jancy Anne Halston, but he could do *this*. Be the person in Marco's bed and a part of this amazing group of people that could at least try to save other people if they had a little bit of time and each other.

As Tor matched Marco's hunger with a voraciousness of his own, he could feel that need to be seen, to be appreciated for who he was, finally, deep in his belly, filled.

He allowed Marco to kiss him back to the bed, the same bed they'd first used only a few days before, and he resisted Marco's attempts to lay him flat on it. Instead, he pulled off his sweater and started unbuttoning the dress shirt underneath, accepting Marco's help on the cuffs and hauling the whole thing over his head when it was done.

He shed the rest of his clothes quickly, watching as Marco started to do the same, and then, just as Marco had freed his belt, Tor saw his opportunity.

He sank to his knees before Marco, tugging on his slacks and putting himself face-to-face with the most intimate parts of Marco's body.

He hadn't had a chance to do this yet.

Marco was such an aggressive lover, assertive in ways that delighted Tor no end, but Tor wanted to play too. He pulled Marco's cock into his mouth, suckling gently as it grew hard and tight against his palate, tasting a little bit of sweat from his time in the kitchen, as well as food smells that were somehow comforting. Marco gasped, hands falling to Tor's head, where he kneaded Tor's scalp through his hair.

"You're still not—" Marco panted. "—going to top."

Tor chuckled, knowing the vibrations from his throat would add to the pleasure. He pulled back, grasping Marco in his fist, keeping the cockhead close enough for his breath to tantalize.

"Why would I want to top?" he teased. "You're so good at it!"

Marco laughed, tilting his head back and giving a dramatic little whimper while thrusting his hips forward. Tor loved the playfulness, the absolute carnal joy that Marco invested in sex. It was as unapologetic as his love of food. There was no shame in Marco's world—not about muffins, not about blowjobs, not about enjoying his job or, it seemed, enjoying Tor's job as well. This time, as Tor thrust his head forward, he lost himself, gorging on Marco's cock with that same lack of apology, indulging in the head in his throat, the precome on his tongue, Marco's happy noises, the sting of his fingers in Tor's hair as he tugged.

A particularly insistent tug pulled Tor back, and he found *he* was the one whimpering, wanting more, wanting to swallow Marco's come down his throat, tasting all Marco had to give.

"Not this time," Marco whispered, running his thumb down Tor's cheek and thrusting it into his mouth. Tor sucked it in, shuddering with arousal, with sudden, electrifying need.

Marco offered Tor his hand and pulled him to his feet, stepping out of his slacks and shoes and helping Torrance clear away his own clothes. When Tor bent to pick the slacks up and fold them over a chair, Marco grabbed them, wadded them up, and tossed them in a corner.

"I have to put those on in the morning!" Tor laughed, but Marco shook his head.

"You'll wear my sweats and love it," he murmured, covering Tor's body with his own. He remembered to pull the covers down this time, and Tor found himself on his back, legs splayed, as Marco simultaneously kissed him stupid and fished for the lubricant under the pillow.

Tor heard the snick of the cap on the edge of his consciousness as he devoured the kisses with the same ferocity that he'd devoured Marco's cock. Long, sweet, and drugging, Marco's kisses took him to a place where Marco's hands on his skin were natural, warm, necessary, and his touch seemed to give life to Torrance's tired body.

A brush of his fingers over Tor's nipple suddenly brought Tor to life, to the land where touch could take his breath away, could pleasure so sharply it hurt, and he pulled Marco against him and arched, crying out, shaking with need as he tried to squash his orgasm from the simple brush of fingers.

"Now?" Marco whispered, his body moving sinuously, every part of him, even his soft furry tummy, seeming to touch Tor just right.

"Now," Tor pleaded. God, that fast, his cock ached and dripped, and his hands shook as he gripped Marco's biceps.

"Shh…." Marco kissed his temples, down his jaw, his throat while he moved one of his hands to position himself. "Open for me, baby. It's fine. I'll go slow."

And there he was at Tor's entrance. Tor shuddered again, sweating, needing him inside so bad.

"Are you good?" Marco asked.

"Yes!"

Slow.

Marco's cockhead was well greased with spit and lube, but Marco apparently wasn't going to shove inside him without prep.

Instead he went slow and pulled back, went slow and pulled back, giving Tor's body the chance to adapt. And again, and stretch, and release. Every stretch drove Tor's heartbeat higher, amped his arousal to nearly unbearable, took his body to a place where he would need to float, helpless, in order to accommodate the size, the sensation, the pleasure.

Finally, Marco was inside, and Tor gave a little gasp and a moan, and his entire body relaxed—not in orgasm but in satiation, because Marco was inside him, exactly where he needed to be, and Tor's restless brain, his constant revisioning, his constant *envisioning* of the past few days, the planning, the strategizing, the overthinking of every move, was suddenly, blissfully, silent.

It was simply Marco, moving gently within him, stretching his pleasure centers while Tor welcomed him where he needed to be.

"How you doing?" Marco whispered as he withdrew softly and thrust forward.

"Good," Tor murmured. "So good. It's like you're the sun and I'm the sky and you belong in me, burning… burning… ah!" Because Marco had thrust forward again, had hit his spot, and Tor's sky filled with lightning at the shock of it.

"Look at you with the words," Marco said, doing it again.

"Oh God," Tor cried, his sky filling with clouds of sensation. Every time Marco fucked him, fucked in, fucked out, the clouds seemed to cover him, to surround him with little electric shocks in every bead of sweat. He needed more. More. A giant shaft of lightning, burning away the fog.

"More?" Marco whispered, thrusting harder, faster.

"More!" Tor demanded, not in a place where he could hold his orgasm, simply at the mercy of the winds of sensual pleasure.

"Wow," Marco breathed. He pulled back on his knees, yanking Tor's hips up off the bed to give him more leverage, and began fucking in a frenzy that left Tor blind, crying out again and again and again, until his body gave a giant climactic snap, like a rubber band, all his muscles drawing taut and releasing with a racking convulsion as come jetted from his cock and across his chest, his vision growing white-blind with orgasm.

Marco kept fucking him as his body spasmed around that amazing cock, everything shaking so hard his teeth chattered.

"Oh God—so good," Marco panted. "That's… that's…."

Tor could only describe what happened to his body then as "blooming." As though all of the muscles that had resisted, had drawn tight and hard with orgasm, then clenched around Marco, grasping him tightly—those muscles had *bloomed*, relaxing, opening him up for complete invasion, welcoming Marco into his soul.

Marco's groan defied description, total and blissful, as Marco slammed against Tor's ass one more time and came.

Tor felt him, spurting and real, scalding inside his ass, and he melted into the mattress, the final act of their consummation filling him with contentment as his body went back to floating, blue skies, blissed out and tranquil, filled and heated by the sun.

Marco fell against him, sliding out, leaving a trail of semen against Tor's asscheeks and thighs, but Tor didn't care. Last time, Marco had taken care of him, and he probably would this time, but it didn't matter.

Tor would lay there, coated in spend, his and Marco's, completely enveloped in a haze of well-being, replete and happy and well.

"Wow," Marco said again. "Every time I think you couldn't get more responsive, you rock my world."

"How is bottoming this good?" Tor mumbled. "Used to be messy and embarrassing and painful…."

"Wrong tops," Marco said with a little laugh, licking the sweat from his neck. "Nobody to take you on a magic carpet ride."

"Magic rocket ride." Tor giggled, and Marco laughed too.

"Wow, you're silly. Hold still a minute while I go get a cloth."

"Won't matter," Tor almost sang. "Gonna smell jizz all night."

Marco chuckled as he ran to the bathroom and rummaged through a box, probably for towels. He came back with a cloth, a towel for under Tor's hips, and sweats, which he had obviously pulled out first.

After a few moments of shivering activity, they were both back in bed, heating the space under the covers and creating their own safe haven.

"How is it," Tor asked, loopy and fine with that, "that there was no indication you were a sex god under the apron and the sweet little face?"

Marco huffed a laugh in his ear and drew him closer. "How do you know I'm a sex god with anybody but you?"

"Confidence," Torrance said, feeling drunk again on their lovemaking. "You… I mean, there's only so many things you can do with a cock, but you seem to know all the right ones."

"I'm used to telling people what to do," Marco murmured. "I'm used to knowing what a thing will need to make it just right. You—you do things independently, but you want someone to order you around. I'm good at ordering people around."

"So funny," Tor said. "I thought you only made muffins."

Marco kissed the back of his neck with so much tenderness, Tor melted. "And I thought all you guys did was sit around being rich and eccentric. It's okay. First impressions are only important if they give you the chance to make a second, and a third—"

"And then apparently a giant happy home impression in my ass," Tor said, cracking up at his own joke.

"Or maybe just a happy home," Marco murmured.

"God—so insistent. I need my office apartment in the city. I can't always stay here."

"I know," Marco said, smoothing his hand down Torrance's shoulder before cupping his hip.

Which left one thing to change. "But…." Tor huffed out a breath. "You know. We haven't even been a thing for—"

"You have a *room* in the *mansion next door*," Marco pointed out, exasperated. "What's the worst that can happen?"

"I move in here, you break up with me because my hours are *insane*, Felix gives my room away to Liam, and if I ever…." Tor's voice grew a little rusty, a little less self-assured. "If I ever need them again, I'm forced to sleep on the bed in Danny's study or the couch in the den."

"And what?" Marco asked, exasperated. "Never eat here again?"

"I know your hours. I'm very good at avoiding people I don't want to see." He'd done it for three years with his parents—and he'd lived in their house.

Marco sighed, kissing his temple. "You should just give it up and move in with me. You're so bad at confrontation, you'll never move out unless I move you out."

"Have you seen me interview people?" Tor asked, legitimately shocked. "I've been described as a pit bull!"

"That doesn't count," Marco dismissed. "You don't know those people and don't care. I think," he murmured, "that if somebody hurts you, they'll never be given another chance to hurt you again."

Tor thought of how he'd moved out of his parents' house and agreed it was a fair assessment, but how did Marco get there? "What makes you think that?" he asked.

Marco frowned. "Because for such a public person, you are remarkably quiet and self-contained," he said at last. "Watching you, *listening* to you at their table, at their strategy meetings—you're like my cousin Liza."

Tor grunted. "You know, someday I'm going to have to meet all your cousins so I know if you're making them up."

Marco chuckled outright. "My imagination only works with food," he said. "Liza loves us all, she participates with the family, but a lot of the time she just sits and lets family wash over her. Not like Stirling, who gets bolder with every interaction. She's sort of a basker. She just... I don't know. Basks in the noise, the love. You bask. But, you know, like most things that bask—lizards, fish, whatever—when shit gets scary, you know how to hide." He shrugged. "Doesn't mean you can't bite when you're going after flies or worms or whatever, but if something can hurt you—you camouflage yourself and lay low."

Tor grunted. "A lizard or a fish," he said, unimpressed. "I feel...." He stuck his tongue out and flickered it before pulling it back in. "Hurt."

Marco's low rumble was reassuring in his ear. "You're very much a warm-blooded mammal in bed, though," he said.

"If you say a pussycat, I'm out of here," Tor threatened, although at this point, he wasn't sure he could move if the cottage was on fire.

"Mmm...." Marco gave a sensual shiver and drew Tor closer. "You are.... I've never even dreamed of a lover like you. One who gives me so much while needing me so completely. It's magic, like spicy fried chicken and waffles. Filling, decadent, delicious, addicting—"

"And not fattening in the least," Tor murmured, sensing sleep stalking him in the lowering dark of his eyes.

"I'll never give you up," Marco said. "You should concede to fate and move your pictures into my bedroom, and we'll be stupid happy and busy and good."

"I have a *lot* of clothes," Tor told him, because right now, this was one of the few things he could think of.

"You keep a lot of them in the city," Marco said with a shrug. "Look—I get it. Not my mom and dad, who haven't spent a night apart in forty years. But that doesn't mean it won't work."

Tor opened his mouth to say... something. Something wise about waiting, but he yawned instead, one of the giant yawns that felt like it unhinged his jaw and enveloped the whole room.

Marco nuzzled him. "Go to sleep," he said softly. "We have so much to do this next week. Don't worry—I'll have you talked into it by the time this whole Hepzibah Coulter mess is done."

"Okay," Tor mumbled, but even *he* wasn't sure what he was agreeing to. It didn't matter—by the time he thought he should clarify that, they were both asleep.

Showtime

MARCO HAD heard about the electronics van, but he hadn't yet been *inside*. But since he and Cammie were the ones going into the meeting with Hepzibah's building manager, the better to let Grace and Frankie in, they had to be fitted with earbuds and small cameras, which they were immediately told to ignore.

"Listen if you can," Josh had said, "or if something's going down and you need to know what it is. But if you're talking to a person, making eye contact with them, being real—that's much more important than what's happening in your ear. We'll make an effort to dampen anything not necessary, okay?"

They both nodded, although Cammie gave Stirling a warm smile as he put a teeny camera on the zipper of her plain black leather tote.

"Don't forget where the cameras are," Josh said, repeating what Danny had told them the day before during practice, "but don't obsess about them either. If your bag gets blocked for a minute, that's fine, as long as you retrieve it naturally."

Cammie nodded, and Marco looked skeptically at the suit jacket they'd fitted him with, which apparently had a camera already installed in the button that Josh was working to activate.

"Be sure to ask for a tour of the working parts of the factory," Josh told them. "And remember—the one cue that you need to hear is the one telling one of you to leave the room and unlock a door—or asking Chuck to go fetch your glasses from the car if that's the way it's going. I mean, he may not be able to accompany you during the tour—it depends on how suspicious the family is. We'll guide you. Cammie, use the old bathroom line, but make sure you're as far away from a bathroom as possible so it's okay if you get lost. Marco—"

"I can't use the bathroom line," he said seriously, all his days of restaurant work coming back to him.

"No, you can't," Josh said on a hint of laughter.

"That would be bad," Grace added from the corner of the van.

"Why?" Stirling asked, legitimately curious.

"Men your age have perfect bladders," Liam said. "A lad like Marco, he disappears into the men's and he's likely going for a snort, yeah?"

"Yeah," Josh said, nodding. "We'll buzz your phone—if you need to go, you need to step out for a call. Answer in four rings as you're walking away, and we'll guide you through the place to find our opening. Cammie, same for you. Women check their phones on the way to the bathroom all the time. We'll guide you in some way when the moment comes."

"Got it," Cammie said, and although her brow was furrowed in concentration, the corners of her mouth were lifted like she was having the time of her life. "Where's Grace and Frankie again?"

The van itself was parked in front of a shopping center. Chuck was waiting outside in one of the deluxe SUVs, because everything, from Cammie's tasteful winter-white pantsuit, glossy french twist, and winter-red wool topcoat, to Marco's contrasting classic gray pinstripe with a man's black topcoat and slicked-back hair, said class, taste, and money. Even Marco's hat—the one Tor had given him—had been temporarily replaced with a black cashmere blend, and Cammie had mittens trimmed with mink.

"God, it's dreamy," she'd said as she slid the mittens on. "I hate that it used to be someone's pet, but...."

"Minks are unpleasant creatures," Grace said. "Now, chinchillas—they're adorable."

"I don't care," she sniffed. "There's other ways to keep warm." She sighed. "Please tell me you got these on consignment."

Josh chuckled. "A lot of my parents' 'go' clothes are bought at estate sales. Think of it as upcycling and enjoy the extra warmth."

Cammie grinned, and in that moment, she was 100 percent Marco's cousin from the neighborhood. "You're a great kid," she said. "Too bad Marco's kind of in love with your reporter or you'd make a good match."

Liam didn't say a word, but Marco watched Josh's eyes dart that way and reckoned nobody had to. "No matches for me until I can make it through an op without falling asleep in my soup," he said grimly. "But thank you, I'm flattered. Tor's a great guy, and I'm glad he and Marco are a thing."

"I can hear all of this," Tor said into their earpieces from the other side of the van, and Marco had to resist the urge to hold his hand to his mouth like a little kid who'd been caught gossiping. "I'm happy you all approve. Now back on task. Do you remember your cover?"

"Marcus and Cameron Metzger," Cammie said, "of the Cape Cod Metzgers. Is that really a thing?"

"They're an old-money family, friends of Felix's," Danny said from their earpieces. He was part of the backup team getting Grace and Frankie past the fence behind the factory. After that, the two of them would hang out by the designated entrance with Carl, pretending to be workers who'd been locked out, while Danny and Felix pulled around the corner so they could watch for any changes in the guard's routine, like the change that ended up with Hunter's split knuckles and swollen hand. They were parked in the older beat-up SUV they'd purchased that month, about two blocks from the factory itself in an often-used employee lot with a view of the security office that served the buildings on the entire block. Marco had seen them dress— everybody was wearing black yoga pants and sweatshirts, but the three men going in were wearing them underneath denim jackets with hoodies and loose jeans. The extra clothes could be easily shed, Marco figured, and in the meantime it kept them warm and helped them disguise their features, particularly with baseball caps over their balaclavas. Nobody would notice them in the influx of construction and warehouse workers in the area.

"The names and all?" Marco asked, and Danny chuckled.

"No, dear boy. The couple is older—Blaine and Denise—and their son is *Marcus*. They're easily researched, right down to their FB profile. Felix asked if we could put in a couple of pictures of Marco—the young men are about the same age and physical type. All he has to say is "whirlwind marriage," and suddenly we have the picture of young and feckless investors."

"These are pretty classy clothes for feckless," Cammie muttered, and Danny laughed.

"They are, lovey—but they're old East Coast money. If your cover was California rich, we'd send you in a Hawaiian shirt and a parka."

"We wear suits in California," Felix muttered, sounding grumpy.

"Made of viscose with skinny ties," Danny retorted, obviously trying to get under Felix's skin.

"Do I have to mute you two?" Josh asked. "Or can we have this discussion at dinner and give Mom one more thing to ban?"

"Where *is* Julia?" Cammie asked, obviously a little nervy. "Or Molly for that matter?"

"We're on standby." Julia's voice came over the earbud, and Marco and Cammie exchanged surprised glances. "If things start to go south, we're casually dropping by for lunch to get Hepzibah and her security to the front of the factory while everybody else flees out the back with their hair on fire."

"Ish," Cammie said, showing all her teeth in an expression of horror. "So you're taking the real risk here?"

"You betcha," Molly muttered. "If we end up taking one for the team, somebody needs to show up at the restaurant and save us. In the name of humanity, don't force us to eat with those people."

"Understood," Danny said. "Operation Bailout is an official contingency plan."

"Glad to hear it," Julia said. "How are our ropers?"

"Looking good, Mom," Josh told her. He frowned and offered the tube of hair gel to Tor, who took it and slicked back a bit of Marco's curls that kept trying to break free. "Remember—you guys go in, tour the factory, sell them some bullshit about investment opportunities, let Grace and Frankie in, and get out. No lingering. No family stories. Be forgettable." He gave Cammie a fond little nose wrinkle. "Hard for you, Cammie, I know, but go for it."

She cackled, obviously flattered. "Marco here—he's good at standing in the background and doing brilliant things, right, Marco?"

Marco grunted. "Sure, Cammie. I'll be Bert to your Ernie."

She cackled again and then took a deep breath, pulling her shoulders back and showing off her ample chest without qualm. Marco had to admit that the confidence he'd always most admired in his cousin was probably what would pull this off.

"How about me?" he asked, but his eyes were more on Tor than anybody else.

"You're going to do great," Tor said. He smiled just enough to make his eyes crinkle in the corners—a reminder that he was nearly thirty, older than Marco, but Marco had heard his sounds in bed, seen him come undone. Something told Marco that no matter how much experience Tor had, in bed or in the line of work they were embarked upon at the moment, he was, in some ways, very much untouched.

It was why Marco was keeping his patience with the moving-in thing. Of course Tor was afraid. He'd had to yank himself out of his family as a whole piece to avoid the pain. The fear of having to do something like that again? That would haunt a man—it would cause him to curl up inside himself and watch the happiness of others, never reaching for any himself.

Marco wasn't used to that thinking. When you grew up in a big, rowdy, loving family, you had to speak up or you'd miss out on dessert, or that last piece of chicken, or the good seat at the movies—or you'd end up doing the dishes again when it totally wasn't your turn. And if the family was *loving*, whatever you asked for or fought for or vied for was acceptable. When it became clear that Marco and his next oldest sister, Bethany, had a crush on the same guy, nobody held it against Marco—and Marco was hurt but not angry when the guy picked Beth. The point was, he hadn't been afraid to ask.

Tor was so used to *working* his way for a place, he didn't realize how much power he had now that the place had found him.

"Marco?" Tor prompted, and Marco realized he'd been staring into space, focused on Tor's amazing eyes.

"I'm here," he said softly, and then he kissed Tor, on the lips, in front of all their friends. "What are you going to be doing?"

"Monitoring feed from Grace and Frankie," Tor said soberly. "The Coulters can't see me in there or know I'm involved until the spots start to percolate. They've got lawyers on retainer—and we already have the first spot out there, so the Coulters can't know I'm gunning for them yet. Timing is everything here."

Marco nodded, because he understood. News cycles were so fast, and the wheels of justice were so slow. In order to indict royalty, they had to have public opinion and interest behind them, screaming for a revolution.

"That's all right," he said with a shrug. "If we have to get our hands dirty, that's what we gotta do."

"You guys get to be our ropers today," Josh said. "Go out and rope 'em in."

"Are we ready?" came Danny's question. "You've got five minutes to get here, and Chuck says it's clear for you to step out of the van and into the SUV."

"Where's Hunter?" Marco asked suddenly, and there was a soft, raspy chuckle on the com.

"Best not to ask," Josh told him grimly, and Marco remembered that brief moment of Hunter falling from the sky to take out the guy who had—however peripherally—threatened Grace.

Yeah. Best not to know too much about what Hunter was doing right now, although Marco assumed he was shadowing Grace and Frankie.

"We set?" Cammie asked, echoing Danny's question.

"Damned straight," Marco said. "Showtime."

"SO DO you get to come in with us into the factory?" Cammie asked Chuck as he was driving them the last few blocks. The road housed a bunch of warehouses and warehouse businesses, all of them surrounded by razor wire and security systems to help guard against theft. Marco had no idea how Grace had breached the razor wire and fences—but given that nobody needed medical attention *yet*, he'd guess that having the thief break in as opposed to the muscle was a good call. Between the grimness of the razor wire, roads pitted and potholed by the big trucks and machinery that drove up and down, as well as the bitter, driving wind off the river, it felt almost absurd to be so well dressed, being chauffeured by this auburn-haired bruiser in a suit.

"If we're lucky," Chuck murmured. "If we're not, you're carrying a device that should pick up on their security feed, which I shall doctor while I'm waiting for you in the car. Otherwise I'll take care of the cameras when we get inside."

"Wow," said Cammie. "So many angles. I can't believe you all accounted for all of them."

Chuck snorted. "If somebody told you we got all of them, they sold you a bill of goods. Every caper's got a glitch. *Every* caper. If there's a wild, wacky coincidence that nobody can account for? You had better believe it's going to happen in the middle of your job. Roll with it, and know…." He huffed out a breath. "We've got your backs, okay? Number one rule? Protect the civilians. You're our civilians. We've got your backs."

"We hear you," Cammie said. "And hey—what's the worst that can happen? I mean, we're nobody. We get busted and we say we traced Clyde to Hepzibah—period. We're not doing more than a misdemeanor here, right?"

"If that," Chuck said cheerfully. "And I like the way you think."

"So we go in, we bluff our way into the warehouse—I mean, seriously, Marco, remember that time Frankie and I crashed your little restaurant-opening party when you were debuting in Boston?"

Marco groaned. "Oh God, I was so embarrassed. I *had* seating tickets for you guys when I took my test, and you all said you couldn't come."

"Yeah, well, we couldn't let you hang like that, kid, remember? But me, Frankie, Beth—who else?"

"Ozzie," Marco muttered, loving his older brother fiercely but also knowing the whole thing had to be his idea.

"Yeah, Ozzie. Anyway, we waltzed in there, pretended we had a table, got all outraged when we didn't, gave fake names. It was a *blast*, and then we *did* get a table, and we got to call you out and compliment you. It was fabulous."

"I remember," Marco said, thinking about how hurt he'd been that nobody could come to his big debut, and how goofily pleased he'd been that they'd gone through *all of that* to come surprise him. His master chef had not been pleased, and the tantrum he'd thrown—yikes. It had been one of the reasons Marco had looked for a job *not* in high-profile restaurant work. The stresses chefs were under—pressure didn't always create diamonds. Sometimes it just smashed perfectly good gems into crappy little bits.

"Then that's what we're doing here," Cammie said, patting his hand. "We got no fear."

Marco grinned at her, suddenly in the moment. He'd taken the entire assignment so seriously—but with Cammie's memories, he was starting to put together the delight the Salingers seemed to take in these endeavors with his own family's chutzpah.

He was starting to feel it. They could do this. And they could have *fun*.

"No fear," he said, grabbing his cousin's hand.

"Good thing you came to that conclusion," Chuck murmured. "Because we're here."

He'd piloted the SUV through the alley that led to the back parking lot and into a small fenced-in lot that led directly to the business office portion of the warehouse. The worker lot was easy to differentiate—the few cars in it were battered and rust-speckled, a testament to how much Hepzibah didn't pay the workers she *didn't* conscript. The fenced lot was surprisingly full, and as Chuck pulled in, he said—obviously for coms—"Josh, run these plates. Recon last week showed us this place usually only has the foreman's car—that's the Kia. This big white Navigator is Hepzibah, but there's two silver Mercedes GLEs and a red Porsche Cayenne that tell me the whole happy family is here, and I've got no idea why."

Chuck eschewed the actual spots and drove the Land Rover up onto the sidewalk apron in front of the offices. He turned off the ignition and got a blank look on his face as he stepped out of the Land Rover, pulled on his overcoat, and ran around to open the door for Camille.

"Oh," Chuck said as the door opened. "So *those* Metzgers. Yeah. The people who invented the pill. I get it. Fucking Jesus, Felix, these people probably think Marco and Cammie are their own personal saviors, here to shake the money tree."

Felix obviously said something tart back, and Chuck grunted.

"No, I don't know any super-rich people who can help us out—"

He paused again.

"No, I didn't know that."

He took a deep breath.

"All I am saying," Chuck muttered, "is that this is a lot of pressure for these kids."

Marco slid out and stepped down to the sidewalk, allowing Chuck to close the door.

"It's fine," Marco said to reassure Chuck. "These people aren't anything to us. It's no big deal."

Chuck shook his head. "I just keep forgetting how rich Felix actually *is*," he muttered.

"One of the twenty richest people in Chicago," Cammie said, flashing her dimples.

Chuck rolled his eyes, and over their coms, Felix said, "That's only the money the government knows about."

In spite of the anxiety he'd had in the car, Marco chuckled. "So we're not just bait," he said. "We're *choice* bait."

"Yes, you are," Tor said. "Chuck, we're running some bugs and cameras to Grace through the fence. As soon as you are in the front, he's going to bug their cars. You'll have to stall for twenty minutes before he's around at the back entrance for you to let him in. You good with that?"

Marco gave Chuck a tight grin. "Well, you did say there were always hiccups."

"Yes, sir," Chuck said loudly, jogging to the steel-framed glass doors to open them ahead of Marco and Cammie. "Right away, sir."

"Is he going to move the car?" Cammie asked Marco in a low voice.

"Nope," Marco said, gesturing Cammie ahead of him with a hand in the small of the back. "We're fucking royalty, baby. We park on the goddamned sidewalk."

"Righteous," she murmured, and together they strode into the lion's den.

IT WAS a testament to how good Josh and Stirling were on coms that Marco, Cammie, and Frankie weren't privy to the absolute chaos that Chuck's comment about the cars engendered.

Stirling took the makes, models, and license plates, and the minute Gregg Coulter's name appeared, the discussion raged.

"Abort?" Josh asked, reluctance clear in his voice. "Abort? Dad, they're civilians."

"Josh, this cover is good for three days—this is our window!" Felix came back with.

"How fucking rich are these people?" Stirling cried, watching a list of financial information scroll across his screen.

"Three times richer than we are—on paper at least," Felix told him. "But they tend to go low profile, and they're very sweet."

"But *Dad*!" Josh protested, obviously reading the anxiety on Tor's face accurately. "Marco and Cammie just went from a distraction to *bait*!"

"Tor, can they handle it?" Danny asked, his voice the clear voice of reason.

They all grunted as Chuck pulled the Land Rover up onto the concrete apron. His and Felix's conversation could be heard loud and clear through the sound system, and Tor had to give him credit—he was not taking this additional danger for Camille and Marco lightly.

Tor swallowed, yearning to pull them from the op, *dying* to put Marco and Cammie back behind the scenes, civilians where they belonged.

For no reason whatsoever, the pale blue visage of Jancy Anne Halston showed up behind his eyes.

It *almost* froze his breath, the image of all the ways Tor could fuck up, all the bad things that could happen to people who depended on him for help. He was a guy with a camera—how could he send these two sweet, innocent people into danger like this?

Well, maybe not so innocent. Marco's eyes, dark and knowing as he took over Tor's body and told him exactly what he needed and exactly what Marco was going to do to give it to him, filled Tor's vision—filled his *lungs* with sweet, necessary, life-giving air.

Marco knew what he was doing. Maybe he hadn't done *this* before, but Marco knew how to think on his feet, how to master his surroundings—how to make the people around him do what he needed them to do. Tor had seen him in the kitchen, completely in charge, and he'd seen him in a group setting, an unfamiliar situation, paying attention to his surroundings and absorbing information.

And Cammie had gone Agent Carter on their asses from the very beginning.

"Tor?" Josh murmured, and he realized everybody was waiting for his answer.

"They'll be okay," he said. "In fact, we should probably take advantage of the fact that everybody's going to be there."

And *that's* when the idea of getting Grace some cameras and microphones to put in the vehicles was born.

"Liam," Josh said, "did you hear that?"

"Time for me to drive the van, boys," Liam said from the front. "Everybody hold on to your arses."

And like that they were in motion and a whole other plan was set forth.

MARCO HAD to admit that Chuck made a rather wonderful chauffeur/valet. He was there to open all the doors, he stood on the warehouse floor in front of what must have been the office, and he bowed quietly to Gregg Coulter as he peered out to see who was there.

"The Metzgers, here to see Hepzibah Coulter," he intoned, as though there was nobody else who would be there for no other reason.

For a moment, Marco thought, "This is preposterous, and the jig is up," because Gregg Coulter's face had gone completely blank, void of emotion and thought, the moment Chuck had spoken to him. In the office a female voice could be heard.

"Gregg—*Gregg*—go out there and greet them! We're right behind you!"

The door swung open, and Congressman Gregg Coulter stepped out in a boxy tan suit, proving that Hepzibah came by her fashion sense through good old-fashioned genetics.

"Hello there!" he crowed heartily. "So, Marcus and Cameron Metzger, yes? So glad to meet you! So glad!" With that, he stepped forward to engulf Marco's hand in a clammy dead-fish grasp of his own. Marco kept his smile wide as he fought the need to wipe his hand on the back of his nice wool slacks.

"Nice to meet you too, Congressman," Marco said, remembering to be friendly but reserved. If he was a rich guy, he'd be sort of contemptuous of the people slobbering all over him to get money. Nobody in the Salinger clan fostered that sort of sycophancy, and Marco was glad.

"Lovely," Cammie said, but her voice had an edge to it, and Marco realized that the congressman hadn't inflicted his loathsome handshake on Cammie—and she wasn't above playing slighted.

"Ms. Metzger," came an effusive voice. "Ignore my husband—he's a throwback to the dinosaurs. Come meet our daughter, Hepzibah."

"Wonderful," Cammie said, keeping her voice barely north of annoyed. "At least the one person we were here to see is actually here."

"I'm so sorry," Hepzibah said, emerging from the back of the office in a power suit made from the brightest red cloth Marco had ever seen, with lapels she could use to float to another country.

"Ms. Coulter-King," Marco said, allowing some warmth in his voice as she strode out to meet them. "I'm surprised your husband isn't here too."

"He is," she said with the grace to look embarrassed. "He's still in the office, on a phone call. If you'd like to start the tour now, I'm sure he'll catch up."

"Darling," Tracy admonished, condescension dripping from her voice, "why don't we invite the Metzgers into the office and offer them some refreshment—they only just arrived."

"I'd love to, Mother," Hepzibah said, her voice like acid ice, "but Byron *requested* he not be disturbed."

Tracy gaped at her, obviously realizing that Byron King's business calls apparently trumped courtesy to potential investors, but also probably thinking that the potential investors could ease some of his business concerns and he should be more polite.

"When we get back from the tour," she said, obviously at a loss. "Hepzibah, where did you want to start?"

Hepzibah turned toward the fit, middle-aged woman wearing a plain gray business suit and sensible shoes who had followed her out of the office.

"This is my foreman—er, forewoman, Jean Campano. She oversees the day-to-day operations here, while I'm more, uhm, on the business and creative end." Hepzibah gave an unctuous smile. "Gotta have the designs to make the clothes, right?"

Jean Campano gave Hepzibah a tight-lipped, sideways look that either called into question Hepzibah's abilities or her contributions period, and Marco and Cammie exchanged glances.

"I read that too," Josh said in his ear. "Potential ally, but don't say anything until you need her."

The oddest thing about having people talk in his ear was that he couldn't respond—but it was reassuring to know that they really weren't alone.

"So," Campano said, a clipped East Coast accent making her sound all business. "Where did you want to start? The design suite upstairs or the production rooms on the second and ground floors?"

Marco and Cammie exchanged glances again, both of them mindful of the suggestion that they give Grace extra time by the vehicles on this side of the factory.

"Design first," Cammie said practically. "It would be good to see where the magic happens."

"Good choice," Tor murmured in Marco's ear, and his stomach settled even further. "Take the stairs."

The stairs hugged the wall, a giant industrial metal framework that echoed loudly with every footfall. Jean Campano made polite noises about "We have an elevator," and Hepzibah loudly declared that her heels would never work in the slotted metal of the stairs.

"We'll meet you there," Cammie said cheerfully. "I've been trapped in the SUV forever. It's good to get some exercise in."

And thus committed, the Coulter family herded into the elevator while Marco and Cammie walked up the noise trap of the stairs.

Jean Campano was more than forthcoming on the trip.

"Look," she told Cammie before they'd reached the first landing. "You seem like nice people—you might want to check on other investment opportunities besides this one."

"Really?" Cammie said, keeping her attention on Jean. "Why is that?" Marco used the opportunity to hang back with Chuck and scan the surroundings.

"Well, for one thing her clothes are butt-ugly," Jean said frankly, "and normally that wouldn't be notable, because Paris fashion, am I right?"

"There does need to be some acknowledgment that not every night is the Met Gala," Cammie conceded, and Tor said, "Nice," in Marco's ear. Well, that was Cammie—surprising in every way.

"There are some designers out there who get it," Campano concurred. "But if it was only the ugly clothes, I'd say go for it. But...." She shook her head. "Look, all I'm saying—there's something hinky going on here with the labor policies. There's all sorts of unregistered workers. They're not on the floor, although those guys get paid rock-bottom scale, but we see them all the time, and they do not look... healthy. And their supervisors? Terrifying. I'm telling you, I'm out of here next month."

"Where you going?" Cammie asked. "I mean, you've got a job lined up and everything?"

"Oh yeah—there's a Dior setup in New York. I'll be on the designer's floor, making three times what I'm making now, but—" She puffed out a breath, and not just because they were working on their third flight of stairs. "—don't tell anyone what I told you. I just—when I was walking out of the office, I heard her husband, the guy who couldn't be bothered when we all know the business is drowning. He was on the phone to a guy named Kadjic—and I'm telling you, after that Gunrunner's Island thing that was on the news last week, that name is raising a lot of red flags."

"Oh shit," Josh said in his ear.

"Oh shit," Tor whispered after him.

"Holy shit," Danny and Felix muttered together.

"You guys," Chuck muttered as they cleared the fourth floor, "where's Grace?"

And then it was like a chorus, led by Hunter, of everybody on coms exclaiming, "*Fuuuuuck!*"

"OH MY God," Josh said. "Okay, everybody—eyes front and center. Everybody's favorite wingnut has just screwed us again."

"I did not," Grace said over coms. "This was not my fault!"

"He's right," Hunter said, sounding breathless. "We were putting the devices on the cars when Frankie gave us a holler."

"They were bringing the workers back early!" Frankie said, sounding like he was holding it together. "I was waiting in the back for the signal to go inside when a couple of trucks pulled up round the west alley and started to unload."

"I couldn't see them," Hunter said, "but Grace did."

"The trucks weren't full," Frankie continued, "but the workers, maybe twenty, looked freezing, and I think one of them is injured. There's guys—leather coats, black pants, bad guys—in each truck. They were heading my way, so I ducked behind a stairwell, but I can see the sort of trapdoor where they're being herded."

"I followed them from the parking lot," Grace said. "Sorry, Hunter—you were on the far side with the bugs, and I didn't want to be spotted. But I snuck in under the guards' radar 'cause my costume is first-rate! Thanks, Mrs. Josh's Mom."

"You're welcome, Grace." Julia's voice was strained. "Just let us know where you are."

"With the workers," Grace said, like, "Well duh!"

"Baby," Hunter said, his voice gruff, "do you even know where *in the building* you are?"

"Well, it's dark," Grace said. "We went down some stairs behind a dumpster, so I dunno. Somewhere underground?"

"Crap!" Hunter muttered. "Guys, I'm on that side of the building on the outside, and I can't see shit. Chuck, Marco, what can you see?"

Tor caught his breath. The visual feed from Chuck, Marco, and Cammie had been moving pretty steadily up the stairs, but getting a look at the building specs from the inside was still hard.

"Hold up a minute," Marco called, probably to Cammie and the woman who'd just name-dropped the atom bomb on them before Chuck realized Grace was getting into trouble. "We're up above the work floor. Let us get a sense of the size of the operation."

"Back to back," Chuck murmured, and he and Marco stood still, sides to the wall, at a slight angle, before they very slowly, very deliberately, turned in a semicircle until almost facing.

The result, Tor realized as Josh and Stirling merged the picture into a panoramic view, was that the entire floor could be scoped out by one person.

"Carl," Josh said. "You got that on your phone?"

"Studying," Carl said.

"Wait," Josh murmured. "What's Marco doing?"

Marco had approached the rail of the metal stairwell and leaned over as though scoping out the operation. They were about even with the second floor—Chuck and Marco had been bent slightly forward as they were taking the panoramic picture of the ground floor. When looking down, they could see the basics of a garment factory; pieceworkers sat at sewing machines, piecing the same parts that had been pinned together and thrown into boxes. When they were done stitching the cut and pinned pieces, the finished garment was hung on a rack near their workstation so it could be taken to the pressing station, where another worker—one with heavy heatproof gloves—wielded the giant steam presser that gave everything knife-edged creases. The noise from the first floor had been muffled by sound barriers between the front office and the stairwell, but up near the second floor, the buzzing of sewing machines and loud calling from the people doing the pressing and stacking was cacophonous and almost deafening.

The second floor, which could be seen when Marco and Chuck angled up, was full of workers with bolts of fabric and pattern pieces, and workers with scissors and strip cutters utilizing every last scrap of the fabric. The completed batch of fabric pieces was placed in a bag, complete with instructions. The bundles were grouped together in boxes, and when a worker on the first floor finished sewing, somebody would run a box down from the second.

The noise from the second floor was not nearly as loud—but it was frightening in its silence. People were concentrating—hard—on cutting the fabric to the last inch of its usefulness, and of not wasting a scrap of what was on the table.

"They do not look happy," Marco murmured, and Tor had to agree. Everybody in the warehouse was working as though their lives depended on it.

Tor murmured, for Marco's coms only, "And these are the workers they pay."

"Yikes," Marco muttered, and Tor had to agree. Tor had seen Flory Gallo's cheerful contracting business. Sure, Flory chivvied the workers when their breaks were too long, and heaven forbid anybody cut any corners, but Flory checked every project out personally before they moved on to county inspections, and Tor had heard from the workers themselves that there was a bonus—even if a small one—for the workers at the end of a successful job.

Hell, Tor worked for Felix Salinger, and not once in the Salinger media building had Tor seen faces this tense—or this afraid.

"Carl's looking at the stills," Tor said, signaling to Josh to let their conversation be private. "We're checking for doors or somewhere that would lead underground from the first floor on the inside. Do you see any movement that's suspicious?"

"Easy," Marco said. "West side of the building. Do you see it, Chuck?"

"Yeah," Chuck murmured. "Tor, Josh, we've got a small door in the back corner, behind a bunch of piecework boxes. The warehouse is so big it's hard to spot, but there's a set of stairs down in the corner and a few bruisers in black leather jackets heading that way."

"Oh shit," Josh muttered. "Chuck, can you get down there? Hunter's headed that way. I don't know if Grace can stay hidden where he is."

They could all hear Marco murmur, "Chuck, go—they need me up there to be a billionaire."

"You sure?" Tor asked, but Chuck was, from his camera feed, already on his way.

Beneath his feet, he felt the rumble of the van as Liam, taking matters into his own hands, began to edge their traveling ops center to the employee parking lot of the factory. It seemed as though they would need to get a lot closer than they were.

"MR. METZGER," came Jean Campano's voice. "I'm sorry, Mr. Metzger—but the Coulters are up here!"

Marco glanced up above him where Jean and Cammie were both leaning against the railing, looking down at the stairs from the third floor.

"I'm sorry," he said with a smile, taking the stairs smoothly, two at a time, grateful for the use of the Salinger gym like he'd never been before. "I was caught up in logistics and numbers. This is a small operation, yes?"

Hepzibah nodded and swallowed down the apparent insult. "Well, yes, but see, it's because the clothes are designer, and we put out limited quantities to boutiques only."

"I meant no offense," Marco said, giving his most charming smile. "I was just thinking about ways to optimize profit—do you have deals for the surplus clothes?"

Hepzibah looked puzzled. "There's no surplus." She smiled adoringly at her father. "Daddy says it's because my designs are very popular."

Gregg Coulter gave his daughter a distracted nod.

"So I'm puzzled," Marco told her. "Where would our money go to build this business higher?"

"Well, the first place it would go," Tracy Coulter said smoothly, "would be to hire a more marketable designer."

The hurt and the horror on Hepzibah's face almost made Marco feel sorry for her. "Mom," she said in a tiny voice, but Tracy continued like she hadn't heard.

"The boutique sales sustain us now, but with some casual-wear lines, with Hepzibah's brand, of course, we could hire some more workers and start to put out some bulk sales as well. Pull in more customers with the bulk sales, and turn them on to the high-level boutique lines."

Marco nodded and looked at Cammie, who was chewing on her lip. "As investors," she said, "would we get some say in the new designer? I know a couple of people graduating from their courses in New York who've got a really nice spin on the casual-to-business-to-semiformal idea. You remember my friend Ellen, Marc?"

Marco nodded because Cammie was referencing a real person who'd grown up in their neighborhood. "Of course," he said, giving his best urbane smile.

"I think you should give her a call," Cammie said. "Ask for her portfolio. I mean—" She gave a smile that was all upper-crust reserve. "—the final decision would be yours, of course," she finished, leaving none of the Coulters under any illusions as to who would be in charge.

"Well," Tracy stuttered, looking at her husband for help.

"Of course," Gregg Coulter muttered, stepping forward, "we would use the first of the cash influx to, uhm, stabilize the business a little before expanding." He turned to his son-in-law, who had just come out of the elevator to join the group. "Isn't that right, Byron?"

Byron King smiled, but it was the sort of smile a fish gave after it had died and a rictus pulled open its mouth. "Of course, once we'd stabilized the business itself, we'd be full speed ahead on the expansion."

"Mmm…." Camille said, tapping her lower lip with a pale pink fingernail. "What sort of stabilization do you need? Are all your paychecks up to date?"

"Of course," Tracy said, while in their ears, Josh said, "They're a month behind."

"Is the overhead taken care of on the building?" Marco asked.

"The lease is good for another five years," Gregg Coulter assured. In their ears, Stirling murmured, "Lease is good, but they're behind on rent by six months."

"What about your vendors?" Cammie asked. "Can we get a list of where you get your fabric and supplies?"

"Of course," Hepzibah chirped. "We only choose the best."

"The best polyester," Carl said in their ears. "But that's not the interesting thing here. Marco, I need you to swing your camera toward the far corner again."

Marco did, pretending to use the movement as impetus for thought. He heard an odd clatter as he did so, but he didn't dare look after Chuck, who had disappeared from the view of the people upstairs while he and Cammie had been talking.

"Well done," Tor said. "Go upstairs and schmooze."

"We will, of course, need to see your books before we agree to invest," Marco acknowledged out loud. "But first…." He gestured grandly to the top of the stairs before finishing the trip up.

"Perfect," Tor said in his ear. "Carl's found a way to get to the corner from outside without drawing too much attention to himself. Good job."

Marco put on his prettiest smile and moved up to the designer floor, ready to tell some more lies so they could get to the part where Tor told him what nobody in their ears was saying.

OH GOD—THE stuff Tor vowed to *never* tell Marco about that day.

"Kadjic?" Josh muttered. "Did he say Kadjic?"

"The fuck?" Danny said over coms. "Who said Kadjic?"

"Byron King," Josh muttered. "Stirling, can you—"

"No time," Stirling told him. "Tienne, somebody is poking at Marco's backstopped ID. Can you jump in and defend it?"

"On it," Tienne said, opening Stirling's spare laptop, already keyed into the ID websites. Tienne's passion may have been art, but his attention to detail made him an absolutely brilliant forger—and part of forging someone's identity these days relied on a certain ability with computers. Tienne would know how to backstop Marco's and Cammie's identities through different layers of social media and bureaucracy, and he could do it efficiently.

"Okay, so, Danny?" Josh said, his voice as crisp and military as Tor had ever heard it. "You can't focus on Kadjic. Kadjic is a job for another day, do you understand?"

"I'm not stupid, Josh," Danny replied irritably, "just stunned. But yes—what else is going on?"

Marco was standing on the stair landing, looking up at this point, and they could see from his lapel camera that all of their principal players were staring down at him, their bodies facing the wall of the factory—which probably saved their asses, because as the Coulters were staring at Marco, behind them, out of their line of sight, Chuck hopped up on the stair rail and *ran down*, bypassing the steps and using the momentum to carry him quickly to the floor so he could open the door and let Carl in. Together they hauled ass to the back corner, where the guys in leather jackets stopped their progress down the stairs and turned to meet the interlopers.

Tor murmured, "Carl's found a way inside," to urge Marco to go upstairs, and hoped a few words of praise would distract from what else was going on with Carl, Chuck, Hunter, and Grace.

Grace was still lost. They could hear his voice, telling them that he was somewhere too dark for the cameras, and it stank. Something about buckets of piss and shit that made Tor's stomach churn, and then, while they could still hear Grace, he wasn't talking to *them* anymore. He was talking to the people who'd been herded down into that dank, cold place, his voice as gentle with them as it had been when Tor had been suffering from nightmares.

"Yeah, I know. I'm a scary stranger," he murmured. "You can have my jacket, but don't be scared. I'm wearing black underneath. Black is no fun as a color. You guys call me Grace, okay? Don't worry. I won't hurt you. I'm bad at hurting people, but I'm good at finding them, right?"

Tor could have listened to the compassion in that kid's voice all day, but they were busy watching the horror show in the corner of the warehouse. Hunter was still sprinting from the parking lot, but the violence between the labor enforcers and the Salinger muscle had already started.

"You guys," Frankie said into his coms, "they left me out here in the back. I can't see anything. What's going on?"

"Stay there," Josh said. "Oh my God—Carl!"

Carl was *supposed* to have gone in through the back entrance that Marco and Chuck had spotted on the cameras—that was his job. Find the entrance, go down the stairs, and find Grace. But two thugs in black jackets had met him coming up the stairs, and as he'd looked around for an exit point, two more came in from outside.

Chuck had done his surfing-the-stair-rail thing down to the factory floor and sprinted across the concrete, letting his chauffeur's coat fall to the ground as he ran. He skidded into the fray as Carl clocked the first guy and ducked a blow from the second, then caught the blow from a third in the kidneys, because he was fit, but he was only one guy.

Chuck caught kidney guy in his own kidneys, and then kept punching. Carl didn't duck an elbow to his eye fast enough, but he countered with his own elbow and caught that guy in the nose. The blood spurted, but the guy didn't go down, and the melee—already fierce—got bloody.

And then Hunter rounded in from outside.

"Where is he!" Hunter shouted into his coms, and there was no doubt who "he" was.

"Down the stairs," Josh said. "He's calming all the prisoners. The place is dark, they can't see, and there's buckets of piss everywhere. Be careful."

"I'll get to him," Hunter said grimly. But first Hunter had to go down the stairs.

Everybody in the van winced as Hunter grabbed the two guys on Carl and cracked their heads together. They crumpled to the ground, and Carl turned to help Chuck as Hunter found the stairs.

For a moment, things seemed under control, but then—

"More thugs," Liam said calmly from the driver's seat, watching the monitor as a carload of muscled, black-clad men came running into the factory. Too many for the two men currently finishing up with the first batch, which explained why Liam was sliding from the driver's seat to the crowded back of the now-parked van. "I'll be back."

"Liam!" Josh called as Liam leapt out of the van. "*He's not miked*!" he shouted, and for the first time in Tor's acquaintance, Josh lost some of his ineffable calm.

"He'll be fine," Danny said. "How many more men in black leather jackets are in there?"

"Four more," Josh said. "They look… slick, Danny, Dad. Like, Gunrunner's Island slick."

"Like Kadjic slick," Danny muttered. "Josh, you keep monitoring—I'm going to do a deep dive on Byron King's and Gregg Coulter's finances. We stopped at the debt, thinking it was a way to lure Hepzibah into exposing herself. We forgot sometimes debt serves a purpose."

"Oh shit," Josh muttered.

"What's wrong?" Tor asked.

"Danny thinks they're in deep with Kadjic. That explains where King's getting some of his money and why Coulter hasn't gone bust yet. They've been letting Hepzibah commit these shitty, penny-ante crimes to save her business, but they haven't told her…." He trailed off, because the entire crime family was too despicable for words.

"She's running a slave operation and two kinds of contracting scams," Tor said, making sure he got this right, "so she can play fashion designer. Her father and husband are letting her because they know she'll lose money anyway, and if *she's* losing money, the mob can buy all her shitty clothes at a loss, and they can give it back through their own bank accounts, clean."

"That's what it looks like," Josh muttered. "So why are they so hungry for investors?" Josh's fingers went flying on a secondary computer keyboard as Stirling fed him information.

Stirling spoke up. "Because it's too little too late," he said. "If I'm reading this right, the mob stepped in about the time Clyde got sucked into the construction scam. The Coulters and King were down almost too much for their cut of the money laundering to save. They're in deep to Kadjic, and their finances are in shambles."

"Oh God," Tor muttered, thinking about all the time he'd just spent trying to tell this story so the public could understand it and the people involved could be punished. This extra layer... it was boggling. It would take forever for people to connect the dots. Hepzibah and her family would be far and away—

"Stop spiraling," Felix ordered. "We run with the original sequence." Tor's hammering heart slowed down a little, allowing him to think—and allowing Felix's words to sink in. "We interview Hepzibah *today*, tell her what we've got on her, let the family blather on and hang themselves, and simply add to the story at the end. Your plan was good, Gray—don't doubt yourself now."

Tor nodded, taking a deep breath. "Interview her today?" he asked, his eyes glued to the screen as—through the factory security feed—Chuck, Carl, and Hunter stood, back to back and bloody, a ring of incapacitated bodies at their feet, another layer of henchman closing in. As they watched, Liam burst through the back door and skidded into the fray. Hunter took the opportunity to disengage from the fighting, and they all heard Carl and Chuck shout, "Go! Find him!" before the fighting started in earnest again.

Fighting that, Tor was certain, the people on the third floor wouldn't be able to hear, insulated by space and the noise of the factory floor from the violence and human-rights violations happening in that corner of the building.

"Yes," Felix said grimly. "And I suggest you get in there and take those stairs two at a time. Get the family at the top floor while Danny and I cut off this van from Minions "R" Us."

"Shit," Danny said succinctly. "Let me secure the laptop, Fox—"

"Secure *yourself*, Lightfingers," Felix snapped. "Let's hope this thing is as safe as advertised."

"Oh no," Josh muttered, and Tor squeezed his shoulder as both of them realized that Felix and Danny were about to wreck their car to keep the fight at the factory from getting out of hand.

"Should I...?" Tor started, not sure how he was going to finish that sentence.

"Mom and Molly," Josh said over coms, "did you hear that? You need to get the EMTs to the crash site stat."

"On our way," Julia said tightly. "Molly, do you want out?"

"I know first aid," Molly said, reluctance in her voice. "You may need me here." Molly, who loved a good fight, had conquered that thing in her that said she *needed* a good fight. Of course, Tor thought, his stomach clenched, she might get what she wanted anyway.

Josh turned to Tor just as they heard the screech of metal from about a block away and Felix and Danny's pained grunts through the coms. "Go," he said. "Stirling, can you take over from Tienne?"

"Done," Stirling muttered, pressing a button to take over Tienne's attempts to safeguard Marco and Cammie's fake identities. "Tienne, hold Tor's camera."

Tor handed Tienne the device and the small handheld light as he slid out of the van, and together they hurried outside, being sure to slam the door shut behind them.

It occurred to Tor that the last time they'd left Stirling and Josh locked in the van, sure it was the safest place to be, someone had planted a bomb on the undercarriage.

"You guys," Tor cautioned, still sprinting for the back door. "You'd better keep an eye out—"

"We have cameras now," Josh said. "We learned. You stay safe and hit those stairs running."

They continued at a dead sprint around toward the back door, where Frankie stood, because it was a shorter shot to the base of the stairs from there, and as Tor and Tienne approached, Frankie jimmied the lock for what was probably the tenth time and held it open for them.

"What can I do?" he asked as they approached, and it was on the tip of Tor's tongue to tell him to get out of there and be safe.

"Block," Josh said through their earbuds. "Tor and Tienne are heading for the stairwell. Keep anybody else from going up after them."

Frankie's cackle was practically gleeful.

"Now we're talking!" he crowed. "Didja hear that, Cammie? I'm gonna fuckin' *fight*!"

Cammie didn't answer him directly, although they could all hear her spinning sunshine and bullshit with Marco, as she had been since they'd walked in, but they did hear Marco's sharp intake of breath.

Tor and Tienne entered the building, and Tor suddenly knew why Chuck had shed his thick wool coat as he'd run into the melee.

It was *stifling* on the factory floor, and he imagined the men battling in the far corner, the thuds of flesh and grunts of exertion muffled by the noise of the factory itself, were also growing hot and exhausted in the steamy warmth generated by all the machines.

Tor gave a yearning glance over his shoulder as they mounted the first flight of steps and watched as Carl landed a particularly powerful punch to a thug in a ponytail whose skin was so pale it glowed from that far away. Now that Frankie had seen Tor and Tienne to the stairs, he headed for the action with uncontained glee. As Tor watched, he skidded in and laid out a guy about to blindside Liam, and the grin on his face as he engaged the remaining men with the crew was fierce and bloodthirsty. It reminded Tor of Marco in a way, and how he seemed to have all the confidence in the world about pretty much anything.

As they pounded up the stairs, Josh kept them updated with the new information, and Tor felt the phone in his pocket buzzing almost ceaselessly with pictures Josh was sending him to back up the queries he was about to lob at Congressman Coulter and his family.

Contrary to what *Hepzibah* believed, this had never really been about her anyway.

Tor risked a glance at Tienne, Stirling's quiet, competent boyfriend, who was sprinting the stairs effortlessly. The young man had the gall to grin at him as they scampered across a landing, and then Tor's eyes were completely on the steps so he didn't break both their necks.

They arrived on the third floor barely winded, and Tor was able to get that wind back as he slowed to a brisk walk and approached the group of people standing a little to the left of four beleaguered designers at drawing tables and a gaggle of piece designers fitting pinned segments over three bored models.

"These are the people who carry out my vision," Hepzibah was saying as they drew near. "I give them my sketches, and they manifest my ideas and translate them into actual garments."

The designer at the nearest table sent Hepzibah a venomous look, as if to tell the world that this wasn't how it worked. Either that or that Hepzibah's "vision" was damned impossible to carry out, and these were the people who picked up that slack.

"When was the last time they were paid, Hepzibah?" Tor asked, small portable mic pulled out of his pocket and attached to his phone.

"They get paid, uhm, monthly," Hepzibah said, sending a green smile to Marco and Cammie—and not even questioning Tor's presence. "Like we told you—"

Tor pulled out one of the first exhibits Josh had sent to his phone. "This is the bank statement that says you haven't," he said.

"We're about to take care of that," Gregg Coulter said smoothly. "Whoever you are." He blinked at the camera, obviously understanding the implications even if he didn't recognize the people in his daughter's factory. If this feed was going live, he couldn't afford to strong-arm reporters—certainly not in front of clients he was trying to impress. He gave his daughter an indulgent smile. "We can discuss my Eppie's lack of business acumen on another day, but let me tell you, those payments in arrears will soon be made up."

Hepzibah turned to her mother in confusion. "But… but Byron told me he would cut the checks." She turned her attention to her husband. "Byron? You… you said we had the money to cut the checks. That all the other stuff I was doing—you had enough money to pay everybody. Why… why didn't you pay everybody?"

Byron sent a resentful glare toward Gregg Coulter. "You'll have to ask your father," he said unhappily, and Hepzibah gave her father a wounded look.

"Daddy? I did side hustles like you told me—why aren't we paid up?"

Gregg Coulter sent Tor a positively murderous glare. "Darlin', can we discuss this another time? You don't need to know the ins and outs of the money here—"

Tor took his advantage there.

"Speaking of extra stuff, Hepzibah—your side hustles—do you mind telling my livestream audience what this 'extra stuff' was?"

Hepzibah's face went white under the giant gold bow she'd worn to pull her thin blond hair back. She turned to her mother again. "My, uhm, mother's a great businesswoman," she said weakly. "She gave me tips on how to raise extra capital with a low overhead to invest in your business."

"Who are you?" Byron asked, as though snapping himself out of a bad dream.

"He's a reporter," Tracy said, her disgust thinly disguised. "He crashed our luncheon last week with some little actress, on Julia Salinger's heels."

Someday, somehow, Tor would make this woman rue calling Molly "some little actress," but now was not the time. "What exactly would those tips be, Mrs. Coulter?" Tor demanded, shoving the microphone into Tracy's face, and Tracy Coulter may have been mean, but she wasn't a fool.

"I look to my husband in all things," she said, throwing the mess directly in Gregg Coulter's lap.

"Well, my little ladybug was the brains behind the outfit," Gregg began unctuously, directly contradicting what he had just told them, and Tor's phone buzzed again. Josh's voice sounded in his ear.

"We've got pictures," he said. "Show them to the Coulters."

"So, you're saying it was your daughter's idea to imprison adults with disabilities and force them to work as fraudulent contractors?" Tor asked. "Because that's a little involved for one person."

"You don't have any proof of that!" Coulter blustered, and Tor held up the phone.

Grace was shown, his back to the camera, coaxing a line of tired, thin, confused people out of the basement chamber in the corner of the factory. Hunter was helping some of the weakest on their way up, and Carl, Chuck, Liam, and Frankie were forming a wall between the mostly unconscious guards and the escaping workers. Everybody's faces were pixilated, but the condition of those being freed was unmistakable. Tired, unwashed, too thin—they all looked as abused as Clyde had when Tor had gotten that footage for his original construction scam story.

"This you?" Tor asked, after showing the phone to the camera in Tienne's hand. "Or I should say, is this the factory we're sitting in *now*?"

"We had no idea those people were there," Gregg began. "I have no idea who they work for—"

"Oh, that's easy," Tor said, holding out the camera to Tienne again so he could film the next set of photos. "They work for *you*. Or rather—" He turned the camera to Hepzibah. "—they work for *you*, but under a series of fraudulently exploited companies who had no idea you were using their company identities to front bad contracting scams and abuse workers."

"Why would I do that?" Gregg asked, before catching himself. "Why would my daughter do that?"

Tor nodded. "That was tough at first—like Hepzibah said, with all that 'extra stuff' she's doing, she *should* have enough in the bank to pay off her company's debts and keep producing"—he had to fight not to editorialize—"*clothing*, which is what she really wanted to do. I mean, I don't approve of her methods—slavery is a *bad, bad thing*," he almost shouted, "but at least her motives were clear. She wanted the money to keep her business going. So very cut and dried. But she should have *had* the money, right, Byron? Right, Gregg?"

"I'm a state congressman," Gregg Coulter stated obviously, but Tor kept talking over him.

"This business is not our only endeavor," Byron King said icily, ignoring his father-in-law's meltdown. "And we obviously have enough money." He gestured around them. "Why would we be in arrears?"

"Because you gambled," Tor said, listening to Josh closely. "Because, unbeknownst to you, Hepzibah had made some *very* dangerous business contacts, hadn't she? They seemed so nice, and they were so impressed by her other moneymaking endeavors, and they had some great business opportunities for you, didn't they?"

Gregg and Byron met gazes, both of them seeming to think the exact same thing.

"Business opportunities that went up in a ball of fire this January, off the coast of Barbados," Tor said, jaw set.

"Are you trying to say," Gregg Coulter blustered, "we had something to do with that… that Gunrunner's Island fiasco?"

"Absolutely," Tor told him, holding up the phone in his hand that had buzzed with financial documents Stirling had sent both to Tor and to the organized crime division of the state's attorney's office. "And you were happy to do it. You told your daughter to find a way to pay off her bills, and she did! But she introduced you to these new and exciting friends who were able to produce a little muscle to make sure her illegal labor schemes had some backup, and you were so excited. They offered to buy her surplus—which she didn't know she had, and you didn't tell her—and told you where to invest your money so you could make up some cash! And it was a pretty sweet deal until Gunrunner's Island, wasn't it? I mean, bless you, you were one of the few investors who didn't get caught up in the sweep—the ties to the factory muddied things, and lucky you. But you're still neck deep in it, and we've got you dead to rights."

"We refuse to answer any questions without a lawyer present," Byron King said, cutting his eyes desperately to his in-laws, forgetting his wife completely.

"But what did I do?" Hepzibah asked her parents, sounding legitimately clueless. "You told me I had to finance my own company, and I *did*! You can't say I didn't! What did I do wrong?"

"For starters," Tor said harshly, "*this*." He pulled up another picture, a little voice in the back of his head asking him who was taking these, but most of him too occupied with what he was doing to care. "See them, Hepzibah? They have *families*. They have caregivers looking for them— and did you let that stop you?"

Her lower lip came out with a pout. "Some of those contractors had been mean to Daddy," she said, as though that excused *everything*. "It wasn't just about the employees."

"*They're not employees when you don't pay them!*" Tor shouted, and she backed up, terrified. "Let's call this what it is, Ms. Coulter-King. This is slave labor, and you used it to add to your coffers, which was bad enough. But in order to pay for your legit workers, what did you have to do?"

She cast a hunted look at her family, who stared back at her helplessly. "I just made a deal with a guy—it was no big thing. He gave me some muscle, bought my surplus, I guess, and I took the extra money and then paid him back for the muscle."

Her father dropped his face into his hands, and Tor knew the jig was up.

"Hepzibah," Tor said softly, "the amount of money they were giving you was *way too big* for those transactions."

"What does that mean?" Hepzibah asked, staring at her parents. "What does that—what does he mean by that?"

"It means, sweet pea," Tracy said tiredly, "you mortgaged your company to the Russian mob."

"And *that*," Tor explained, aware that the ungodly racket on the ground floor had ceased and sirens from outside were loud enough to reach the news feed, "is why your parents weren't paying your bills with that money." He turned to them. "And why you so very much wanted investors."

Marco and Cammie had been standing off to the side since Tor and Tienne had barged up to the floor; he finally had a chance to meet their eyes.

Marco was grinning at him, adoration written in every line of his face, and heat crept up Tor's cheeks, the relief and triumph of that moment made complete in a way it never had been before.

God, the intoxication of that look. The man he loved was gazing at him like he could hang the moon. Tor could be drunk off it for the rest of his life.

Right now, he gestured toward the two of them. "I have it on good authority," he said, giving the Coulters a meaningful look, "that if you take the freight elevator, you can hook up with your chauffeur and avoid the unpleasantness to come."

The two of them nodded soberly, although their eyes sparkled.

"Very kind of you," Cammie said, grabbing Marco's hand. As they passed the silent and pale Coulters, she spoke loudly. "God, that was a close call. I'm so glad that reporter got there in time, because I would have hated to invest in those *hideous* clothes."

Hepzibah let out a little whimper, as though that was the unkindest cut of all, and Tor turned back toward them and *really* got to work.

The Patter of Falling Straight Pins

"DAD," JOSH muttered unhappily from the couch in his suite, "make her stop."

"She won't stop for me, she won't stop for you," Felix replied, trying without success to thrust a plastic straw under the cast on his arm to scratch the skin underneath.

"Both of you, stop," Julia told them irritably, finished with replacing the ice on Josh's eye. "Of all the bollixed, slapdashed, dumbassed capers we have ever pulled, that had to be the one that aged me the fastest."

"Dearest," Danny murmured in a conciliatory tone, "it was for a good cause."

"Do you want me to stop bringing ice for your knee?" she asked waspishly.

"No, no," Danny said, holding his hands out. "And by all means, keep the ibuprofen flowing. I'm only saying…."

"You're only saying that trashing a perfectly good SUV was the smartest play you could bring at the time?" she snapped.

"Well," Felix said, apology in his voice, "it worked."

It had too. Not only had the EMTs arrived in record time, but they had actually listened as Felix pointed to the fleeing henchman and directed law enforcement attention to the Coulter warehouse. Maybe half of the "guards" hired by Andres Kadjic to reinforce his hold over the Coulters got away— but half of them were in custody, and that was not a bad ratio.

"Danny, give me your cane," she growled.

"No," Danny said crossly. "I just got him back. You cannot beat him senseless."

"Tor," she muttered, glancing to Tor and Marco as they stood in the doorway, late lunch on the trays in their hands, "please talk some sense into them."

"Uhm, Leon's home," Tor said, and nobody missed the relieved sighs of the five injured men in the room. "He was irritated you went without him."

Julia gave him a sulky look. "Did you make it clear that was not part of the plan?" she asked. "It was supposed to be reconnaissance only?"

"Hm," said a deep voice behind Tor and Marco. "I seem to recall something like that happened at Gunrunner's Island. I'm starting to think you people enjoy planning so you can scare the hell out of us when the plans fall to shit."

Tor stepped aside to let Leon into the room, and he paused for a moment to survey the carnage.

Chuck and Carl were on Josh's bed, both of them holding ice packs to various parts of their bodies. Chuck had one draped across both eyes and his nose. Michael had been the one to bring up a bucket to put the old ice packs in, and he was doling out ibuprofen for the two of them with narrowed eyes. As Tor and Marco had approached with food they'd heard him threatening to call Lucius and make him take a plane to Chicago to nurse Chuck back to health. Chuck's reply had been a whimper, and Michael had stopped yelling at him, because with two black eyes and a broken nose, it was very clear that Chuck's entire head hurt.

Carl wasn't much better, but Michael's hurt silence and tender touches to the nonbruised or swollen parts of his face and body seemed to be more recrimination than he could bear.

"I'm sorry," he mumbled as Michael smoothed his hair back. "We don't know why the workers came back early. But once they were there and Grace had found them, we couldn't just leave them, right?"

"Here, gentlemen," Leon murmured to Tor and Marco. "I'll start handing out soup since all the flat places to put the trays are taken."

"Thanks, Leon," Marco replied. "We were thinking we'd have to use the floor."

The room was a mess, littered with bandages, ice packs, and painkillers—and, of course, the walking wounded.

Very few of them had escaped unscathed.

"Where's Grace and Hunter?" Leon asked quietly.

"They're in the den, being tended to by Stirling and Molly," Julia explained. "They were all too mad at Josh here to even stay in the same room with him."

Josh had been the one taking pictures of the freed workers and sending them—pixilated—to Tor as he'd needed them. He'd been popped in the eye—and the kidneys—by a guard who hadn't been incapacitated *enough*, and he had spent a good two hours at the hospital being tested to make sure none of his fragile healing organs had burst. Given that Danny and Felix had needed a trip to the ER after their car wreck—and Julia insisted the others went to have their concussions assessed and their noses, wrists, and ankles set—he'd been in good company.

"That's not true," Josh told her, sounding grumpy at the thought of his friends mad at him. "Grace was…." He sighed. "Grace needed Hunter time.

And he needed to not worry about me. I made Hunter take him down there to play video games with Stirling and chill him out."

"Poor soul," Julia said with a sigh. "He was devastated by those people he helped out of the basement."

Tor had heard him sobbing on Hunter's shoulder after the rescue units that Julia had planned to have in place *tomorrow* had been called in for emergency service that afternoon. Once again, he remembered Grace as the reluctant angel during his own time of need, and he thought that it was a good thing he had his own Hunter to protect him against the harshest parts of the world—and his own tender heart.

"Where's our young copper?" Leon asked, and a pained look crossed Josh's face.

"After they set his wrist, he had to call his home office and explain how he knew that Andres Kadjic had been actively involved with an American politician," Josh said. He let out a sigh. "He was super proud of the broken nose, by the way. Asshole."

Tor and Marco winced, and Marco added, "If it's any consolation, Frankie hasn't been so happy to have a black eye since one got him laid in high school."

There was a collective groan.

"We're so sorry," Danny said. "Marco, I cannot apologize to you enough for dragging your family into this—"

"We dragged you!" Marco said, and now that Leon had handed out the last bowl of the life-giving soup that had been waiting for them as they'd trickled home in twos and threes, he could set his tray down in a corner and shake out his arms. When he took Tor's tray from him quietly, Tor did the same, because the full bowls had been heavy and it had been a long day.

"Yes," Felix said, and Tor heard him pulling his "boss" persona on, which was particularly impressive given he'd changed into sweats and was sporting a broken wrist and his own broken nose. "But we promised to help and…." He grimaced. "Usually we're more professional than this."

Leon laughed so hard he almost spilled the soup he was handing to Michael.

"Oh my God!" he guffawed. "Since when!"

Danny cast him a narrow-eyed glare. "You know, we *were* starting to approve of you. Don't ruin it now!"

Leon laughed again, a rich, stomach-rolling sort of laugh that seemed to make the rest of the misery diminish with every breath.

"Danny, Felix, I love you like…." He sobered, so they knew this was real to him. "I didn't love my brother more," he said softly, speaking of

Josh's father. "This entire family—you have pulled me in and touched my heart like no other. But let's face it, my brothers. What you told Grace about being trickster gods and agents of chaos? It was the most truthful thing anybody has ever said about any member of this household."

Marco chuckled. "You have given my cousins stories to tell for the next ten years," he said kindly, and Tor wanted to hug him. Then he sobered, and Tor wanted to cry. "And you have given my family back my uncle, and my uncle back his friend's son. Clyde was…." He let out a sigh. "My aunt Marie was in tears, she was so happy. And I know Tor has more reporting to do—and the business may never recover completely—but my family won't let my uncle suffer, and my uncle and aunt won't let Clyde suffer. And he was one person. You… you freed over twenty people today—Cammie and I counted. We called our mothers and had them come help Julia's friends so they could be part of the rescue." He turned a look of adoration on Tor, the same adoration he'd shown in the warehouse. "People complain about stuff all the time—about politics, about corruption, about what bad people can do to helpless people. I work for a family that actually *does* something about it, and I don't care if nobody knows but us—I'm really proud of that."

There was an awkward blushy silence in the room, and oddly enough it was Michael who broke it. "That's sweet and all," he said, "but you'd better not let Grace hear you or he'll steal all our wallets and catapult them into outer space so we can believe the worst of him again."

Tor was grateful to Marco. With his characteristic honesty, he had broken through all the bravado and swagger that the Salingers were so good at, and he'd said something real.

And Michael had put them back in family legend land, where this group of thieves, bruisers, and hackers were comfortable again.

"I heard my name," Grace said, and his voice sounded clogged. "You'd better not say anything rotten about me. I'm ouchie."

Josh's face lightened, and he sat up carefully from his reclined posture on the couch. "They said you weren't here," he said. "You were supposed to be all ouchie on Hunter, but if you want to be ouchie on me, you can."

"Hunter's downstairs on the phone, trying to convince Lucius to calm the fuck down," Grace muttered, sitting right next to Josh and putting his head on Josh's shoulder. "I needed my woobie, not my boyfriend."

Josh put his arm around Grace's shoulders and leaned his head on Grace's.

"I'll always be your woobie," he promised, his own voice sounding a little clogged.

"Good. Now stay in the truck for another six months," Grace said, but unlike the *rest* of the family, he didn't sound angry—just like he was reminding Josh of something.

"I'll try," Josh promised, letting out a sigh. The young man looked all of the things he'd been over the past six months—exhausted, sick, fragile—but he also looked... proud. Tor thought of all the times Josh had pushed himself, had been left behind, and had pushed himself again. This was his first full involvement with the team since his diagnosis back in the summer, and suddenly Tor understood why Josh kept trying to keep Liam at arm's length while he was healing.

Josh wasn't made to sit in the van. He needed to know Liam could love him when Josh was in the middle of the fight.

He risked a glance at Marco, who was starting to take empty bowls from most of the people in the room and stack them on trays. Marco had seen Tor—the man behind the curtain—and so far he was okay with who and what Tor was. And his de facto family as well.

Was Tor ready for that?

He'd started helping again, collecting soup bowls and spoons, when Marco put his hand on Tor's wrist. "Let me," he murmured. "There's something you've all been dying to talk about—I can tell."

Tor gaped after him as Marco hefted the trays of empty bowls and headed toward the stairs.

"I'll help," Michael said, grabbing the other tray and putting it on his shoulder, restaurant style. Liam held the door for them as they disappeared down the hallway toward the stairs, and Tor swallowed, turning back toward the room.

"Move over," Liam said, but grimly and with no play at all, forcing Josh to scoot Grace over a little as Hunter, Stirling, Tienne, and Molly all entered the room.

"We couldn't have done this in the den?" Julia complained, and Leon wrapped an arm around her shoulder and pulled her back to sit in Josh's desk chair while Hunter lowered himself stiffly onto the floor and Stirling and Molly did the same in front of the couch.

"What's this about?" Leon asked softly.

"We *should* make you leave the room," Danny told him. "Plausible deniability and all that. I must say, it's lucky Lucius is in the air so he doesn't have to be involved."

"He'll want to be," Chuck murmured, sitting up with his back against the wall to match Carl. "Hunter, don't sit on the floor, brother. If your body's feeling anything like mine...."

Hunter gave a grunt and scooted back a little farther so Grace could stroke his hair, and Chuck stopped.

This was it. This was as comfortable as they were all going to be.

"I've been thinking about it," Danny began conversationally.

"No."

Everybody in the room said it. They didn't yell it, just stated it as an incontrovertible fact.

"People," Danny began gently, and from his position of leaning against the door, Tor saw the look Josh sent him, a look of such anger, such hurt, that Danny's tongue must have cleaved to the roof of his mouth.

"You can't say it's only your problem," Tienne said softly, and Tor stared at him. The young man had been quiet, stalwart, and surprisingly game, and while he was not exactly a forceful personality, Tor was getting the feeling that there was something... unflappable about Tienne. He was a stone in the river. The river may have worn him smooth, but he stayed put, part of the bedrock, the thing that changed the river's course without the river being any the wiser.

The silence was the smoothness. Everything else about Tienne was quiet strong.

"You, my boy," Danny murmured, and Tor was brought forcibly back to how Danny had saved the boy's life from the monster none of them were talking about. "I wanted to keep you out of it. I wanted to keep you all out of it. I—"

Felix broke in. "There might not be anything we *have* to do," he said hopefully. "I mean, is it really that much of a surprise the man's name came up? He's come up in a lot of our dealings. He's an international criminal, after all!"

Liam grunted. "He's a criminal that needs to be taken down, Felix," he said after a minute. "I would prefer none of you be involved either, but the fact is—" He shrugged. "—you're perfectly placed. All of you. You've become a thorn in his side, whether he knows it or not—"

"He knows," Stirling said from Josh's feet.

"How do you know that?" Josh murmured. Tor wasn't sure if the boy knew it or not, but while he and Grace snuggled, holding each other like "woobies," Liam had seized his hand, and Josh was gripping Liam's hand tightly in return.

"Because," Stirling said, holding up the laptop he'd brought in. He opened it and pulled up a screen. "This is my personal laptop," he told them. "It's encrypted and bounced off over twenty IP addresses. This morning I would have said it's impossible to trace."

With a few more taps of the keys, he continued. "Do you all remember, when shit started going south, how I told you somebody was taking a poke at Marco and Cammie's backstopped IDs?"

Everybody nodded—while Frankie, Cammie, and Marco had been on limited coms by that time, the rest of them had been on full coms, their practice at listening through the chatter—and at not contributing to excess noise—serving them well.

"I gave my laptop to Tienne to keep the IDs intact, and he did, but as he did, the person poking at them was tracing my IP address."

Everybody was staring at him, riveted.

"Did they find us?" Josh asked after a breath.

Stirling shook his head. "No. I have a fail-safe, five addresses away." He glanced up at Danny. "It's something you taught me. When somebody gets that close with a trace, it wipes out everything—the backstopped ID and any alterations we've made to regular IDs to fortify it. Marc and Cammie Metzger ceased to exist, and my connection to the twenty IP addresses is completely gone. I have to rebuild the entire network from the ground up on a clean computer."

Those in the room who dealt with computers all sucked air in through their teeth, thinking about the time it would take to do that.

Stirling grinned fiercely. "Oh, I'm looking forward to it," he said. "Teach that fucker to try to hack *me*." He pulled in a breath. "And he's going to try again—but worse," he said, holding up the laptop screen so they could all see it, "he *thinks* he knows who I am."

"Oh no," Danny said faintly.

The screenshot had been taken just before the screen went blank—Tor could see the code in the corner that indicated the complete annihilation of any of the data the hacker had been looking for.

There, in basic coding, were the words Hello, Lightfingers.

"Leon," Julia said, her voice the slightest bit thready, "I don't suppose you would consider returning to Belgium for the next few months?"

Leon snorted. "Only if you have an operation planned from my home there," he said. Then, almost cajolingly, "Although I'd love to have you and the others come visit."

"Belgium, Josh," Grace said. "We missed the last trip, remember? Hunter said it's like a boring stuffy movie there with big houses. We should see it."

Josh gave a sigh. "I like it here," he murmured. "Besides, all the diamonds are in Belgium. Don't tell me Andres Kadjic doesn't have his fingers in those pies either."

"Please, everybody," Danny tried again, sitting up in the recliner and gazing beseechingly at Felix. "This is my mess, and I should go clean it up—"

"I absolutely will not forgive you if you go out and get yourself killed," Felix said, and while the tone was slightly irritated, the expression on Felix's face was... *devastated.* "No. Absolutely not an option." Felix glanced around Josh's crowded bedroom suite. "Look around you, Danny. *Look* at this absolutely terrific mass of talent. Wasting the potential of all these people who love you to fix this terrible wrong—that would be a sin." And finally, finally, Felix's voice broke. "And we love you, Danny Lightfingers. All of us. And our lives would be sad and bereft without you in them, and I would be heartbroken, and I'll never be able to put those pieces together again. Once was all I had in me. You can't leave me again. You can't leave any of us, but not Josh, or Julia, and especially not me—"

Tor was the first one out the door, but the rest of the room followed him, including Leon, leaving only the original grifters, Felix, Danny, Julia, and Josh, the family that should never have been but that had forged itself into an unbreakable whole.

"So what are we going to do?" Tor asked, not wanting to be the one who said it but wanting to know.

"You, mate," Liam said cheerfully, "have some work to do. Don't you need to be editing and doing voice-overs and all that crap? Felix told you to keep on with the original plan to destroy the Coulters. Don't tell me you've forgotten that."

"Oh no," Tor muttered, the stress of the work falling on his shoulders. "I haven't forgotten." He still had at least two weeks of twelve-hour days to solidify the media blitz that would completely ruin the despicable Coulter family. Tor was going to present *all* the dirt, in excruciating detail. He had already fielded some absolutely heartbreaking phone calls from family members who were so relieved to have their brothers or sisters or children returned to their care, and from some of the contracting companies who were begging for his help to regain their reputation so the business could live to see spring.

"So you're busy," Liam murmured. "In fact, we all are. We've all got day jobs to manage, people to see, plans to make. But in the meantime...."

"In the meantime," Grace said, having listened unashamedly to their conversation, "Josh and Danny are going to plan." He sounded absolutely sure of himself. "Josh won't leave me, and Danny won't leave his family. Not again. They're in there already, making plans to stay."

"Then all we have to do," Stirling said as they neared the landing, "is make plans to stay with them. It's very simple."

At that moment, there was a clatter in the kitchen, and Phyllis's hurried, "He's fine, Lucius, in fact he's up in Josh's—oh—"

And Chuck's boyfriend, who had been off managing his own company, came charging into the hallway to cluck over his great brawny lover and reassure himself that Chuck was okay.

The Way to a Man's Heart

THREE WEEKS after the confrontation at Hepzibah Coulter's factory, Marco woke up and felt the spot next to him in bed—and growled.

Empty again.

The day of the confrontation, after the meeting in Josh's room, Tor had spent hours in his room at the mansion, putting together the news releases that would indict the congressman's family on a thousand crimes. Including being horrible human beings. Marco had managed to pull him away, seducing him as far as the bed in his room, kissing him senseless until Tor's body was pliable and needy and everything in his heart and mind was burned away by Marco's possession.

The next day, Tor had given him an absent kiss on the way out the door, saying he was going to work in his apartment for a few days, but he'd be back.

He had been, every four days or so, looking exhausted and worn thin. He chose his times carefully, exercising with the rest of the group and haunting the kitchen for breakfast with them as well, their banter as free-form as it had always been but somehow… closer. As though the family was closing ranks. The fences they were building were more white picket than barbed wire, but Marco had grown up in a neighborhood in which none of the neighbors built fences, instead letting all of the neighborhood kids run from house to house in a giant knot. The only thing that had been fenced was Mrs. Culliver's swimming pool, and if you asked her nicely for the key to the gate and had enough supervision, she'd give it to you.

Marco did not like fences, and he was particularly suspicious of one that seemed to have him on one side and his lover on the other.

Three times since the big confrontation, he'd managed to corner Torrance Grayson somewhere in the mansion and kiss him senseless, taking him to bed ruthlessly, reminding the man why he needed Marco Gallo in his life.

"He's probably busy," Cammie had said the week before, on one of their regular phone calls. "I mean, he hasn't broken up with you. That's important."

Marco had "*hmm*ed." "Something happened that day—the day of the factory," he told her. "Something they didn't let us hear."

And then his cousin said something very wise. "Marco honey, they've done this a lot. I mean, a *lot*. It was fun and games for us to participate, and I'm telling you, Frankie's got a girl on the hook right now who's absolutely convinced he's James Bond, but… but for them to do what they did? And not get mentioned at *all*? These people are Chicago royalty, honey. They've *got* to have friends in high places. And, you know, friends in high places have…."

"Enemies in low ones," he said softly. His aunt and uncle had called him once a day, separately and together, to thank him again for calling in help. Flory was slowly starting to build back his business, and Clyde was an employee again. The man's late father had paid for him to have a place in a halfway house, living semi-independently, but he got so excited when his bus took him to Flory Gallo and Sons that Flory was reluctant to let him go back there every day. The family had embraced him for Sunday dinner, taking turns picking him up, making sure he was happy and comfortable, and Marco had heard him say more than once that the world had sunshine again, because he thought all the sun had gone away when his father did.

So his family had reaped the benefit of Torrance Grayson's hard work—and that of the rest of the Salingers. But the Salinger crew didn't seem to be celebrating, and neither did Tor.

"Baby," Cammie said, sounding serious.

"Yeah?"

"If you're absolutely committed to this guy, you gotta let him know."

"Know what?" Marco asked, not sure if he could make himself any clearer as far as Tor was concerned.

"That his enemies are your enemies. And that includes somebody planning to hurt his family. I mean, I saw them working together—they worked together the way Pop and the guys work together. That wasn't just a bunch of assholes with the same job, honey, that was—"

"Family," he supplied.

"Yeah," she agreed. "And you need to let him know you're in."

So Marco had caught Tor's attention at family dinner a few days after that conversation and had worked *very* hard at letting Tor know he was "in." But now, waking up alone in his bed, he realized that maybe he'd concentrated a little too hard on the wrong kind of "in."

Furiously, he jumped out of bed and showered, hating to wash Tor's smell off his body but needing to feel as professional as possible before he walked across to the house to start work. It was Sunday morning, which meant Felix, Danny, and Julia were having one of their "private" brunches. The staff was good at having their food—and Marco tried to go all out for these—ready and dished up by eight in the morning, and then…

disappearing. Sometimes the other members of the household joined them, but more often than not, it was the three of them, talking very seriously about something they felt very private about.

It was as good a place as any for Marco to make a stand.

Marco made sure he was one of the people who carried in the plates—in this case it was lobster eggs benedict, fruit parfait, and slabs of perfectly browned bacon—and he remained in the dining room to pour the orange juice and coffee, something the three of them normally preferred to do for themselves.

Felix was the first one down the stairs, looking tired but clean-cut and ready for Sunday brunch.

"It smells delicious," he said, smiling at Marco, and then his eyes sharpened. "But you didn't deliver it by happenstance, did you."

Marco shook his head and discarded his pride over his shoulder. "Tor," he said softly. "He... he's been pulling away from me."

"Oh," Felix said, lips parting slightly. He glanced around almost wildly for a moment. "Danny's usually better at these things," he said, sounding uncomfortable.

"But Tor's your friend in particular," Marco said, trying not to panic. "He thinks of you like an older brother—family he's reclaimed after he left the other one in the dust. And... and I think he's pulling away like the rest of the family is pulling away. There's something nobody is saying, and—"

Comprehension dawned, and Felix held up a hand. "He's... something worrisome came up," he admitted. "During our little adventure at the factory. I imagine Tor simply is trying to keep you safe."

Marco felt his expression—and his resolve—harden. "I meant what I said that day, sir. I'm all in. This family is my place—that includes him. That includes whatever he's afraid of. But—" He threw out his hands. "—I need to be able to pin him down to tell him that!"

Felix laughed weakly. "I believe I saw Chuck on his way out to the gym on my way in," he said. "He was going to drive into the city today with Grace and Hunter. Perhaps...." He gave a shrug. "If you send Phyllis in here, I'll tell her you have the day off, and they could give you a ride too?"

Marco nodded. "I'll pack an overnight bag," he said grimly. "Tomorrow's my day off."

Felix smiled. "Thataboy. Good luck, young Marco. Tor deserves a mate in the midst of all this madness. I think... I think he feels that he had to sacrifice his relationship with you to stay with us. Feel free to tell him that *I* said I'd rather he not do that."

Marco smiled, feeling hope for the first time since he'd awakened to that cold, empty spot in his bed. "Can I… uhm, can I have some help before I go, sir?"

"If you're going to move his stuff into your little cottage, I suggest you hit up Hunter and Chuck before you leave." He gazed at his brunch longingly just as Danny and Julia came in, looking like he did—tired and unhappy about having to conduct their own business on a Sunday morning.

"And in the meantime," Marco murmured, "I'll leave you all alone."

Felix nodded gratefully, and Marco went to tell Phyllis. When he told her why he was taking the evening off, she gave a happy cackle.

"Oh, it's about time," she said. "Everybody's so damned serious. We *need* you two together."

"I'm working on it," he vowed. And then he went to hit up Chuck, Hunter, and Grace.

TOR HAD been deep in editing when the knock came on his door, telling himself devoutly that he was glad to finally be working on something besides the Coulter case. Felix hadn't changed his mind about wanting Tor to have his own show, and Tor was putting together a "pitch tape" for his ideas throughout the season.

Felix had warned him that he might need some extra episodes in the can for some point in the year, and Tor wanted to be ready.

Still, all of that fled his mind when he opened the door, wondering if he'd ordered takeout and forgotten, and found Marco there, an overnight satchel over his shoulder and a bag of takeout—Thai if Tor knew his food—in his fist.

"Uhm," Tor managed, staring at Marco's beautiful sloe-eyed, sharply chiseled features with a hunger that had nothing to do with Thai food. "I'm not sure I—"

"No, you didn't order it," Marco muttered, pushing gently past Tor's body and into the apartment. "Close the door, and for God's sake, let's crack a window or two—it's stifling in here."

"It's *February* out there," Tor managed as Marco—true to his word—cracked one of the old-fashioned windows a hair's breadth and some of the fusty air closer to the vaulted ceilings began to dissipate.

"It's *sad* in here," Marco retorted, setting the food up on the counter. "I'm done with sadness."

Tor managed to get hold of himself. "But… but Marco, what are you *doing* here?"

"Claiming you," Marco said with no self-consciousness whatsoever.

"I'm sorry?" Tor was so confused, but Marco wasn't having it.

"You should be!" he snapped, turning around, and for the first time, Tor saw hurt, writ large across Marco's beautiful features. "I ask you to move into my cottage fifty-zillion times and you sleep with me and disappear? Not once—*three times*—and I'm left to wonder what I did wrong."

"You didn't do anything wrong," Tor mumbled, not sure how to explain this.

"No, *you* did," Marco said crossly. "When you assumed I couldn't deal with whatever the family is dealing with. You didn't even give me a chance to say yes or no, you just… just pulled away, like a coward, which I know you're not. So why? Why would you do that?"

"Because I'm weak," Tor confessed, hating himself for those nights. Marco had simply grabbed his hand when Tor had made to go fetch his car. One minute Tor was saying goodbye to Phyllis in the kitchen, and the next, Marco had stalked through the kitchen, grabbed his hand, and was hauling Tor to his cottage and his bed.

Tor had been lost from the first brush of their lips.

"You're not weak," Marco told him, crossing his arms in frustration and leaning back against the counter.

"Oh, I am," Tor said, knowing it was the truth. "I-I should have broken it off. But…." He gave a self-conscious smile. "I… you're so pretty. And my heart wants you so bad."

Marco uncrossed his arms and strode up to Tor in two big steps. "Then take me," he murmured and then smiled slightly. "But still from the bottom. You're not ready to top yet."

Tor gave him a sad smile. "Marco, you don't understand—"

"That the Salingers have a big bad enemy and you're all planning what to do about him? You think I don't understand?"

"Marco," Tor said, firming up his voice the best he could, "it's dangerous!"

"I'm Italian, Torrance," Marco retorted. "Even if we're not all gangsters, I've seen the Godfather movies about six-thousand times. According to my father, it's what happens when your great-grandparents met on the boat from the old country. You like wine, you love food, and you watch the Godfather movies six-thousand times. I'd say he's full of shit, but that's my family. A walking talking stereotype—fucking sue us. I get it. Your big bad crime-fighting family has pissed off a big bad crime boss. You'll give me the details later."

"You need the details *now!*" Tor responded, panicked. Oh God, he couldn't let Marco go into this thinking it was no big deal. Andres Kadjic knew Danny Lightfingers was *alive*. And more than that—suspected that he was actively involved in operations that lost him money. Kadjic was a *serious* criminal, and Tor couldn't let this man—*this* man—put himself in harm's way in any way, shape, or—

Marco kissed him—but more.

His lips didn't just move over Torrance, his *soul* moved over Tor's. His lips were a conduit. Tor found himself turned around and pressed up against the apartment door as he fell down the Marco rabbit hole where no thoughts or doubts existed, only the gorgeous, pure desire that flooded him whenever Marco decided that they absolutely must make love.

Tor made a sound of protest, and Marco pulled back. "What?" he asked. "Is this the part where you tell me that you don't want me in harm's way?"

"Yes," Tor panted, almost weeping with the space between them. He *missed* Marco, missed their quiet conversations in the morning, missed Marco's once-constant presence in his life—missed his touch, missed his smell, missed *him*.

"Tough," Marco whispered harshly, taking his mouth again.

Tor's next protest was a little weaker. "But I love you," he half moaned. "I love you so much. I'm so afraid—"

Marco took his mouth again, this time carnally, not merely insistent but *dominating*. When Marco pulled away this time, Tor found himself backed up against his couch with Marco's hands shoving down his yoga pants.

"Fear is nothing," Marco told him once the pants were down around Tor's ankles. He thrust his hands under Tor's shirts and pulled them over his head. "You just said you loved me."

"I do!" Tor tried to argue, wrestling with the shirts. When he emerged, Marco had shimmied out of his own pants and kicked off his shoes, and it took a minute before Tor found his tongue. For a moment, all he could do was stare at Marco, naked and aroused, and remember that he'd had this man inside his body the night before.

"I love you too," Marco murmured, dropping his coat to the floor and pulling his shirts over his head. He emerged completely naked and bore Tor down to the couch, kissing his chin, his neck, his throat, his shoulders as he spoke. "That seals it," he murmured, kissing with his mouth while his hands reclaimed Tor like conquered territory. "I've never been in love before like I am with you. And you love me a little—"

"So much," Tor moaned, opening his throat to Marco's touch, admitting he was lost.

"So we're in this together," Marco told him, nipping at his earlobe while Tor bucked up against him. "We're in this together, and you can't back out now."

"Okay," Tor admitted, wrapping his legs around Marco's hips.

Marco pulled back enough to fumble with a small ampoule of lubricant, and Tor opened himself, raising his hips and giving Marco access. The sweet invasion of Marco's fingers was enough to make him shudder, and then Marco's cock took over his senses completely. The words, the vows, the explanations ceased as Marco's body resumed explaining what Tor's words never could.

With Tor's first whimper, the lovemaking slowed down, became sensual, and Tor's climax rolled through him slowly, triggering Marco's. Tor arched his back, feeling Marco's lips on his Adam's apple, his teeth nibbling at Tor's clavicle, his body where it should always be, sheltering Tor from the raging oceans of a turbulent world.

Finally their breathing stilled, and Marco's welcome weight was on top of him, anchoring him to the planet.

"So," Marco mumbled, sounding winded, "I moved you out of the mansion into the cottage. You understand?"

"Yeah," Tor agreed. "Don't you even want to hear what we're dealing with?"

"Frankly, no," Marco told him. "You'll all bore me to death with details later. What you need to know right now is this." With an arch of his back he ground himself inside Tor again, making their joining, their connection, absolutely carnally clear. "You understand?"

"I understand I've been fucked into submission," Tor said grimly, but then he relaxed, suddenly accepting the inevitable. "But that's fine."

"Fine?" Marco prodded—and prodded again.

"Perfect," Tor conceded, melting into him. "I need you," he confessed, his voice shaking. "I… life, my job—even my time with the crew—none of it was any fun without you."

Marco rolled his hips again, and Tor could feel the rhythm begin in their bodies. "You need me," he said again.

"I need you," Tor echoed.

"You love me," Marco told him.

"So much," Tor agreed. The weight of the last weeks seemed to lift off his shoulders as he said these things out loud, for real, his heart gaining freedom with every word.

"Then we'll be fine," Marco said, thrusting in earnest this time.

Tor cried out, tender and receptive, and they began round two.

It didn't matter. Round two, round six, round ten, Tor's apartment, Marco's apartment, the mansion—Tor understood that now.

They were joined. They were together. And Marco would be part of his heart, part of his job, part of his family, in all ways.

"I'll never block you out again," Tor promised before his body took over again and he lost all control over his words.

"I'll never let you go."

Later, after their climaxes had rolled through them once more and Marco had covered them with a blanket, Tor would tell him about Kadjic, the big scary word, and Marco would nod and accept it and ask questions and learn.

And Tor would be safe in his arms, ready to plan, ready to protect his family—ready to conquer worlds with Marco beside him.

Conquering the world—or at least fixing it—was so much easier on a soul filled with love.

These two ficlets take place at the end of The Tech—it felt like a lot of people would have some reactions to the events in that story, but Stirling and Tienne were too self-contained to tell those parts. Hunter and Grace, Danny and Felix—even Josh and Liam—all had a little more to do at the end of that one.

More Time—A Long Con Ficlet

HUNTER NOTICED first.

He looked around the lounge in the yacht and did an automatic head count. Danny and Carl had just returned from the hospital in Barbados, and they were ensconced on cushions and being catered to within an inch of their lives. Carl had to order Michael to stop waiting on him and to just… just *sit* for God's sakes and let Carl hold him.

Danny was more accepting of all the attention. He let Felix hold him, Julia wait on him, and Leon debrief him about what all had happened in the two days since they'd taken down Harve Christopher and the arms cache on the desert island that had been supposed to be Stirling and Molly's inheritance. He looked tired but happy, and even from across the room, Hunter could watch Danny's amazing brain clicking everything into place as he was fed details from the fallout. Between Interpol, the Barbadian authorities, and the charges pending on Harve and all his accomplices in the US, there was a lot to tell.

Every so often Torrance Grayson would add a detail that had gone into his broadcast on the island itself, and everybody at that table would light up and cheer. The fact that Tor had started the epithet "Gunrunner's Island" seemed to be especially delicious.

Stirling, Molly, and Etienne were sitting in a corner of the room, watching something funny on Stirling's laptop, and Hunter knew it was hard to find your center when your brain was as special as Stirling's or Etienne's, so he was going to just leave them.

Chuck ambled up to him, hands full of snacks for Lucius, who was hanging on Leon's every word, and mumbled, "Where's your pretty half?"

Hunter grunted. "Was just asking that myself."

"He's upstairs," Josh said behind them, and Hunter turned in surprise. He'd thought he'd backed up in a corner, facing the wraparound window, but he'd forgotten there was a cushion next to the couch, and Josh was there, leaning his head against the arm of the sofa itself and looking exhausted.

"Did you see him go?"

Josh nodded unhappily. "I… I couldn't go after him. I guess missing sleep is bad."

Hunter got a better look at him and swore. "Where's Liam?" he demanded.

"I sent him after Grace. You weren't in the room yet."

Hunter growled. "Dammit, Chuck!"

Chuck was unceremoniously dumping two platefuls of fruit, bread, and pastries on Lucius's table. "Yeah, yeah," he said, handing Lucius a napkin and giving him a wink. "I'll get Josh to his room, and you go talk Grace down."

Hunter waited just long enough for Chuck to pick Josh, too tired to complain, up in his arms before he charged down the corridor, aiming for the stairwell that would take him to the top deck.

He shuddered to guess what he would find there.

LIAM SWALLOWED hard and watched as Grace, ethereally beautiful and graceful as his name, tried hard to give him a heart attack.

"Dylan, mate," he said, his East End coming to the forefront in his agitation. "If you could maybe come down from there for my sake?"

Grace had been pacing the slippery rail that wrapped around the top deck in the wind from their stately pace through the water. It wasn't gale force, no, but it was breezy, and the rail was wet from brine. And, well, heights made Liam a little squidgy. Yes, he did all the scary things Grace and Josh did—when he needed to. BASE jumping, fine. HALO jumping, fine. Bungee jumping, also fine.

But not fun. Not really. Liam was more than competent at these things because he had to be, but unlike Grace and Josh—or Hunter, Chuck, or Molly for that matter—Liam was never the guy who hauled off and leapt into oblivion, drunk on the fall itself.

"Cool your jets, bobby—"

"Bobbies are more a British cop. I'm actually an agent for Interpol. It's a thing," Liam said tartly. He got that Americans did not always get the thing, but he thought maybe he should say something so they would.

"Oh," Grace said, suddenly contrite. He executed a perfect turn on one foot so he could look at Liam as he stood leaning against the rail. "My bad. Sorry. I didn't mean to be a prick, Mr. Interpol guy." For a moment his face crumpled, and his ankle wobbled, and Liam's heart jumped into his throat. "I never mean to be a prick," he mumbled. "Not really."

Liam took a breath, and suddenly he knew what this reckless moment of daredevilry might be coming from.

"Nobody's mad at you," he said softly, "for jumping on the boat when you figured out where it was going."

"They should be," Grace said, and then he leaned forward and put all his weight on his hands, clutching the rail and walking on them as smoothly as he'd walked on his feet. "It was stupid. All this up here," and he actually took a hand off the railing to point at his head, "and I lead my friends into danger because I'm trying to solve it all by myself. See? Dumb. Yell at me."

Liam swallowed. "What I'm going to yell at you for," he said, allowing some of his crossness to surface, "is scaring the piss out of me right now."

Grace grunted—not as though he was in trouble, just as though he thought Liam was stupid. "Just tell Josh you couldn't find me," he said, as though that was ever going to happen.

"You are daft," Liam snapped. "Do you know how long it took that boy to trust me? To talk to me like a person and not his father's friend? And now I'm just going to watch you jump ship? If you land in the water—"

"Oh, please," Grace muttered.

"Fine, you can land in the water. Whatever. How do you know we're not shallow? How do you know there's not a reef fifteen feet below? How do you know a gust of wind won't shove you against the boat and beat your brains in? Your best friend—your brother—sent me up here when he looked like warmed-over death because he was freaking out. And now you're going to do a saber dance while I watch? No offense, Dylan Li, but fuck that shit. If you go in the water, I'm jumping in after, because if I did any less, Josh Salinger would never speak to me again!"

Grace paused to stare at him before launching into the air, doing a flip above the deck, and landing squarely on his feet with a thump. He threw his hands above his head in the classic "stuck the landing" pose and then frowned right at Liam, as though this was the entire reason they were on the deck of the ship in the rapidly waning light in the first place.

"That matters to you?" Grace asked curiously.

"Of course it does!" Liam snapped passionately, and then, oh God, he remembered who he was talking to. "Danny's a friend, and I would like it if his family liked me too."

Grace blinked his remarkable tawny eyes. "Weak sauce, Mr. Interpol Agent. If you're trying to talk me off the ledge, you can't lie to me—might tip me over." He raised a mocking eyebrow and put all his weight on the arm holding the rail, lifting himself up almost horizontally while Liam lost his shit.

"No no no no no… come down. Fine. The boy's… pretty," he said with dignity, although Josh Salinger was more than that. He was magnetic, with his dark eyes, his narrow face, and his easy grin. "And… God, he's got a fine brain, right?"

"If you tell me his brain gets you hard, big deal, Agent Cop-man, I'll laugh in your face and then do a swan dive off the side of the ship just so you can stop being more stupid than me."

Liam stared into Grace's eyes and realized that the young thief was absolutely, positively not fucking around.

"What do you want me to say?" Liam asked wretchedly. "I… I've got feelings for the boy, obviously. But he's getting better. I don't want to be his woobie! I want to…." He'd caught a lot of sun, and the zinc oxide had only gone so far. Still, his cheeks knew the difference between a sunburn and a blush, and even in the fading light, he figured Grace knew too.

Grace let out a sigh. "I hear you. I get it." He looked wistfully over the railing. "What am I going to be, do you think, when you and Josh get together and he doesn't need me anymore?"

Liam's throat was suddenly too thick to swallow. "Frankly, mate, I don't see that happening. Ever."

Grace rolled his eyes. "Everybody says that—"

"Because it's true!" Liam blurted. "Can't you see… don't you see what a rare and special thing it is? What you and Josh have? It's not going to be contaminated by sex. You'll never outgrow it. You two could go on a year-long trip, and whether you were together or apart, you'd come back and still finish each other's sentences. I don't want to be his woobie—but you've been his woobie since you were in knickers. And he's been yours. I'm not taking your woobie away, Grace. I want a whole different side of the man."

Grace sighed and slid bonelessly down the plexiglass wall under the railing. "Fine," he said, but he sounded lost and disconsolate. "I don't believe you, but I won't pitch myself off the boat either. Boring. I'm done with the water today."

Liam gazed at him, feeling helpless, and at that moment, Hunter stepped off the stairwell leading to the deck.

"Good," he said. "I'm done with water too. Let's go downstairs and watch movies."

Grace stared up into his lover's face, and something about Hunter's drawn brows and worried expression must have touched him. The edges of his mouth turned up a little, and his eyes crinkled at the corners. Until that moment, Liam would have said a person's face could not actually "light up" when they were happy, but Grace's did.

To his surprise, Hunter didn't just offer Grace a hand. Instead he crouched down and met Grace eye to eye.

"Whatcha doin', Grace?"

"My brain got so busy," Grace murmured, and Liam heard the tears there. "All I could think was that I almost got all my friends killed, and I hated my own skin."

Hunter let out a breath and leaned forward until they were touching foreheads. "Your friends love you so much, they would literally follow you into hell, Dylan Li. That puts a lot of power in your hands. Be gentle with it."

Grace nodded, and a wounded sound issued from his throat. Hunter sank cross-legged on the deck, pulled Grace into his arms, and just sat there, whispering things that Grace apparently needed to hear.

Liam wanted to cry himself. God, he'd been so worried. Telling Josh he'd let Grace jump off the fucking ship had not been on his to-do list that morning.

Or ever.

With a sigh of relief, he took a few steps off the deck, but Hunter stopped him with his voice.

"Liam?" he said, sounding vulnerable for the first time in Liam's acquaintance.

"Aye?"

"You… you did me and Josh a real favor tonight. I… I… I owe you."

Liam shook his head. "Not at all. Dylan Li—you remember this moment, yeah? People love you."

Grace's reply was muffled against Hunter's shoulder. "Thanks, Mr. Interpol Cop. Take care of my brother."

"Sure."

Liam didn't add that Josh Salinger had a thousand people who wanted to take care of him, and most of them could probably do a better job than a boy who grew up in the East End of London and worked hard to grow into a larger world.

He wanted to check on the boy, and figured he should keep those kinds of insecurities to himself.

But Chuck was waiting for him when he got down to the lounge, and he pulled Liam aside before he could get roped into any other conversation.

"He's asking for you."

"Which room?" Liam asked. They'd put Josh into Liam's room in the beginning, and Josh had preferred it, although it was smaller and not as poshly outfitted as his own. Liam had split his time between the nicer stateroom and Josh's room, where they played a thousand games—from

Mad Libs to Cribbage—to occupy Josh's busy, busy brain when his body couldn't keep up with the rest of his family.

"The little one," Chuck said, rolling his eyes. "Because it has Liam cooties all over it."

"I thought he just liked the smaller—"

"God, spare me," Chuck muttered. "Go see him!"

Liam did, pausing for a couple of big glasses full of fruit juice and a pocket full of snacks before he went. He knew dinner would be served soon but he was hungry, and he figured Josh would be too.

When he got to the room, he set the drinks and the snacks down on the tiny end table by the bed and saw, to his surprise, that Josh wasn't asleep— he was staring at Liam hungrily instead.

"How is he?" he asked softly.

"Confused and rocketing around in his own head," Liam said frankly before sitting on the bed next to Josh. Josh scooted to make room and smiled a little.

"You know…?" He sighed. "Never mind."

"What?" Liam asked softly before smoothing Josh's hair back from his brow. God, he was pretty, even sick. His dark eyes loomed large in his peaked face, but someday he'd be healthy again, and Liam could maybe take advantage here and bend and kiss his full mouth and….

"I need Grace to be okay before I…." He made a sound of frustration.

"Before you find your own bloke," Liam said softly. "I hear you. And I need you to be okay before—"

"Before you become my bloke," Josh said, smiling as he co-opted the slang.

"Aye. We'll just be friends, then," Liam said, although his chest ached with the words.

"For now," Josh said, like he was exacting a promise.

"For now," Liam agreed, and the ache in his chest was soothed with the words.

"So," Josh said softly. "Tell me in excruciating detail how many heart attacks Grace gave you before Hunter got there to talk him down."

Liam laughed. "At least two hundred and three."

"Gotta get used to that," Josh told him. "Because he's my ride-or-die."

"I get it," Liam said. "He's your sidecar guy. I'm your garage."

Josh grinned. "That's a terrible metaphor, but I'm too tired to think of a better one."

"We can spend an hour trying… until dinner," Liam told him, smoothing his hair from his forehead. Again.

Josh let him.

They hadn't come up with a good analogy for the two of them by the time Chuck brought them a tray, but the hour seemed to go by at lightning speed, so maybe they just needed more time.

Only a Flesh Wound—A Long Con Ficlet

"MOVE SO I can take off your bandage."

"No."

"It's time to clean and disinfect and rebandage, Danny. You said you'd cooperate." Felix crossed his arms in front of his chest and glared.

"I said I'd be conscientious about my health," Danny said, making a good show of defiance even though he felt sick and out of sorts on the hotel bed. "I didn't say I'd let you baby me to death."

"I'm not babying you to death, Danny—you won't let me baby you at all!"

Danny gave a little shiver and tried not to sulk. Their three days in Venezuela after their cruise around the islands had turned out to be three mandatory rest days for Danny and Carl, who had both been injured during the last part of their little adventure. Carl, apparently, was out in the shade, allowing his boyfriend to feed him grapes or some such adorable gooey bullshit, but Danny... well, Danny's skin did not turn a luscious gold in the sun. Instead, it turned pink, with lots of freckles, much like Liam's. So while Carl could sleep in the shade and rest up that way, Danny had been told—in no uncertain terms—that he got the luxury hotel, the air conditioning, and the overprotective husband who was currently trying to look at the ugliest part of his body.

"I don't want to be babied," he told Felix grandly. "I want to have sex. Can we have sex?"

Felix stared at him, putting his hands on his hips. "Are you deranged? You were shot."

"It's only a flesh wound," Danny said, trying to smile prettily. When they were twenty, it would have worked.

But then when they were twenty, they wouldn't have spent ten years apart, eating their own hearts out. When they were twenty, they wouldn't have almost lost the boy they loved more than a son. When they were twenty, they hadn't known enough to even be afraid.

"Said the Black Knight after both his arms fell off with gangrene," Felix said staunchly.

Danny gasped in outrage. *Monty Python and the Holy Grail* was sacred to their people, as were Michael Mann's *Heat, Ocean's 11, Logan Lucky*, and the *Italian Job*—both versions.

"That is *not* the way that movie goes!" he all but shouted. "How dare you!"

"And how dare *you* try to make light of the fact that you got *shot*! How dare you risk infection by not letting me dress your goddamned wound! Come *on*, Danny, could you at least let me tend your damned wound!"

"No," Danny said sulkily. "You'll get all weepy, and all 'Oh Danny, I almost lost you,' and you'll contemplate the shortness of life, and seriously, Fox, haven't we done that enough this year?"

"No," Felix said, a look of grim determination on his face. "But obviously I'm not the one to smack some sense into you. You may not have learned anything in the last ten years, but *I* have learned to call in reinforcements."

"Reinforcements?" Danny gaped. "Who else do you trust to come in and tend to my—"

"Julia!" Felix thundered, stalking out of their suite and heading down the hall to where Julia and Leon were—thank God—housed in a room and a bed of their own. "Julia, he's being unreasonable!"

"Fox! Felix, come now—it's really just a—"

Without warning, Josh took advantage of the slightly open door and slipped into the suite, followed by Liam. Liam, who looked as sunburnt and freckled as Danny felt, was carrying a first-aid kit. With a little click, Josh closed the door behind them, and Felix's voice faded as he stalked his way toward the elevators.

"Hello?" Danny asked, still irritated. "Who invited you?"

"You and Dad," Josh snapped. "You were yelling so loud it's a good thing we take up the entire floor, because if none of us knew you had a gunshot wound when we got here, well, we sure do now, don't we!"

Danny groaned and used his good hand to drag through his brown hair, which—barring a few strands of pubic gray—was curling wildly in the humidity. "I'm sorry, son," he said, feeling pathetic. In front of his own kid—not classy, and not adult in the least. "I just—"

"Didn't want Dad feeling sorry for you," Josh said, shooting Liam a meaningful look. "Because that's not sexy at all, is it."

Liam scowled back. "You don't have to feel sexy to form a real bond with someone," Liam said, as though this were an old argument.

"But if you want to have sex with someone, it sure helps," Josh snapped, and then he sat heavily on the bed next to Danny while Liam

moved to the en suite sink to wash his hands. "Sorry, Uncle Danny. I...."
He yawned. The events on Gunrunner's Island (as they had taken to calling
it after Tor broke the story) had exacted a toll on everybody. Josh was still
recovering from his cancer—and the treatment—and would be for a few
more months.

"You got tired," Danny sighed. "Join the club." With an effort, he
released the latch on his sling and then, using one hand, unbuttoned his
Hawaiian shirt so Liam could bare his shoulder. "Are you good with that?"
he said, nodding to the first-aid kit in Liam's hand as he returned from the
sink. "Are you going to bandage my shoulder to my knee?"

"No, Lightfingers. Turns out they teach us basic first aid in Euro-cop
school," Liam said, his good humor reappearing. Interesting how he only
seemed to grow snappish with Josh. Sort of like Danny only had knockdown
drag-outs with Felix. So interesting. So tale-as-old-as-time.

"Well, thank God for that," Danny murmured, wincing.

"Have you been taking the antibiotics?" Liam asked, probing the
stitched wound carefully for redness.

"As ordered," Danny told him dutifully.

"How about the over-the-counter painkillers?"

Danny turned his head away, sheepish. There was nothing addictive
about ibuprofen, but he felt terribly superstitious about any chemical
designed to ease his pain.

"They're also anti-inflammatories," Liam said firmly. "Take them for
that. Trust me—a day taking ibuprofen as directed and this—" He made a
gesture around the swollen wound. "—will fade. Please, Danny?" He smiled
then, and Danny saw in the boy what he'd seen nine years ago when a green
Interpol cop had saved his life and dragged him to rehab. He had curly
brownish hair, freckles, and his teeth were slightly crooked in front—Danny
and Josh knew many classically handsome men who would outshine Liam
Craig like the sun in the looks department. But not the heart department.
The fact that Josh seemed drawn to young Liam like Felix had been drawn
to Danny seemed poetic somehow. They had raised a boy capable of seeing
Liam Craig's stalwart, kind, good-humored heart.

"Please?" Josh yawned, curling up at the foot of the bed. Danny had
assumed he'd nodded off and had, in fact, drawn his knees up to let Josh
catch his nap.

And that was it. Danny caved. With a sigh, he patted the boy on the
head and asked Liam humbly for the meds and a glass of water, which Liam
supplied. When he was done, he disinfected Danny's shoulder with some

lidocaine to take the edge off before he rebandaged it and helped Danny back on with his shirt and sling.

"I wonder where Felix went?" Danny mused as Liam went to dispose of his gloves and the soiled bandage before washing his hands.

"He went to find Mom," Josh said on a yawn. "Grace told him Mom and Leon are down on the beach, so he went down there. Probably so he could cool off, because if he came back in here when you were being stubborn, he would have pitched you out the window."

Danny chuckled. "My God, that man loves me."

"So much," Josh mumbled, finally falling truly asleep.

"Here," Liam murmured, pulling Josh to the other side of the bed and covering him with one of the throws left about the suite. Josh rolled into the throw and curled up to Danny's side, and Liam took advantage of his sleep to ruffle his hair.

"You two seem to be getting on?" Danny asked delicately.

Liam gave him a sad look. "No dating," he said with a sigh, "until Josh is back to strength."

"Your idea or his?"

Liam shrugged. "Moot," he said philosophically. "But don't tell him that."

Oh. Poor man. That far gone already.

"I'll keep my fingers crossed," Danny promised and then sighed. "In the meantime, do you want to watch a movie? Keep me company until Felix comes back? Maybe by then, Josh will be up to walking back to his own room."

"It would be my pleasure," Liam said with a pretty smile. "What shall we watch?"

Danny nodded to his laptop, which was already connected to the hotel screen. "There's only one movie we can watch after Felix's little tantrum— you know that, right?"

Liam's voice assumed the shrill tones of a very irritated guardian troll. "What is your name? What is your quest? What is your favorite color!"

"Green! No, blue!" Danny answered, and Liam scrolled through the movies and started it up before pulling the comfortable chair in the corner of the suite next to Josh's side of the bed.

WHEN FELIX finally returned, Julia not in tow because she'd managed to calm him down, he practically barged through the door, an apology on his lips.

He was violently shushed by Danny, who was still on the bed where he had been, but with Josh curled up and sleeping next to him, and next to

Josh, a dozing Liam Craig, head lolling to the side in the very comfortable stuffed chair.

Monty Python and the Holy Grail was playing on the television, and Felix sent his beloved a droll look.

"Really?"

"Sh…," Danny murmured. "The part with the flesh wound is coming up."

Felix snorted and pulled the room's other chair next to Danny, making note of the closed first-aid kit on the end table. "I take it you let Liam dress your wound?"

"What can I say, Fox? Josh has a corner on the guilt market. Always has, ever since he was a baby."

Felix sighed. "I'm glad somebody does," he murmured, reaching out to pat Danny's knee. Danny captured his hand and raised Felix's knuckles to his lips.

"You've captured my heart, Felix. Forever and ever and ever. I think we've established that."

"I just want you to be well," Felix said softly. "Forever and ever and ever." He leaned close and kissed Danny's temple. "Is that too much to ask?"

Danny grinned and turned quickly, catching Felix's mouth in a real kiss, one that was soft and not urgent, but filled with promise.

"I'll do my best," Danny whispered. "Now hush. Here's the line."

They both turned to the screen to see the Black Knight, bobbing about with no arms and no legs as he screamed, "Come back, you coward! It's only a flesh wound!"

Felix had to admit—of all the times he'd seen the bit, this was the time he laughed the most.

Continue Reading for an Excerpt from
Under Cover
by Amy Lane

Prologue

CROSBY TRIED to slide out of bed stealthily, but he must have failed. When Garcia wrapped an arm around his middle, he mumbled something about going to the bathroom.

Shit.

He used the facilities, but he also put his socks on while he was in there because that got tricky when you put them on after you put on your jeans. He was trying for casual here. No big deal. Two colleagues who'd hooked up after a drink or two when the workday was over.

Happened all the time.

They were professionals, right? And it had been a sucktastic case.

Crosby made the mistake of looking at himself in the mirror when he was washing his face in the bathroom, and unbidden came that moment when the nine-year-old girl had been in his sights as he'd aimed at the murderer behind her.

"Don't take it if it's not good," his AIC had said in his earpiece, but the guy had a knife in his hand. They'd been hunting him, one crime scene after another. So much blood.

And here he was, knife dripping, holding it to her throat, and Crosby wondered which one would make him feel worse—if the killer got her or if Crosby got her, aiming for the killer.

And that hadn't been the worst of it. Garcia... he'd been so close. In Crosby's sights. If Crosby had been just a hair off....

He shuddered then and tried not to retch and splashed more water on his face. Garcia had toothpaste and a fresh toothbrush in the cupboard; Crosby took advantage of it. What was raiding the guy's cupboard when he'd had your cock in his mouth the night before, right?

The memory of the moment overwhelmed him.

Garcia, slighter body moving quickly down the street, Crosby's big blondness lumbering behind him. Crosby had never felt clumsy before in spite of the breadth of his chest, the muscular thickness of his thighs, but Garcia was so tightly wrought.

"Naw, man, I should go home," Crosby had said halfheartedly in response to Garcia's suggestion that Crosby not go back to his uncomfortable living sitch.

"You said she's not your girlfriend!" Garcia laughed. "Besides, you're just crashing at my place!"

From behind Crosby could see the slenderness of his hips, the wiry refinement of his ass and thighs. Garcia wore his black jeans tight—Crosby liked that.

"She's not my girlfriend," he defended. "I knew that from the beginning. We haven't been together since I got hurt."

It would have been awkward to hit her up after nearly six months of not so much as a text. And he didn't want to be needy, although God, tonight he needed somebody.

And Garcia hit him that way. Some girls did, some guys did—just hit.

Even in the spring chill, sweat dotted Crosby's chest under his fleece jacket. He wanted to take off his watch cap, but it was still in the thirties at night, and he knew his ears would be bright purple by the time they got to Calix Garcia's neat little house in Queens.

Sometimes, guy or girl, they hit *hard*.

Garcia had been hitting him pretty hard since he'd shown up in their unit six months ago. Small, quick, compassionate, and with zero ego, the guy was a dream agent. Crosby had looked forward to working with him every day.

And as he followed his fellow agent, and friend to the door so he didn't have to drive crosstown to the place where he roomed with his old college buddy who was throwing a constant party, he thought hungrily about *working* Garcia, from toes to nipples, from mouth to cock to ass.

Working him. So hard.

Garcia let Crosby in first. Crosby had paused in the doorway, letting his eyes adjust so he could find the light, when Garcia closed the door behind him and came up hard against Crosby's back.

"Tell me to turn on the light," Garcia murmured in his ear, and Crosby's heart pounded. Oh wow. Oh *wow*.

His mouth went so dry he had to clear his throat twice to speak. "No."

Garcia let out a breath, hot and violent, into his ear. They were both still wearing jackets and hats, but Garcia's hands came to rest on his hips, then snuck under the hem of his jacket, and Crosby quaked at the chill of his fingers near his flat, molded abdomen.

"Tell me to back off," Garcia murmured.

Crosby's entire body shuddered violently, and he turned in Garcia's arms and shoved him back against the door. For a moment, they stared into each other's eyes in the darkness, Garcia's gleaming black and excited, before Crosby lowered his head enough to whisper in Garcia's ear for a change.

"No."

"No what?" Garcia baited.

Crosby ground their groins together through their jeans. "Not backing off."

"Good," Garcia breathed and nipped his lower lip.

Crosby nipped his in return, and then Garcia teased the seam of his pursed mouth with his tongue. Crosby shuddered again, and Garcia thrust his package against the placket of Crosby's jeans.

"You gonna tell me it was an accident in the morning?" Garcia taunted him. "You tripped in the dark and fell on my ass with your dick?"

"No," Crosby said, tracing Garcia's jawline with his nose, bumping along his temple, working his hands into Garcia's jacket so he could feel the tight, wiry muscles underneath.

"Gonna tell me you got a girlfriend?"

"I *had* a hookup," Crosby told him, thinking it was honest.

"Now you got two." Garcia grinned and dropped to his knees, dragging Crosby's jeans and briefs down his ass.

Crosby's cock flopped out, mostly hard, and the twinkle in Garcia's eyes as he looked into Crosby's face, mouth open, and engulfed him to the root, almost made Crosby come before the first touch.

It didn't get any worse after that.

NOW CROSBY looked at himself in the mirror and remembered those sparkling eyes, and his cheeks heated.

He couldn't betray those eyes.

With a sigh he wet-combed his hair and used a cloth on his pits and all points south. He was going to be wearing the same outfit back to work that morning; he didn't want to smell bad.

Then he returned to Garcia's bedroom, taking in the redwood floors, the cream-colored area rug, and the gray-blue and brown bedding, all of it masculine and inviting and clean. He'd been to Garcia's flat before, a couple of times. Spent Christmas in the spare room, which had a bed and everything. Had shared the occasional late-night takeout when Garcia had taken pity on him and rescued him from his living sitch. Garcia had even had the team over a couple of times—once to celebrate his birthday and once to celebrate Crosby's.

This guy had his life together. His room was a little messy but not a pit. He had solid modern furniture in the small living room and even a dinette table in the kitchen/dining room.

Garcia could bring people to his place because his place was *his* place.

Crosby took turns rooming with his old college buddy or with his bestie in the unit, Gail, because he had no place in the city.

He admired someone who could make their mark in a little New York house, and he admired anyone who could work Special Crimes Task Force.

And he really liked Garcia.

With a sigh he went back to the bed and thrust his stockinged feet into one leg of his jeans and then the other. He left the placket open before grabbing his T-shirt and sitting down on the edge of the bed.

Garcia was watching him, head propped on one hand, the covers sliding down his bare chest, revealing a scattering of dark hair between the nipples.

"You going to go back to work and pretend this never happened?" he asked, and his eyes were bright—but not twinkling.

With a sad shock, Crosby realized he could hurt Garcia—hurt his friend, his partner, his colleague—if he played this wrong.

"No," he said, sliding the T-shirt on. It was chilly in the room, although he'd heard the thermostat click on. Probably on a timer.

"Then this was a onetime thing, and we still respect each other in the morning, and I see you with your girl hookup and you see me with other guys and we think, 'Yeah, I'm glad he's happy'?"

There was an edge to Garcia's voice, and Crosby's chest grew tight, his throat swelling as he tried to imagine that exact scenario. He'd never seen Garcia with other guys—had really only intuited that Garcia might be gay… until he'd closed the door last night. But the thought of that, of *his* partner, *his* guy, on the arm of another man was like a big, ugly beast in his stomach.

What came out next was more like a growl.

"No."

"Then wh—"

Crosby turned on the bed and took Garcia's mouth, not wanting any more scenarios, not wanting any "What are we now?" questions. He just wanted the taste of Garcia, and as he swept his tongue inside that warm, willing cavern, he tasted his own come and remembered that last slow, painful orgasm, the final of three, because Garcia had wanted to taste him before they fell back asleep.

Crosby's cock strained against his briefs, the whole works threatening to bubble out of the unbuttoned fly, and he pulled back, breath laboring in his chest.

"I haven't hooked up with Gail's roommate since you started at SCTF," he blurted as he pulled away.

Garcia tilted his head. "Yeah?"

"Yeah." Crosby nodded. He held his hand up because they'd done this quietly, under the table the night before, surrounded by colleagues. It was where they'd started.

Garcia gave him a guarded look and threaded their fingers together. "So what do we do?"

Crosby looked at his sex-swollen mouth, remembered his head tilted back, his eyes closed, as Crosby had pounded into his body and Garcia had begged so sweetly.

"We can't come out to the squad yet," Crosby said, wanting to do that again. Wanting to feel Garcia's come spurting between their bodies. Wanting to hold Garcia's cock, his home, in his mouth again.

Garcia started to withdraw his hand, but Crosby captured it.

"We couldn't even if one of us was a girl," he said, knowing he sounded like a meatloaf and not caring. "'Cause protocol. 'Cause it's dangerous. 'Cause we'd worry every time we had to draw our weapons."

Garcia's eyes, black-brown infinity pools, sharper than daggers. "I already worry about you every time we have to draw our weapons," he said, the brutal honesty stripping Crosby to the skin. He remembered the week before, Garcia catching a shelf to the back of the head, being sent sprawling, and how Crosby had needed to run right past him while Harding checked to make sure Garcia was okay because Crosby had point and there was an asshole with a gun and a death wish who wanted to make everybody else die first.

"But we still do our jobs," Crosby said soberly. The job—it meant everything.

Garcia nodded, and they were on the same page.

"But you don't hook up with Gail's roommate anymore," he reiterated.

Crosby nodded, not bothering to speak the truth one more time. Gail's roommate hadn't been a thing since Calix Garcia had walked in the door at the SCTF six months before. "And you don't hook up with—"

"Nobody," Garcia whispered. "I haven't hooked up with anybody, not for a really long time."

Crosby remembered the sweet yielding of his body, the way he'd devoured Crosby's cock, like he'd been starving for it. Apparently only Crosby's cock.

"Only me," Crosby said, feeling possessive.

"Yeah."

"You only hook up with me."

"Yeah."

They stared into each other's eyes for a moment, and Crosby took his mouth again, holding Garcia's hands over his head and ravaging, claiming, knowing his short beard would leave marks, stubble burns, proof that he'd been there.

But Garcia submitted, took the kiss, made it more, until the buzzing of both their phones from the charger on Garcia's dresser shocked them apart.

"We have work," Garcia murmured.

"Yeah."

"We can do this. Only hook up with each other."

"Yeah."

"Get dressed, *papi*. We can get coffee and bagels on the way in."

That got Crosby to move. He stood and buttoned his jeans, then gathered his sweater, his fleece, his boots. Garcia ran to the bathroom, probably to give himself the same sort of regimen Crosby had, and Crosby picked up his phone and texted Harding, their Agent In Charge, that Garcia would pick him up on the way.

Nobody would ask, he knew. Buddies coming to work together. Like him sleeping on Gail's couch before the roommate complication. Nothing to see here, folks; no mind-blowing sex, no uncomfortable emotional attachment.

But even as he thought about that, thought about making it clear he wouldn't be sleeping with the roommate again, he fought off the obvious, the thing neither of them had said.

If they only hooked up with each other....

If they worried when weapons were drawn....

If they pretended they weren't doing the thing....

If Crosby marked Garcia like Garcia marked his home, making the man his and fuck anyone else who looked at him....

If these were the truths they were living with now....

It wasn't a hookup anymore. It had never been one in the first place.

Covert—Backing Up to the Beginning

Six Months Earlier

JUDSON CROSBY woke up on his best friend's couch and groaned.

"You awake?" Gail Pearson had long blond pigtail braids and cornflower blue eyes—and some of the keenest knife skills Crosby had ever seen. Unfortunately those knife skills hadn't saved her from a kick from a perp that had caved her knee in exactly the wrong direction knees should go, and she'd been laid up for the last two months, acting as their team's backup hacker because Kylie, their regular hacker, had just gotten married and taken a year's leave of absence.

Gail was going nuts, and she was driving her roommate nuts, and Crosby had been called in to mediate a week into her "incarceration" at home. Crosby had shown up to be Gail's legs and her ride to work, and had stayed—on and off—for the sex with Iliana, her roommate. Iliana, who was as tall and dusky as Gail was tiny and blond, worked as a commander in Active Crimes in a precinct next door to the precinct that patrolled their street. To say Iliana's sex life was a closely guarded secret was to say Fort Knox was closely guarded. Crosby knew he was a means to an end, a flesh-covered dildo, as it were, because Iliana was straight with him—and that was fine.

But it meant that on the nights they weren't doing the quick and dirty, he was out here on the couch, because Iliana's room was Iliana's room, and he wasn't welcome, and he knew it.

It was a good thing their couch was a sweet, sweet ride to dreamland, or he'd be forced back into his own apartment, where his roommate's other guests had probably had sex on every surface, including the ceilings, with every gender known to or yet to be discovered by humans.

Toby Trotter was a great guy, but he was not—*not*—an ideal roommate.

Crosby's days often turned into weeks in the Special Crimes Task Force. A collaboration that borrowed officers from the police, the FBI, NCIS, ATF, and probably a few other alphabets as well, the SCTF was funded by the military but under the management of Lieutenant Commander Clint Harding. Clint—formerly covert ops, though some speculated CIA while others speculated black ops, deep—answered to no other master than the

Attorney General of the United States, and sometimes they had words. His job—his only job—was to track down felons who had eluded capture in their particular jurisdiction, often felons who were in the middle of a crime spree.

Clint's unit's job was, in his words, to keep the blood from spilling and to bring the bad guy in. He preferred alive, and he made that plain, but he also preferred his guys alive to the bad guy if it came down to that, and his unit was grateful.

Crosby had been tapped for SCTF as a homicide cop in Chicago, but he'd lived in New York for a year to be part of the unit. He'd managed to find a roommate—his old college roommate, actually—who was making a lot of money as a DJ and was happy to let Crosby stay in his spare room. Toby was a great guy, and he'd stayed true to his offer of showing Crosby around the city. The deal had seemed too good to be true when it had first been offered.

After a year and a half of dragging his bloody, bruised, exhausted ass into the apartment to find the party he'd left two days ago still going strong, Crosby had recognized that seeming too good to be true was often *being* too good to be true. He'd jumped at a chance to help Gail out and get some sleep, and then he'd awakened one night to Iliana taking off her robe in the middle of the living room and saying, "I don't want strings, I just want dick. You in?"

Well, if nothing else he'd needed to work off some stress.

With a moan he turned his head now to see Gail holding out a mug of coffee. He whimpered and sat up, taking it from her hands. "We got a call?" he asked.

"Yeah. I told Clint it would take us half an hour. You showered last night, because you're considerate as fuck, and I just need to change." She shook her head. "You know, if you weren't banging my roommate, I'd be afraid you'd perv out on me when you had to help me change, but you seem to be a perfect gentleman."

Crosby sipped his coffee—hot, with cream—and smiled a little. "She make it back last night?"

"Yeah. Late, though. Does she really only let you sleep in the bed when you're having sex?"

He grimaced. "She actually asks me to leave if we don't fall asleep. Don't worry. I have no illusions as to intimacy or monogamy. I know what I'm here for."

Gail sighed, the breath stirring the fine strands of gold hair that curled from her tight braids. "You have to forgive her. I mean, I was super excited when you guys started hooking up—after Danny….” She trailed off. Iliana's boyfriend, Danny Aramis, had been killed in a train derailment up in Pennsylvania on a business trip. Apparently it had been true love for them, and according to Gail, Crosby was Iliana's first step into the land of the living in over two years. Her job at the Forty-Third Precinct—she was in charge of the Active Crimes Division—kept her too busy to have much of a social life, and here, neatly delivered, was a person who got law enforcement hours and was pretty decent (if Crosby dared say so) in bed.

It was starting to dawn on them both that Crosby was a means to scratch an itch—he was most assuredly not an emotional act of bravery.

“Yeah, well….” He shrugged. “I was willing. But the good news is I can get up now and get us dressed, and I don't need to kiss anybody goodbye.”

Gail didn't answer back. They both knew Iliana didn't care where he went when they weren't fucking, and that was not going to change.

But the thought gnawed at Crosby. He sat through the briefing with Clint and looked over their little unit: Natalia Denison, Clint's second in command, a former ADA with a lawyer's sharp mind and hand-to-hand fighting skills the likes of which Crosby had never seen, who wore a little silver goddess pendant that looked like something from an assassin's catalog; Joey Carlyle, former Marine with the speed and stamina of a gazelle and the patience to stalk a perpetrator through miles of woodland in the snow without a single word of either complaint or victory in case he gave away his position; Gideon Chadwick, Navy covert ops, weapons expert, and psychology major; and Clint Harding, their boss, former top-secret badass, who had an uncanny way of looking at evidence and figuring out what their suspect would want, where they would go, and what they would need.

Then there was Gail, who was small, sneaky, and uncanny when it came to judging what a suspect would do in the heat of a confrontation, and Crosby, who, as far as he knew, was only there because he'd run down a serial killer in the middle of a drug war and brought the guy in alive. Doing so had also stopped the war. It had started because two neighborhoods had been losing their young people at a terrible rate, and Crosby had figured out that they hadn't been lost to gang violence, but to Cordell Brandeis, who was currently rotting in a supermax prison with over two hundred kills to his name.

It was either that or the thing that had made his entire department in Chicago want to kill him. Okay—maybe there were two reasons Crosby was in the SCTF.

These were good people, he thought seriously. They had families and kids and spouses or parents who worried about them and a special set of skills he could understand would work in the situations they'd been thrown into.

He'd been with the unit for a year and a half, and he still didn't know—really—what the hell he was doing there.

And that right there was about what he'd been thinking when trouble walked through the door.

Award winning author AMY LANE lives in a crumbling crapmansion with a couple of teenagers, a passel of furbabies, and a bemused spouse. She has too damned much yarn, a penchant for action-adventure movies, and a need to know that somewhere in all the pain is a story of Wuv, Twu Wuv, which she continues to believe in to this day! She writes contemporary romance, paranormal romance, urban fantasy, and romantic suspense, teaches the occasional writing class, and likes to pretend her very simple life is as exciting as the lives of the people who live in her head. She'll also tell you that sacrifices, large and small, are worth the urge to write.

Website: www.greenshill.com
Blog: www.writerslane.blogspot.com
Email: amylane@greenshill.com
Facebook:www.facebook.com/amy.lane.167
Twitter: @amymaclane

A LONG CON ADVENTURE

The Mastermind

AMY LANE

"Delicious fun." — *Booklist*

A Long Con Adventure

Once upon a time in Rome, Felix Salinger got caught picking his first pocket and Danny Mitchell saved his bacon. The two of them were inseparable… until they weren't.

Twenty years after that first meeting, Danny returns to Chicago, the city he shared with Felix and their perfect, secret family, to save him again. Felix's news network—the business that broke them apart—is under fire from an unscrupulous employee pointing the finger at Felix. An official investigation could topple their house of cards. The only way to prove Felix is innocent is to pull off their biggest con yet.

But though Felix still has the gift of grift, his reunion with Danny is bittersweet. Their ten-year separation left holes in their hearts that no amount of stolen property can fill. A green crew of young thieves looks to them for guidance as they negotiate old jewels and new threats to pull off the perfect heist—but the hardest job is proving that love is the only thing of value they've ever had.

www.dreamspinnerpress.com

A LONG CON ADVENTURE

The Muscle

AMY LANE

A Long Con Adventure

A true protector will guard your heart before his own.

Hunter Rutledge saw one too many people die in his life as mercenary muscle to go back to the job, so he was conveniently at loose ends when Josh Salinger offered him a place in his altruistic den of thieves.

Hunter is almost content having found a home with a group of people who want justice badly enough to steal it. If only one of them didn't keep stealing his attention from the task at hand….

Superlative dancer and transcendent thief Dylan "Grace" Li lives in the moment. But when mobsters blackmail the people who gave him dance—and the means to save his own soul—Grace turns to Josh for help.

Unfortunately, working with Josh's crew means working with Hunter Rutledge, and for Grace, that's more dangerous than any heist.

Grace's childhood left him thinking he was too difficult to love—so he's better off not risking his love on anyone else. Avoiding commitment keeps him safe. But somehow Hunter's solid, grounding presence makes him feel safer. Can Grace trust that letting down his guard to a former mercenary doesn't mean he'll get shot in the heart?

www.dreamspinnerpress.com

A LONG CON ADVENTURE

The Driver

AMY LANE

A Long Con Adventure

Hell-raiser, getaway driver, and occasional knight in tarnished armor Chuck Calder has never had any illusions about being a serious boyfriend. He may not be a good guy, but at least as part of Josh Salinger's crew of upscale thieves and cons, he can feel good about his job.

Right now, his job is Lucius Broadstone.

Lucius is a blueblood with a brutal past. He uses his fortune and contacts to help people trying to escape abuse, but someone is doing everything they can to stop him. He needs the kind of help only the Salingers can provide. Besides, he hasn't forgotten the last time he and Chuck Calder collided. The team's good ol' boy and good luck charm is a blue-collar handful, but he is genuinely kind. He takes Lucius's mission seriously, and Lucius has never had that before. In spite of Chuck's reluctance to admit he's a nice guy, Lucius wants to know him better.

Chuck's a guaranteed good time, and Lucius is a forever guy. Can Chuck come to terms with his past and embrace the future Lucius is offering? Or is Good Luck Chuck destined to be driving off into the sunset alone forever?

www.dreamspinnerpress.com

A LONG CON ADVENTURE

The Suit

AMY LANE

A Long Con Adventure

Two and a half years ago, Michael Carmody made the biggest mistake of his life. Thanks to the Salinger crew, he has a second chance. Now he's working as their mechanic and nursing a starry-eyed crush on the crew's stoic suit, insurance investigator and spin doctor Carl Cox.

Carl has always been an almost-ran, so Michael's crush baffles him. When it comes to the Salingers, he's the designated wet blanket. But watching Michael forge the life he wants instead of the one he fell into inspires him. In Michael's eyes, he isn't an almost-ran—he just hasn't found the right person to run with. And while the mechanic and the suit shouldn't have much to talk about, suddenly they're seeking out each other's company.

Then the Salingers take a case from their past, and it's all hands on deck. For once, behind-the-scenes guys Michael and Carl find themselves front and center. Between monster trucks, missing women, and murder birds, the case is a jigsaw puzzle with a lot of missing pieces—but confronting the unknown is a hell of a lot easier when they're side by side.

www.dreamspinnerpress.com